Peter H
Crawford

Peter's Pence

Peter's Pence

A Novel
by
JON CLEARY

WITHDRAWN

1974
William Morrow & Company, Inc., New York

Library of Congress Catalog Card Number 73-20709

ISBN 0-688-00252-8

1 2 3 4 5 78 77 76 75 74

FOR EVE AND ERIC McCLINTOCK

1

Fergus McBride stood at the side of the nave of the Basilica and watched the scene with a mixture of amused contempt and reluctant admiration; and yes, he admitted, maybe even a little awe. You never got the virus out of your system, no matter how hard you tried. The Jesuits, temporarily sacrificing logic for prophecy, had got it right: give us a child till he is seven and he is ours for his lifetime.

Well, maybe not quite, thought McBride. There was a difference between being a true believer and being someone awed by the pomp and ceremony of the Church at its most magnificent. Occasion had no logical relation to faith; he would prove that tomorrow night when the culmination of three months' planning would be achieved. Stealing certain of the Vatican's treasures would be an occasion; he liked the thought that some day his name might figure with those of Charles V and Napoleon. Neither of those two was a hero to the Irishmen who had suggested tomorrow night's operation, but that didn't worry him. He would not have nominated the two emperors as his own heroes, but if he was caught tomorrow night it would be some reward if some imaginative journalist named him in the company of those two illustrious looters. There was enough Celt in him to be thinking of possible failure and wondering what dividend could be salvaged.

The Pope raised the gold chalice and the five hundred bishops in their red robes made bloody ripples as they leaned forward. Martin the Sixth, offering this Mass to celebrate his saint's day, was a man with a sense of theatre; there were few stages anywhere in the world that offered the spirit of drama one could achieve here on the papal altar in St Peter's. He held the chalice aloft, nothing of humility in his action, the leading actor in his own drama. The Vicar of Christ, McBride thought: he's ready to turn the Holy Trinity into a Quartet. But he was

7

not the first pope with an appreciation of his own importance. Pride had never been a bar to election as pope: the cardinals, the electors, were too aware of the sin in many of their own breasts.

McBride felt a tug on his sleeve. 'Signor McBride, His Holiness wants to see you in his apartment when Mass is finished.'

Monsignor Arcadipane, Pope Martin's private secretary, was a man to whom the whisper was a natural tone of voice. Small, grey-haired, eyes forever restless behind thick-rimmed glasses, he always made McBride think of a spy who had come in out of the cold but was not yet warm; the impression was heightened by the big briefcase that he carried with him wherever he went, as if he was still burdened with secret papers he had not yet been able to unload. He was a Roman and therefore infected by the endemic local disease; Mussolini had cleared the Pontine marshes and relieved the city of its other disease, malaria, but no Roman would have wanted to be cured of the urge for intrigue. Yet McBride had never seen any evidence that Arcadipane had anything but absolute loyalty for his papal employer.

'What does he want to see me about?' McBride kept his own voice low: even the statues of the saints in the Basilica had ears.

Arcadipane shrugged. 'He doesn't confide everything in me,' he said sharply, as if McBride had placed him at a disadvantage by asking the question. 'Perhaps he wants to make a statement on something.'

McBride nodded, cursing himself for feeling on edge. He would have to keep a tighter rein on his nervousness; the job would not be done till tomorrow night and he would be here for a long time after it. He was, after all, the Special Projects officer in the Vatican press relations bureau and it was not the first time the Pope had summoned him. When the current Bishops' Synod had been announced, Pope Martin had issued a statement that the Vatican had been bitterly criticised for its poor press relations in the past and that he was appointing an experienced layman journalist to make sure that matters were improved. There had been some muted grumbling and protest from the Vatican staff at the fact of an outsider's being brought

8

in, but Martin was not a man to listen to muttering: genuine protest, he had once remarked, deserved a clear voice.

'You have got us a lot of space in the newspapers,' said Arcadipane grudgingly.

Not as much as I'll get you the day after tomorrow. 'I'm dealing with a man who is newsworthy. The Holy Father is like Pope John was – editors are always looking for stories on him.'

Up on the altar, beneath the baroque canopy of Bernini's *baldacchino*, Martin was taking communion. Soon the bishops would begin filing up to the altar steps; already the older ones were straightening up, getting their rusty knees ready for the short walk. McBride decided it was time to leave. In his five months here in the Vatican he had never committed the hypocrisy of taking communion: not out of fear of mortal sin but out of respect for his own principles: if you were a true unbeliever, you had to have faith in your disbelief. When he had got the post as Special Projects officer no one had bothered to ask him if he was a *good* Catholic; so long as he *was* a Catholic, had not committed murder or rape and had kept his heresies quiet, they had engaged him on his professional qualifications and the recommendation of the head of *Time*'s Rome bureau and the Rome correspondent of *The New York Times*, for both of whom he had worked as a stringer. He knew his Church history, politics and protocol, and he was not afraid of work. At the time he had been nominated for the post he had also been broke, which had given him a suitably humble look, an appearance not necessarily common among professional Christians.

'Are you taking communion?' Arcadipane asked.

'Some other time. I don't think His Holiness will be offended.'

Arcadipane nodded. Here at the heart of the Church no one kept tabs on another man's devotion to his religion. McBride guessed it was the same at the White House and Buckingham Palace; saluting the flag was taken as deed if the thought was there. And so far he had done a good job of disguising his true thoughts.

He turned, moved down a side aisle and pushed his way out through the crowd. He nodded to several of the photographers manipulating their own sacred instruments, saw the television and newsreel cameramen juggling with their lights as the slow red tide oozed out of the bishops' stalls; then he was outside the Basilica and standing on the steps in the bright November sunshine. He breathed deeply, glad to be in the open air again. Fear of confinement, to a single office, to one job, had been one of the reasons he had become an itinerant newspaperman. He had said nothing when he had taken the Special Projects post that there was no knowing when he would want to move on again.

Though the tourist season was over, there was a large crowd in St Peter's Square. Normally the citizens of Rome took the Vatican and its activities for granted; it was only another bureaucracy and the Romans already had enough of those. But Martin the Sixth, German, the first non-Italian pope in over four hundred and fifty years, still fascinated them after a year in office. Each time he made a public appearance he was sure of a big audience who, with that dichotomy in the Roman character, bent their knee in genuflection while they looked at him in critical judgment.

McBride wondered what sort of judgment they would pass on himself if they knew his plans. If any of them looked at him at all they would have seen a man of medium height, anonymously good-looking in a broad-featured way, somewhat dandified in his dress; he could have been an Italian man who had reached a certain level, confident of his position on the ladder but with an eye cocked at the rungs above him. He was the sort of man who might be missed in a crowd but who would make an impression on intelligent people when met at close quarters. There was an alertness in his eyes that attracted the observant stranger to him, and the wide mouth suggested humour to those who were looking for a man who did not take himself too seriously. The fact that he was an American, born and brought up in Boston, was only evident when he spoke. His Italian was reasonably fluent, but America was there on his tongue like a visa stamp.

He looked out on the square, once again examining the escape route the others would have to take tomorrow night. The Via della Conciliazione ran straight down to the river; it was the most exposed route but they knew it would be the quickest for their immediate getaway. Once past the Castel Sant'Angelo and on the banks of the Tiber they would head north, cross the river by the Ponte dei Risorgimento and take the Via Flaminia, then the Via Cassia, for Florence and the villa that had been rented there a month ago. The plan was to stay off the autostrada, where the exits were limited and where they could be trapped if they were pursued, and keep to the lesser roads all the way to Florence. There the others would hole up, while he remained in Rome and Phase Two was set in motion.

He went down the steps of the Basilica, keeping to the north side of the square, and passed behind rows of cars parked in front of the northern colonnade. He saw the television and newsreel trucks in the special area he had reserved for them and nodded to Seamus Smith, the chief of the Paragon Films unit which was doing a special documentary on the Synod. The tall silver-haired Smith gave him a friendly smile and held up a cine camera, jokingly suggesting he should take a shot of McBride. The latter grinned, shook his head and turned in through the tall columns of the colonnade.

He went up the steps, nodded to the Swiss Guard on duty there, had a masochistic thought as he wondered what it would be like to be impaled on the guard's pikestaff (thank God *they* didn't stand guard on the Vatican museums!), then turned right up the stairs that led to the Pope's private apartments. He knew he had fifteen or twenty minutes to spare, but he resisted the temptation to detour and glance in on the Library; the layout there was stamped like a blueprint on his mind and he knew the exact location of what was to be taken from that source. Over the past week he had stayed away from all the museums that were to be plundered; Luciana had scouted them all yesterday to make sure that nothing had been changed that would alter their plans. When they came into these buildings tomorrow night they would be operating to almost split-second timing.

On the third floor of the palace he knocked on the door of the private apartments and was admitted by Sister Caterina, the Pope's housekeeper. She was a formidable woman who could have run an army camp as efficiently as she ran the papal household; she would not go into Heaven on her knees, unless St Peter happened to open the gates while she was scrubbing the front steps, which McBride knew wouldn't be up to her standards of what an entrance should look like. She did not like men, especially fancily dressed laymen who winked at her.

'None of that in here, Signor McBride,' she said in her Calabrian accent, still rough after thirty years in Rome. 'Did His Holiness send for you?'

'He did.' He smiled, winking at her again; he paid court to all women, even those who saw no need for the existence of men. 'He's suggested that I need a mother, someone like you.'

She led him into the study, not responding at all to his sweet talk. 'A man your age, signore, doesn't need a mother. He should have a wife.'

'Are you proposing, Sister?'

'I'm not!' She made no reference to her religious vows; she just rejected him as any man-hating woman might. 'All you men are the same – so full of yourselves!'

Including His Holiness? But he didn't ask that question, even in fun: his uncle in Boston, the Irish ward boss, had taught him the political limits of joking. 'We have to be, to survive in a woman's world.'

Sister Caterina, a second-class citizen as every woman was in the Church, gave him a sour look. 'I'm preparing His Holiness's supper. I'll leave you here.'

'I promise not to steal anything.'

She curled her lip and went out with a swish of thick skirt that sounded like a hissed sneer. Charity was not one of her virtues; she would get into Heaven purely on the merit of being hard-working. McBride, despite her dislike of him, respected her more than he did some of her more sanctimonious sisters who went around wearing their piety like this year's fashion.

When the Pope came into the study he had divested himself of his altar garments and wore a simple white soutane that made him look a bigger man than he actually was. He was handsome, though running a little to flesh around the jowls, with thick grey-streaked hair on a boldly sculptured head. He had the build of a light-heavyweight boxer, and McBride knew that up till a year ago he had been a regular tennis player and an occasional skier. He had been known as the sporting cardinal and was said to have been one of those who had argued most strongly for the Olympic Games to be brought to his see of Munich. But popes were not expected to be athletic, as if athleticism and spirituality did not go together, and though he still had an occasional game of tennis out at the summer palace at Castelgandolfo, those activities were no longer publicised. McBride personally thought that it was a pity, but popes, like kings, are the prisoners of their courts.

'Mr McBride!' Martin spoke English as well as he spoke German, Italian and French; unlike some holders of his office, he believed the Head of the Catholic Church should have a catholic tongue. 'Always available when I call on you. Is that American politeness? Some of those others who work for me here – !' He raised his hands in an Italian gesture; Rome was already beginning to infect him, as it had so many before him. 'But don't quote me, please!'

'I was always a discreet newspaperman, Holiness,' said McBride, responding to the good humour of the other man. He admired Martin and thought he might prove the best pope of recent times, but he knew the rough road that lay ahead of the German. A road to which McBride himself was going to add a few bumps within the next forty-eight hours. 'I think that was my main qualification when they recommended me for this job.'

Martin rang a bell and Sister Caterina was at the door on the instant, like an aggressive guardian angel. 'Some whisky for Signor McBride – or is it bourbon? Bourbon, Sister. And a glass of wine for me. Rhine wine, Sister, not Italian.'

'Yes, Holiness,' said Sister Caterina, but her tone implied that any pope worthy of the name would drink only Italian wine. She disappeared but was back within seconds with a tray on which stood the drinks her master had ordered. 'Shall I pour, Holiness?'

'No, I can do it.' When the nun had gone Martin said, 'I have a butler somewhere around here, but Sister Caterina never allows him near me except on official occasions. There is no protector like the female of the species.'

McBride smiled, but said nothing. Though the atmosphere

13

between them was easy, almost man-to-man, he knew that Martin had an acute sense of office; there were several tales of senior clerics in the Vatican who had mistaken the attempt to put them at their ease as an invitation to familiarity.

They sipped their drinks while Martin looked carefully at McBride. 'Do you mind if I say I've sometimes wondered why you took this job? You're a man who, I think, likes the good things of life. Don't be embarrassed – ' He held up an apologetic hand and smiled. 'So do I – but who would tolerate that in a pope these days? I had more luxuries when I was the Archbishop of Munich than I have now.'

'I didn't think it was so obvious, Holiness – I mean about me, not you.' He smiled and the Pope smiled back. McBride wondered what all this was leading up to. He had had an audience with Martin no more than half a dozen times and only once with him alone. On none of those occasions had the Pope shown any hint of the personal note that he was pursuing now. 'I thought I'd been discreet about that, too.'

'I notice small things, Mr McBride. The way people dress, for instance. When I was in Munich I used to watch some of my flock work their way up the ladder of affluence, getting better dressed as they climbed each rung. Those shoes of yours – hand-made English, aren't they?'

'A splurge, Holiness.' The shoes were five years old, walking memoranda of better days. 'I was working in London and I sold a feature story to *Life* – '

'Do I sound critical of you? I'm sorry. I'm rambling on, but the truth is, you interest me, Mr McBride. I *like* you, you have an air of independence, and that's why I sometimes wonder about you. The Vatican doesn't pay well – the Church is the fount of charity, except when it comes to wages. Why did you take the job? Are you really interested in propaganda?'

What is this – a confessional? McBride was suddenly cautious, wondering if someone had split and this unconventional pope, instead of calling in the police at once, was going to hold his own investigation. 'As a matter of fact, I am,' he lied. 'That was the sole reason for taking the job – I thought I could improve things. If you'll forgive the impertinence, Holiness, I think the Church's propaganda has been too long in the hands of the Church.'

Martin threw back his head and laughed. 'Oh, you're so right! We have too often been our own worst enemies. Relax, Mr McBride. I am not going to have you dismissed. You have done such a splendid job over this past week that I want you to do something else for me.'

'Whatever you wish – ' McBride did his best to look professionally interested.

'I want you to prepare a statement for release tomorrow that we – ' Martin used the royal or papal pronoun: the man disappeared into the pope for the moment ' – are going to send certain of the Vatican treasures on a world tour.'

McBride's hand tightened on his glass. 'May I ask why, Holiness?'

'I think the treasures belong to the Christian world and there are far too many people, the great majority, in fact, who will never be able to afford to come to Rome to see them. I have been having discussions with the Director-General of the Museums, he has been in touch with various museums throughout the world who have agreed to co-operate, and now we are ready to announce the project.'

'You have kept it all very quiet.' McBride hoped his voice was steady.

'You know as well as I do that some of our brothers here don't want the focus on the Church ever to shift from Rome – it has been a bone of contention for centuries. But now I am going to present them with a *fait accompli* – it is one of the prerogatives of being Pope – and I want you to prepare the announcement.'

'Why me, Holiness?' McBride was still suspicious: this was too close to home.

'Because I can trust you.' He took another sip of wine and McBride waited for the sardonic pay-off. But then Martin went on, 'I can trust you to see that the statement is released promptly, instead of being put away in the innumerable pigeon-holes we have here in the Vatican, and that it is released without any editing. This is *our* project – ' the dignity was there now, plus the authority ' – and it will be implemented exactly as we want it.'

McBride could feel the stiffness in his joints, as if he had been suddenly afflicted with arthritis; he eased himself in his chair, trying to hide the shock that had hit him. If the announcement was released tomorrow, attention would be focused on the museums and their treasures. The Romans, careless of their heritage, might suddenly start rushing to look at what had been available to them all their lives; the guard would be doubled as it was in the tourist season, to prevent any repetition of what had happened a few summers before when a crazed Hungarian-Australian had smashed Michelangelo's *Pieta*. If the reaction among the Vatican conservatives was what Martin expected, then it was possible that the guard would also be doubled at night to prevent the treasures being removed until there had been a discussion on the project. And despite the Pope's autocratic authority, McBride knew how Vatican discussions could bog down any project.

'What treasures are to be taken abroad? There are so many – '

Martin opened a drawer in his desk, took out a typed sheet of paper and handed it to McBride. 'We have been selective. There are certain works, of course, that cannot be moved – '

McBride ran his eye down the list, feeling himself growing cold as he did so. It could have been their own list, plus other items they had considered but had rejected because of the difficulty of removing them. The Reliquary of the True Cross was there; the Joshua Roll; the Vatican and Roman Virgils; Exekias's amphora: the list was a typed joke, a cruel jest worthy of some of the bad popes who had degraded their office. He looked up, expecting to see the smile on Martin's face as the Pope told him the game was up.

'I left the selection to the Director-General – I must confess I have never had time to look at our treasures, nor to appreciate them. Everything there can be easily transported, as you can see.' The Pope's voice was an echo in McBride's ears; the men who had come to see him three months ago had said exactly that: *everything there can be easily transported*. 'Since the treasures are priceless – I sometimes wonder what their value would be if someone tried to steal them – '

Fifteen million Deutschmarks, roughly six million dollars: that was the ransom they were going to ask for less than a tenth of what was on the list in McBride's hand. 'What will the security be like while they're being transported?'

'The tightest, I hope.' Martin smiled. 'I want you to stress that in the statement you prepare. Do you personally like the scheme?'

'I am all for distribution of treasures, Holiness.' He could feel a weakness inside him, a trembling of unreasonable anger that all the meticulous planning, the aid to *their* cause, was being wrecked by the whim of a man who had done nothing else but shock the Vatican Establishment ever since he had ascended to St Peter's Chair. The anger was more disturbing for the fact that up till entering this room McBride had had nothing but admiration for Martin and his efforts to open up the Vatican to the changing world outside.

'Do I note a little reservation?' Martin, wise and experienced in the politics of the most political of churches, had developed an ear for nuances.

'None at all, Holiness.' McBride was recovering; all his life he had been adaptable. He just hoped the others would be the same; if they weren't, then their plans would have to be deferred until the treasures were returned to Rome or the heist would have to take place in another city in another country. And then he and Luciana would not be needed and Joe McBride would never be personally avenged by his son. 'How long will the exhibition be on tour?'

'Possibly two years, possibly more. I want it to go wherever it will be welcomed.'

Two years: the others would not wait that long. He put down his glass and stood up. 'If you will excuse me, Holiness, I'll go see the Director-General now and get the details from him. I'll prepare the statement tonight, bring it to you first thing in the morning and we'll release it at midday at a special press conference. Do you want to attend the press conference yourself?'

'I think not.' Martin smiled again, finished his wine. He was outgoing, believed in a more open Church than any of his predecessors; but he also believed in the mystique of the office he had inherited, knew it would be destroyed as soon as he exposed himself to open questioning by journalists who believed in the mystique of nothing. He was surprised that McBride, who had claimed to be discreet, had suggested such exposure. 'I am not here to solicit votes, Mr McBride. Unlike your unfortunate presidents, I don't come up for re-election every four years.'

McBride recognised the rebuke. 'If you will excuse me, then?'

'You have our permission.' Martin's tongue slipped from the personal to the official with no difficulty at all; certainly he did not have to pander for votes, but he was a man who would have been no different had he been placed in that position. From the day he had first achieved authority as a parish priest, he had been absolutely certain of himself, a characteristic by no means endemic among those in power. He could talk to McBride on the personal level because he knew the American recognised the level above which he, McBride, could not impose. 'You are most efficient. I wish you were one of my bishops.'

McBride smiled for the first time in five minutes. His facial muscles creaked as Lazarus's must have when it was possible for him to smile again. 'A bishop who liked the good life? I don't think I'd do you credit, Holiness.'

Martin laughed, stood up and came round his desk. He put out his hand and McBride, after a moment's hesitation, kissed the ring on it. But then the Pope took McBride's own hand, shook it with a firm grip.

'In our position we get so few opportunities to talk on a personal level. One appreciates the few people who are not here to ask something of us.'

How about postponing your statement for forty-eight hours? 'Thank you, Holiness. It is a pity we met so late.'

'So late?'

'I mean, late today.' It had been a slip. 'I'd have enjoyed staying on and talking with you.'

'There'll be other times, I'm sure.' For the first time McBride saw the sadness behind the smiling blue eyes. When this man

18

was young, he thought, he must have looked the epitome of Hitler's Aryan ideal. And yet . . . 'Once, a long time ago, when I was in Dachau, I used to pray for someone to talk to, just to keep my sanity. Sometimes I feel just as lonely here as I did then.' Then the sadness was forced back behind the eyes, into the past, and once more he smiled. 'But again, don't quote me.'

2

Heinrich Kessler sat on a bench in the Borghese Gardens, staring at the Temple of Aesculapius without seeing it. The small artificial lake caught the glow of the setting sun; a tiny brown cloud of ducks floated across the golden reflection. But Kessler's sombre eyes never saw beauty these days, they were blind to delight. He stared bitterly at the nursemaids and mothers making more noise than the ducks which their children were trying to feed: God, how Italians molly-coddled their kids! A small child sneezed and its mother instantly smothered it in a thick overcoat, as if a blizzard had just swept in from the north. A young mini-skirted English *au pair* girl looked at the mother and child with amused contempt; then she removed a sweater from her own small charge and took off her jacket, exposing a bosom that was a proclamation of what a cold climate could do for someone strong enough to survive it. But Kessler was in no mood for amusement nor the contemplation of prominent bosoms.

He got up and began to wander through the gardens. He passed a father and son walking hand in hand, the boy clutching a child's football under his arm. He would have been about the boy's age when he had last walked with his own father in the Englischer Garten in Munich. He could not remember if he had ever carried anything, certainly not a football; he had never been a sports-minded child, preferring his mineral collection and the badges his father used to bring home for him. Those days were dim in his memory, anyway, the edges of the images always fogged; there had been years when there had been no memories at all, after the bomb had fallen on the house in the suburb of Au. There were later memories of his father, but they were so faint he always got a headache trying to retain them in his mind. His father wore a uniform, but he was not the same father who had walked with him in the Englischer Garten; sometimes he would remember that his mother had cried when his father came home in the uniform, but she had never told him why she cried. Perhaps she had meant to when he was older, but she had died in the bombed house. Sometimes in the asylum he wished he had died too.

Then he would never have learned what they had done to his father.

He walked down out of the gardens and down the road to the top of the Spanish Steps. At the bottom of the steps the artists were packing up and going home; at this time of year they really came here only for each other's company and to exchange comments on the suckers of the summer. A young man, long-haired and thickly bearded, looking like a yak in jeans, strummed a guitar and sang about the blues in a second-hand Alabama accent: when he stopped singing and spoke to the two girls with him he had a thick Glaswegian accent that wasn't helped by an over-abundance of adenoids. Kessler looked at the youth and the two girls with contempt, but no amusement. He had forgotten how to laugh: the memory of that delight was lost forever.

He looked out across the roofs of the city, over the river to that other city where the man he had come to Rome to kill lived and reigned. He had been in Rome two weeks and he had seen Kurt Stecher, Pope Martin the Sixth, three times. He had been surprised to find that Stecher looked exactly like his photos in the newspapers and magazines: so many people did not. But there was no mistaking Stecher. He even looked like the young priest who had stood in the box at Nuremberg and pointed his finger at Wolfgang Kessler.

Heinrich Kessler, mind still recovering from the bomb burst, had still been in the asylum when that had happened. It was four years later, when he was twenty years old, that he had discovered by accident, reading a copy of *Stern*, what had happened to his father. He had been released from the asylum by then, was living in the small town near Munich and working as a gas attendant and general handyman at a garage. He had made no friends and the men he worked with respected his

20

reserve; they knew none of his background and they didn't care to know; in 1950 Germans were still trying to salvage their own identities out of the wreckage of the past twenty years. But he had left the garage and the town, moved closer to Munich and got a job at the BMW motorcycle works. He had begun to collect photographs of Kurt Stecher, just as he had collected minerals and badges back in those dimly remembered happy days with his father.

But the idea of killing Stecher had not occurred to him till this year. It was only then he had realised he had no other reason for living.

There was still one more photograph to be collected, but it was not yet taken: the one of the dead Pope lying in his car on the road to Castelgandolfo tomorrow afternoon. He would take that photograph himself if they gave him time before they shot him or took him away.

3

Sister Caterina showed McBride out of the apartment, looking at him with new interest now. His Holiness had been holding the American by the arm when he had turned McBride over to her and she had never seen him do that with anyone, not even the cardinals from the Curia.

'You should look happier, Signor McBride. You are obviously a favourite of His Holiness.'

'That look you mistake for unhappiness is supposed to be one of humility.' But he would have to watch it: there must be no cause for suspicion for the next few hours.

'I'd never have known,' said Sister Caterina, and flung open the front door as if she were opening the gates on the Outer Darkness.

McBride retraced his steps down through the palace and out into the northern colonnade. Seamus Smith, Turk Toohey and Des Ryan were packing up their camera equipment and loading it into their Paragon Films truck. He stood in the shadows of one of the huge pillars, wondering if he should go out and approach all three of them. So far his relationship with them, to anyone who had bothered to study them, was purely professional, that of a press relations officer dealing with men of the various media. It had been a successful cover-up till now, enabling him to introduce Smith and the others into the Vatican without arousing suspicion, and it would be foolish to blow it.

He went out of the colonnade and past the line of television and newsreel trucks, nodding affably to the other technicians finished with religion for the day and headed for what sin they could find tonight. He passed the Paragon truck at the end of the line, hissed at Smith out of the corner of his mouth, 'Come after me!' and walked on. For a moment he thought Smith had not got the message and he had to resist the urge to look back. Then he heard Smith calling him.

'Oh, Mr McBride! A moment, please!'

He stopped and turned. He was well out towards the middle of the square, just by one of the fountains, in the most exposed and yet the best position for discussing a secret arrangement; no one could overhear them out here and what would be more natural than that a documentary film director should have a question or two for a press relations officer? He waited for Smith to catch up with him.

'When you get to me,' he was already saying before Smith reached him, 'turn around and point back towards the truck as if you're telling me now that it's broken down.'

'Something has gone wrong?' Smith was as good an actor as the Pope, although more theatrical; he pointed back towards the truck with an outflung arm, even affecting a troubled expression. 'Why must the truck have broken down today?'

'Because we are going to have to pull the job tonight.' A group of Irish nuns went past, faces pinched with piety, voices thick with brogue and excitement; they had heard Mass said by the Holy Father himself and churchgoing in Connemara would never be the same again. McBride waited till they had gone, wondering how much passion they had for the other religion of true Irishmen and women, then he looked back at Smith. 'I can't explain now, but we have to advance everything by twenty-four hours. The plans are exactly the same, but they happen tonight instead of tomorrow night.'

'It can't be done.' Seamus Smith gestured again towards the

truck, even more dramatically this time; Toohey and Ryan had stopped loading and were looking in puzzlement out at their colleagues in the middle of the square. *We're going to blow the whole goddam thing in a minute*: McBride turned his back on the distant Toohey and Ryan and looked at the spouting fountain. Smith said, 'The necessary equipment for our friend Turk is not in the truck.'

'Jesus!' said McBride, and two priests passing by looked at him and nodded their heads; if one had to mention the Lord's name, this was the obvious place for it. 'I'd forgotten that!'

'The truck can't break down now – we have to take it away and bring it back with all that we shall need.'

Smith looked at his watch, making even that a dramatic gesture. He was the unlikeliest IRA man one could imagine; McBride hadn't quite believed him when he had first met him. His mother had been a minor actress with the Abbey Theatre, one who had believed that all the world's a stage and had acted in a suitably panoramic style; only her extraordinary beauty had kept her in the company. His father had been an unsuccessful publisher, an Englishman who had reversed the usual literary trek and had gone from London to Dublin, en route passing a dozen Irish writers going the other way. Smith himself had been educated at a minor English public school; was now fifty years old, tall and handsome, with silver-grey hair sleeked back from an arrogant, aristocratic profile; and owned a small but profitable farm in Westmeath. He hated his father's countrymen with a passion he never attempted to explain and that McBride, a milder man, found a little frightening.

'It will take us at least an hour to collect the stuff,' Smith said. 'What excuse will we have for coming back here?'

The sun had already gone down behind the dome of the Basilica; it would be dark in less than an hour. But darkness was the last thing a documentary film crew wanted: there was no night-life around St Peter's worth filming. The truck had to be left here in the square for transporting the loot when they had it; Turk Toohey's equipment would have to be brought in now by some other means. McBride looked up at the silver-blue dome as if for inspiration, but miracles are not visited on crooks. Or if they are, he thought ruefully, the Church doesn't

23

recognise them nor would it. Because, since the reason for the heist would never be made public, he and Smith and the others would be damned as nothing but crooks, criminals inspired only by greed.

'Okay, meet me at my apartment at eight o'clock. Same arrangements as for tomorrow night, only we'll bring everything ahead.'

'We leave the truck where it is?'

'You got any other suggestions?'

'The truck will stay, but don't think you are going to make all the decisions, dear chap.' The theatricality of Smith's gestures and the affected languid drawl of his voice were conflicting characteristics that McBride found unsettling. 'We have not spent all this time preparing this operation to have it buggered up by a Johnny-come-lately like yourself.'

'Don't start threatening me, Seamus.' McBride smiled broadly at Smith as two typists from the press relations bureau went past. Both young good-looking girls, they glanced with interest at the tall handsome man talking to the Special Projects officer; Roman girls placed no age limit on a man's attraction for them. Smith preened himself under their looks, almost stepping out of himself to share their enjoyment; and McBride kept the smile fixed on his face like someone posing for an old time-exposure photograph. 'I'm not working for you but for the organisation. I'll talk to Dublin as soon as I get home. What they say, goes. I'll see you and Turk and Des at my apartment at eight o'clock.'

Still smiling broadly, he waved a hand in farewell, turned and went across the square and up through a side door of the Basilica. It was the long way round to where he wanted to go, but he could not take the chance of retracing his steps; he had to look like a man who had been going somewhere when he had been intercepted by Smith seeking permission to leave the truck in the square overnight. He found the chief of the security guards, told him the truck would not be moved tonight because it had broken down, and moved on towards the museums.

It had been a long way round to what was going to happen tonight, a road that for most of his life had never really looked like leading to any destination. The road, he guessed, had begun to unwind in the village of Cavanreagh in the spring of 1920 when the Black and Tans had swooped down in reprisal for a raid on a police station; someone had fired a shot at the Tans and the latter had opened up as if on a duck shoot. Brigid McBride, Fergus's grandmother, had died at once with two bullets in her; Joe McBride, Fergus's father, sixteen years old and innocent then of even sympathy for the IRA, had had his left arm shot off at the elbow. That day the Black and Tans had infected Joe McBride with hatred, had turned a mild easy-going boy into an enemy whose bitterness had increased with the years.

Joe McBride, on his discharge from hospital, had been pushed off to relatives in America by his uncles: the boy's stump had been more useful as a fund-raising symbol than for holding a gun. Joe had settled in Boston, been found a job with an Irish family printing firm, and spent the next thirty-five years helping to raise funds among those Irish-Americans who had fought the good fight at a good distance. Several times he had gone home on a visit, but always only to observe; the IRA men at home, recognising his worth on the other side of the Atlantic, had never given him a gun. Each visit home had only increased his bitterness and widened the gap between himself and Nora, his wife.

Nora herself had left Ireland tired of the fighting and the talk of fighting; but that had not stopped her from marrying Joe, with whom she had fallen in love at first sight. That had been in 1938 when Joe had just come back from his fourth visit home. A year later she had married him, only to have their honeymoon cut short when Joe had to go off to raise funds for the campaign of bombings in England. Blinded by her love for him, she had not really realised the depth of Joe's bitterness towards the English; but her eyes were soon opened and from then on she had done her best to protect their only child from inheriting what was in her eyes a disease. Fergus McBride could still remember in acute detail the arguments between his mother and father. He could also remember the day, when he was eleven years old and there had been a particularly harsh argument, his father tearing off his shirt and shoving the ugly stump under his nose, shouting at him never to forget it, that the missing half of his arm was buried in Brigid McBride's grave.

But Fergus had never responded to his father's exhortations, had always sided with his mother because *she*, he had seen even as a boy, was the loser in the war that could never be won. In 1956, when Fergus himself was sixteen years old, Joe McBride had gone home to Ireland for his tenth and last visit, Nora refusing to go with him. He had crossed the border into Ulster and there persuaded someone to let him join a party planning to blow up a power station. He had been fifty-two years old, slow-gaited by then, diabetic, and his eyes short-sighted behind his thick glasses: a perfect patsy for the ambush that had been waiting for them. Some traitor, never discovered, in the IRA had set them up; the other members of the party, recognising at once the hopelessness of their position, had surrendered. But Joe McBride, the fighter who had never been in an actual fight, who would never have surrendered his cause even to God, had turned and tried to run. He died with the same number of bullets in him as his mother had.

All this Nora and Fergus had learned when they had come back to Cavanreagh for the funeral. As they had lowered Joe into the grave Nora had already begun to join him; her life started to run out of her as tears. Fergus, standing beside her, knew even then that he had already lost both parents. He had stared around at the grim-faced men and the weeping women, suddenly hating them: these were the strangers for whom his father had died.

But then, walking back to the village from the graveyard, his mother had said, 'Don't blame them, Fergus. They have their reasons for believing in what they do.'

'*You* don't believe in it.'

'I do believe in it, yes.' She had never lost the Irish habit of adding *yes* to her statements, as if to convince herself that what she had said was the truth. 'I've always believed in it. But I was always afraid that I'd lose your dad if I'd let him come back here to fight. And I did.' She walked in silence for a few yards, the tears rolling down her cheeks. Then: 'We're not going back to Boston. I can't leave your dad now.'

So they had stayed on in Cavanreagh and within a year Nora McBride was dead. She died of pneumonia, the village doctor said, but he and the villagers and Fergus knew she died of a broken heart, which is a cause of death the English won't accept on their death certificates. At seventeen Fergus said goodbye to Cavanreagh and the Six Counties and went back to Boston. His uncles put him through college, then got him a job on the Boston *Post*. But restlessness had taken hold of him, twelve months of any place had produced claustrophobia, and he had begun to wander, everywhere but back to Cavanreagh and the two graves on the hill where, his father had once told him in one of his softer moods, the wind always blew from the west and never from the east and England. He had spent twelve months in London and liked the English, had wondered how people who could be so tolerant about so many things could tolerate all that had been done to Ireland in the past. Several times he had found thoughts in his head that were silent echoes of words he had heard his father shout in fury; but he had quickly put them out of his mind because he knew they would eventually lead to the gun and the bomb in the hand. Letters from his uncles in Boston and relatives in Cavanreagh had followed him round the world, asking him what he had to contribute to the cause and to the memory of Joe and Nora McBride. And always his answer had been the same: nothing while they all thought violence was the only means to their end. Some day he hoped his father, and his mother, would be avenged. But he would never fire a gun or throw a bomb to achieve that. And so he had continued to wander, running away, he knew, from the voices on the hillside, the furious shouts of his father and the soft prayers of his mother.

Then three months ago the two men had arrived from Dublin, one of them a survivor of the abortive raid on the power station back in 1956. They had talked to him for three nights, with as much fervour but more effect than Joe McBride ever had; but they had had the advantage of Joe's and Nora's ghosts, which Joe had never had. And at midnight on the third night McBride had agreed to what they had proposed.

'The museums are closed, Signor McBride.' The guard, even more officious now that he was about to go off duty, stopped him in his tracks. 'Unless you have special permission?'

There was a challenge in the thin harsh voice: *I'm a working man, don't keep me here longer than I'm paid for.*

'No. I wasn't thinking – I came this way by mistake. Has the Director-General gone?'

The guard shrugged: *How would I know, does the Director-General tell me anything?* Warped and surly, he went on his way down the long corridor. Christ, McBride asked the walls about him, why does the atmosphere of religion make so many of them unhappy? But the frescoes that coloured the corridors had no answer: muscle-bound saints were too intent on climbing up the walls to Heaven. He went on his way looking for the Director-General.

He found him in his office, a small thin man with a bald head and the tight suspicious eyes of the curator who was always having fakes pressed on him as masterpieces. He was like the Devil's Advocate in the Sacred Congregation for the Causes of Saints: one challenged nominees for canonisation, the other so-called works of art.

'Ah, yes, the exhibition!' Barzelli showed an enthusiasm that McBride had never seen in him before. He had stiff awkward movements that suggested his limbs did not belong to him; he moved two rigid arms as if he were semaphoring his excitement. 'Did you know His Holiness is sending me around the world to arrange it all? Oh, it will be a relief to be out of Rome in the winter!'

If we can get in here tonight we may spoil your trip. 'When are all the items to be removed from the museums?'

'First thing tomorrow morning. We'll bring up other things from the storehouses to replace them. We have so much,' he said, and tapped his foot on the carpet as if he stood on a gold mine.

The paper in McBride's hand trembled a little, but he did not look down at it. 'Nothing has been removed so far?'

'Ah, no. No.' Barzelli jerked around his office like a puppet whose strings had been turned into charged wires. 'The timing had to be right – the announcement and the beginning of the packing must be on the same day. You know the politics here.' He winked: a desiccated museum piece himself,

28

he had suddenly shed centuries. 'We must surprise everyone.'

You've certainly surprised me. It was imperative now that the robbery had to take place tonight. 'No one will be working on the removal and packing tonight?'

The stiff arms were spread wide. 'I am eager to start working myself this very minute! But whom can I get to help me? Tomorrow, tomorrow – isn't that our way? But first thing in the morning – ah!' McBride waited for the Director-General to get down on his mark like a sprinter; he began to worry that Barzelli might not even go home tonight. 'I can hardly wait!'

'Likewise,' said McBride, and left him.

4

McBride parked his car in the garage near the Hotel Eden and walked down Via Francesco Crispi. His apartment was one of the few perks of his job; it was in a building that was one of the Church's numerous real estate holdings in Rome and it came to him at a rent that was almost nominal for this part of the city. As the Pope had said, he liked the good life and since going to work at the Vatican he had supplemented his income by writing, under a pseudonym, for various overseas newspapers and magazines. He knew he was not the only one in the Vatican who wore two hats: it was said there were more correspondents *inside* the Holy City than were accredited to it from outside.

Gina and Rosanna were already on the beat on the front steps of the building. They smiled good evening to him and he asked them, as he did every evening, how business was.

'Slowing down, signore. The tourists have gone and now we have to bargain with the local men.'

'Tough, eh?'

'Italian men think *we* should pay *them*. They are all peacocks.'

Gina was eighteen, a synthetic redhead from Salerno who was lucky to have been allowed on this beat so young and especially since she was a non-Roman. This was one of the best beats in the city and it was reserved mostly for older girls like Rosanna, who had served long apprenticeships and worked their way up from the cheap beats in the bushes out by the

Circus Maximus. Romans were born bureaucrats and the whores of Rome were no exception.

'I am trying to teach her to be patient,' said Rosanna, twenty-eight years old and a fourteen-year veteran. 'The winter is just a working holiday. One keeps at it just to stay in practice.'

'All I want,' said Gina, 'is to get rich quickly and retire.'

'Don't we all?' said McBride, went into the dark shabby entrance, shoved ten lire into the elevator's coin box and ascended slowly to his floor. In his five months in the apartment he had seen three of Rosanna's partners come and go; Gina was the latest and she had been here a month. He had never seen any pimp checking on the girls, but he knew someone ran them and the organisation was excellent. He hoped the IRA was as efficient.

Luciana was waiting for him in the apartment. She came into his arms as soon as he opened the door; she was not nymphomaniacal, but he sometimes suspected it was a condition she trained for. She was warm, beautiful, and he wished to hell now that she was not involved in tonight's operation.

'Signor Smith telephoned me. We are in trouble?'

'I'll tell you about it in a minute.'

He kissed her, went into the bedroom and dialled the phone number of the house on Crumlin Road in Dublin. The voice that answered was guarded, but he recognised it. The man who owned it had been one of those who had talked to him for three nights three months ago; McBride had phoned the same number once before, to report the arrival of Smith, Toohey and Ryan, and had been answered by the same guarded voice. Even in Dublin one couldn't be sure that the wires weren't tapped.

'This is the General Manager.' McBride would never become accustomed to his code name. There was a romantic streak in him, the Celtic blood in him would have dried to powder had there not been; but he saw the need for a mundane code name, realised the danger of using some legendary hero's name. 'We have a problem.'

He explained the need for the change in the timetable, never once mentioning any place. 'I just want one thing clear. When you put the proposition to me, you agreed I was to run it, at least till Phase One is completed. This is *my* territory, I'm the only one who knows it thoroughly. That was why you picked me to manage it.'

'Who's giving you trouble?'

'No one – yet. But I think our grey-haired friend, the Sales Manager, thinks he is the only one who can manage an emergency.'

'You don't get on with him?'

'Who does?' said McBride carelessly.

The voice 1300 miles away was sharp. 'He is one of our best men. There is no one in the company who can bring in the figures that he does.'

That was probably true, McBride guessed. Once they had the fifteen million Deutschmarks they had to be carried across Europe to the bank accounts that were waiting for them; Smith, he had been told, knew the best routes and had never once been stopped and questioned while carrying other sums. But that would be Phase Three and the rest of them would have dropped out of the operation by then.

'Okay, he's necessary. I don't argue with that. But he doesn't run Phase One. Can I tell him that on your orders?'

For the first time the voice in Dublin softened; there was a chuckle. 'That's always been the trouble with Irish business – too many chiefs. But – ' The voice hardened again. 'Don't fail us, man. We need those sales or we go bankrupt. Good luck. God be with you.'

The line clicked and McBride hung up. *God be with you*: they really believed He was on their side. Well, why not? Despite the boast of John Aylmer, the Elizabethan Bishop of London, God was not an Englishman. He belonged to everyone who believed in Him. McBride believed in Him, but made no claims.

Luciana was standing in the bedroom doorway, leaning one hip against the jamb. She was a mixture of hauteur and occasional commonness; she could look like the aristocrat she was or like one of the whores downstairs. She looked common now, the moll of a gang planning a heist: he shut his eyes against the image. But when he opened them she had straightened up, came and sat on the bed beside him, leaning forward intently.

31

'Darling, I can't be with you tonight! I have to stay home with Papa. He has an important dinner for some men from New York. I am his hostess. I have to be there!'

'You'll just have to let your father do his own entertaining.'

Count Augusto Pericoli came of an old, once influential family, but now he had nothing but his name, which he lent to foreign businesses looking for a cachet on their letterheads. He and his daughter fought like gladiator and lioness, but they loved each other. McBride wondered what the Count, another romantic, would say if he knew what his daughter was involved in.

'I'll have to stay with him, darling. He says tonight is most important to him – he won't tell me why. I can meet you somewhere when it is time for us – '

There was a ring at the doorbell. He kissed her and went out to the front door. Turk Toohey and Des Ryan slipped into the apartment with the practised ease of men who rarely made an honest entrance through a doorway. McBride led them into the small living-room, where they gave Luciana only a cursory nod. In their respective games they were both misogynists: there was no place for women.

'Smithy tells us things have gone crook on you.' Toohey was a small stringy man in his late forties, balding and with a complexion that suggested he had never quite washed off the coal dust of his early years. It was his story that he had been actually *born* in the coal mines of New South Wales and he had taken to crime only to get out of them. His first attempt at escape into a better world had been to tunnel under a bank in the mining town of Cessnock, blow the safe and finish up doing three years in Sydney's Long Bay gaol. He was only casually sympathetic to the IRA cause: he was on this job for a percentage of the take, the professional for whom the men in Dublin had been able to find no substitute. 'You can't trust the bloody churches. They're all the same.'

Des Ryan nodded emphatic agreement. He was that rare animal, an almost silent Irishman; he was slightly taller than McBride, with the shoulders of a weightlifter and the face of a boxer who had lost too many fights. Which was what he had been; he had begun fighting the English in the clubs of Liverpool, Manchester and London and had been no more successful than the organisation he had later joined. But all his defeats, and theirs, were now behind him: he was convinced that from tonight on the Irish were going to win.

McBride was about to explain what had happened when Smith arrived. There was no slipping through the doorway for him; he came in as if looking for welcoming applause. Toohey raised his ragged eyebrows halfway up his lined forehead and sank resignedly into a chair. Ryan grinned at McBride and retired to lean back against a wall. Only Luciana showed any positive antagonism to Smith. She looked at her watch.

'You are ten minutes late.'

'Being ticked off by an Italian for being late? Wonders will never cease.' Smith took off his gloves and slipped the light-weight topcoat from his shoulders. McBride, elegant though he tried to be, always felt like Li'l Abner alongside Smith. 'My dear girl – '

'I am not your dear girl – '

McBride put his arm round Luciana, doing his best to squeeze the breath out of her while trying to look affectionate. 'We don't have time for arguments – ' He hurriedly explained to them what had caused the sudden change in plans. 'We do it tonight or we wait two, maybe three years, unless our friends in Dublin can organise another heist in some other country.'

Turk Toohey stood up. 'Well, that's it. I'm going home.'

Ryan, his battered face looking even more battered with worry, spoke for the first time. 'It's not possible, Fergus. The truck's still there in the square, like you planned, but it's empty. How are we going to get all Turk's gear into the palace?'

'I'll take it down in my car.'

Toohey's eyebrows went up again. 'An Alfa sports? You want your head read, mate. I need at least a dozen lengths of four-by-two for shoring up that opening you want me to dig – I don't want the whole bloody papal palace coming down on my head. I reckon the timber will need to be about five feet long – '

'Could you get by with four-foot lengths? That's the longest I can fit into the trunk or the back seat. And I can only take eight pieces of timber.'

'It's not gunna give me much room for working. I ain't a

33

bloody mole, mate. Then there's my gear – ' Toohey shook his head. 'It's not on, Fergus. Better forget it.'

'We are *not* going to forget it!' Smith turned from admiring himself in the gilt-framed mirror over the small fireplace. Mirrors attracted him as much as women; he looked for a reflection of himself in everything he passed. 'We shall never get another opportunity like this – and we need the money *now*! Our job is only the first part of a wider campaign – and it has all been carefully timed!'

That had been the theme the two men from Dublin had, quietly but persistently, hammered at McBride when they had come to Rome. 'We know you are against the means we have had to use up till now,' they had said. 'Your dad, God rest his soul, told us that.'

'I'm dead against it,' McBride had said. 'Violence has its own backlash. Freedom isn't worth the lives of innocent people.'

'There are still some in the organisation who think it is. But the majority of us want to try another course. Money is the answer – we should have seen it years ago. The English are sick of the Six Counties, they'd give 'em away tomorrow if they knew what to do with the bloody Protestants. We're going to buy them back.'

'Buy them – ?' McBride had wanted to laugh, but the two men were too serious to be ridiculed. 'Do you think the English will set a price?'

'Not the English. We're going to buy the Protestants. One of your uncles came over from Boston, told us how he and his brothers ran their ward for years on money. Corruption is the name of the game, Fergus – Irish politicians have used it all over the world, got their men in every time, but we've never used it enough at home where we've needed it. Don't ask us why – maybe it's been because we've never had the cash, maybe it's because there's no glory in corruption and we've all wanted to be heroes. Padraic Pearse wouldn't be a saint to us if they'd jailed him for bribery instead of shooting him. But that's the way, Fergus boy, that's the way. We're going to run men for Stormont, spend money like water, buy the scrutineers when the votes are being counted – it's the way! Violence isn't winning for us – but money will, if we have enough of it! And you're the key, Fergus boy, you're the one can lead us to it! In three years the Six Counties will belong to us and we'll have done it with the greatest weapon there is – money!'

'And when you're in power in Stormont, when you've bought all these seats – how *are* you going to buy a majority? The way the electorate is gerrymandered, you'll never have a majority, no matter how much money you spend.'

'Infiltration, Fergus, infiltration. We have men in the Unionists already – we know others who can be bought.'

'As soon as they vote in Stormont for *any* sort of union with Eire, the fanatics in the Loyalists will assassinate them. You guys would do the same to anyone in the Dail who voted for reunion with England.'

'Some of our friends were planning to kill them anyway. Now, if their own people kill them, at least their families will have money in the bank.'

McBride had shaken his head in wonder at the cold, almost callous acceptance of other men's death. 'Is that what they call Irish logic or something? Is that always the Irish alternative to everything – death? Jesus!' He almost wept at the futility, the wastage, of such a philosophy.

The older of the two men, the one who had been with Joe McBride when he had been shot, said quietly, 'No, Fergus, it's not. That's what we're trying to prove this time. Sure, the fellers in Stormont are going to be in danger for a while, but we'd hope to break the back of the fanatics in the Loyalists. The gun isn't going to win the fight for either of us, us *or* them, and there are a lot of the Ulstermen who know it. We're going to do it by peaceful means – electioneering, bribery, corruption, handouts here and there – but the organisation is going to need more money than it's ever had in its life before. We've got it all worked out, Fergus, a grand strategy, but we've got to have the money first!'

McBride had sat there bemused, not quite believing what he was hearing. Yet there was a mad logic, Irish logic maybe, to what the two men were proposing. He had seen first hand what money could do in politics back home; this was only the same approach but on a grander scale. It at least had the merit of being an alternative to the gun.

35

'You're the means, Fergus boy – the Lord Himself put you in the Vatican. He doesn't believe in violence any more than you do and he's given us the sign!'

The interminable rosaries, the priests' surreptitious blessings: McBride had seen it all in his year in Cavanreagh, the calling on God as if the IRA cause were another Crusade. Not all the IRA men were Catholic believers, but these two old timers still clung to their faith: one religion was part of the other.

'With you as our inside man, Fergus – '

The job would not be too difficult. The Vatican had its security guards, but it was not an impregnable fortress. Given an insider who knew the pattern of the security, who would be in a position to discover means of entry to the Vatican museums other than by way of the guarded doors, the robbery was not an impossibility for a team of professionals.

'Could you get me good men – professionals? I don't want any other amateurs in it – one, *me*, will be enough.'

'We have three fellers in mind – this won't be the first job they've pulled. One of 'em we've never used before, but we're told he's the best in the trade. There's one thing, Fergus – '

'Yes?'

'Does it go against your faith to be robbing the Holy Father himself?'

McBride was about to say *What faith?*; but he let it pass. 'Didn't you say the Lord Himself put me here?'

'Ah, good man!' The two men from Dublin looked relieved. For a moment McBride wondered if they had been waiting on him, the voice from the Vatican, to say everything was above board; he had the feeling he had just blessed them. 'Fergus, you don't know how much we've been relying on you – '

That had been three months ago and McBride had at last seen a way of answering the voices on the hillside. Maybe Joe McBride, another of those who believed in glory, would not have approved the campaign. Even Nora, who had stood in awe of the Papacy and Rome all her life, might have had her doubts about the means of raising the money. But no other alternative had ever offered itself to McBride and until it did he knew he would always hear the pleading echo of those voices. And so he had said Yes.

And now Smith was saying, 'If circumstances say the job has to be done tonight, then we do it tonight!'

'Then you find another bloke to do your tunnelling,' said Toohey. 'I'm a professional, that's why your mates in Dublin engaged me, and I don't do things on the spur of the moment.'

The bantamweight Australian had never tried to hide his dislike of the heavyweight Anglo-Irishman. Their lives and their life styles were at the opposite ends of a wide spectrum; the only link between them was the job they were discussing. But the clash of personalities had always been one of the continuing sores in the IRA.

Smith ignored the interruption. 'I suggest we take a vote. I am for attempting the job tonight. All those in favour?'

McBride raised his hand automatically: if the job wasn't pulled tonight, he would no longer be needed. Smith looked about the room, nodded in satisfaction. 'Luciana, Fergus, myself. Three to two.'

Toohey picked up the battered trilby he always wore. 'Okay, you dig the tunnel. I'm not having a bar of it.'

McBride said, 'Turk – '

Toohey shook his head. 'No, it's not on, Fergus. I'm the one who's got to risk his neck carving out this bloody hole. You people don't have to come into the tunnel until I've made it safe. I don't mind risking being caught by the demons and locked up for a few years – that's all part of the game. I'm sympathetic to what you blokes are doing – my old man was Irish and he had to get out of Ireland because things got too hot for him in 1916. Your mates reminded me of all that when they came to see me in London. But I told them and I'm telling you now – I'm in this for the ten thousand quid they're paying me because I'm the best tunnel man in the game. But I got out of the mines because I was always scared stiff of a cave-in, and every tunnel job I've pulled since I've made sure I've never had even a cupful of dirt come down on me. Your mates could have got a dozen Irish miners to do the job, but they knew none of them was as safe and quick as me. That's why they met my price – against the price you're gunna ask for the ransom it's nothing, because they knew I could guarantee to get you into the muscums. But not now.'

'They should have checked on his guts, not his skill,' Smith said to McBride. 'It must be the first time they have ever recruited a coward.'

Toohey was unruffled, laconic; his temper never seemed to get above freezing point. 'Don't ever meet up with me, sport, when you're not on IRA business – I'll chop you down for sure. That's a promise.'

McBride jerked his head at the little man and walked out on to the narrow balcony. Toohey hesitated, put on his hat, then followed him. Below them in the street a car had pulled up at the kerb and Rosanna was having a bored argument with the driver over price; their low voices floated up like the murmur from some distant auction. Toohey looked down at them, then glanced at McBride.

'If I had any cash to spare, I think I'd take that Rosanna on a holiday with me. She's a good sort and I think she'd like to get off the beat for a couple of weeks.'

It was the first time McBride had ever seen the Australian show any sentiment. 'I didn't know you knew her.'

'Not that way, I don't. I've spoken to her a coupla times, but, when I've been coming in here. She's all right.' He lit a cigarette and blew out smoke. 'But we didn't come out here to talk about a troll. What's on your mind?'

'The job, Turk. We can't do it without you.'

'Too bad – '

'No, listen to me. Okay, it's going to be more dangerous for you than we'd counted on. I'll call Dublin and try and raise your price, if you like – '

'It ain't that, Fergus. It's just – well, that big son-of-a-bitch inside is right. I'm shit scared when I've got to take risks underground. I'd give it up if I knew some other way of pulling a big job. I ain't a hold-up man, that ain't my line. I do a fair job as a peter man, I can crack most safes they have around in offices, but there's nothing in it. Office safes never give you much more than a few hundred quid, you're working flat out all the year round just to keep up with the cost of living.'

It had never occurred to McBride that professional crooks were affected by inflation. 'Do this job for us and the cost of living shouldn't worry you for a couple of years at least.'

38

Toohey pushed his hat back, looked down into the street. Rosanna was getting into the car; her price had been met or she had surrendered to the fact of a falling market; she, too, had to worry about the cost of living. Ever since he had left home all the women in his life had been whores: he had always bought love, or what passed for it, with the same casualness as he bought his cigarettes or his beer. The thought of marriage, or even living with a woman, had never crossed his mind; he was entirely self-contained, a classic loner. If he had taken Rosanna away for a month, he would have brought her back here, said goodbye to her on the pavement below and left her without a backward glance or even a memory of her.

He leant on the railing, glanced sideways at McBride. He liked the American, but he recognised him for what he was, an amateur who would never attempt another job like this, whether it succeeded or not. He wasn't in it for the money and he didn't have the IRA passion that Smith and Ryan had. 'You oughta talked to me tonight before you talked to Dublin.'

'It was my decision, not Dublin's.'

'Well, too bad, mate.' Toohey tossed his cigarette down into the street, straightened up from the railing and turned to go back into the apartment. He stopped when McBride roughly took hold of his lapels: he had never thought of the American as a standover merchant, someone who might try a bit of the knuckle. 'Don't get rough, mate. You might get done over some night when you're not expecting it. I'm a sneaky bastard when it comes to the rough stuff.'

Christ, thought McBride, what sort of nightmare country am I entering? This was the territory his father had talked about, the knife or the gun in the dark. He heard himself say, 'The men in Dublin gave me a dossier on you, *mate*.'

'Yeah?' Toohey looked at him warily. 'Why?'

'Because I demanded it. We argued about it a whole night, but I told them I wasn't going into any job, not one like this where I could finish up with fifteen or twenty years in prison, without knowing everything about the jokers I had to work with. I know all about Smith and Des.'

'What do you know about me?'

'That the Police Judiciaire in Paris are still looking for the guy who dug the tunnel into the Banque National in the Place Vendôme in July 1971. Scotland Yard would like to talk to the guy who did the tunnel work into Barclay's Bank in Holborn, London, in April last year – '

'You can let go my coat.' Toohey stepped back as McBride let him go. His temper and his voice were still even; McBride could have been a tailor measuring him for alterations to the jacket. 'The demons in both places know I did the job, but they've got nothing on me that can take me into court.'

'The dossier doesn't stop there. There's a bit in it about what happened to the cop who surprised the gang that was trying to break into the National Westminster Bank in Belfast in June 1970.'

Toohey leaned back against the railing. Across the street a man and a woman were arguing in their apartment, raising their voices against the blaring of a radio: the woman shouted hatred to the accompaniment of syrupy strings. The little Australian's own voice was soft and casual, not the voice of a murderer: 'Who told them I did in that copper?'

'I don't know. The point is, they do know. And so do I.'

'Yeah. It was an accident, but nobody's ever gunna believe that.' Toohey nodded to himself, still leaning negligently back against the railing. Then he straightened up, looked across the street at the quarrelling couple and shook his head: the loner never had to run into *that* sort of punishment. He spat down into the street, barely missing a passer-by, looked back at McBride, said casually, 'You grass on me, mate, and no matter how long I've gotta wait, I'll kill you too.'

5

Smith, Toohey and Ryan had gone, taking their gritty atmosphere with them. McBride, out on the balcony again, heard Gina offer them an invitation and be rebuffed with some remark that brought an abusive curse from her. Beside him Luciana, her arm linked in his, said, 'It is not going well, darling.'

'Do you want to back out?'

'No. I promised I would help.'

40

'You're in this by accident – the others wouldn't hold you to any promise.'

'The others would be glad to be rid of me. But you need me, darling. Don't you?'

He couldn't give her an honest answer. She had been recruited for the job only two nights ago, an hour after the phone call had come in from Dublin to say that Maire Fitzgibbon had been picked up at the border while driving down from Belfast. Dublin suspected there might have been a leak; the picking up of the Fitzgibbon woman had been too coincidental. Fortunately she had not yet collected her air ticket to Rome, so the police had no idea where she had been heading. But it had made Dublin suddenly cautious; God knew who else was being watched; could the job be pulled with just the four men? McBride, Smith, Toohey and Ryan had been discussing the emergency when Luciana had walked in.

She had met them all only once before, when she had come, again unexpectedly, to the apartment six weeks before. She had a key to the front door and after that initial encounter with the other three men McBride had wondered how he could get it back from her; but that would only have aroused her rage and her curiosity and in the end he had let it go. She had not taken to any of the men nor they to her; McBride had told her they were documentary film men trying to get special privileges out of him for the Bishops' Synod and she had accepted his story. Smith, Toohey and Ryan had not come to the apartment again until two nights ago when Luciana was supposed to be out of town visiting relatives. When McBride had proposed that Luciana should be the look-out girl, Toohey and Ryan had looked dubious and Smith had emphatically rejected her.

'Honey,' McBride had said, 'would you mind going into the bedroom and closing the door?'

For a moment it had looked as if she was going to hit him with whatever was closest to hand; she looked wildly around for a missile. He knew her temper and he had hurriedly steered her into the bedroom, closed the door and kissed her. That had been a mistake, for she had bitten him.

Clutching his lip, he had mumbled, 'Honey, for Christ's sake trust me! I'll tell you all about it as soon as those guys give me the okay – but I can't tell you until then.'

'Tell me what? What's this about a look-out girl?'

He shook his head, in answer to her question and at his own dilemma. 'I've got to talk to *them* first. Then I'm not even sure you'll agree. Just trust me – *please.*'

She had stared at him, then abruptly softened, put a gentle finger on his lip. 'I'm sorry I did that, darling. All right, talk to them, though I don't trust any of them. I promise not to listen through the keyhole.'

But to be on the safe side he had taken Smith and the others out to the kitchen. 'Look, we have to have someone to keep an eye on the truck. If there's no one there, we could come out into the square with all the loot and walk straight into the arms of the security guards. They'll check it anyway, even though you'll have permission to leave it in the square overnight. But we don't want them hanging around at the wrong moment – when we come up out of the grotto, we've got to know the coast is absolutely clear. We're not going to be able to load the loot *and* Turk's gear in a matter of seconds.'

Des Ryan had been the first to look as if he might agree. 'Fergus is right. *Someone's* got to stay up there in the square. And none of us can be spared.'

'I don't like the thought of using women at all,' said Smith. 'They're a hindrance. I was against using the Fitzgibbon woman, but I was over-ruled.'

'How much do you have to tell her?' Toohey asked.

McBride pondered a moment. 'Pretty well everything, I guess, except who is directing us from Dublin. She's a radical – or was when she was at university. That was how I met her – I did a story on radical students at Rome University when I first came here. She's quietened down now she's graduated, but she'd understand what we're trying to do.'

'Women are unreliable, yes.' Ryan's soft voice and the use of *yes* was a too acute reminder of Nora.

'How do we know we could trust her?' said Smith.

'How do we know we can trust each other?' McBride looked around at the three of them. 'You and Des know each other. But Dublin doesn't really know that much about me and Turk, and neither do you.'

42

'We've all got Irish blood,' said Ryan, and looked as if he believed that was some sort of guarantee.

'You can't trust the Eye-ties,' said Toohey, fifteen years away from Australia and still xenophobic in his outlook. 'You never know whose side they're gunna be on.'

'If I ask her, she'll be on *my* side,' said McBride. 'I'd trust her.'

There was silence in the kitchen. The small refrigerator started up, hummed away like a timing device. Then Smith said, 'As Des says, we have to have *someone*. So it may as well be her.'

Toohey chewed on his lip, then at last nodded, saying nothing. Ryan seemed the only one with any degree of enthusiasm for McBride's suggestion. 'I think we can trust her, yes. Go and ask her, Fergus.'

It had been more difficult to convince her that he and the others were in earnest than it had been to persuade her to join them. 'Steal the Vatican treasures!'

'Look, if it's against your religious principles, forget it – '

'No, darling.' She had stroked his hair, like a mother soothing a child woken from a nightmare. 'I'm like so many Romans – the Vatican is nothing to us but a lot of smug pious bureaucrats. The Pope – '

'What about *him?*'

'Ah, he is different. He belongs to Rome – even the German one. But we wouldn't be stealing from him, would we?'

'Not the way I see it, no. But I want you to be sure you agree with what we're doing. I'm in this because I think it's the only sensible way they can ever reunite Ireland. I'm not passionate about it, but I'll be pleased and proud if we bring it off – not just the robbery but the reunion of Ireland. Maybe it will give my father the answer he was always looking for in me but never found. My mother knew the answer, but she could never convince Pop of it.'

'What was the question?'

'Whether I believed in freedom. What Pop could never understand was that I didn't believe in the gun and the bomb. Will you help us?'

'If there's to be no guns and no bombs – yes.'

That had been two nights ago and now she had asked if he needed her. He did: he was not like Toohey, a loner. He pulled her to him, felt the curve of her belly against him, put a hand on her bra-less breast. It was her one concession to Women's Lib, though he doubted if she ever gave a thought to that movement now she had left university; she had dedicated herself to him and sometimes the total surrender of her love frightened him. She moved her belly against him: down below Gina propositioned another passing man.

'There isn't time.'

'There's always time,' she said, being more Italian than ever; somewhere over the city a clock struck but he knew no one would count the strokes. 'Half an hour, darling. The men are coming for dinner at ten o'clock. I want to comfort you – '

He was tempted: she knew all the advantages of a bed besides sleeping in it. But he was worried and worry did nothing for a man's potency. He gently pushed her away. 'In another week this will be behind us, we can go back to being just like it was.'

'I had begun to worry. These past two weeks you weren't yourself – I even thought there might be another girl.'

He shook his head, kissed her. 'Never. But I've never done anything like this before – it would take the sap out of any man.'

'Are you afraid?'

He hesitated, then said, 'Yes. Not just for myself, but for you. I'm sorry I asked you.'

She locked her arms round his neck. 'Darling, whatever you believe in, I believe in. Don't be afraid for me. Let's go to bed.'

He patted her unsheathed bottom; she protruded temptation like a silk bag of whores. But unlike the girls downstairs, she would always offer love with her tempting: it would always be her weakness.

'One o'clock in the truck. Here's the spare key. Get into the driver's cabin, lock the door after you and keep out of sight. If you see anyone hanging around from two-thirty onwards, you know where we'll be making our exit – get around there and wait for us, don't let us come out into the square. We should be finished and out of the museum by three o'clock at the latest. It all depends on how long 'Turk takes to tunnel into the grotto. If we're ahead of time I'll send Des up to let you know.'

'Good luck, darling.' She kissed him and slipped reluctantly out of his arms.

When she had gone he looked at his watch: nine-twenty. Three hours to wait before he had to drive out to the house in Quattromiglia where Toohey and Ryan had all the gear and timber. They would now be sawing the timber down to four-foot lengths to fit into the boot and rear seat of his own car instead of into the back of the truck; in his imagination's car he heard the low, toneless swearing of the Australian as they literally cut down the safety odds. Toohey had estimated that he would need three times the amount of timber they were now going to take in; in their argument out on the balcony he had seen the point of the little man's rejection of the new timetable, but he had not been able to concede it. But he had seen that Toohey was scared and now, alone and with nothing to do but wait, something of that fear had begun to infect him. He would be glad when it was time to go up and get his car.

He had established a pattern since the Bishops' Synod had begun of occasionally turning up at Vatican Radio late at night to hand in special stories; the Radio broadcast twenty-four hours a day, seven days a week in thirty languages; staff and related personnel like himself were coming and going all the time. The guards on the Santa Anna gate would not query him when he drove in tonight, though he hoped they would not look too closely into his car.

He sat down, feeling worry begin to gnaw him. He was surprised to find that he was halfway through a prayer before he realised what his mind was doing.

2

McBride pulled his car into a parking spot in the deep shadow of the tower that housed Vatican Radio. There had been no bother with the guards when he had come through the gates; at one o'clock in the morning not even the most officious guard wanted to inspect the car of a senior staff man. He switched off the engine and got out of the Alfa as Smith, Toohey and Ryan slid up into the shadows beside him.

'Any trouble?' he whispered.

'They should have better locks on their gates.' Smith, somewhere, had picked up a skill for picking locks; though he did not like him, McBride was coming to appreciate that the man was a complete professional. 'Even a nun could have picked the one where we came in.'

The Alfa was loaded down like a small delivery truck. While Smith and Ryan unloaded the trunk, McBride and Toohey took the gear out of the car's back seat. A pick, a crowbar, a shovel, a drill with the two heavy batteries needed to drive it, a workman's plastic helmet, eight lengths of timber, four thick blankets, four brown friars' robes: it looked to McBride like the working gear of a Franciscan construction crew. Ryan picked up the batteries in their cradle as if they were no more than a milkman's crate of empty bottles; then he loaded four lengths of timber on his shoulder and looked at McBride. The latter waited for the young Irishman to be asked for a pick to be shoved between his teeth.

'It's nice to be back on the job, yes.'

'Do we have to stand around here gabbing?' Toohey, glancing at the inadequate timber they had brought, was nervous and irritable; he almost wished they would be disturbed before they could begin the job. 'Which way, mate?'

McBride, the friars' robes slung over one shoulder, four lengths of timber over the other, led the way across the shrub-

47

shadowed gardens. Above them the moonlight glimmered on the dome of the Basilica: in the pale blue light the huge dome seemed translucent, an inverted gossamer cup which seemed as if it might break beneath the weight of the lantern and globe that surmounted it. But none of the men looked up as, bent over beneath the weight of what they carried and the desire to be invisible, they hurried towards the rear of the papal palace.

The photostated plan McBride carried in his pocket put an unsuspected grotto at the north-east end of the Museo Chiaramonti. Long before he had joined the Vatican staff he had heard rumours of still undiscovered grottoes, but exploratory work had been suspended in this particular area; because it was so close to the Basilica itself, any further excavation had been forbidden because of the danger not only to the workmen but to the foundations of St Peter's. When he had agreed to the Dublin project he had insisted on his own scheme of action. Diligent searching and some luck had brought him to the old plan among stacks of ancient, crumbling papers in the storehouse of the Vatican Library; there had been no date on the plan but he had·known enough of Church history to put the date as pre-Constantine. The grotto was in the danger area, but the plan showed that it finished right beneath what was now the long gallery leading down to the Sistine Chapel. Above the gallery was the Vatican Library, their first target.

At the rear of the apse of the Basilica there are steps that lead down to the basement. To those who work in the Vatican they are known sardonically as the tradesmen's entrance; the ghosts of the Apostles are said to use it when calling on the ghost of St Peter. Some tradesmen, though not apostles, used it now. At the bottom of the steps they came up against a stout wooden door that McBride knew was kept locked by two iron bolts on the inside. At the time the doors had been fitted Italian design had been at the *nadir* of its functionalism: the hinges were on the *outside*. It took Toohey only a few minutes to remove the hinges, despite the fact that the bolt-heads were rusty and seemingly hadn't been touched in centuries. Then the four men pressed their combined weight against the door and the bolts inside, with only a faint whisper of protest, yielded. The door opened inwards and the four men, picking up their gear again, slipped through. They pulled the door back into place so that the damage to it would not be apparent to any guard who inspected it from the top of the steps. They were now in the basement of the Basilica, down among the ghosts of history if not of the Apostles.

McBride switched on a flashlight and led the way. He could feel himself sweating with exertion and excitement and nervousness; the ray of the torch trembled like a blind man's white stick. He wondered for a fleeting moment if his father had felt like this on his one, ill-fated expedition to the power station.

The four men passed among the conglomerated spare parts of religion: statues in need of repair, rusted candlesticks, dusty banners, huge candles stacked like preserved icicles. They came to a flight of stairs and McBride, as sure of himself as a guide-dog, led them up it. He was the only amateur among them but he was determined to prove to the others that he could be as professional as any of them. He had done his homework, the mark of any professional, had scouted every inch of the route he had chosen.

They were now in the Basilica itself, hurrying silently down one side of it. Out of the corner of his eye McBride saw the glow of the altar lamp, following him like a red suspicious eye as he slipped by each of the side pillars. All the old superstition came back: he was a thief in the house of God. Abruptly he quickened his pace, as if he were being pursued by furies he had long forgotten. Suddenly he held up the arm carrying the friars' robes and they all stopped, stiff as statues that had been taken down from their pedestals and then left while someone made up his mind what to do with them. From the far corner of the Basilica there came a cough, then a low voice said something; peering across the vast dark interior, McBride saw the half-open door and the black silhouetted figure of the security guard standing there. McBride felt the silence of the huge church pressing down on him: the wrath of God was not a terrible roar after all. The lengths of timber rattled on his shoulder; for a moment he had the awful fantasy that he was carrying his own cross to be made up. The guard came out of the room, moving out of the line of the lighted doorway; he was lost in the shadows and McBride strained his ears for the

49

approaching hurrying footsteps. Then the man moved back into the doorway, paused a moment, then went back into the room.

The four men moved on, went down another flight of steps, and McBride was through purgatory: again the old superstitions came back.

He could feel the cold sweat running on him as Smith picked the lock of the grille door that barred their way into the grotto before them. This was the last grotto to have been opened; further excavation had stopped here. Smith opened the door with a flourish, they all passed through and the door was pulled to behind them. Smith and Toohey had now switched on their flashlights and the mosaics on the walls, gold and green and blue, glimmered like countless tongues of flame. Christ climbed a hill, handsome and robust: the artists of this period had still been under the Hellenic influence. Smith stopped for a moment, reached across the protective rail that ran round the inside of the grotto, and ran his hand lovingly over the surface of the wall.

'Forget it,' said Toohey sourly. 'We can't take anything like that.'

'The interest was purely aesthetic,' said Smith. 'A word I doubt you could spell.'

'Quit it!' McBride hissed as the voices were amplified in the narrow, low-roofed grotto.

They had come to the end of the chamber, to be faced by a brick wall. Steel girders held up thick beams that supported the roof. Toohey swung the ray of his torch up to the mosaic-patterned ceiling: a long crack ran across it, past the beams to disappear into the top of the brick wall.

'What's behind the wall?'

'About six or eight feet of rock and earth, I think – maybe a bit more. Then there's the other grotto I told you about. That's the one that leads up beneath the gallery.'

All four men had put down their loads and Toohey, a craftsman at work, was inspecting the wall. The others stood about like land speculators awaiting an estimate: was St Peter's worth knocking down? McBride wiped the sweat from his face, aware that none of the others seemed to be troubled by any such sign of apprehension.

'If I make a hole in the wall,' said Toohey, 'I could bring the whole bloody lot down on us. If you'd brought me here at the start, mate, I'd have told you to forget it.'

'How could I get you down here?' said McBride, voice edgy. 'That door and grille back there is only meant to keep out tourists who wander off limits, but if we'd come down here before and I'd got you in here to look at this and we'd been discovered – '

'All right, you've made your point,' said Toohey.

'The real point,' said Smith, 'is that we're here now and the time for debate is long past. Get to work, dear chap.'

'Get stuffed,' said Toohey casually. 'I'll start work when I'm ready.'

But McBride was relieved to see that the little man, hat pushed back on his head, was still examining the brick wall and the steel supports. He might be afraid of what could happen, but he had the pride that so many craftsmen can't resist: this was his trade, none of the others could do it, and he had to show them how good he was.

'Okay,' he said at last, took off his hat and began to strip off his jacket and shirt. He put the plastic helmet carefully on his head and pulled on a pair of work gloves. 'You buggers can sit down and watch.'

He connected the batteries to the drill while Ryan went back and hung the four blankets over the entrance. McBride knew the blankets would provide only flimsy insulation against the noise of the drill, but it was the best they could do. Their best protection was Toohey's own soundproof chamber.

From the long box he had been carrying he produced a bundle of aluminium rods. He fitted them together into a framework; then he fitted a large plastic cover over the frame. To McBride it looked like the sort of cover he had seen repairmen using above manholes in streets back home, only it was clear plastic and not canvas. One end was completely closed; the other end, which faced the wall, was open. Toohey finally took out a light face mask and an air cylinder mounted on a back pack.

'There's no air in there once I start working,' he said. 'When I get in there, you blokes push the tent flat up against the wall and keep it there. Put some weights, the lengths of timber will do, on those flaps at the bottom to keep it down. There's gunna be *some* noise, but you'll be surprised how little. Keep an eye on me and when I give you the signal, let me out. I'll have to come out every once in a while because the tent is gunna fill up with dust pretty quick. Okay, let's get started.'

McBride picked up one of the friars' robes, threw it to Ryan. 'Okay, Des, go upstairs. You know your act if you're picked up. You're Father Brian and you've stayed inside the Basilica to do twenty-four hours' penance. They're not going to believe you, but don't make your break till they've got you outside. If they try to come down here, you better start a brawl with them.'

'I thought you said the guards came around only every two hours?' said Smith.

'They do.' The Patrol of the Hundred Keys, a security guard carrying a ring holding the keys to all the main doors, accompanied by a fireman, made the rounds of the Vatican during the night. 'But it's just as well to be sure, isn't it?'

Ryan put on the robe and went back upstairs, carefully putting the blankets back into place behind him. Toohey put on the mask, nodded to McBride and stepped into the plastic tent. McBride and Smith pushed it flat up against the wall; a suction rubber channel ran right round the edge, taking hold of the brickwork where Toohey had brushed it clear of grit. The little ex-miner, looking like some helmeted gnome trapped under plastic for exhibition, went to work on the wall.

There *was* little noise, no more than a grating hum that the blankets absorbed as soon as it reached them. Dust rose up around Toohey and soon he was just a dim shape, a thickening of the dust itself, in the cocoon. Then the humming stopped, a hand spread itself like a brown crab on the plastic, and McBride and Smith pulled the tent away from the wall.

Toohey took off the mask, wiped the dust from his face. 'I'll be through it in another go. How was the noise?'

'Great,' said McBride. 'I mean, there wasn't any, none they'd hear upstairs. Who dreamed this up?' He nodded at the tent.

'I did. I once read about a kiddy who smothered under a plastic bag, put it over his head and couldn't get it off. His mum was in the next room and didn't hear him yelling. I just started to experiment and I come up with that. Noise has always been the problem in my job. Well, time for another go.'

It took him only another five minutes' work with the drill. Then the tent was pulled away, he took off the mask and air cylinder, and he began to work with a lightweight pick such as miners use. He pulled the last bricks out one by one, easing them out carefully by hand and watching all the time for subsidence in the rest of the wall. McBride stood close by, every nerve cracking inside him like snapped tendons, and even Smith, watching the break in the roof, had begun to sweat a little. At last Toohey stood back, looked at the earth and rock that showed through the hole in the wall.

'What do you reckon?' McBride asked.

'I'll go through that like a bandicoot,' said Toohey, and did not bother to explain what a bandicoot was. Underground again, he was becoming more and more Australian, the youthful miner of long ago. 'Trouble is, soft stuff like that crumbles like stale cake.'

'How do you feel?'

'Well, I couldn't kick the arse off an emu, if that's what you mean.'

It wasn't what McBride meant, since he didn't know what it meant, but he just nodded. 'Well, it's up to you, Turk.'

'I take it you're not feeling very confident or perky?' said Smith.

'You're getting on my tit, that's what's wrong with me,' said Toohey, and picked up the short-handled miner's pick and began to chip at the earth and rock as if he wished it were Smith's head.

McBride looked at his watch: the patrol would be coming into the Basilica on its inspection in another fifteen minutes. 'Will you need to use the drill again?' Toohey shook his head and McBride looked at Smith. 'Better go up and tell Des to come back.'

For a moment it looked as if Smith was going to argue: he had never been anyone's messenger boy. Then abruptly he went out of the grotto as Toohey turned and looked over his shoulder at McBride.

'They sent you a pain in the arse there, mate. We're gunna be cutting each other's throat before this is over.'

McBride nodded. To give himself something to do and keep his mind distracted, he began to dismantle Toohey's tent. Then Smith and Ryan came back, and they and McBride stood watching like three kibbitzers who did not know each other while Toohey dug deeper and deeper into the rock and earth behind the brick wall. Then McBride looked at his watch, gave the signal and Toohey stopped work. All the flashlights were extinguished. McBride crept back through the absolute blackness of the grotto, feeling his way along the protective rail, to the blanket-covered door. He pulled the blankets aside and listened carefully. Up in the Basilica he heard the hollow clack-clack of footsteps, the murmur of voices, a hoarse hacking cough: the awesome splendour of the huge church was reduced by the ordinariness of its caretakers. The men went on their way, keys jangling like harness metal, dying away in the vast stillness. No doubt they were convinced their job was a sinecure, that no one had any intention of breaking into the house of God. Those days were over, gone with the barbarians.

McBride switched on his flashlight and went back to the other end of the grotto. Smith and Ryan switched on their torches and Toohey went back to work. Within ten minutes he was two feet into the wall of rock and earth, putting up his first lengths of timber shoring. Each time he shoved in a piece of timber he looked up at the crack in the roof of the grotto, but he said nothing. He was four feet in behind the brick wall, lying on his back and working into position the length of timber Ryan was passing to him, when the trickle of earth began to pour slowly into his face. He came out in a rush, his feet pushing Ryan out of the way, and sprawled on the floor of the grotto.

McBride, holding his breath though unaware of it, looked quickly up at the roof. The crack had widened, spreading slowly like a black vine across the mosaic on the ceiling: Adam and Eve stood on either side of an ever-widening gap, the Serpent was chopped in two. All four men watched, saw the earth spill through the crack and fall like a thin brown muslin curtain between McBride and Toohey on one side and

54

Smith and Ryan on the other. It slowed to a thick trickle at the widest end of the gap, then stopped. The movement of the roof, for the moment anyway, had come to a standstill.

Toohey slowly picked himself up, brushing the dust from his face. He said nothing, but turned back to look at the brick wall. It bulged like a huge red-brown abscess: at any moment it might burst. Slowly, keeping an eye on the wall, Toohey began to gather up his gear.

'That's put the kybosh on it. I'm going home.'

'You can't!' McBride's voice came out of a bone-dry throat. 'We're nearly there! You can't have more than three or four feet to go!'

'Look, mate – '

'No, *you* look!' McBride grabbed Toohey by the front of his singlet; he could smell the sweat on the little man. 'If you pull out now, we're done. Christ, what do you want for ten thousand pounds? You're paid to take the risk!'

'I want to go on living, that's all – '

'Don't we all? If that roof comes down, it kills me as well as you!'

'Let him go,' said Smith. 'We don't need him. We'll do it ourselves.'

'You walk out now,' said McBride, 'and I'll see you don't get a goddam penny. And Dublin just might let the Belfast cops know where you can be picked up.'

'Let's give it a try, Turk,' said Ryan. 'If you like, I'll go first, yes – '

Toohey had not looked at Smith or Ryan. He stared at McBride, eyes as hard as the end of the drill at his feet. 'You're gunna need watching, mate.' Then he looked up at the crack in the roof; there was no more trickling earth. 'If any of you remember any prayers, you'd better say 'em.'

'Who'd listen?' said Smith.

Nobody had an answer to that. Toohey looked around the grotto, then said, 'I'm gunna need more timber. You better start breaking up that railing.'

He slid gingerly back into the narrow tunnel, while Ryan at once moved to begin breaking up the protective railing. Toohey gestured for more timber and McBride pushed in another length. Toohey shoved it into place, lay on his back looking up at the rock and earth only a foot from his face, then he motioned for his pick.

'Here goes.'

It took him another forty minutes to tunnel through the remaining few feet of earth and rock. The actual digging out was not difficult; the rock came away *too* easily. The dirt and rock were passed back down the tunnel in a child's plastic bucket; each bucketful had the potent threat of a bomb. McBride took over from Ryan, crawling in on his stomach to help shore up the roof and sides with the lengths of timber. The boards themselves were no problem, but even with the timber from the broken-up railing there was not enough. Earth kept trickling down from the roof of the tunnel, and each time McBride withdrew he came out with his face mud-streaked from sweat and dirt.

Then suddenly, so abruptly that his arm jerked and he brought down a shower of earth on himself, Toohey broke through into the far grotto, the one that had lain undisturbed for almost eighteen hundred years. Centuries-stale air came out in a rush like poison gas; Toohey flung a hand over his nose and mouth and cursed. But he stayed in the tunnel, widening the hole into the grotto. At last, covered in dirt, he came scrambling out.

'It's all yours. But take it easy – that tunnel's as shaky as an old crow's tit.'

Holding his flashlight ahead of him, McBride crawled cautiously through the tunnel and slid on all fours down into the far grotto. He flashed the beam of the torch around him, but saw nothing that excited him; the mosaics were only a repetition of those in the grotto he had just left. Only his sense of history gave him any thrill other than that this was the way to the treasures above him. God alone knew who was the last man who had stepped in here; the world had suffered a dozen empires since a light had last glowed in this darkness. He turned and called through the tunnel for the others to follow him.

Ryan came first, scrambling through as if afraid that the tunnel would cave in on him. Smith was next, fastidiously brushing the dirt from himself as soon as he was in the grotto. Toohey was last, pushing his gear and the friars' robes ahead of him: if all went according to plan they would not be coming back this way.

Toohey slid into the grotto, picked up his shirt, jacket, hat and his drill and gestured to the others to take the rest of the gear. McBride's flashlight was focused on the little man as he put the drill on his shoulder. A grotesque shadow of him was flung on the mosaics behind him: a huge black hunchback, he stood among golden angels.

'Where do we go from here?'

'Upwards this time,' said McBride. 'Through the floor of the gallery, then it's just a walk up the stairs to the Library.'

'Sounds easy,' said Ryan.

'Yeah,' said Toohey, raising an eye towards the roof. 'But we're still down the bloody mine.'

Then McBride saw the dirtfall trickling down through the beam of his torch. He looked up, jerking up the beam, and saw the rapidly widening crack in the roof of this grotto.

'Run!'

The rumbling, at first, had the sound of a faraway thunderstorm. McBride, still standing stockstill despite his warning to the others to run, saw the roof beginning to tremble, breaking up, as Toohey had warned, like a piece of stale cake. Angels, saints, Christ Himself, all began to disintegrate: pieces of mosaic fell like blue, gold and green gems through the beam of the torch. The head of Christ came down in one piece, shattered as it hit the floor, was covered at once in a fall of earth. The rumbling grew, became a roar.

Toohey, clutching his drill, brushed by McBride. The end of the drill caught McBride and swung him round; he snapped out of the trance that had gripped him and he went after the other three men in a mad scramble. The roof of the grotto came down with a thunder that deafened them; an explosion of dust enveloped them. Though the men hung on to their flashlights, each one's finger slipped from the button: they were suddenly engulfed in a thick blackness that threatened to choke them.

McBride, stumbling headlong through the black dust, certain

57

that he was dead but wondering why it took so long for consciousness to die, hit something that gave, grabbed at it and realised it was one of the others. Whoever he was, he was not dead; he struggled in McBride's frantic grasp. The writhing body, alive and fighting to stay that way, suddenly made McBride realise all was not over. He fell away from the other man, all at once determined to survive. The rumbling was still going on, but it was receding; there was another loud roar and somewhere beyond the blackness the roof of another grotto caved in. McBride pressed the button on his torch and the beam flashed on. The dust was still thick around them; but nothing more was falling through it. They were safe, at least for the moment.

McBride felt a hand reach out and grab him. Then another hand came at him from his other side. He opened his mouth to shout to the others, but at once knew his mistake; he gulped in a mouthful of dust and he began to choke. His eyes filled with tears, the tears turned to mud; his nose felt stuffed with solid earth. He was going to be stifled to death, not killed by falling masonry.

He stumbled around, the hands still clinging to him, and bumped his knee against something hard and solid. He fell over it, throwing out the arm that still held two of the friars' robes to cushion his fall; but he did not fall all the way to the ground, was brought up sharply against another obstruction. Still coughing, his lungs full and bursting now, he felt his way up the obstruction: it was a slope of some sort, earth, rubble, masonry: something that seemed solid and climbable. He began to crawl up it, not really expecting to get anywhere but above the choking dust. His torch had gone out, but he still clung to it. The hands had let go of him, but now he could hear the scrambling behind him.

Then he saw the glimmer of light beyond the thinning dust. He quickened his pace, clambering up the pile of rubble that had been the roof of the grotto; he had no idea where his feet trod, but they crunched down on the faces of angels and saints; then he was above the killing dust, was pulling himself up on to the floor of the long gallery that led down to the Sistine Chapel. He lay on the floor, gasping hoarsely, trying to clear his lungs and eyes of the dust; he wanted to laugh at the sardonic accident that had brought them out here at the very spot at which they had been aiming, but his throat was too dry for anything but a harsh grunt. Dimly he was aware of the other three men crawling up on to the floor beside him.

He got painfully to his feet, spitting out dust, trying to work up saliva to clear his mouth. He blew his nose, wiped the mud and dust from his eyes. The others were on their feet, coughing and spluttering; his eyes cleared enough for him to see what a sorry gang they all were. They would be even sorrier looking if they did not get out of here soon.

He threw one of the robes at Toohey and pulled his own over his head; Smith and Ryan were already donning theirs. They all hastily brushed themselves down, wiped their faces and hair free of dust; they were still far from immaculate, but McBride had seen shabbier friars. With Toohey still clutching his drill, looking now like a wizened mother in a brown dress holding a child to her breast, they fled up the gallery away from the Sistine Chapel.

They reached a corner just as a security guard came round it. McBride was in the lead and he was past the man before he realised what he was; he pulled up sharply, turned round and saw Smith bring his heavy torch down on the man's head. The guard went down without a sound, dead or unconscious before he hit the floor. McBride felt sick: he had the sudden feeling that everything from now on was going to go wrong, that the worst was still to come. The others, without a backward glance at the still form of the guard, ran on and up a flight of stairs that faced them. On the landing they turned to wait for McBride.

'Which way?' Smith said. 'Quick, man – which way?'

They could hear voices and running footsteps now; the corridors and stairwells echoed with panic and puzzlement. An elderly guard came galloping down the stairs; he went past them with hardly a nod at them. McBride pulled the cowl of his robe closer about his face: he was back in home territory.

'This way!'

He led the way at a run up the stairs. He had reached the top, was still running too fast to pull up, when he saw the familiar figure standing in the doorway to the Vatican Library.

2

Pope Martin, standing in the Library, heard the rumble some-where beneath his feet and a moment later felt the building tremble. An earthquake in Rome? Didn't the Lord think he had enough to test him without visiting natural disasters on him? He waited for a second tremor, the one that would collapse the building, but none came; he heard a second rumbling roar, but this time the building did not move. Then he knew the Lord had heard his instant and involuntary prayer: if the first rumble had been a tremor, at least it was not going to be followed by an earthquake. Unless it was a warning to get out of here as quickly as possible, that the worst could still happen.

This was no place for him at almost two o'clock in the morn-ing. He had gone to bed a little after midnight and had lain awake as if it were midday. A recent sufferer from insomnia, he had replaced the Spartan cot of his predecessor with the comfortable four-poster that had helped him sleep in Munich. But tonight no amount of comfort or willpower had been able to relax him. His mind had been livelier than a gallery of cherubim: *they* always tired him in paintings with their smug, smiling athleticism. He had tried prayer and other diverting thoughts, but always his mind, prowling in the darkness of the room, had kept returning to the project that would be an-nounced tomorrow. Had he done the right thing? How passion-ate would the attack from the conservatives be, would they see it as another thumbing of his nose at their influence? In itself the sending on tour of the treasures was not that im-portant; but he was losing the support of the conservatives and he had begun to learn the lesson of all men in power. One opponent won over was worth two committed supporters; converts, as the Church knew, always worked harder than those already committed. The past year had been difficult, but the year ahead promised worse. Perhaps he was tilting at windmills, ignoring the storms that might demolish the windmills and himself.

He should have allowed the Director-General of the Museums

60

to choose the treasures, put out the news of the tour as a routine announcement. There would have been repercussions, but that way there would have been an avenue of retreat if the opposition proved to be as strong as he feared it might. Why, he hadn't even seen half of what had been selected!

It was an excuse to get out of bed and he recognised it for what it was. Anything to tire him out, to bring him back to bed too exhausted to do anything but sleep. If one was preparing for another fight, one should at least know what one had chosen as weapons. He slipped on a plain black soutane over his pyjamas, debated whether he would need a coat and decided he would be warm enough. Still in his slippers he opened his bedroom door, ready to move through the apartment to the front door. Then he remembered the Swiss Guard who would be on duty there: twenty-four hours a day they stood guard against the furies, whatever they might be, sworn to defend him to their death. They hadn't fought a major battle in defence of a pope since 1527 when 147 of their complement of 200 had died protecting Clement the Seventh against the marauders of Charles the Fifth; but their standards were still so high, so fiercely loyal, that any corps in any professional army were like chocolate soldiers beside them. Martin admired them, but tonight he did not want to be under their protective and, no matter how they might hide it, curious eye.

He turned, made his way towards the rear of the apartment. He let himself out by a back door and made his way downstairs through the palace. The corridors and stairways were deserted; he was thankful that the staff went to bed as soon as he himself retired. Only when he finally came to the main doors of the Library did he meet anyone: a sleepy guard who looked at the Holy Father as if he were the Holy Ghost.

'Do I look so frightening, Giulio?' A politician as well as a priest, Martin had learned the value of a memory for names; in his twelve months in Rome he had come to know the names of everyone, high and low, who worked for him. 'I just want to go into the Library.'

'*Now*, Holiness?'

One of the virtues he had had to teach himself since coming to Rome had been patience: people expected so much more of a pope than of a cardinal. He sighed. '*Now*, Giulio.'

'*Alone*, Holiness?'

'I'd prefer it, Giulio.'

The guard stifled a shrug; it wasn't his place to criticise crazy popes who went wandering through museums in the dead of night. He broke the alarm connection, unlocked the big doors, stepped inside the Library and switched on the lights. The long pillared room blazed with the colour of its frescoed walls and ceiling, but Giulio turned his back on it.

He made a gesture and Martin read it: *It's all yours, Holiness*. But it wasn't all his, it was the Church's and everyone's in it, including Giulio himself. But it was no use explaining that to the guard: he would want no part of it.

'Close the doors, Giulio. If anyone sees the lights and comes inquiring, don't let them in.'

He moved into the long room as the guard, with a final shrug that Martin caught out of the corner of his eye, closed the doors. The richly decorated walls and ceiling of the Library were not to everyone's taste, but they suited his; austerity depressed him and he had sour memories of the concrete box, inspired by the Bauhaus influence, that had been his first parish church. He felt an urge to touch the luxuriant walls, but he resisted it; sensuality was frowned upon in a pope, at least since the times of the Borgias. He smiled to himself: *the old days are gone forever, Kurt*. The new name, Martin, still hung on him like someone else's suit; he doubted if he would ever talk to himself as Martin. Kurt Stecher was the man under his skin and he would never be driven out by the man who wore the papal robes.

He was standing by one of the glass exhibition cases, admiring the beautiful illuminated books it contained, when he heard the rumble. The case trembled on its thin legs and he instinctively put a hand on it to steady it. He waited for the second tremor, but none came, only the second rumbling roar; he said his quick prayer of thanks. Then the door swung open and Giulio, walnut face cracked apart, stood there on legs that threatened to fold under him.

'Something downstairs has collapsed, Holiness! Everything may fall down!'

Smiling, he walked to the door, took the guard by the arm and said calmingly, 'Giulio, have a little more faith. Do you think the Lord is going to let his house fall down around my ears?'

Giulio still looked afraid and unconvinced: his wages didn't cover a guarantee of faith. 'It would be safer outside, Holiness – '

'Go downstairs and see what has happened. I'll take up your guard post till you come back.'

Dubious, scared, Giulio shuffled off towards the stairs. The gabble of excited voices and the clatter of running feet came up from the floor below; the sounds seemed to give Giulio confidence that the palace was not about to tumble down and he suddenly quickened his pace and galloped down the stairs. Martin stood outside the Library doors listening to the hubbub below, smiling almost benignly even though he was puzzled; whatever had caused the commotion, he understood the staff's reaction to it. Unlike many foreigners, he was never critical of Italian excitability: he just wished there were more of it and less chill restraint over in the Curia.

He was looking at the stairs, waiting for the return of Giulio, when the four Franciscans, their brown robes dusty, their cowls pulled low over their heads, came running up from below. They pulled up sharply when they saw him; he had time to notice that one of them, the shortest, carried some sort of drill that he hugged to himself as some musician might hold a valuable instrument. Then the four friars hurried towards him, pushed him roughly back into the Library and slammed the doors shut. The last man in took the keys out of the doors and locked them from the inside. Then he stood with his back to the doors, his head turned as if he had changed his mind and wanted to go out again.

'I beg your pardon, Father,' said the tallest friar, 'but we don't have time for niceties. Tie him up, Des.'

'What with?' All their voices were muffled by the cowls pulled close about their faces and each held by a pin.

'The cord round his waist, stupid. Isn't that what they're for, Father? Tying up the doubting Thomases – ' Then the tall man stopped, the brown cowl stiff as a block of wood on his shoulders; then he turned slowly and spoke to the Franciscan

63

who stood with his back to the closed doors. 'Do you recognise whom we have here?'

The man against the door nodded, keeping his hooded head turned down. He gave a muffled growl that was barely distinguishable as 'Let's get out of here quick!'

'Oh, we're going to get out of here,' said the tall man. 'But it is a pity we can't take with us what we came for. Unless we take a substitute?'

'No!' The man against the door grabbed at the cowl about his face as if afraid that it would fly open with the explosion of his protest.

There was the sound of running feet out in the corridor and a moment later Giulio began to bang on the doors. 'Holiness! Are you in there? Are you all right?'

Martin opened his mouth, but the tall man clapped a hand over his face and shook his head. The cowl fell open slightly and the Pope caught a glimpse of a long nose and dark angry eyes; the features were familiar but only because he had seen so many like them since coming to Rome; he had come to believe there was a Vatican face. Then the tall friar was behind him, hissing in his ear, 'If you know what's good for you – !' The strong fingers tightened on his mouth, hurting him.

'Where do we go from here?' The little friar with the drill under his arm spoke for the first time, looking at the man against the door.

The latter hesitated, then skirting the group, passing behind the Pope and the man who still held him, he led the way down the long room towards the far end. The doors were still being hammered on; other voices had joined Giulio's. The tall man took his hand away from the Pope's mouth, pushed him in the back, and all five men, one reluctantly, went hurrying down away from the commotion behind the locked doors.

The man leading them knew his way: he led them through doors and down passages like some guide in a crazily speeded-up film: Martin passed through parts of his palace he had never seen before. Then they were out in the night air, in a garden where the sculptured bushes crouched like green-black animals wrapped in sleep; an alarm bell was ringing somewhere and lights were going on in windows like startled eyes. Far away

64

there was the sound of a police siren, but it seemed to be getting no nearer. Martin looked up and saw a star fall like a thrown blue stone across the corner of a building that he recognised as his own palace: was it a sign? Then he chided himself for his superstition and tried for some prayer. But what prayers were there against kidnappers?

The man who was leading them suddenly stopped, stepped back into the shadow of a wall till he was invisible, then said, his voice still muffled, 'Now we'll leave him.'

'Ah no, we're taking him with us.' The tall friar dug the Pope in the back; for the first time in years Martin felt again the hard, chilling threat of a gun-barrel. '*He's* our treasure now. He's worth a dozen Joshua Rolls.'

He looked at the other two men and after a moment the shorter of the two said, 'Fair enough. He'll be easier to carry, too.'

The man in the shadows said, 'What's that you've got? I thought I said no guns?'

'I always carry my own insurance.' The tall man's voice was sharp; Martin felt the gun go harder into his back and again he prayed. I'm abject, he thought, afraid of death. But only because this was not the sort of death he would have chosen for himself; it would achieve nothing, only a sort of empty martyrdom that would inspire nobody.

'For Christ's sake, quit arguing!' the little man said. 'The demons will be here soon!'

The sirens were now getting closer, coming from three directions: up from the river, down the hill from the Via Gregorio Settimo, from the north along the Viale Angelico: the modern furies, whee-whaaing through the night, were descending on St Peter's. Shouts were coming from the palace and the museums; the corridors echoed with shouts and, once, a woman's scream. Martin, despite his predicament, smiled: someone must have broken into Sister Caterina's room.

'Let's get out of here!'

Martin sensed a growing panic among the men; the gun kept rubbing nervously against his spine. So far he had said nothing; how did one talk to one's kidnappers? But now he said, 'You'd do better to leave me.' He spoke in English, the language the men had used. 'You can get away on your own – I promise to stay here, give you time – '

'Afraid, are you?' the tall man snarled.

'Yes,' Martin admitted. He had been afraid before, when he had preached against the persecution of the Jews in the box-like church in that suburb of Augsburg, when he had been in Dachau and every dawn had been a threat and not a promise; he was wise and experienced enough not to be ashamed of being afraid. He said quietly, 'Just as much as you are, my friend. We could both die – you could kill me and the police will kill you. We can prevent that by being sensible.'

'Let him go,' said the man in the shadows, voice still indistinct. Something hovered on the edge of Martin's memory: an accent, an inflection. But he couldn't pin it down and he peered into the shadows, trying to identify the shapeless, darker shadow. 'We'll never get away with him.'

'We can try – '

On the other side of the small garden a covered flight of steps suddenly blazed with light like a cubist fire; from farther up the steps, out of sight, came the clatter of running footsteps. Martin was pushed forward by the gun into the shadows; he stood side by side with the man he thought he knew but could not recognise. The tall man said, 'Better get us out of here. You know all the exits.'

For a moment Martin thought the tall man was talking to *him*; then the man beside him moved away from the wall and the Pope felt the gun dig into his back again. They slid along the wall, keeping to the shadows, slipping behind the shrubs and hedges, and came to a door.

'It's locked.'

The tall man moved past Martin, took something from a pocket under his friar's robe, worked on the padlock and a moment later slid back the bolt. They went into utter blackness, closing the door behind them, and stood close together like peak-hour commuters in a train that had broken down in a blacked-out subway. Martin could smell the after-shave lotion on the tall man; something tangy and manly, he supposed the advertisements would call it. He could smell the little man, earth and sweat, and the one called Des whose breath smelled

66

of the gum he had just begun to chew rapidly. There seemed
no smell at all about the fourth man, unless it was that of fear.

'You stink of incense,' said the tall man.

'An occupational disease,' said the Pope.

'Quiet!' whispered the man who had led them in here and, a
moment later they heard the footsteps, half a dozen of them,
go hurrying by outside.

A man said, 'Who would want to kidnap him?'

'The Curia?' said a second voice, and laughed.

'It's no laughing matter,' a third voice joined in. 'He could
be already dead. No one is safe these days – '

Then the searchers were gone, their footsteps dying away in
Martin's ears like the last vestiges of hope. His body, taut as
those around him had been, suddenly slackened; the gun
grated hard against his backbone, but he didn't flinch. He could
feel the indecision among the men surrounding him; except
for the tall man, they really didn't know what to do with him.
Father, forgive them, for they know not what they do. But irony
had too sour a taste at a time like this.

A flashlight was produced, swung round the room in which
they stood, then flicked off. But there was time to see they were
in a gardener's storeroom. 'This leads nowhere.' The man who
knew all the exits was obviously disguising his voice; it was no
more than a croak in his throat. 'We've got to go out through
the gardens.'

'Half bloody Rome's outside there now!' Out in St Peter's
Square sirens were arriving every few seconds: the night
moaned with painful excitement.

'We can't stay here,' said the tall man. 'They'll have been
through every nook and cranny of this place by daylight.'

'What about – ?'

'No names,' croaked the man who, Martin guessed, had been
the leader when this business had started; but he was no longer,
at least as far as the tall man was concerned. 'If she hasn't
gone by now, she'll be trapped in the truck and they'll find her.'

'Too bad,' said the tall man. 'I hope she can keep her mouth
shut.'

Even in the darkness Martin felt the stiffening of the man
beside him. Then the door was opened cautiously; stars

glimmered in a thin wedge of sky. All the sirens but one had stopped; it went on and on like a crying forgotten child at some party. There was a rising babble of voices coming from somewhere, but the garden for the moment was silent, deserted. The door was pushed open wider, Martin was dug in the back again by the gun, and all five men stepped out into the night.

The man who had been the leader slipped away along the shadowed wall and the tall man growled, 'He had better come back.'

'He will,' said the little man. 'For Christ's sake, stop bitching.'

'He'll come back,' said Des confidently, and a minute later the ex-leader, almost as if determined to reassert himself, came running back.

'Okay. But we'll have to leave *him*.'

'He goes with us,' said the tall man stubbornly.

'Seems a pity to leave him,' said the little man. 'He's worth Christ knows how much – '

Des said, 'We could be caught, anyway. If we're going to take the risk of getting out of here, let's try for a dividend.'

There was a rustle of the leader's robes that could have been a shrug, then he croaked resignedly, 'Okay. But we don't harm him.'

'Why should we?' said the tall man, but Martin felt the hard contradiction of the gun in his back.

It was the gun, Martin decided later, that was the deciding factor. He did not think he was a cowardly man, but he knew he was not a foolhardy one. The gun was kept pressed into his back as the four men, two in front of him and two behind him, walked across the garden, through a door in a wall and down a long path that led to one of the northern gates. Twice Martin was pushed roughly and quickly into the shadows as groups of men, security guards, Swiss Guards, even half a dozen priests, crossed and recrossed the gardens.

As they moved on the tall man said, 'You're a wise man, Holiness. Not a peep out of you then.'

'Not wise,' said Martin. 'I'm just afraid of violence, that's all. Towards myself or anyone else.'

'Is there a guard on that gate?' the tall man asked the leader.

'Usually just one at night. There could be more now.'

'If you are afraid of violence,' said the tall man to Martin, 'don't try any tricks when we get to the gate. I shan't kill you – you're too valuable – but I'll kill the guard. You understand?'

Martin nodded, feeling the old sickness that he thought he had forgotten . . . *We want the Jew you are hiding, said Kessler, the SS man. We shan't hurt you. Just give us the Jew* . . . Oh Lord, let them take me from here without anyone being hurt!

'I understand.'

The gate was locked and there was still only one guard on duty. He peered in at them through the bars, only his chin, like a hunk of blue rock, visible under the shadow of his cap. 'Where do you priests think you're going? This is no time of night for you – '

Des stepped up close to the gate. 'Listen – '

The guard leaned close and Des's arm went through the bars and circled the man's neck. From up the street there came the sound of an approaching police car; the siren wailed its warning, as if trying to play fair with the men it was hoping to catch. Des pressed hard on the man's neck, while the little man put his hand through the bars and took the keys from the guard's pocket. It was done with a minimum of fuss; these were professionals, Martin noted with a sinking heart. The unconscious guard slid down the bars, falling on his face as the gate swung open before him.

The lights of the police car were now in sight; the siren wailed and shutters flew open in response; in a few moments the street outside would be a crowded circus of curiosity and excitement. The five men hurried down along the high wall, out through a final, open gate, round a corner and into a side street.

They paused in an alley, pressed back into the shadows. Dimly Martin saw the torn posters on the wall: half a dozen faces with blackened teeth and grotesque moustaches peered out at him, pleading for his vote at the last elections. There could be another election soon, for someone to replace him if these men killed him.

'We need a car,' said the tall man. 'We'll never be able to get round to the truck now.'

69

'You're the expert,' said the leader, or ex-leader, to Des. 'Find us one. A big one, not a Fiat 500.'

Des slipped off the robe. 'I don't need this now.' In the shadows Martin could see only a burly young man who still remained a stranger to him; his only identification was his first name and his Irish accent. 'I'll try and see if our girl-friend has got away.'

He went out of the alley, moving noiselessly on rubber soles, and Martin, feeling the cold solidity of a wall behind him, leaned back. He pressed his shoulders hard against the wall of someone's home, trying to convince himself of reality. But the nightmare was growing and he shut his eyes and began to pray, as he had in that other nightmare.

3

Luciana, standing with the small group of spectators between two pillars of the northern colonnade, felt the tug on her sleeve and looked over her shoulder. She gave a choked gasp when she saw Ryan.

Ryan nodded warningly at the back of the policeman who stood ten or twelve feet away from them, as curious as the spectators he was holding back. Ryan slipped out of the group and Luciana followed him. They stood by the base of one of the huge pillars, lovers whose tryst had been interrupted by all the commotion.

'I got out of the truck as soon as I heard the first police car coming,' Luciana said. Ryan had his arm round her, the first time he had ever touched her; she could feel the tentativeness of his embrace, as if he were afraid of betraying Fergus. 'Nobody has spoken to me so far. They don't suspect – ' Then suddenly she gripped his arm. 'Where's Fergus? Is he all right?'

'He's all right.' Ryan was looking over her shoulder, out through the pillars at the square. He was acutely conscious of her, embarrassed by her closeness. He had never had the money nor the time for girls; he was not a virgin, but he guessed he knew a lot less about women than did the Pope himself. He was as disturbed by Luciana as he was by the policeman standing just a few yards away.

'Did you get what you were after?'

'Not exactly.'

A family scrambled by, the five small children in their pyjamas and dressing-gowns as wide awake as if it were the middle of the day. One of the children, a boy about nine, stopped and looked at Ryan and Luciana, his shrewd big eyes looking expectantly for lust as he stared at the lovers. Ryan made a threatening gesture at him – when *he* had kids, he'd see they were all in bed by eight o'clock and stayed there – and the small boy was plucked away by his mother, who threw out abuse in equal doses at her son and Ryan.

'What do you mean – not exactly?'

'Keep your voice down.' Ryan leaned close against her, telling himself this was Fergus's girl; he whispered in her ear, smelling the perfume behind it. 'I'll pick you up down on the corner of the Piazza del Risorgimento. Hurry down there, but don't *run*. When I pull up beside you, jump in.'

Luciana started to move off, then saw the small boy watching them round the base of the next pillar; behind him, the boy's father was also staring at them. She put her hand behind Ryan's head, pulled his face towards hers and kissed him on the cheek. She felt him stiffen, imagined she felt the heat of the blush in his face. She hadn't thought there were any virtuous men left, but maybe the Irish were like that. They were all such damned good Catholics, much better than the Italians.

She walked away from him, trailing her fingers down his sleeve; if anyone else besides the inquisitive child and his father was watching them, they would be convinced that the lovers were only parting for the time being, that as soon as the excitement was over they would be resuming what had been interrupted. But she worried as to what had gone wrong and for the first time she felt the grit of doubt.

People were hurrying up the Via Ottaviano as she walked quickly down towards the Piazza del Risorgimento. Whole families scampered by, none of them fully dressed; they could have been refugees fleeing from some disaster had it not been for the gay, if puzzled, excitement that gripped them. They ran towards St Peter's Square as if expecting a miracle to be taking place there, right in the front yard of the Holy Father himself.

She had been waiting five minutes on the edge of the piazza, worry fretting at her even more, when she saw the police car coming down from the direction of the Square. It swung in towards her and she knew she had been mistaken for what she had feared: a prostitute waiting for business. What a way for the night to end! She panicked, unable to think what she should say when the police got out of the car and grabbed her; but there was no strength in her legs, she could not run. Then the door of the car swung open and Ryan said, 'In the back – quick! Lie on the floor!'

She scrambled into the car, fell on the floor as Ryan slammed the door shut after her and swung the car round the piazza. She rolled over and looked up at the back of Ryan's head as he crouched over the wheel.

'Des! A *police* car – are you crazy?'

'It was easy, yes. Nine cars there and only one copper standing by to guard them – everyone else is inside the Vatican. There's so much confusion there, sure it's just like home!'

He turned the car down a dark alley, pulled up. Luciana sat up as three friars and a priest got in. She guessed who the three friars were – but a *priest*? It was cramped in the back with her on the floor and Smith, Toohey and the priest on the seat above her. McBride got into the front seat beside Ryan and she heard him say in a hoarse voice that she hardly recognised, 'For Christ's sake – a *police* car!'

'It's always the same,' said Smith, the disgust in his voice distinguishable despite the hood over his face. 'The organisation falls down every time when it comes to transport. Once there were eleven of us in the one car trying to get away from a raid.'

'And you call yourselves bloody professionals,' said Toohey.

'We'll survive,' said Smith, and looked down at Luciana. 'Allow me to introduce you to our substitute treasure – His Holiness himself.'

Luciana tried to think of some sarcasm, but in that moment they passed a street lamp and she saw that the priest *was* the Pope, or his double. She flung up a hand to her mouth, then all at once she did something she had never done in her life before. She fainted.

'Bugger!' said Toohey, and chewed on the cowl pinned across his face. 'She's passed out.'

The Pope looked down at the girl lying across his slippered feet. 'You should not have chosen a Catholic girl. The nuns always put too much of the fear of God into them.'

'She'll survive,' said Smith callously, and in the front seat McBride stiffened, turned halfway round, then thought better of it.

'Where do we go?' asked Ryan, turning the car north along one of the streets that ran parallel to the river.

'We can't go all the way to Florence in this,' said Toohey.

'That's right,' said Ryan matter-of-factly. 'I made a mistake when I picked this car. The fuel gauge shows almost empty.'

'Christ Almighty!' said Toohey, and chewed on his cowl again. 'Demons who run around with empty tanks!'

McBride leaned across and whispered in Ryan's ear and the latter nodded, picked up the car's speed at once. McBride had been resisting the urge to see how Luciana was, but now concern for her overcame his need to remain unrecognised by the Pope. Pulling the cowl closer round his face he turned round, knelt on the seat and reached down to touch Luciana's face. As he did so she stirred and looked up at him.

'Where am – ?'

He put a gentle hand over her mouth, afraid that she would mention his name, and shook his head. She struggled up, sat with her back against the door and looked up like a puzzled and frightened child at the men in the car. Then she stared at the Pope as the passing lights flashed on his grey exhausted face. This was a terrible dream.

'Don't worry, child,' said the Pope with a tired smile. 'I am not the Devil.'

'You had better blindfold him.' McBride had slumped back in his seat, was facing forward again. He was still disguising his voice, hoping the Pope would not recognise it. He was utterly dispirited by the turn of events, certain that this road they were on would come to an abrupt end: the old guilt-punishment syndrome came back like a childhood malady, the measles of religion. But there was no turning back now: he would have to go on, hoping for one of the miracles he had

73

always denied. Was this what they meant by Irish luck?

Toohey took a handkerchief out of his pocket. 'You're lucky, Pope. It's clean.'

'I appreciate the thought.' Martin leaned his head forward as Toohey tied the handkerchief round his eyes.

'You're pretty good-tempered.'

'Thank you.' Martin sat back, resting his head against the leather behind him. 'I hope we all remain good-tempered.'

'That depends on you,' said Smith, and Martin recognised the real enemy he had in this car.

They crossed the river by the Ponte del Risorgimento, skirted the gardens of the Villa Borghese and headed east through the city. On this side of the river Rome was sleeping; they passed through deserted streets, past silent shuttered houses. A wind had sprung up; torn papers flew down a gutter like a flock of night birds.

Ryan drove cautiously through red traffic lights, taking the prerogative of a police car – 'if coppers can't break the law,'he grinned, 'who can?' Once they saw another police car parked by a waterless fountain, like some huge animal beside a dried-up waterhole; it flashed its lights at them, a sleepy blinking of yellow eyes, and Ryan, grinning again, responded. Then they were out of the city and heading along the Via Tuscolana.

Luciana twisted her head and looked out over the car door. 'We're not going – ?'

'I'm afraid we are.' McBride did not turn round. 'There's nowhere else to go.'

'It's too close – they'll find us there. Let him go!'

'Shut up,' said Smith, and shifted his foot; Martin felt the movement and for a moment thought the tall man was going to kick the girl. 'Where *are* we going?'

'I'll tell you when we get there,' said McBride. 'You'll just have to trust me.'

The Pope, listening with the heightened ear of the man who cannot see, detected that the man who spoke suddenly had no trust in himself. His own trust lay in God, but he wondered if this kidnapping was an act of God's designed to bring about a larger fate than his own small destiny.

3)

It was raining, a steady drizzle, as McBride drove the police car back towards Rome. He was following a narrow country road that ran down between the fields that surrounded the Villa Pericoli; behind him the Alban Hills were hidden in the mist of rain that also obscured the street lamps of Frascati, four miles beyond the villa. It was perfect weather for getting rid of a police car one didn't want, but he knew he didn't have much more time. Already dawn was starting to sketch in the outline of the hills to the east, illuminating the ragged clouds; farmhouses grew out of the fading darkness as if they did not exist during the night. He would have to dump the car within the next fifteen or twenty minutes, yet it would have to be somewhere within the city limits. To abandon it out here would only narrow the search when the police came looking for the Pope's kidnappers.

The Pope was now in an upper room in the Villa Pericoli. Luciana and her father had a small apartment in what had once been the Pericoli palazzo on the Via del Corso and they owned the villa out here in the country; both properties heavily burdened with mortgage, it was all that was left of the once considerable Pericoli fortune. McBride knew the villa was not a safe hideout, too close to Rome and too exposed in the middle of the surrounding fields, but in the circumstances that had trapped them this morning he had been unable to think of any other alternative to the villa outside Florence. It would have been pushing their luck too much to expect to drive one hundred and seventy miles in a police car without being intercepted somewhere along the road.

They had reached the Villa Pericoli without any interception at all. The night had still been fine when they drove up the lane to it and Luciana, crouched on her knees and leaning forward with her face close to the cowled head of McBride, had kept whispering, 'No, darling, no! Let's go somewhere else!'

But she had been in a minority of one; even the Pope, the silent voter, had prayed to be taken out of the car as soon as possible. Ryan had driven the car into the stables, the door had been locked on it and then the five of them, taking the still blindfolded Pope with them, had gone into the villa.

'Ideal,' said Smith, flashing his torch around the large room into which Luciana led them. It was sparsely furnished, chipped and faded relics of the luxury the Pericolis had once known, but it would do if their stay here was not too long. 'A pity we can't turn on the lights.'

'The electricity is cut off,' said Luciana. She did not add that it had been cut off because her father had been unable to pay the bill. She was not going to lower her pride in front of this arrogant Irishman who looked and sounded so much like an Englishman.

'It'll do.' Toohey laid his drill down gently on a dust-sheeted couch, sat down beside it and by the light of his torch began to clean the dirt from it. 'We'll be out of here by tomorrow night.'

Ryan said, 'You think they'll pay as quickly as that for him?'

'Oh, they'll pay,' said Smith, and tapped the Pope on the arm. He had put his gun away and thrown back the hood of his robe; he was relaxed now and the cutting edge of threat had gone from his voice. 'They are probably already taking up a collection for you. What will they use to buy you back – Peter's Pence?'

Martin, despite his weariness and unease, appreciated the irony of the tall man's humour. Only two weeks ago, in every Catholic church throughout the world, the annual collection known as Peter's Pence had been taken up: it was a personal contribution to the Pope, to be distributed by him to the poor. This being his first year in St Peter's Chair, he had no idea how much the collection would total; whatever it was, he did not have enough ego to think that an equal amount would be subscribed for his release by these men. Popes came and went: the poor of the world remained.

76

'Or they might sell off some real estate,' said Smith. 'The Church must still be the biggest landlord in Europe.'

'Cut it out!' McBride growled.

Martin sighed silently, already recognising how the dialogue would go during his captivity. *It had been that way with Kessler, though the SS man had had less sophistication than the tall man.* Clerics were always easy marks; their profession made them natural butts; even the faithful made jokes at their expense. 'You forget that popes are expendable. They have been in the past.'

'Not you,' said Smith. 'You haven't been in office long enough for them to know whether they want to get rid of you.'

Little do you know, thought Martin. 'How much are you asking for me?'

Smith looked at McBride. 'I think we should raise the fee, don't you?'

'Don't let's get too greedy,' said Toohey. 'If we ask for too much, maybe they won't be able to raise it in a hurry.'

'What do you think you're worth?' Smith said to the Pope.

'Treat him with more respect!' Luciana snapped. 'He is not an ordinary man — one doesn't put a price on him!'

'Shut up,' said Smith. 'No one asked your opinion.'

McBride wanted to smash his fist into the handsome mocking face. He took a step forward, but Smith's hand went to the pocket of the robe, where McBride had seen him put away the gun. The American hesitated, then he took Luciana's arm and led her out into the big entrance hall. She leaned against him and began to weep.

'Hush,' he said, and after a few moments her weeping stopped. 'We're in no position to argue with them, honey. This wasn't my idea, bringing the Pope here with us.'

She looked up at him. 'What went wrong? Everything was so well planned – '

'The roof caved in in the grotto – it brought down the whole floor above us. We were lucky to get out alive.' They stood in the darkness of the hall, holding each other close. 'We were just trying to get away when we ran into – *him*.'

'I can't believe it is *him*.' They could have been discussing the Second Coming. 'We have to let him go – it's too dangerous – '

77

'The others won't let us. Anyhow – ' He paused, looked back into the main salon; the narrow light from Toohey's torch outlined only half of each man, like a trick photograph. 'We have him now. We may as well ask for the money.'

'But if they catch us – ' The voluptuous body was cold and stiff in his arms. 'Do they have the death penalty for kidnapping?'

'Don't talk like that. They won't catch us.'

'Will you go back to your office in the morning, just as you'd planned?'

'I have to. If I don't – ' No suspicion must fall on him, he must keep up the charade of being what he had been for the past five months, a Vatican civil servant. 'We have to go through with everything just as it was planned.'

'We can't.' Her voice was harsh with worry and delayed shock. 'He's seen me – he will tell them what I look like. I'll never be able to go out in Rome – I'll have to leave Italy – '

'No.' But there was no conviction in his reassurance; this was a complication he had not foreseen. 'Did you leave any note for your father, saying you wouldn't be back tonight?'

'Yes.' When she had left the apartment the New York businessmen, three of them, had still been there with her father. They had not talked business at the dinner table and she did not know nor care what the subject was to be; she knew that her father's role was no more than that of a figurehead, that he would have no say in any decisions. She had left the note she had written pinned to her father's pillow; it had said she was spending the night with Fergus. She had done the same two or three times in the past; it had been one of the major causes of fights between her and her father; but she was her own girl in such matters and her father knew it. She had taken a small vanity bag and slipped out of the apartment without any trouble. 'But I'll have to go back in the morning.'

'You better stay here till I find out what's happening.'

'I just wish we hadn't brought him *here*.' She looked around in the darkness of the hall; the eye of memory didn't need any light. 'We lived here when I was a child, in the summers – '

He remembered the summers of his own childhood, the day-trips to Buzzards Bay, his father driving the ten-year-old

78

Plymouth and his mother sitting in the back seat saying how she wished they could live always by the sea. There had been an innocence to his life then, unspoiled even by the shirtsleeve pinned over his father's stump.

'Does your father come out here to the villa now?'

'In the summers, yes. There are no servants – we can't afford them any more – but a woman comes over from the farm up the road and looks after Papa when he's here.'

'Does she come over in the fall and winter?'

'I don't know. I don't think so.'

'We should be here no more than forty-eight hours. Let's hope she doesn't come over while we're here.'

They went back into the salon and Smith said, 'You've given her a lesson in economics, I hope?'

McBride squeezed Luciana's arm as he felt her stiffen again. 'I'll take the car back before it gets light. I'll come back tonight, but it may be late before I can get away.'

'You'd better bring some tucker,' said Toohey. 'The money's gunna be no use if we starve to death before we get it.'

'I took these out of the police car.' Ryan held up two bars of chocolate. 'That's all we have. All the tinned food we have is still in the truck.'

McBride felt Luciana stiffen yet again and he looked at her sharply. 'What's the matter?'

'My vanity bag – it's in the truck!'

There were sharp curses from Smith and Toohey. 'Is there anything in it that would identify you?'

'I don't know. Perhaps. It was just make-up, a nightgown, some underwear – '

'Do you send your stuff out to a laundry? Would there be a laundry mark on it?'

'Those sort of things I wash myself.' She said, not very convincingly, 'I'm sure there's nothing in it that will identify me.'

'They were trying to get into the truck when I took the police car,' said Ryan. 'They'll have found her bag by now, yes.'

'The truck's got to be moved,' McBride said. 'You better come with me. You can bring the food back with you.'

'No,' said Smith. 'He stays here with me. If Toohey wants

79

his money, then he's got to do more than he's done. So far he has only done half a job.'

'We're still in my territory! We run it my way – '

McBride, in his anger, had spoken out clearly. The Pope, sitting in his chair, ignored by his kidnappers, raised his head, then dropped it again. Behind his blindfold he had no idea if anyone had seen his reaction; he prayed that they hadn't. But he knew the voice and his mind spun with shock and disappointment.

'The Vatican was your territory, dear chap. When we crossed the Tiber your authority ran out. I'm running things now.'

'We're the Regulars, yes,' said Ryan. 'You fellers are only one-job men.'

'I'll go in and get the truck.' Toohey stood up, slipped out of his friar's robe, put on his trilby which he took from his jacket pocket. 'I'll earn my money, don't be afraid of that. But don't start coming your authority with me, mate. Either side of the Tiber, you don't matter a bugger to me.'

'We'll see about that,' said Smith.

Toohey spat an imaginary speck off his lip, stared at Smith a moment; then he looked at the blindfolded Pope. 'Can you eat anything, I mean nothing upsets you? You got ulcers or anything? I'm talking to you, Pope.'

Martin smiled wryly beneath the handkerchief round his eyes. 'Ulcers? Would you expect me to have?'

'I wouldn't be surprised. It's a bugger of a job, I'll bet.'

'It is indeed,' said Martin, 'although I've never heard it described in exactly those terms. The only buggers I've had reference to were the Albigensian heretics.'

'Then your education has been widened a bit, ain't it?' Toohey sounded almost friendly. 'So you can eat anything?'

'Anything,' said Martin. 'And thank you for your consideration.'

McBride kissed Luciana on the cheek. Aware of the Pope again, he once more disguised his voice, lowering it to a hoarse whisper. 'Look after him. I'll be back tomorrow for you as soon as I can.'

'Be careful, darling.' She was not calm, but she had gained some control of herself.

Smith followed McBride and Toohey to the back door. 'Don't make any more mistakes. We've had enough blunders.'

'Bringing His Holiness was the biggest,' said McBride, and went out of the door before Smith could reply.

Now he and Toohey were driving towards Rome in the police car and Toohey said, 'You oughta picked someone else but that Smithy, mate. He's nothing but trouble.'

'I didn't pick him. All of you were wished on me, you know that. Are you going to stick with us till the job is finished?'

'I'll have to think about it. Kidnapping ain't my line. But I need the money. It might take me six months to plan another job where I'd be sure of ten thousand quid.'

'You don't really care about the Irish cause, do you?'

'In the long run I don't care about anyone but me. That's the way it is with everyone in the end – yours truly is the only cause that's worthwhile.'

Ah, no, Turk, you're wrong. That's what I thought; but the voices from that hillside were too persistent. But he couldn't hear the voices now, and wondered what they would say if they knew of the turn of events. His mother had prayed every morning and evening of her life, a devout Catholic who revered the Pope, no matter who he might be. If spinning in the grave was possible, the hillside outside Cavanreagh must be heaving now.

They had circled round the eastern end of the city and came in on the Via Casilina. It was daylight when they parked the police car in a side street near St John Lateran, pulling it into a lane full of other parked cars; in the grey morning the cars looked like a long line of hippopotami and the police car might remain undetected among them for several hours. Both men carefully wiped the inside of the car of fingerprints, then they got out, locked it and dropped the keys down a nearby drain.

The rain had stopped, but the pavements were still wet and glistening and there was a thin edge to the wind that met them as they walked up the street towards the bus stop. McBride, wearing a thin sweater and a lightweight jacket, felt he could have done with the Franciscan robe he had been wearing last night, but it was a disguise he hoped they would no longer need. He shivered as the wind bit into them across the open space in front of St John's and looked at Toohey, but the Australian seemed oblivious of the chill air.

'It's too early to pick up the truck,' McBride said. 'Go have some breakfast somewhere, then go over to the Square about eight o'clock. The cops will question you, but just play it straight. The truck wouldn't start last night when you finished work and you've come back this morning to pick it up. If you'd got away last night, I could have just said that as far as I knew, you'd finished your job, packed up and gone. They wouldn't have started looking for you for at least twenty-four hours. If the truck is left there and none of you turn up, they'll start looking for you at once.'

'Our plans seem to have gone a bit skew-wiff, don't they? That's the trouble with the Irish.'

'It wasn't the Irish,' said McBride, but didn't add who he thought it might be. Toohey, he was sure, wouldn't believe in Divine intervention. He was surprised that the thought had occurred to himself. The old superstitions were hard at work, all right.

Toohey ambled off into the grey morning, towards the Terminus Station and breakfast, and McBride, hungry, worried and exhausted, caught a bus that would take him closer to his apartment. There were a few other passengers, the unfortunates whose day began so much earlier than most of the city's workers; they looked at the well-dressed newcomer, not one of the regulars, but they were too sleepy to wonder why he should be sharing their misfortune. McBride sat among them, staring at the floor, burdened by his own troubles.

He walked the last few blocks to his apartment. Rosanna and Gina had gone home to whatever beds they slept in when they were not working: he hoped that *they* had had a good night. He let himself into the apartment just as the phone rang. He looked at his watch: 6.55. With a trembling hand he picked up the instrument, had to clear his throat before he answered.

Father O'Hara, the Assistant Director of the press relations office, was on the line. 'Fergus, I've been trying all night to get you! You should leave a message at your flat where a man could get you.'

'I'll do that next time, Pat.' McBride, the charade at last

begun, tried to sound good humouredly sarcastic; he had to convince himself as well as O'Hara that so far he knew nothing of what had happened last night. 'The only thing is there'll be no one here to lift the phone to give you the message.'

'Ah, yes, that's good logic. I see your point, man. Well – ' O'Hara drew in a deep breath; McBride could hear it being sucked down the line. 'Fergus – they've kidnapped His Holiness!'

'Who are *they*? Pat, I'm in no mood for jokes at this hour – '

'Glory be to God, would I joke about a thing like that?' Sometimes O'Hara sounded *too* Irish; when he became excited his brogue thickened like cold soup. 'You'd better get over here right away. It's just bloody bedlam here and nothing else!'

McBride showered and changed quickly, was fortunate enough to get a taxi up at the Hotel Eden and was over at the press bureau within half an hour of O'Hara's call. He went into the office, gearing himself like an actor stepping on to a strange stage. O'Hara and two lay staff men were waiting for him, faces cobwebbed with sleep they had been denied.

'The Director is over with the Secretary of State,' said O'Hara. 'He's a bit upset we couldn't get you before this.'

'I was with my girl.'

'Maybe we should have called her apartment, eh?' Goffi, one of the staffers, fat and married thirty years, leered; he had seen McBride's girl once or twice, the sort of girl he had dreamed about when he had been thin and young and unmarried. 'You'd better leave us her number, eh?'

McBride ignored him, looked at O'Hara. 'You better tell me everything that's happened. It still sounds pretty incredible to me.'

O'Hara slumped in a chair. He was a thin, intense man with grey hair that stuck out stiffly from a long thin head; he always reminded McBride of a toilet bowl brush. Certainly he got a lot of dirty work: he was always given the job of rewriting those press release items that might upset the ultra-conservatives in the Curia. He looked up at McBride and carefully, as if he were reciting some heresy, he told what had happened during the night.

'The guard on the gate said four Franciscans attacked him.

83

They were obviously not Franciscans – their habit was just a good disguise, as it has always been – '

'Spoken like a true Jesuit,' said McBride, trying for a joke but knowing at once that he had made a mistake.

O'Hara glowered. 'You don't seem to appreciate how serious this is. They could kill him, Fergus.'

'I don't think they'd do that.' McBride tried to keep the emphatic note out of his voice. 'Why the hell should they do a thing like that?'

'One never knows.' Pirelli was the other staff man, short, bald and cynical, the sort of newspaperman McBride had seen on rewrite desks all around the world. 'With the madness there is in the world today – '

'It can't be just a criminal gang,' said O'Hara. 'It's got to be political. It could be Arab guerrillas, those Tupamaros from South America, even the Communists.'

Even the IRA? But O'Hara, an Irishman whom McBride had never heard mention Irish politics, seemed not to have given a thought to them. McBride said, 'Has there been any ransom demand or anything?'

'Not yet. Not a word.' O'Hara took out a handkerchief and blew the long horn of his nose. 'I hope they don't harm him. I was just beginning to like him. Never had much time for the Germans before, but I liked him.'

'He was one of the *good* ones, you mean?' said Pirelli, who had been a Fascist when it had been fashionable. 'I thought you Irish always got on well with the Germans.'

'Only in wartime,' said O'Hara, and McBride looked at him sideways. Was O'Hara an IRA sympathiser?

Then the Director, Monsignor Lupi, appeared in the doorway, looking, even at 7.45 in the morning, more like a film star than a priest. He was too short to attract attention in a crowd, but he was the handsomest man McBride had ever seen, with dark wavy hair and eyes that had all the women on the staff wondering what they could do about his celibacy.

'Fergus, where the hell have you been?'

'He's been with his girl,' Goffi volunteered, and leered again. Thank Christ we don't run a gossip column here, McBride thought, or you'd be worse than Winchell ever was.

'At a time like this?'

'The timing was not intentional,' said McBride sourly. 'I just didn't happen to know His Holiness was going to be kidnapped. Next time – '

'All right,' said Lupi testily. 'Cardinal Moroni wants you to continue handling the press relations – you know all the men here covering the Synod. They think you should have a press conference as soon as possible. I've suggested eight-thirty.'

'That will be too early for most of the press guys I know – '

'They're already here – or anyway down the street in the Espresso bars having breakfast. They've been all over the Vatican most of the night – more on the job than you were.' McBride said nothing and Lupi went on, 'Why is it one can always get a hundred per cent coverage for a disaster?'

'I think they'll all turn up for the Second Coming,' said Pirelli.

'Your blasphemy is going to get you fired one of these days,' said Lupi, and rubbed his sad beautiful eyes with the back of his hand. 'I could fall alseep, and the day is only beginning.'

'I'll keep them out of your hair.' McBride decided it was time he looked and acted positively. 'Go home and have a nap.'

'Cardinal Moroni,' (the Secretary of State, the man who, rumour said, had just been beaten for the papacy by Martin), 'wants us to stand by for any emergency announcements. I'd better stay here. He thinks we may be the means by which the kidnappers will want to communicate with them.'

'If they want to talk with us at all,' said Pirelli, sounding not cynical but sad. 'Madmen have no use for dialogue.'

We're not madmen! McBride wanted to cry out; but all he said was, 'We can just hope – pray for the best.'

'They're already saying Masses all around Rome,' said Lupi. 'They have ordered a universal day of prayer.'

Goffi said morosely, 'It may be too late. He may already be dead.'

'Then we'll pray for his soul,' said O'Hara, Irish and always able to find a use for prayer.

McBride knew he had to escape from this atmosphere: it was both binding and throttling him. He looked at his watch. 'I'll have to get over to the Palace. What's the approach to all this?'

85

'Cardinal Moroni will tell you.' Lupi couldn't keep the slice of malice off his tongue. 'He's virtually acting as Pope.'

The priests of Rome, McBride thought, the bureaucracy of venial sin. He went out of the office and up the Via della Conciliazione, colourless under the grey sky, crossed the Square, where the fountains had been turned off, and went into the papal palace. The Secretary of State's apartments were on the floor immediately below those of the Pontiff, symbolic of his position as next in line, the man who acted as regent in such emergencies as the present bizarre one. McBride climbed the thronged stairs, held up every few yards by guards who were now over-reacting with their security precautions.

As he reached the Secretary's apartments, Monsignor Arcadipane was coming out, clutching his briefcase to his chest like an oxygen tank. 'Dreadful, Signor McBride, dreadful! One shudders at the fanatics that are abroad today – '

Madmen, fanatics: McBride wanted to recite to the weeping monsignor a little of the history that had occurred around here: it was as if Arcadipane thought the Vatican had never known murder, rape, looting and torture. And kidnapping: Leo the Third had suffered much worse at the hands of his Curial enemies than Martin the Sixth was suffering at this moment.

'How's Sister Caterina?'

'Desolate,' said Arcadipane desolately, and went stumbling off.

McBride was shown into the Secretary of State's office, a big room that befitted the rank of a man who was both prince and diplomat. Moroni sat behind his huge desk, a tiny man who looked like an altar boy born with an old man's face. He said good morning to McBride and gestured to the plump, grey-haired man in the too-tight uniform sitting in a chair beside the desk.

'You know General della Porta, head of the Carabinieri. He personally is taking charge of the case.' Cardinal Moroni picked up the cigarette he had put down when McBride had entered, drew on it, then blew out a cloud of smoke. He had lung cancer, but so far only his doctor and the Pope knew; he had intended announcing his retirement when the Bishops' Synod ended, but that might have to be delayed now. It would be ironic . . .

But he put that thought out of his head before it could take root. You did not contemplate another man's death, even if it might open up the possibility of your realising your long-held ambition. Now was his opportunity to practise pure charity, without any thought of reward. 'He will be working with the Rome chief of police, but he will be in charge.'

McBride wondered how the Rome chief of police would feel about that: there was as much rivalry among the forces of the law in Italy as there was in the Vatican. Knowing della Porta was in charge didn't make him feel any easier. 'Has there been any word from the kidnappers, Eminence?'

'Yes,' said Moroni, and McBride suddenly had to clamp down on his surprise. 'They phoned in a few minutes ago. They want fifteen million Deutschmarks for his safe return.'

Smith had jumped the gun: he would have it out with that Irish son-of-a-bitch when he saw him tonight. This was Smith's answer to his remark as he had walked out the door of the villa; this was to show him who ran the territory now. McBride sat down, containing his anger.

'Deutschmarks? Are they Germans, then?'

'We don't know. The man who called in spoke poor Italian. Passable, but not good.'

McBride looked at the Carabinieri chief. 'Have you any leads, General?'

Della Porta stroked his thick military moustache with the knuckle of his forefinger. He was a man in whom vanity and disgust with that fault fought a seesaw battle; there were days when he dressed and strutted like a peacock and other days when he would have worn sackcloth if a good tailor would have accepted the order. Today was a sackcloth day, hence the five-year-old uniform that was too tight for him. But for all his vanity he was, as McBride knew, one of the best policemen in Europe.

'A few, signore, but very sketchy. One might almost say it looks like an inside job – '

McBride kept his gaze steady as he listened to the Carabinieri chief.

' – but there are almost a thousand employed or residing in the Vatican and only God knows how many coming and going

87

every day with legitimate reason. Like yourself, for instance – '
He spread a well-manicured hand; a signet ring tightly en-
circled a plump finger like a gold tourniquet. 'The leader of the
gang could be an historian or an archaeologist. They knew of a
secret grotto that, as far as we've been able to find out, no one
else knew existed.'

McBride made a note, looking professional. 'I'll use that at
the press conference. The guys will want something more than
noncommittal garbage.'

'Do we have to tell them *anything*?' asked Moroni, vague
behind his smokescreen.

'With all respect, Eminence, that's been the trouble in the
past – the Vatican has never wanted to tell them anything.
That's why the Press has been left to indulge in conjecture,
most of it not good for the Church.' *And if we leave them to
conjecture now, some too-imaginative son-of-a-bitch may come up
with a flight of fancy too close for comfort. Let's put the blame on
the historians or archaeologists for the time being: they never get
enough notoriety.*

'I think Signor McBride is right,' said della Porta; his
vanity started to reassert itself. 'I'll go with him to the press
conference. They may want to ask *me* some questions.'

'The fifteen million Deutschmarks – ' McBride could feel a
dryness in his throat as he asked the question: 'Can it be paid
over at once?'

'It will take twenty-four hours.' Moroni waved a hand and
emerged from behind his smokescreen. 'How the world
changes! There was a time when kidnap currency was American
dollars.'

'The German mark is the most stable currency now,' said
McBride, then hastily added, 'I guess that's the reason they've
asked for the ransom in marks.'

'Good thinking, signore,' said della Porta, knuckle at his
moustache again. 'You must have a financial brain. Or no
confidence in your American dollar.'

The effort to stay calm was straining every muscle in
McBride's body; the Inquisition racks had never tortured a man
more. 'I'm just a pragmatist, General. It's a favourite role with
Americans these days.'

'All your bishops are the same,' said Moroni. 'Whatever happened to the American dreamer?'

McBride ignored that: too many dreamers finished up in hillside graves listening to west winds with empty messages. 'When do we have to deliver the money and where?'

'They said they would call again with instructions.' *So Smith recognised he didn't know* all *the territory.* 'Whatever they ask, we'll do it exactly to the letter. The only thing is to get His Holiness back safely.'

'Well, I better go and open the press conference.'

'There's no more you want to know?' said della Porta.

McBride, on his feet, looked at the Carabinieri chief. 'Is there any more?'

'No, not much. But I thought an old newspaperman like yourself would have asked more questions.'

'Such as?' *I'm never going to get through this role, I'm too much the amateur.*

'Whether we thought the kidnappers might have other demands, how the money is being raised, all those sort of details.'

'I guess I'm still suffering from the shock of what's happened. I was with His Holiness only last evening – '

'Why did he see you?' Moroni slipped off his chair, came round the desk. He was only five feet in height and his soutane, ash-spattered and too long for him, swished on the carpet as he walked. 'He didn't tell me he planned to make any statement to the Press. He always consulted me – '

Not this time, he didn't. 'He'd have talked to you this morning, I'm sure. He has – had a plan to send some of the Vatican treasures on a world tour. It was to be announced today.'

Chagrin deepened the lines on the elderly altar boy's face. But Moroni was too experienced to parade intra-Vatican conflicts in front of della Porta; the other Romans were always looking for something to gossip about when the Holy See was mentioned. 'Ah, yes, *that*. His Holiness did mention it – it slipped my mind.'

There's no smoother liar than a clerical one, McBride thought. 'I suppose we better hold back that announcement?'

89

'Oh, yes, yes. I'll call the Director-General of the Museums and tell him.'

'I wonder if there would be any connection?' della Porta mused. He stood up, pulled down his jacket as it crept up over his hips. He was more concerned than he showed; he knew that for the next few days or weeks he was going to be spotlighted as no other police chief in the world had been for years; vanity did not blind him to the fact that he would be the target for all the criticism that would already be building up like thunderclouds on the horizon. 'Could someone else have been in the Library when the Pope had that guard let him in?'

'Such as?' said Moroni almost belligerently.

Della Porta shrugged. 'Anyone. It does seem coincidental that he should be down there alone in the Library – it's almost as if someone knew he would be there and was waiting for him. Don't you think so, Signor McBride?'

'I wouldn't know.'

'I thought the connection might have struck you. In your profession you must come across a lot of coincidence.'

'A good newspaperman sticks only to facts.'

'Were you ever a crime reporter?'

'No.' *What's he getting at?* McBride's fingers involuntarily tightened; he tried to straighten them, like a man fighting arthritis. 'You have to have a flair for that.'

'Ah, indeed yes. Just like us policemen. They always say the best policeman would be a reformed criminal. Well, shall we go to the press conference. Some of the questions may illuminate our befogged minds.'

You and I, thought McBride, are going to get different reactions from whatever questions the smart-ass newsmen ask. 'Let's hope so, General.'

'Is there anything I can do?' said Moroni.

'Pray, Eminence,' said della Porta. 'What else?'

Moroni made a gesture that could have been a blessing or a dismissal, and opened the door for them. Two carabinieri stood outside in the corridor, Toohey, sullen and uncomfortable, between them.

They had taken the blindfold from around the Pope's eyes and now he lay on the dank mattress on the big bed, covered by the two blankets they had given him, and gazed up at the small skylight in the ceiling some fifteen feet above his head. *Damn high ceilings!* But then that other room where he had been kept prisoner had had a ceiling that had been no more than a few inches above his head, that had seemed to press like a weight on him. He should be thankful for God's and the long-dead architect's small mercies. He had checked the windows; but the tall man, when he had come up here during the night, had nailed them down so thoroughly there was no chance of opening them or the shutters outside. The skylight, though it might taunt him as an impossible way to freedom, did give light.

He was not afraid of the dark, but he did not *like* it. The SS had kept him in darkness for forty-eight hours after they had arrested him the second time and ever since then he had preferred the light to the dark. Hell, if by some dreadful mischance he should arrive there, would, he knew, be utter blackness.

A key was turned in the lock and the door opened. The girl came in, her face covered by a rough cloth hood in which she had cut eyeholes. She looked ridiculous, but because he was a naturally polite man he tried not to smile. She carried a steaming cup of coffee on a small tray.

'We found some stale coffee, Holiness. It doesn't taste too bad.'

He took the cup, sipped the coffee. 'Wonderful.' He sat up in bed, pulling the blankets up about him against the chill of the room. He still wore his soutane over his pyjamas and he was glad of the extra warmth. 'Why don't you take your mask off, my dear? I've already seen you, you know. You'll be more comfortable.'

Luciana instinctively put a hand up to the mask, then just as quickly withdrew it. 'No, you may have forgotten what I look like by the time we let you go.' The mask, covering her face, fluttered as she spoke. 'All women should look alike to men like yourself, Holiness.'

'You mean to priests? Unfortunately they don't.' Martin could feel the coffee warming him; and even talking to this girl warmed him. The hours in this room had been long and chill, not only because of the coldness of the room but from the thoughts that had gripped him like the ague. When he had been held prisoner that other time there had been only the Jew and himself to consider. Then, he had been no more than Kurt Stecher. But now . . . He felt the weight of a whole world on him, and he smiled at the girl, seeking distraction in small talk. 'If they did, perhaps we should not lose so many priests every year.'

'You should do away with the celibacy law.'

He shook his head. 'Actually, celibacy is not a major problem. It counts, but not to the extent outsiders would believe. I was only half-serious, my dear. Women are not the temptation to priests the journalists would have you believe. Frustration is our major problem, the frustration of wanting to do things and not being able to. That goes for all of us, from myself down to the poorest parish priest.'

'You must be able to do what you wish.' Even the mask did not hide the surprise in her voice.

Martin drained the cup, handed it back to her. He got off the bed, began to walk up and down to increase the circulation in his legs. He had been wonderfully fit when he had come to Rome a year ago, but lately he had begun to feel he had turned a corner: age stretched ahead of him, a downhill road. 'One wishes one could.' There was so much he wanted to do, a whole world to conquer with charity; but till he had come to Rome he had never realised the strength of the chains of tradition and the responsibility of power. He sought distraction again: 'Is this your first – caper? Is that the word?'

'It's no longer a caper,' she confessed. 'Your Holiness was never meant to be involved in this.'

'I know,' he said. 'What did they want?'

She shook her head. 'I'll let them tell you that.'

'Tell him what?'

There was a movement at the door and Smith stood there, dressed again in the Franciscan habit and with the cowl pinned across his face. An hour ago he had sent Ryan up to Frascati to make the phone call to the Vatican with the ransom demand; he had told him to walk both ways and not to thumb a lift from anyone who might later identify him. He knew Ryan would not be back for at least another hour, but already he was beginning to feel nervous, a condition that normally never affected him.

'What's he been asking you?'

'Nothing!' The two masked figures snarled at each other like grotesque beings in which the mutations had gone wrong. 'We were just talking.'

'Well, watch him. These chaps know how to get things out of you. That's what the confessional is all about, isn't it?' He looked at Martin. 'Bare the soul and go to Heaven.'

Martin gave no reply and Luciana said, 'Don't talk to him like that!'

'Why not?' One could imagine the raised eyebrow and the mocking smile behind the cowl.

'Because he should be respected! He wasn't brought here to be mocked by someone like you!'

The cowled head turned back to the Pope. 'She's obviously one of yours, you know. You'd collapse without the women to support you.'

'That goes against the grain of an Englishman, I suppose?'

'I'm not English!' The edges of the cowl fluttered with the force of the denial. But then the voice was controlled again, once more a drawl. 'Make us some more coffee, there's a good girl.'

It was a dismissal of Luciana and her body stiffened so abruptly Martin expected a cracking sound. She slammed the cup on the tray and stamped out of the room, her heels rapping like hammerheads on the tiles. Smith looked after her and once again one could imagine the mocking smile on the hidden face. The cowl turned back to Martin. 'You chaps have the right idea. You know how to keep women in their place.'

It was one of Martin's aims to raise women in the Church from their status of second-class citizens and there had been fierce argument about his proposal to name women to certain committees. But the tall man obviously did not take much interest in Church politics and knew little, if anything, of the

93

battles Martin had begun since becoming Pope. He wondered what the tall man's interests were, why, when he sounded so English, he had so angrily denied being an Englishman.

'Women have their place,' he said noncommittally. He watched the hooded figure carefully, for he had decided that this was the dangerous one among those who had kidnapped him. Perhaps it was because he was the one who had the gun, but this man was the only one who gave him the same prickling sensation he had felt every time Kessler had come into his cell. Kessler, he knew, would personally have killed him if Schoppel, the senior SS man, had not overruled him. Martin doubted that anyone could overrule this tall man if he wanted to do some--thing.

'Only in places where you priests would have no use for them.' The voice was callously lewd. 'They are a hindrance in a situation like this.'

'Don't harm her on account of me.'

Smith had been about to go out of the room; but now he turned slowly and said, 'What did you say?'

'I said don't harm her on account of me. You're looking for the opportunity to do just that, aren't you?' Oh, God, he thought, stop my tongue! This was how he had given away the Jew.

'What gives you that idea?'

Martin knew he was playing with the girl's safety, perhaps even putting her life at stake; but he had to throw sand into the cogs of the machine that was this gang, had to start them working against each other. One part of him, his conscience, shouted at him not to repeat the error of thirty years ago; but he knew he had to escape from here and though he had no clear idea of what he intended to do, he had to make a start. He knew from experience, having seen it from parish level right up to the papacy, that the body divided among itself sooner or later took its eye off the outsider. And here, more than anywhere else he had ever been, even Dachau or the Vatican, he was the outsider.

'I think it would please you to hurt your leader through her. She is his girl-friend, isn't she?'

'My *what*?' The laugh behind the cowl was harsh with incredulity. 'He's no more a leader than – '

94

'Than I am? Is that what you were going to say?'

'No,' said Smith grudgingly. 'You're a leader, from what I've read. Not that I've read much – religion doesn't interest me. It's for fools – and fools are easily led.'

'True,' said Martin, who was too sensible to deny an evident fact. 'That fools are easily led, I mean. But not all people who believe in religion are fools. I believe in it and I'm no fool.'

'Arrogant, eh? Aren't popes supposed to be vessels of humility? Whosoever shall exalteth himself et cetera et cetera . . . Don't you subscribe to that little homily?'

'I don't think you are the one to lecture anyone on arrogance.'

'My dear chap – ' The voice was almost too languid now, almost comically so; the iron control bent under the seething anger. 'If you're no fool, contemplate the thought that when we get the money for you, we don't *have* to return you. You are what the anti-pollution cranks would call a disposable container. A nuisance, in other words.'

He went out of the room, locking the door behind him, and Martin was left to contemplate the threat. Looking up at the sky he saw the break in the clouds, the flash of blue like a promise; but he had never believed in such simple omens, his faith had never fed on superstition. He knelt down on the tiled floor, blessed himself and began to pray. To some, he guessed, that might be only another form of superstition. But God, if you believed in Him, had to be addressed in some way. And He had sustained him before, in that other place.

3

'We held him on suspicion, General,' said the carabinieri sergeant, one eye on Toohey and the other on promotion. 'He was trying to drive away a truck that has been parked in the Square all night.'

'Mr McBride,' said Toohey, all indignation and hurt pride, yet still at low boiling point, 'tell them who I am. You gave me my pass yourself – '

'It could be a forgery,' said the sergeant, suddenly looking uncertain.

'Do you know this man?' della Porta said to McBride.

'I can't remember his name – '

'Johnston. Bert Johnston,' said Toohey. 'Paragon Films. We're making a documentary. Our truck broke down last night and I understood you'd personally given permission for the truck to be left there – '

'Sure, I remember,' said McBride. 'I've handed out so many passes during the Synod. Sure, Mr Johnston is okay – '

'Perhaps,' said della Porta, knuckle at work on his moustache again. 'Perhaps not.'

'There was a case, a large one, of canned food in the truck, General,' said the sergeant, confidence revived. 'And a woman's vanity bag.'

'All film crews carry food.' Toohey looked sourly at the sergeant as if he expected any man of normal intelligence to have known that. 'Sometimes we don't have time to stop for a proper meal.'

'What about the vanity bag?' said della Porta.

'I wouldn't know about that.' Toohey looked elaborately candid. 'It could belong to a model we used the day before yesterday – '

'A model – a girl, you mean? In a documentary film about bishops?'

Toohey had got out of his depth and he looked at McBride to rescue him. 'You saw the director's script.'

McBride could feel his brain turning cartwheels in his skull. 'I can't remember it all. I think he wanted some contrast – '

'Who is the director?' asked della Porta.

'His name is Lamington-Bass, hyphenated. He's English.' It had been agreed that the Irish connection should be hidden as much as possible; even Ryan, the only one with an Irish accent, had been given the Welsh name of Jones. 'He should be around later in the day.'

'I'd like to see him.' Della Porta looked at Toohey, then nodded to the carabinieri sergeant. 'Take him away, sergeant. We shall hold him for questioning.'

'You can't do this, sport,' Toohey said to della Porta. 'I'm an Australian citizen travelling on an Aussie passport – '

'You won't be the first we've held, Signor Johnston. Our relations with the Australian embassy are very good. They realise the best confidence men in the world are Australians.'

'I'm no con man.' Toohey managed a genuine look of professional disgust.

'Then you won't mind our questioning you.'

Toohey looked at McBride. 'I expect you to get me outa this, Mr McBride. And pretty bloody quick, too.'

Della Porta waved his hand in dismissal and Toohey, with a hard backward glance at McBride, was led away by the two carabinieri, their dreams of promotion and reward already making them handle him more roughly than was necessary.

'He seemed to think you were his friend, Signor McBride.'

'Only in a professional sense.' McBride was wondering how far he could go in pressing for Toohey's release. He would wait a while, sure that Toohey would give nothing away, then try and have him released without creating any suspicion. 'That's what press relations officers are for.'

'Oh?' said della Porta. 'I often wondered.'

They left the Palace and walked down across the Square and down the Via della Conciliazione. Several carabinieri fell in around them to protect them from the marauding photographers; these were the new barbarians, McBride thought, the looters of one's privacy. The group had to stop as a taxi, horn hooting, forced its way through; McBride caught a glimpse of a man in a hat leaning forward in the rear seat urging the taxi driver on. A carabinieri sergeant shouted at the driver, but the latter was already out of earshot.

'A law unto themselves,' della Porta said to McBride. 'Taxi drivers think every city in the world belongs to them.'

He was basking in the glare of the photographers' lenses; the ultra-violet rays of publicity gave him health. But at the door of the press building he gestured for the photographers to be kept out: he knew when enough was enough. And at a press conference, answering unexpected questions, one could not always offer one's best profile.

The conference was the most hectic McBride had ever attended, let alone conducted. Questions flew like shrapnel; McBride managed to dodge most of them, but some cut home. All the time it seemed to him that della Porta never took his eyes from him.

'Does the Vatican think this is a political kidnapping?' asked *Suddeutsche Zeitung*.

'No,' said McBride, and wondered if he sounded too emphatic. Out of the corner of his eye he saw della Porta look at him under lowered eyebrows, then stroke his moustache again with his knuckle. It was the sort of mannerism you saw in actors who played the same part week after week and at another time it would have amused McBride; but now he found himself watching for it as a danger sign, a hint that della Porta was underlining another mental note. 'The ransom demand was just a straight demand for money.'

'It will be paid, of course?' said *The Wall Street Journal*. Fifteen million Deutschmarks was nothing in today's market; General Mills had paid the equivalent of that last week for some fried chicken franchise in Arizona. 'Will it come out of capital reserves? Or will you have to seek a loan?'

'The Vatican doesn't need to borrow,' *l'Unita* interjected. 'With its vast fortune from all sources, the poor as well as the rich – '

'This is not a propaganda session.' McBride's voice was sharp with authority; he wasn't going to let this conference get out of hand. 'For either Catholicism or Communism. We are just trying to see that a man, regardless of his position, is returned safely.'

'That's all very well,' said *Taas*. 'But he would not have been kidnapped if he had not been Pope. Are you sure politics is not involved?'

'The Arab terrorists?'

'The German Underground?'

McBride abruptly closed the conference. All the sensible questions had been asked in the first ten minutes; now the correspondents were just looking for angles on which to hang their stories. The wire services had already sent out the bare news of the kidnapping and now each correspondent had to justify his salary and expenses by sending back a story that would not be duplicated by a rival. McBride went out of the conference room by a side door and waited for della Porta in the corridor.

'It is a pity they are so necessary,' said the Carabinieri chief.

'Perhaps there is something to be said for a controlled press.'

'I don't agree,' said McBride, the old newspaperman in him rising to the bait.

'They could frighten the kidnappers, panic them into doing something foolish and perhaps tragic.'

'Not if the money is paid over at once.' Della Porta made no comment and after a moment McBride went on, 'You're not suggesting the ransom should *not* be paid?'

'I am against any sort of deal with kidnappers or terrorists. Even for popes.'

McBride could feel the sweat starting in his palms. 'I don't think Cardinal Moroni agrees with you.'

'No. But some day we are going to have to put a stop to these demands. The Israelis have the right idea – never any deals '

'Do you want the ransom money held back while you try to – to catch the kidnappers?'

'If I can persuade Cardinal Moroni and his associates – yes.'

'But you have no leads.'

'No. But we have found the police car they stole. And we have that man Johnston. Nothing much, Signor McBride, perhaps nothing at all. But a policeman is like a priest he has to have faith or he would never get anywhere.'

'An apt remark in the circumstances. May I quote you later?'

'If things go badly – yes. You look tired, signore. A late night last night?'

'Too late. And I didn't expect to be as busy as this so early – '

'Who did?' said della Porta sympathetically. 'Was there anyone else in that documentary film crew besides Johnston and Lamington-Bass?'

He was torn between an outright lie and equivocation. He settled for the latter; he had no idea what lies Toohey would tell under pressure. 'There could have been – I can't remember all the passes I made out.'

'There'll be a record of the passes, of course?'

'Yes.' He was afraid to look down: the sweat seemed to be running off the ends of his fingers now.

99

'I'd like to talk to Signor Lamington-Bass. You'll have his address, of course?'

'It'll be in the files. Do you want me to contact him?'

'You have enough to worry about, Signor McBride. No, my men will find him.'

4

Heinrich Kessler, vexed and disappointed, hovered on the edge of the restless crowd in St Peter's Square. When he had heard the news on his transistor radio in his pensione room this morning he had thought someone was playing a dreadful joke on him. The radio had been his only companion in the past year, and he had come to know that disc jockeys (a term that sounded like a madman's invention) often had a juvenile, macabre sense of humour. But the announcer this morning had been no disc jockey, even though the news had been macabre. Kessler's head had begun to throb and he had lain on his bed while the excited voice drilled at his brain; he knew only a smattering of Italian but it was enough. *The Pope was kidnapped this morning by four men dressed as Franciscan monks . . .* It had been an hour before he had felt well enough to rise from the bed. He retched drily as he sat up and the tears ran down his lined and sunken cheeks. He had put on his glasses and peered about the room, as if he expected better news if he could see properly. But the pensione, the cheapest he had been able to find, had never been a place for good news. Even the coloured print of Lake Como on the wall, faded and fly-blown, was only a sneering reminder that the man who booked into this room could afford no better.

The news when he had reached St Peter's Square had been no better. Rumours fluttered as thickly as the pigeons, but there was only one hard fact: the Pope was still missing. Wrapped in his overcoat that was thin as a sick dog's hair, he moved among the crowd hoping to hear something encouraging, like a derelict looking for cigarette butts. He could feel the gun in his pocket, the Mauser H SC 7 mm that would be fitted with the silencer he carried in his other pocket, but it looked now as if he might never get to use it.

Cars came and went in the square, people criss-crossed each other's paths: Vatican business seemed to be going on as usual.

They are accustomed to calamity, he thought; and felt an odd spark of sympathy for them, an emotion he had almost forgotten. A car wheeled its way across the square towards the bottom of the steps that led up to the Basilica; it pulled up and two bishops got out, their purple hats suddenly prominent as large flowers in the blaze of sunshine that broke through the clouds. A bell tolled somewhere: for a Mass, to mark the hour? Whatever the reason, no one took any notice of it: bells were the music of Rome and it was a sign of hope that they were still ringing.

Kessler was standing behind the police barrier that had been put up near the north colonnade when he saw the two carabinieri, a sergeant and a corporal, grab the small man in the trilby hat. The man was opening the door of a truck on which was lettered *Paragon Films*; the carabinieri swooped on him as if he had been about to throw a bomb. Kessler moved closer, heard the small man protesting in English in a strange accent that the truck was *his*, that he had a pass, that he had no time for bloody demons who came the rough stuff. Most of it was incomprehensible to Kessler, but because nothing else was happening elsewhere in the Square he stayed close to this argument and listened.

The carabinieri sergeant said something in Italian, then changed to English. 'Your name, signore?'

'Johnston,' said the small man, straightening his hat as the other carabiniere let him go. 'I'm working here, doing a fillum on the bishops. The bloody truck broke down last night and I've come back this morning to try and shift it – '

The sergeant nodded to his colleague and the latter got up into the driving cabin, checked some papers he found there, tossed them aside, then got out of the cabin and held out a woman's vanity bag. Even from where he stood Kessler could see the sudden change of expression on the face of the small man.

'I dunno anything about that – '

The corporal went round to the back of the truck. Kessler could not see him, but he did see the photographers now converging on the scene. They arrived like a flock of well-dressed vultures, cameras sharpened; at once, Kessler noticed, the small man tilted his hat forward over his eyes and lifted his hand to hide his face. The corporal came round from the back of the truck, young face as wide open as the lenses aimed at him. His voice carried with the excitement that gripped him: Kessler heard something about food. The sergeant grabbed the small man again by the arm and the cameras clicked like gun hammers.

'A case of tinned food? Why is it in the truck? You will have to come with us – they will want to question you – '

'*Dove?*' yelled one of the photographers.

'General della Porta,' said the sergeant, swollen suddenly with importance, and he and the corporal hustled the small man away up through the colonnade. Kessler noticed that the small man, hat still tilted over his eyes and his hand covering his face, had said nothing when questioned about the case of tinned food in the truck. It seemed to Kessler that the small man all at once wanted to be out of the limelight, that he had something to hide, even if it was only himself.

The photographers drifted away, scavenging for more titbits, complaining because so far they had nothing that editors would pay money for: disasters were becoming less and less an economic proposition. Kessler stayed where he was, watching the colonnade into which the carabinieri had disappeared with the small man. He felt suddenly hungry, but he did not want to go away for breakfast; he looked around, saw a boy selling peanuts, crossed to him and bought two packets. It was a poor breakfast, but he had become accustomed to poor food; all taste in his mouth had died when he was a child, he ate now only to stay alive to avenge his father. He chewed on the peanuts, leaning against the police barrier, waiting with all the patience of a man who had forgotten the meaning of time.

If the small man came out alone, got into his truck and was allowed to drive away, he would not be worth following. If he came out still in the custody of the two carabinieri and was taken away in a police car, then it would be reasonable to assume that the police suspected there was a link between him and the kidnappers. The assumption might be tenuous, but Kessler had to grab at anything that came to hand. In his own way he was as much a scavenger as the photographers.

He did not have to wait long. The two carabinieri, faces flushed with triumph, came down the colonnade, the little man almost running to keep up with them as they dragged him towards a police car. The photographers had come back; in the shadows of the colonnade their flashguns blazed in ambush. The crowd along the police barrier congealed into one excited throng; Kessler struggled to free himself, not wanting to be trapped. He looked wildly about for a taxi, saw one pulling up in the Square and three bishops getting out. He plunged across the Square on stiff, awkward legs, came up into the middle of the argument as to who was to pay: the bishops, on expense accounts, fought among themselves to hand out charity to each other.

'Permit me – ' Kessler thrust money at the taxi driver, jumped in and slammed the door. He waved across the Square towards the police car moving slowly through the inquisitive crowd. 'Follow that car!'

Then he giggled, the first expression of mirth he could remember uttering in years; the phrase brought back another memory, of American gangster films his father had taken him to see, of how his father had enjoyed them even more than himself; his father, too, had laughed every time anyone said, *Follow that car!* The amusement and the memory of his father suddenly warmed him; all at once he even felt a revival of hope. He sat forward in the seat as the taxi began to gather speed across the Square, following the police car as it headed down the Via della Conciliazione.

2

'You're going to have to go back in there,' said McBride. 'Play it straight, finish off the picture.'

'Nothing doing, dear chap,' said Smith. 'I'm surprised that you even suggest it.'

'What about Turk? If they take his prints, and they're sure to, they'll know within twenty-four hours who he is. Interpol has him filed.'

'He'll have to look after himself.'

'That's pretty goddam callous! He went back in there

because you said he hadn't earned his money. He could have walked out – he doesn't owe the cause anything.'

'He could split on us,' said Ryan, 'especially if he knew we were deserting him.'

'Not friend Toohey. He's uncouth, but he's not the type who would ever give information to the police.' Smith spread some stracchino cheese on a piece of bread, bit into it, made a face but kept eating. He swallowed, went on, 'I'm needed for another important phase of this venture – taking the money to Beirut and lodging it in the banks there. I'm not going to expose myself to any risk just to get Toohey off the hook. You may check with Dublin, if you think I'm wrong.'

'You didn't trouble to check with Dublin about putting in the ransom demand! You pull another one like that on me, either of you, and I walk out!'

Ryan said, 'Maybe we were a bit hasty, yes. But we're too close to Rome, Fergus. And we've got him upstairs – the sooner we get rid of him the better.'

'You may walk out if you wish,' said Smith. 'You're not really necessary from now on.'

Ah, but I am, thought McBride. Somehow he knew he was the only guarantee of the Pope's safety: even Dublin seemed to have realised that. It was now one-thirty in the morning and he was almost certain that no one had tailed him as he had left his apartment and walked up to the garage to collect his car.

He had quit the Vatican at ten o'clock after the hardest day he could remember ever having worked, got his car from the parking lot where it had been all last night and today; then, going through his regular pattern, he had taken it to the garage, left it there and crossed the road to the small restaurant where he ate every night. He had eaten a meal he hadn't tasted, then gone home to the apartment.

Rosanna had been standing in the doorway. 'You look tired, signore.'

'A little, Rosanna. How's business?'

She shrugged. 'So-so. Ours must be the only business that doesn't have inflation. One man wanted to know tonight if I operated on hire purchase.'

Despite his exhaustion and worry, McBride smiled. 'I hope

you told him where to get off. Some things are sacred, aren't they?'

'Sure. But if things get worse, next time he comes around – ' She shrugged again, shivered a little at the cold night air; she wore a tight jersey dress that showed off her wares but did nothing to keep out the cold; whoring, like ice-cream selling, was a summer trade. 'I'm tired, too. You want me to come up and keep you company? Ten thousand lire for the night. A bargain.'

'I'm sure, Rosanna, and I appreciate the offer. But some other time.'

He had gone past her when she turned round. 'Hey, that was terrible about Il Papa, eh? I went to Mass for him tonight on my way here.'

'You're a good girl, Rosanna.'

'You kidding?' She laughed. 'Not in twenty years. Good night, signore.'

Once upstairs he had found a carton in one of the kitchen closets and filled it with food, everything that he could find in the refrigerator and cupboards. He waited out on the balcony till he heard Rosanna bargain with a client, get into his car and be driven off down the street. There was no sign of Gina and he could only guess that she was taking a night off or had an all-night client. He picked up the carton of food, went down in the creaking elevator. Rosanna was just coming back to take up her stand in the doorway again.

'How about that? He wanted it to be a family affair – him and his three brothers! And their father to watch!' He knew she was not a golden-hearted whore, if anything her heart was probably pure slag; but she had her standards, she had a dim memory of what decency was. He just wished she had chosen some other night to be righteous. 'You're loaded down, signore.'

'Just rubbish. I'm taking it out to one of the dumps.'

'You Americans are too clean. Leave it here – they'll take it away eventually.'

'I'm anti-pollution.' It was his turn to be righteous.

'Ah, who cares? The world stinks anyway.'

He had never realised she had a bent for philosophy, but now was not the time to debate it with her. He said good night and went up towards the garage, keeping to the shadow of the walls. Several times he stopped and looked back, but he saw no one following him. Then he wondered at his ultra-caution: why should he think he'd be a suspect? He was reading too much into della Porta's attitude; the Carabinieri chief probably acted the same way on his day off. Sure he had to be cautious, that was the name of the game from now on, but he didn't have to invite suspicion by acting suspiciously. If he was going to survive he would have to rid himself of his feeling of guilt.

The old man who took care of the garage after midnight was accustomed to men coming and going at all hours, taking their cars out or bringing them in. In this neighbourhood lovers and husbands came and went like service maintenance men, which, in a way, they were. The old man waved sleepily to McBride and went back to his comic book and the girls with their forty-inch busts, the one dream he still had from his youth.

McBride drove out of the garage and down to the central telephone exchange. He was able to dial directly to Dublin; technology had improved the conditions under which conspirators and crooks had to work. He knew he had been too cautious in not phoning from his apartment, but already he had begun to think in terms of his phone being tapped.

The voice in Dublin, hoarse with sleep, said, 'Yes?'

'You read the market report today?'

'That we did. You bought a commodity we never wanted – it's upset some of the board members.'

'It was unavoidable. Our Sales Manager will explain it all to you when he gets back to head office. If we want to realise our sales quota, we're stuck with this commodity. But I'm still having trouble with our grey-haired friend. He jumped the gun this morning on our quota. He's also *carrying* a gun.' McBride looked over his shoulder, but there was no one near him; over behind the counter a male operator was eating his midnight supper. 'I was told by you there was to be none of that.'

There was silence in Dublin. Then: 'He was specifically instructed he was not to take anything in that line. He'll need watching. His methods have given us trouble in the past.'

'Jesus! *Now* you tell me! What do I do – send him back to you?'

'You can't. He's necessary to the rest of the operation. But you'll have to watch him, see he doesn't step out of line. That commodity you have has to be protected.'

'You want it sold at the quoted price?'

McBride hoped fervently that they would say no, that the deal was off. But Dublin said, 'The board has talked it out. We need the money for our expansion programme. Sell it, but see that it isn't harmed. When will you report again?'

'Christ knows,' said McBride, and hung up in Dublin's ear.

No police car or any other vehicle had followed him out to the Villa Pericoli. He had turned off his lights as he had approached the villa and driven up the dark lane almost at walking pace; the moon was out but it came and went behind the clouds like a wall eye behind thick strands of blown hair. The car was now in the stables at the back of the villa, but he knew if he had to come out here again he would need to hire a less conspicuous job. A bright red Alfa was not a badge of anonymity. Another amateur's mistake . . .

'Get one thing straight,' he said to Smith. 'I'm running this whole show from now on. You take that gun out of your pocket once more and I'll beat the daylights out of you!'

'I thought you said you were anti-violence?'

Smith's smile was a mocking goad, but McBride held himself back. 'I'm against *killing* people. But there's enough Irish in me not to hang off if some son-of-a-bitch won't go along with the rest of us!'

Smith held out his cup and Ryan lifted the pot and poured him some coffee. 'You raise a fist against me, McBride, and I'll certainly take the gun out of my pocket again. That goes for anyone who tries the same caper.'

Ryan suddenly tilted the pot upright, leaving Smith's cup only half-filled. 'Don't start threatening me, Seamus. I've used a gun before, but when Dublin decided against it, I gave it up. But if any man drew a gun on me, I'd still kill him. Yes.'

That's two of us against him, McBride thought. He stared at Smith, saw just the flicker of doubt in the tall man's eyes.

'You know where we stand, Smith,' he said. 'And what I

say goes from now on. You can check *that* with Dublin.'

'I think we should let Il Papa go.' Luciana had been sitting quietly in a corner of the big salon, looking like a dark ghost among the dustsheets.

Smith picked up the coffee pot and filled his cup. Then he looked at McBride and said, 'If what you say goes, you had better tell your girl-friend she has no vote.'

'That's right, Fergus,' said Ryan. 'I'm not happy about the way things have turned out. It's too dangerous, for one thing. And if it ever got out what we'd done, the IRA would lose half its support back home. But now we have him, they'll pay the ransom money quicker than they would have for those museum treasures.'

'So far the Pope doesn't know who you belong to,' said Luciana. 'Let him go unharmed, he can tell them it was all a terrible mistake – '

McBride shook his head, though he wanted to agree with her. 'The money is the important thing, not him. We'll release him in the next twenty-four hours, *unharmed* – ' he glanced at Smith, but the latter had his face buried in his coffee cup ' – and the Church won't have suffered. Maybe it will even have been drawn closer together – I've seen that in the Vatican today. But we'll have the money to do something the whole world will applaud – bring peace to Northern Ireland.'

'Do you really believe that?' Luciana said.

'Yes!' snapped Ryan, and thumped the table with his fist.

'Yes,' said McBride, aware that his own voice must sound like only a faint echo of Ryan's.

Luciana looked at Smith. 'I didn't hear what you said.'

'I don't owe you any answers, my dear girl. I'd be pleased if you just shut up.'

Luciana came out of the shadows like a greyhound out of a trap; McBride caught her as she flung herself at Smith. He struggled with her while Smith spread more cheese on a slice of bread and watched the two of them with amusement.

'Honey – ' McBride, worn out, all his patience at last gone, suddenly slapped Luciana hard across her rump. Equally worn out, she just as suddenly burst into tears, pulled herself away from him and ran out of the room. He heard her stumbling across the dark hall, crashing into chairs and tables, but he was too exhausted to go after her. He sat down at the table, poured himself a cup of coffee and looked at Smith.

'You open your mouth again like that to her and I'll break your teeth!'

'She should never have been brought into the job.'

'I know that – but we had no alternative. If the organisation in Dublin had been better, they'd have had a stand-by woman to take Maire Fitzgibbon's place. You might tell them that when you get back to Dublin. I hope their goddam organisation is better when they start the campaign in the Six Counties.'

'Are you suggesting we could do with some American know-how?'

'We won *our* revolution.'

'Vietnam, too?'

'Quit it!' Ryan, his battered young face flushed, leaned between the two older men. 'We've got enough trouble without creating our own.'

McBride sighed, sat back. 'You're right, Des.'

Smith hesitated, then nodded. He had had a cold bath this morning, a reminder of his public school days, and washed all the dirt of the grotto from himself; he had found an old razor belonging to Luciana's father and given himself an adequate shave; he had washed his hair and brushed his clothes and now sat at the table in fair imitation of a gentleman at leisure. But McBride, perception heightened by his own tension, saw the whitening of the knuckles on the hand that held the cheese knife.

'All right,' Smith said coldly. 'What do we do?'

'We'll tell them to deliver the money tonight.' McBride felt better as he began to outline the programme; his old adaptability came back. 'We'll make it the same time for the pick-up – seven-fifteen, right at peak hour.'

'They may not have the Deutschmarks by tonight. Roman banks don't hold that much German currency – '

'It'll take them no more than a couple of hours to fly it down from Munich or Frankfurt. Des can come back into town with me and phone the Vatican from the Terminus Station. There's just one thing – if Turk isn't released by tonight, we'll have to use you.' He looked at Smith.

'That's not in the plan. I was to stay out of sight until the Fitzgibbon woman took over the money from Des. Then she was to bring it to me and I was to take it to Beirut.'

'There's no Fitzgibbon woman now and there's no guarantee Turk will be free in time. And even if he is, there's the chance they'll put a tail on him.'

'It's the only thing, Seamus,' said Ryan. 'I've got to dump that suitcase before I get off the train, yes.'

'Who watches him upstairs?'

It was McBride's turn to hesitate. Then: 'It will have to be Luciana, I guess.'

'Not her,' said Smith. 'She'd release him as soon as our backs were turned.'

'I'll talk to her,' said McBride, and left the room before there could be any further argument.

When he found Luciana, searching for her throughout the ground floor of the villa as if they were playing a game of hide-and-seek, she was watching him from the landing on the stairs that led to the upper floor. She sat on the top step, saying nothing as he went up towards her. He sat down, turned off his flashlight and put his arm round her. There was a faint glow from the candles in the salon downstairs, but up here the darkness enveloped them like the ghost of the villa itself.

'Luciana – '

'We should never have become involved, Fergus.'

Fergus: they always use your name when they're about to lay down the law. It had been a characteristic of all the women he had known, as if formality were another weapon in their armoury. 'I'm sorry I brought you into it. But I *had* to be involved.'

'Fergus, it's dangerous now – '

'It's always been dangerous, you knew that.'

'But it's much more so now. Is it worth it?'

He wondered what Joe McBride had thought in the moment before he had died, if he had only then realised what danger he had stepped into. 'I think so.'

'Please let His Holiness go – '

'We can't,' he said flatly.

'I'm afraid – '

'What of? Divine retribution?' He was more brutal than he meant to be. 'We fell from grace too long ago. You can't turn back once you've jumped.'

He sensed rather than saw her puzzlement; he felt the movement in her shoulders as her head turned. 'What are you trying to say?'

'Nothing.' Suddenly he was too tired for explanations; sitting with your ass being frozen by a cold marble step, it was difficult to think of yourself as a fallen angel. Lucifer had at least kept himself warm. 'I need you. We want someone to keep an eye on His Holiness tonight while we pick up the money – '

'I'm not staying with him, darling.' Her voice had softened. 'I thought I'd finished with religion, that I didn't need it any more. But when I saw *him*, talked to him – ' He felt her shake her head. 'I couldn't be his jailer, darling. I found out tonight I still believe in Hell. And I suppose that means I believe in all the opposites. God and the Catholic Church. And him.'

Then they heard the banging on the door upstairs. 'What's up with him? Have you got your mask? You go up – '

'I told you – I don't want to have anything more to do with him. Please, darling – '

He went downstairs into the salon. Smith sat at the table sipping another cup of coffee while Ryan cleared away the dishes. It was almost as if a master-servant relationship had been established. 'The Pope's banging on his door. You better see what he wants.'

'You go and see what he wants,' said Smith. Ryan had stopped with the plates stacked in his hands, like a gambler about to deal from a china deck. 'You're the boss. Perhaps he wants to come to some arrangement with you.'

McBride picked up one of the robes, slipped it on and went upstairs, pulling the cowl about his face and pinning it. Luciana was still sitting on the step on the landing; she looked up at him as he went past but said nothing. The banging on the door stopped as soon as he turned the key in the lock.

'I want to go to the bathroom.' There was no light in the bedroom but for the weak filtering of moonlight through the dirty skylight. The Pope stood in the beam of McBride's torch, a blanket wrapped around his shoulders, his hair awry from the movement of his head on his pillow. 'If it's not too much trouble?'

McBride made no reply. There was no point in risking identification just to be friendly to this man who, in earlier circumstances, he had begun to like. He led the Pope along a hall, waited outside the bathroom with the door half-closed to give Martin some privacy; then he took him back to the bedroom, waited till the older man was back in bed. Then the Pope looked at him.

'Good night,' Martin said. 'And thank you, Mr McBride.'

3

Turk Toohey sat in the small, minimally furnished room in the Carabinieri headquarters in the building on the Via del Quirinale. His hat was pushed back on his head and he sat with his short legs stretched out in front of him and his hands in his trouser pockets. The image would never have struck him, since he had never been in an employment exchange, but he looked like a man waiting to be called for a job interview. There was no sign of concern on his thin, blotched face, only a patient boredom, the look of a man who was a veteran of dozens of such interviews and who really didn't care about their outcome.

He had already had eight interviews today, all by different carabinieri officers. Some of them had been as patient as himself and polite with it; others had been angry and sarcastic, and one had lost his temper and slapped him hard across the face. None of them had got anything from him but his fictitious name, Bert Johnston, and his fingerprints, the only honest identification he had. By morning, he reckoned, they would know all they needed to know about him. After that their only problem would be what charges to file against him so that they could continue to hold him.

So far he had not been questioned by any Public Security police. He knew of the rivalry between the different police authorities in Italy and he guessed that General della Porta was not going to turn him over to anyone else while there was

still some mileage in him. He cynically accepted the situation:
the fewer demons you had to face, the better. But deep inside
him, despite all the outward bored calm, he was worried and
angry and disappointed. He could get Christ knew how long
for this job; kidnapping had never been his line and he had no
idea what the cop for it was in Italy. For all he knew it could be
life or even the rope; thank Christ the Eyeties didn't have that
Frog invention, the guillotine. He wasn't afraid of death in
itself, though he had always been scared of dying in the bowels
of a mine; but if he had to die up here on the surface he wanted
to go out all in one piece, not with his bloody noggin lying in a
basket and the rest of him kicking like a headless chook. All
his living, for what it had been worth, hadn't been meant to end
that way.

He shivered and looked across at the sleepy carabiniere sitting
on the only other chair in the room. 'What's the time, sport?'
He held up his watch to indicate it had stopped. 'I'd like to get
a bit of shut-eye.'

The carabiniere held up his own watch: 1.50. But he just
looked blank at the rest of Toohey's remark and the Australian
lay farther back in his chair and made a pantomime of sleeping.
Then he opened his eyes again and said, 'What about it, sport?'

The carabiniere shook his head and Toohey called him a good
old Anglo-Saxon name; the carabiniere looked slightly puzzled,
as if he had heard the word before somewhere. But he just
shook his head again and Toohey closed his eyes, trying to
doze off in the chair.

But his mind gave him far more discomfort than the hard
wooden chair and sleep was as far off as freedom. He knew he
should try to break out of this place, but he had never been one
to go for long odds. This building was alive with demons and
without help he wouldn't get ten feet beyond that door there
before they'd chop him down. And he knew he could expect
no help from McBride and the others; they didn't need him
any longer, though they might be scared he'd split on them.
He knew he wouldn't do that; he had his code of ethics or
whatever it was called. A man couldn't look at himself in a
mirror if he talked to the demons about his workmates.

He wondered how the Pope was making out, cooped up out

there in the villa; was he too being kept awake by a mind that wouldn't lie down? Bugger the man: why did he have to go wandering around in the middle of the night making himself such an easy target? If he'd been in bed, like a joker like him should have been, there would have been no temptation to make him the substitute for the loot they'd missed out on. Toohey knew that he himself would never have thought of taking the Pope; as he had said to himself, kidnapping was not his line and after the collapse of the grotto roof he'd have been happy to call it a night.

There had been, and still was, a sense of bitter disappointment at how the caper, like the grotto roof, had fallen in. For the two months he had been in Rome he had been noncommittal in his attitude towards the success or failure of the job; he had looked on it as no more than that, a job, and he had prepared for it with all his usual professional care. He had never suffered from the Australian characteristic that 'if it's close enough, it's good enough'; in his own way he was more of a perfectionist than Smith, who made such an act of his talent. He would have preferred not to have had to rely so much on the amateur, the Yank, but there had been no way round that; the Vatican demons, the Swiss jokers in their fancy dress, wouldn't have turned a blind eye to him scouting around on his own down there in the locked-off grottoes. But he had been as well prepared as he could possibly be when the job had come to be done and over the past week, as the time for the actual haul had got closer, he had allowed himself to dream about the future. He had never had any long-term dreams; it was enough to have escaped from the past. But a comfortable retirement had all at once begun to look good: no more tunnelling, no more fear of being buried, no more worrying about how much the demons had on you. But now the retirement might be of a different sort . . . The disappointment came up like bile in his mouth and he looked around for a place to spit.

Then the door opened, pushed back tentatively as if whoever was about to enter was not sure if he had the right room. A thin, stooped carabiniere, wearing glasses and carrying a large manilla envelope, came in, looked around, then closed the door behind him. He nodded to Toohey, gave a sort of half-smile.

Then he took a gun, fitted with a silencer, out of the envelope and shot the other carabiniere.

He looked at Toohey, said in halting English, 'You are free to go,' and went out of the room, leaving the door open behind him.

4

'The shoes, Mr McBride,' said the Pope. 'Religious orders, particularly Franciscans, don't wear hand-made shoes. Some cardinals, perhaps – ' He smiled. 'I told you I used to notice the small things about my parishioners – and your voice gave you away on one occasion. I don't suppose you would call yourself one of my parishioners now, would you?'

McBride, shaken, came into the room and closed the door behind him. He pulled back the cowl, almost glad to escape from its confinement, and sat down in the uncomfortable high-backed chair on the far side of the bed from the Pope. The only illumination they had, apart from the weak moonlight through the skylight, was that from the flashlight. He kept the beam focused on the bed and sat in the darkness behind it, like an army regathering its resources after a setback. But recognition, he was realising, was almost as much a relief as a shock.

'Do you want an explanation?'

'Am I entitled to one?' Martin asked. 'I don't think you are seeking absolution, are you?'

McBride shook his head slowly. 'You wouldn't give it.'

'I might. I once – ' But Martin couldn't go on with his own confession. His gift of charity had failed him once and Wolfgang Kessler was dead because of it. He would never again be lacking in charity, not if he could possibly help it. Charity, they said, was the overflow of pity; but for him it had also become a penance. It would be his test, to see how much he could forgive. 'But I'm not going to be your only judge, you know that. There'll be the police – absolution isn't one of their talents, I'm afraid. And there'll be the Church – the clergy and the laity. Some of them may go as far as thinking you've committed heresy by kidnapping me – and heretics have always been fair game for certain groups in the Church.'

'I know, Holiness. But believe me, no heresy was intended. You know we didn't plan to bring you with us.'

'I don't understand what you were doing there last night. Were you after the treasures – one of your colleagues mentioned the Joshua Roll. Was that what you were after?'

'That and some other things.'

'Did what I say to you yesterday bring on the idea?'

'No, it had been planned months ago.'

'You couldn't dispose of treasures like that – no collector would dare buy them.'

'We were going to sell them back to you – the Church would have paid for them.'

'And what were you going to do with the money? Live the good life we spoke about?'

McBride shook his head. 'The money wasn't for any one of us, Holiness. I can't tell you what it was for, but it was for a good cause. Or anyway one I believed in.'

Martin pulled the blanket up further around him; he felt cold with a sense of despair that was familiar. There had been the same feeling of hopelessness in the cell in Dachau, though the cell had been less comfortable than this room and Kessler himself had been part of the chilling atmosphere . . . 'Are you going to let me go when they pay over the money?'

McBride looked up in surprise, but Martin couldn't see him in the darkness beyond the torch: a shiver of the beam itself was the only sign that there had been a reaction. 'Of course! Why should we want to keep you?'

'I'm sure your friend downstairs, the tall one, could give you several reasons.' *Kessler had always had only one reason: I was a protector of Jews, the capital sin of all sins in his eyes.*

'We'll let you go. We're not – ' He couldn't say the word *murderers*: the awful possibility wasn't within a comprehension of himself. I'm only capable of minor sins, he told himself; but kidnapping was a capital offence, in some countries they executed men for it. Just as they did murderers. 'We'll let you go,' he repeated with some desperation.

'Are you afraid, Mr McBride?'

'Let's say I'm uncomfortable.' You could take confession too far. 'I'm not used to this sort of thing.'

The Pope said soberly, 'I know that. But you see, I've been in this situation before – or something like it. They were asking for a different sort of ransom – they wanted a Jewish doctor I was hiding. I only managed to keep going by being – philosophical, as you call it. Jokes, even bad ones, are sometimes the crumbs of sustenance.'

'I had a sense of humour once.' Confession again. But he heard himself going on, 'I lost it somewhere back there in the Vatican, I think.'

'Last night?'

'No, quite a while ago.'

Martin smiled quietly to himself, nodding his head, looking down the slope of the blanket as it fell from his shoulders and chest. The blanket was thin and worn, an old one; for the first time he noticed there was some sort of crest woven into each corner of it. An identification of the owner of this villa, if that was what he was looking for; but he was not interested in clues, he took the cowardly way out of not wanting to know so that he would not have to forgive. Dear God, he prayed, help me.

He involuntarily leaned back on the pillows, suddenly burdened. He tried to remember all the popes who had been held captive, wondered how they had stood up to their ordeal. He was not afraid for himself, but he carried the burden of the knowledge that millions throughout the world saw him as their Rock. To have that Rock snatched from them might seem an omen . . . 'Do you believe in omens?'

'If there are such things, Holiness, we've both had our share of them in the last twenty-four hours.'

'Indeed we have. What are you going to do about yours?'

Then the door opened. McBride, moving with a reflex action, not at that moment knowing why he did what he did, whipped the cowl back on his head and over his face. Smith, wearing his robe, cowled also, stood just inside the doorway, a candle in its bottle holder held out in front of him like a votive offering.

'I beg your pardon, Holiness,' he said mockingly. 'Are we intruding in the confessional?'

'You might have been,' said Martin, hating this tall cynical stranger and hating himself for the feeling. 'But as it happens, your friend has nothing to confess.'

'Oh, he has something to confess, don't let's delude ourselves. But perhaps he feels no sorrow for his sins. That would deprive you of doling out penance to him. You chaps enjoy that, don't you?'

'I'm not prepared to listen to your insults.' Martin's voice was low but cold; he spoke with the authority that recalcitrant cardinals and bishops had come to recognise. 'Close the door.'

Smith's cowled head moved from side to side: he admired style and this man had it. 'You're cool, no doubt about it.'

'You asked for it,' said McBride. 'Shut the door and lock it.'

He brushed past Smith, aware of the sudden stiffening in the other man, and went out of the room. It had just occurred to him that he and the Pope had arrived at an unspoken agreement to keep secret Martin's recognition of him; and he knew then why he had whipped the cowl back over his head. He had become the protector as well as the captor of the Pope.

As he went down the stairs Luciana stood up from the step where she was sitting and took his hand, an armistice gesture. They went down to the salon hand in hand and Ryan, still clearing the table, looked up at them in surprise as they came in. Then he smiled, his big buck teeth almost like another illumination in the dimly lit room. He seemed to be the only one whose good humour hadn't diminished.

'I can't get used to seeing a friar with a girl-friend. The village where I came from, the priest would never talk to a woman or girl alone, except in the confessional. I used to be a good Catholic once,' he said, almost a little incredulously. 'Yes.'

'We don't want any of those here now.' Smith came into the salon, pulling the cowl back from his head; he looked at the other friar as he put the candle back on the table. 'I hope that upstairs you weren't getting any ideas of reconversion?'

'I was just finding out from him if there would be any opposition in the Vatican to paying the ransom for him.'

'I'm surprised you have any doubts about it.' Smith slipped out of his robe.

'I know the Vatican better than you do.' *I'm lying and I'm lying badly.* But he was too tired for better invention: he could think of no other lies.

Smith shook his head as he smoothed back his silver hair.

'What goes on in the Vatican doesn't matter in the slightest. We're asking the *Church* for the money, not the Vatican. Martin is popular with the ordinary Catholic in the pews – and they'll see that the money is paid. You've been too long in the corridors of power, dear chap.'

'There's della Porta, the Carabinieri chief. He doesn't want the money paid. He's flatly against deals of any sort.'

'Nobody listens to the police in other countries – the Church certainly won't. They'll pay the money and they'll pay it when we want it.'

'Okay, that brings us back to tonight,' said McBride, still holding Luciana's hand. 'Luciana won't stay with the Pope.'

Smith looked at Luciana. 'Why not?'

'I have my reasons,' she said, matching his voice for coldness. 'I don't have to tell them to you.'

'So what happens now, *leader*?' Smith's voice was heavy with sarcasm.

'I'm not committing her to anything against her will,' said McBride. 'If we have to, then we leave the Pope here alone, tied up as well as we can do it. And you take over the pick-up job from Des.'

'I told you, I'm not taking that risk – '

'And I'm telling you, I'm not taking any more risks with Luciana's safety. She's done all she was supposed to do, be the look-out in St Peter's Square, and now she's opting out. And that's okay by me.'

He stared at Smith and Ryan, aware that the younger man had quietly moved closer to Smith. These two were the Regulars, as Ryan had described themselves: the full-timers, the volunteers for whom the war went on all the time. They hadn't had to be recruited by three nights of persuasion, they wouldn't be opting out the day after tomorrow as he would be free to do and would do. Smith was the dangerous one, but Ryan was no less dedicated.

'We better be going.' McBride turned his back on the other two men, gently pushed Luciana towards the door. There, he stopped and looked back. 'If there's any hitch about the pick-up of the money this evening, Des will come back this afternoon. Otherwise we stick exactly to the plan, except you'll be taking Maire Fitzgibbon's place.'

'How do I get back to Rome?' Smith seemed to have accepted the situation.

Luciana answered McBride's unspoken query to her. 'There's a bus goes down the main road right through to the Terminus Station. It will take you about an hour, perhaps a little more. It passes the end of our lane at about a quarter to the hour.'

'There had better not be any hitch,' said Smith.

'There won't be on our part,' McBride said. 'But della Porta could shove his nose in. If they listen to him – '

'They had better not,' Smith said softly; it was a stranger's voice, full of more menace than his usual tone. 'And you had better see that they don't, dear chap.'

'They're not going to listen to me!'

'Then persuade someone whom they will listen to. Perhaps they need another phone call – to tell them he dies if we don't get the money – '

'No!' McBride had come back to the table. He slammed a hand down on it and the candles in their bottles wobbled; shadows trembled like dark breaking waves on the walls. He leaned forward towards Smith. 'We don't do that! If I hear of any phone call that comes in with that message, then I blow the guff. I'll be out here with della Porta and if you've as much as laid a hand on the Pope, I'll give them your and Des's names and I'll tell them where the men can be found in Dublin!'

'You do that,' said Smith, voice even softer, 'and you wouldn't last a week. We've never shown any mercy to traitors.'

'I'll take my chances. But I only came into this because I was promised there would be no violence. And nobody, you or anyone else, lays a hand on him upstairs!'

There was silence in the room for a moment; then Ryan said, 'He's got the whip-handle, Seamus. We have to do it his way. There's too much at stake. Dublin would never forgive us if we buggered it now with the wrong approach.'

'Let's go,' said McBride, and once more turned his back on Smith, knowing he had won, at least for the time being.

He led Luciana and Ryan out to the stables where he had put the Alfa. Without lights he drove slowly down the lane.

As they reached the end of it Ryan nodded across towards a small building silhouetted against the thin moonlight.

'What's that?'

McBride waited for Luciana to reply but, seated cross-wise in the small back seat, she said nothing. At last he said, 'It's the Chiesetta Sant' Augusto. It used to be a church, but it hasn't been used for ages. It belongs to Luciana's family. It's a true Roman temple – the oldest parts of it date back to the second century A.D. It's in some of the old guide-books, the Baedekers of last century, but it seems to have been forgotten after Mussolini came to power. The Pericolis don't care about it and neither does anyone else, I guess.'

'I'm sorry we had to come here,' Ryan said. 'I think Seamus would have been easier to get on with if we'd been in a safer place, like the villa outside Florence.'

'He'd be a son-of-a-bitch wherever he is. I don't know why you continue to work with him.'

'I do what GHQ tells me. I'm a soldier.'

'Yes, I guess so.' But McBride found the idea hard to digest. His mind was too deeply stamped with the image of the traditional soldier, he was too much a stranger to guerrilla warfare. And yet, he told himself, I'm right in the goddam middle of it!

He looked back at Luciana. But she was staring out of the car, paying no attention to the two men, and the rest of the drive back to Rome was made in almost complete silence. Once Ryan said, 'There's a police car. I wonder if they're looking for us?'; but he got no answer from either McBride or Luciana and he lapsed back into silence. When they had parked the car in the garage and come out into the deserted street, Luciana spoke for the first time since leaving the villa.

'Find me a taxi, Fergus. I am going home.'

'No, come back to the apartment with me.'

'No, I'm finished with all this.'

'I don't think so,' said Ryan quietly. 'You had better tell her that, Fergus.'

'I shan't – what's the word? – *split* on you.' Luciana was on the verge of tears. 'Please, Fergus – let us both be finished with them!'

'I can't,' he said, and heard the note of despair in his voice. *God, how I wish we both could just walk out!* But even as he thought of the possibility he knew it was hopeless. Whatever his faults he had always kept his promises; and there was the promise to the men from Dublin. Things had gone disastrously wrong, but if the Pope was returned unharmed and the money was paid over, then the object would have been achieved: the base would be there for the peace campaign, for the reunion of Ireland without need of the gun: it was a cause he had to stay with while he could still contribute. And there was another, more personal reason why he could not walk out now: he could not abandon the Pope. The man back there in the villa had a hold on him that was tightening every minute. His mind was too disturbed to grasp the reason right now: it could be Martin himself, the man who was a symbol of peace for millions, it could be a revived spark in his own religious ashes, it could be that he could not sacrifice any man to the possibility of his being murdered. 'Come home with me – we'll talk about it – '

'I think you'd better, Luciana,' said Ryan, still quietly; but now there was a note of command in his voice that McBride had not heard before. 'I don't want to hurt you. Or you, Fergus,' he said as McBride made a move towards him. He held out his hand and the light from a nearby street lamp glittered on the long-bladed knife that Smith had used to cut the cheese back at the villa. 'When Seamus started talking about killing again, I thought I'd better take this, just in case.'

McBride looked down at the knife, feeling the tightness in his stomach. He put an arm round Luciana, feeling the rigidity of her, as if her whole body had turned to bone. 'I thought you were on my side – no violence?'

'Call it habit, Fergus. I've been at this game too long, yes. My grandad and my dad and two of my uncles, they all died for the cause. One of my brothers was killed in Belfast last year. And now the coppers have Maire.'

'Maire? Maire Fitzgibbon?'

'She's my sister – that's her married name. When she heard they wanted a woman for this job, she volunteered. That's the sort of family we are. The sort that's not going to let this job fail because someone might let something slip. Luciana stays with us, doesn't talk to anyone, till this is over.'

'If I told her to walk away, what would you do?'

'I'd have to kill her, Fergus. Yes.'

'You'd have to kill me too.' Ryan said nothing and McBride went on, 'That would foul up the job completely. Because you need me, Des. At least until tonight.'

They stood there in the silent street, silently challenging each other. Then down the line of cars parked at the kerb an engine started up and headlights blazed; Ryan turned his head quickly and just as quickly slipped the knife back into his pocket. The car drew away from the kerb, went roaring up the street: McBride caught a glimpse of a man and a woman sitting close together in the front seat. Ryan looked back at McBride and Luciana.

'We'd better get down to your flat pretty quick.'

'Does Luciana go home?'

'No,' said Luciana. 'I'm coming with you.'

McBride could feel the tight pressure of her hand on his arm; he knew she was as much concerned for him as for herself. 'If Luciana comes, Des, you don't pull that knife on her again.'

'Not if she promises not to walk out.' Ryan was giving nothing away: the blunted boxer's face, marked by scar tissue, was like a mask.

'I shan't walk out,' said Luciana. 'Not till Fergus's part of the job has been done.'

Ryan hesitated, then nodded. They began to walk down the street and after a few yards Ryan seemed to relax. They passed the entrance to the Hotel Eden as a taxi drew up and two couples got out; McBride recognised the accents as American and Australian. One of the men took the arm of one of the women and helped her out.

'Why, thank *you*, Stanley. You Aussie men are so *gallant!*'

'I've got funny noises in my head.' The Australian woman tapped the heel of her palm against her ear as if trying to clear it of water. 'I thought I heard you say he was gallant. He used to bite his mother's bosom if her milk wasn't warm enough.'

The American woman screeched with laughter, and all four of them went into the hotel on a surf of mirth. Ryan stopped

5

'I'll tell you about it upstairs,' said Toohey.

All four of them crowded into the elevator and McBride, after feeling in his pocket, said, 'Anyone got ten lire?'

Cramped together like peak-hour commuters suddenly asked for extra fares, everyone searched for the necessary coin. 'No,' they all said at once.

McBride sighed, slid back the doors and they all got out. This whole operation had Irish notes to it; he had read of major IRA raids that had failed because some almost inconsequential detail had been overlooked. A rendezvous missed because an out-of-date map had been used, an important telephone call unable to be made because the man responsible for it had forgotten to bring pennies for the call-box: McBride wondered if he had forgotten some minor detail that might prove disastrous before today was out.

They tramped up the stairs and were halfway up to McBride's floor when the lights in the stair-well, operated from a time-switch in the hall below, went out.

'I left my flashlight in the car,' said McBride. 'Where's yours, Des?'

'I didn't bring it. I didn't think we'd need it.'

'You wouldn't read about it,' said Toohey disgustedly. 'There are more amateurs here than at the Olympic Games.'

They groped their way up the rest of the stairs. McBride fumbled in the darkness with his key, trying to find the lock in his front door.

'Isn't there a time-switch on the landing here?' Toohey asked.

'It isn't working. They're going to fix it, they say. *Domani, domani.*'

'Bloody Italians and bloody Irishmen!'

'What about the bloody Irishmen?' said Ryan.

McBride, still fumbling to find the lock, changed the subject. 'How'd you get in downstairs, Turk?'

'I picked the lock. Smithy's not the only one who can do it.'

'Why didn't you come up and pick this one? You'd have been safer in my apartment.'

'No, that's your place, mate. I believe in respecting another bloke's privacy.'

In the darkness McBride shook his head at the little man's mixed code of ethics. His fumbling fingers at last found the lock and he opened the door. They all went in and he switched on the lights, glad to return from the shadows he had been swimming in for the past three hours.

'I'll make coffee,' said Luciana, not helpfully but to effect her own escape from the company of the three men. She was not curious as to how or why Toohey had suddenly turned up here; she had lost interest in all the men Fergus was involved with. She had reached a stage of utter dejection, of worry for Fergus. She was afraid not only for his safety but for the feeling between them. She felt something had happened to that feeling; once, there had been a warmth in him that had generated an answering fire of love in herself and though she had always known she might love him more fiercely than he might feel for her, there had been no fear in her mind that she might lose him. She could be vain and flirtatious, but they were only sparks from the blaze that was the core of her being; she knew she sometimes acted and sounded selfish, but if he had asked her she would have given her life for Fergus. But he was no longer the gentle considerate man she had fallen in love with, and she wished she knew where and when that man had been lost. He had disappeared some time in the last twenty-four hours and, so complete was her dejection, she wondered if he would ever reappear. In her misery she also had one of those quick returns to faith that lapsed Catholics are prone to. The convent sisters had been right: God proved his existence with his punishments.

She searched around in the cupboards of the kitchen, opening and slamming doors as if she were slapping Fergus's ears, suddenly angry with him. She went back to the door of the living-room.

'There's no coffee. And there doesn't seem to be anything to eat but ice-cream.'

'Goddam,' said McBride. 'I must have taken everything out to the villa.'

'Bloody Americans too,' she said, and looked at Toohey. 'Nobody's perfect.'

'I'm an Aussie,' said Toohey, and for the first time ever actually smiled at her, a lopsided grin. '*We're* perfect.'

Luciana didn't return his smile: he was one of the enemy, one of the men she was finished with. There was nothing she could do in the kitchen, so she crossed the living-room and went into the bedroom, slamming the door behind her. She gazed at the bed, the meeting-place of their love, then she fell on it, rolled over on her back and stared at the ceiling. She was surprised to find that she could not weep, that her misery had dried her even of tears.

Out in the living-room Toohey was saying, 'You wouldn't read about it. This joker just walked into the room and shot the other demon stone cold dead with a silencer.'

'Nobody heard the shot?'

'He shut the door, it was one of them old-fashioned very thick jobs, and the silencer he had was pretty effective. Silencers make a bit of noise, but most people wouldn't recognise it, not even coppers. Ask any number of 'em and most of 'em would tell you they'd never heard a silencer fired. I'd only heard it m'self once before,' he said, and looked at McBride.

McBride made no comment on that: what had happened in Belfast in June 1970 no longer interested him. Now he knew there was going to be no coffee, he was pouring bourbon for himself and the other two men: Jack Daniel might prove a stiffer crutch than Chase and Sanborn. 'You sure it wasn't a fake, a put-up job? He could have used blanks.'

'The bloke he shot was bleeding like a stuck pig. He was dead, all right.' Toohey took his drink, gulped a mouthful and shook his head vigorously, getting rid of a memory. 'I didn't know whether to skedaddle or not – for a minute I thought they were trying to frame me or something. But nobody came into the room and then I thought I'd better get outa there. If anyone had come in, who'd have believed me if I'd told him another demon had come in and done the shooting?'

'Did you have any trouble getting out of Headquarters?'

'It wasn't easy, but I managed it.' It had taken him fifteen minutes to make it to a rear exit; at one time he had been huddled in a cleaner's closet while two carabinieri stood outside the door and complained about the extra duty they were all being drafted for. 'That time of night the place isn't crowded. There were some other blokes in civvies around, reporters or clerks, I dunno, and in the end I chanced my luck and tried to look like one of them going out the back to the dunny. They'd taken me out for a piss once, so I knew where it was.'

'Did anyone follow you?'

'If I'd seen anyone tailing me, do you think I'd have come here?'

'Sorry.' McBride sipped his drink. He had never been a three-o'clock-in-the-morning drinker and his taste buds were dead asleep; the whisky didn't even provide the prop he had hoped for. He put down the glass and said, 'Why did you come here?'

'Where else could I go? I couldn't find my way back to the villa on my own. I'll be safe here.'

'We'll look after you.' Ryan had not touched his drink, but sat holding the glass in his big hands, occasionally glancing down at it suspiciously, as if it were some sort of quack medicine that had been offered him as a cure-all. He was not a spirits drinker and he wished suddenly for a long glass of stout. 'We've had a few troubles while you've been gone.'

McBride forestalled Toohey's queries by keeping to the immediate subject. 'You've got no idea who this killer was?'

'Not a clue. I didn't really look at him, everything happened so quick, and I was pretty sleepy. I know I've never seen him before, but. He was sorta tall and skinny and he wore glasses – that's about all I can remember about him. I'm buggered if I know what he was up to. Was he helping me to get away or was he just paying the other demon back for something the bloke had done to him?'

'These Italians can be pretty drastic when it comes to revenge – ' Then McBride stopped as he remembered the Irishmen who had their ideas about revenge. 'It's my bet the guy didn't belong to the Carabinieri. Something stinks about the whole business. I'm getting superstitious.' He picked up his glass again, gulped a mouthful of the whisky. 'Too many things are going wrong.'

'This one went right for me,' said Toohey. 'I'd have been up to my eyeballs in trouble if I'd still been there in the morning, when my dabs come back from Interpol. When they took my prints, they told me they were gunna check on me.'

'You'll be in trouble over your head if they say you killed the cop,' said McBride. 'Have you thought of that?'

Toohey nodded morosely. 'Like you say, too many things are going wrong. If I believed such crap, I'd start to think The Bloke up there was getting his own back on us.'

'I believe it,' said Ryan, suddenly drinking from his glass. 'I'm superstitious too. That's the bloody trouble with being Irish. Our mams suckle it into us along with their milk.'

McBride looked at him hopefully. 'Does that mean you've changed your mind, you think we should call the whole thing off?'

Ryan kept his eyes on the whisky in his glass, measuring it as if he were conducting some chemical experiment. 'No. I'm fatalistic too. I don't think I've ever really believed I'll die in my bed.'

'Jesus Christ!' McBride thumped his glass down on the table, spilling some of the liquid. 'You all want to be fucking martyrs!'

'Didn't you know that?' said Toohey, sourly realistic.

'Yes,' admitted McBride, forcing himself to sit back in his chair. 'Sometimes I think it was my old man's main ambition.'

Ryan looked up from his drink. 'None of us backs out. Right?'

McBride and Toohey looked at each other, then the Australian said, 'I guess that's about the strength of it. We don't split up till we've got the cash. I'm broke. I need that ten thousand quid, because when I leave here I'm gunna have to run a bloody long way. And right now if it cost only a dollar to go round the world, I couldn't get outa sight.'

'We've already put the word on them, Turk,' said Ryan. 'We collect the money tonight.'

'I know. The demons told me about it. One of them got shit on his liver and belted me one – he didn't think much of people who went rounda kidnapping his Pope. I don't think it's much of a lark m'self, but we're stuck with it now.' He stood up, yawned and stretched his arms. He looked unconcerned, almost his old phlegmatic self, a workman who had had a longer than usual day at his trade. 'Can I kip down on this sofa, Fergus?'

McBride got blankets and pillows for both men, said good night and went into the bedroom, closing the door behind him. Luciana, fully dressed, still lay on her back on the bed. Without moving her head she looked at him, waiting for him to speak first.

'Do we share the bed?' he said, not bothering to take off even his tie till she answered.

She got up, pulled down the coverlet, kicked off her shoes, took off her dress and her panty-hose. Wearing only her slip she got in between the sheets. Only then did she say, 'We don't make love.'

'I feel as if I've been castrated today.' He began to undress, suddenly feeling old, stiff and weak.

'Not today,' she said. 'It happened some time ago.'

He was sitting on the edge of the bed, his back to her. He looked at her over his shoulder: he had the feeling he was about to get into bed with a stranger. He put on his pyjamas, the first time he had ever worn them when going to bed with her: we're not strangers, he thought, we're an old married couple. He opened the window, leaving the outside louvred shutters closed, put out the light and got in beside her. They lay side by side on their backs, each staring at the dark ceiling.

'We're not going to get away with it,' he said at last. 'The Pope knows who I am.'

She lay stiffly for a moment, then he heard the rustle of her hand beneath the sheet and then it touched his hip, felt for his own hand and held it. 'Was he angry?'

'I don't think so.' There had been no surprise at Martin's calm recognition of him, only the shock of the recognition itself. It occurred to him now that he had not expected any display of anger from the Pope; the man, if he was capable of it and

McBride was sure he was, would never show it. It had nothing to do with the image of holiness he was expected to project: Martin's control stemmed from some other reason, one buried in the character of the man, not the pope. 'But he's not going to make the sign of the Cross over us and tell us to get lost.'

'Does he know why you want the money?'

'No.'

She still held his hand, but she said shrewdly, unable yet to expend her own forgiveness fully, 'Will he tell the police who you are when you release him? They'll question him, even though he is Pope. He'll have to respect Italian law.'

'I don't know the extent of his charity. Popes should have more than anyone else, shouldn't they?'

She slipped her arm under his head, held him to her without passion. Italian women, she told herself, were meant to mother their men. *Mamma mia!* was more than just an exclamation, it was an admission that Italian men knew where their real strength lay; she would prove to this American it was where all men's strength lay, in their women. She settled herself comfortably, prepared to have him sleep all night within the circle of her arm, within the circle of power she had only just discovered in herself. She was not even surprised to find that lying here with Fergus, mother now as well as mistress to him, was as satisfying as making love.

2

Kessler stood at the corner of the narrow street that ran off the Via Francesco Crispi, sheltering himself from the cold breeze that blew down the hill from the east. Normally he was oblivious to the elements, but he had been awake now for almost twenty-four hours and his body was beginning to rebel. Revenge was a fire, but it didn't always keep a man warm.

He watched the closed door where he had seen the little man pick the lock and disappear into the building last night. Some time later he had seen the three people, two men and a girl, come down the hill and go in the same door. Several minutes later a light had come on in a room on the fourth floor; someone had come to the doors that led out on to the small balcony and closed the curtains. Kessler had crossed the road and with the aid of a lighted match had checked the names on the plate beside the door: Sr. Fergus McBride lived on the fourth floor. He had gone back to the side street, sat down in a doorway and begun his vigil. Sooner or later the little man would come out of the building where he was hiding and would lead him to the Pope.

He knew nothing about the little man, not even his name; but the fact that the man was a cipher did not matter, he was just a means to an end. Yesterday morning the taxi had followed the police car across the city to the Via del Quirinale, the taxi driver enjoying every moment of the chase through the hazardous traffic.

'Get out of the way, fools!'

Their first hazard had occurred before they had even got out of St Peter's Square. The taxi driver, urged on by Kessler, had had to horn his way through the crowd of photographers enveloping the two men walking across the Square towards the Via della Conciliazione. Kessler, impatient to get after the disappearing police car, had glanced angrily at the two men in the middle of the besieging photographers.

'Who are they?' he snapped.

'General della Porta, chief of the Carabinieri. The other man I don't know. Your Italian is not good, signore. We'll talk German, if you like. I learned it during the war.'

'You fought on our side?' Like so many Germans he had never thought of the Italians as allies; like so many of them he believed they had fought the war alone. 'Against the American and the British?'

'At the beginning,' said the taxi driver, hoping this was not one of those Germans who still believed they had not lost the war. 'Then I saw how things were going. It was better to be practical.'

At last he got the taxi free of the obstructing photographers and he went down the Via della Conciliazione as if every kilometre per hour on his speedometer meant another thousand lire on his meter. You had to earn your money where you could, even from ex-allies.

'You a journalist? What paper do you work for?'

'*Die Welt*,' said Kessler, thinking he might as well claim the best as an employer. A sediment of humour was beginning to stir in him, as if someone had poked a long stick down into the deep dark well that had been the last thirty years. 'I'm on special assignment.'

The driver had gabbled on, mixing his wartime German with his native tongue, but Kessler, unable to follow him, had just sat nodding, his eyes never leaving the police car threading its way through the traffic up ahead. When he had got out of the taxi and was paying the fare, tipping lavishly as he had not done since he had left Munich, he was suddenly aware that the driver had made a remark that was more than just chatter.

'What did you say?'

'I said I hope they don't harm him.'

'Who?' Kessler, eye on the big doorway down the street into which the two carabinieri had disappeared with their prisoner, looked puzzled. 'You mean him?'

'No, no. Your Pope.' Then the taxi driver, mistaking Kessler's look for one of reproach, added hastily, 'Sorry. *Our* Pope. I meant he was yours because he's German – '

Kessler left him, uninterested in anything further the driver had to say, and walked slowly back along the street. The clouds had begun to lift and the sun blazed on the bleached ochre of the walls of the Quirinale Palace. Cars came screeching up the Via 24 Maggio, almost clipping the corner of the building where Kessler stood as they raced across the square and up past the palace, the screech of their tyres one long jeer at the seat of authority. Kessler, a German living in the past, shook his head at how Italians flaunted their disrespect for law and order; no wonder they had been such unreliable allies during the war. After he had killed Kurt Stecher he would, if he were still alive and free, be glad to get out of this mad country.

He waited there on the Quirinale hill all day, sometimes walking along the street past the palace, sometimes standing on the corner of the square, once going up into the park to buy more peanuts from the old man he had seen going in there. By nightfall he was convinced that the little man, still held there in the Carabinieri headquarters, held the clue to where the Pope could be found. If he was innocent, the carabinieri

135

would have let him go by now; the fact that they were still holding him meant they suspected him of knowing more than they had so far been able to get out of him; if they had been able to get anything worthwhile out of him there would have been a flurry of movement out of the headquarters, but all day there had been no more than a steady coming and going, no wild rush that suggested the police had at last got a clue to the Pope's whereabouts.

General della Porta had arrived at the headquarters just before eleven and left again at five; other senior officers had come and gone. Kessler, watching them come out of the building, had seen no excitement on the faces of any of them, just stiff glum concern. Newspapermen and photographers had gone into the building, then come out to lounge about in the sunshine like casual workers waiting for some contractor to come out and give them the call.

Late in the afternoon Kessler had crossed the street and approached one of the older photographers who sat with his behind perched on the fender of a police car. 'Do you speak German?'

The photographer, lean and grizzled, eyes squinting as if from years of peering through a view-finder, looked at him suspiciously. Was this a German *paparazze* trying to muscle in on the Rome scene? Then he saw that Kessler carried no camera and, as if reassured, he nodded. 'A little. What do you want?'

'I'm a freelance journalist,' Kessler said. 'For some German Catholic magazines. The man the carabinieri arrested this morning – have they charged him?'

The photographer shook his head. 'Not yet. But they're not telling us anything.'

'Do they think he had anything to do with the Pope's kidnapping?'

'I don't know what *they* think, but I know what *I* think. The police have got no other lead but this fellow and the way they're hanging on to him, I'm guessing he knows something. If I can get a picture of him – ' Suspicion sharpened his eyes again. 'You're not going to take any pictures?'

'Oh, no, no.' Kessler tried to smile, to appease the man; he found dealing with other people so difficult, almost an agony. 'I wouldn't dream of invading your territory.'

He thanked the photographer and retreated to his post farther down the street. At midnight, when the newspapermen, the photographers and the few idlers had at last drifted away and the street was virtually deserted, Kessler decided he would have to rescue the little man from the Carabinieri headquarters.

It never occurred to him that no sane man would have contemplated what he was about to do. A madman's logic is not necessarily mad logic; it can have a certain innocence to it. He reasoned that the Romans, though they had no respect for their law officers, did not kill them casually in cold blood; therefore any carabiniere, on his way to or from duty, would not be on his guard against any attempt to murder him. It was just one-thirty in the morning when his victim, chosen only at the moment he emerged from the Carabinieri headquarters, a man destined for death because he was the right size, appeared and began to walk down across the square.

He was about the same height as Kessler but a little heavier, a desk man with the stiff cramped walk of someone who had spent too long a day in his chair. He had a raincoat slung over one arm and in the other he carried a large, stuffed manilla envelope. He went down the steps that led into the narrow streets that eventually came out at the Trevi Fountain, walking with his head held back, breathing in the night air after the smoke-stale atmosphere of the office he had just left. Kessler shot him in the shadow of a house in a tiny piazza; the man fell beneath a plaque on the wall honouring the memory of a Partisan hero who had been shot by a German firing squad; but neither the dead man nor Kessler saw the plaque. It took only a minute to strip the man of his uniform and pull the body in behind a barricade of garbage cans. Kessler emptied the manilla envelope of the papers it contained, put his gun in it, picked up the uniform and went back up the steps. He went down the side street opposite the palace and there in a dark doorway he changed out of his own clothes into the uniform. He folded his clothes neatly, as they had taught him in the asylum, wrapped them in his overcoat and pushed the bundle under one of the line of parked cars. A motor scooter was

137

parked behind the car, its rear wheel locked by a chain. Kessler wrestled the scooter closer to the rear of the car so that the bundle of clothing was completely obscured by the scooter; he did not expect anyone to come along here at this hour peering under cars, but that was one of the characteristics he had inherited from his father: to be meticulous about everything he attempted. Then, carrying the manilla envelope under his arm, he went back up the street and made his way into Carabinieri headquarters.

He was not to know it, but there would be an inquiry later that day into how easily he had gained admittance to the building. General della Porta would suspend all those who had been on guard that night and several officers would be posted to hill villages or to Sicily where the Mafia might teach them to be more vigilant. But General della Porta would be unfair: it was years since he had worked at two o'clock in the morning and he had forgotten it was the low point in the day's rhythm. He had also overlooked the fact that in any bureaucracy, and even a police headquarters is no more than that, a man with a piece of paper or an envelope in his hand is part of the essential pattern; malingering Roman centurions with papyrus rolls in their hands had wandered around Caesar's headquarters with the same unchallenged freedom as Kessler wandered into General della Porta's headquarters. Once in the building it had taken him some time to find the room where the little man was held, but eventually he had opened the right door.

He had shot the carabinieri guarding the little man without feeling of any sort: death, his own or anyone else's, was only another condition of life. He put the gun back in the envelope, told the little man he was free to go, and went down the corridor and waited round a corner till the little man emerged cautiously from the room. His quarry was obviously a man accustomed to making himself scarce; he acted with too much professional slipperiness for an honest man. There was a delay while he hid in a closet to escape two gossiping carabinieri; but finally Kessler saw him slip out of a rear door that led to the lavatories. Kessler followed, keeping just far enough behind not to be noticed. In his own way he was more professional than he knew; Toohey never once saw the man who was trailing him. The chase went on for over a mile, with Toohey several times doubling back on his tracks, but eventually it finished in the Via Francesco Crispi.

Kessler had waited in the side street till he saw all the lights go out behind the curtains in the McBride apartment. The doors to the balcony opened and a figure stepped out, stood for a moment in the moonlight; Kessler recognised the shape of the little man. Then the man went back into the apartment, closing the shutter doors behind him. Kessler, trusting to luck that the little man had gone to bed for at least a couple of hours, then retraced his steps to the Quirinale. He retrieved his bundle from beneath the parked car, changed back into his own clothes and pushed the uniform under the car. He was about to walk away when he looked at the motor scooter. He needed transport: the little man was not going to go everywhere in Rome on foot, not if he was trying to avoid the police.

The chain locking the back wheel of the scooter was only a deterrent, almost a joke: one shot from the silenced gun broke a link in it. Kessler threw the chain in the gutter, straddled the scooter and pushed it down the street. At a corner, under a street lamp, he familiarised himself with it, got it started and rode it sedately, if a little shakily, back to the street off the Via Francesco Crispi. The longer he rode the more daring he became; he quickened his speed a little, felt the breeze rushing into his face, and by the time he dismounted he was laughing, almost as young as he had been when he had last seen his father.

Oh, Father, he cried suddenly in the middle of laughing; and sat down in the doorway and began to weep. He finally dozed off, for an hour, and woke in a panic that the little man might have gone while he was asleep. But he knew that if the door up the street had opened he would have woken instantly; there was an animal instinct in him that would never let the little man get away from him. Daylight, no more than a grey blush, began to slide down the walls above him and soon church bells began to toll, their sound mingling into the one sad, light song on the cool clear air. The sky turned blue, promising a fine day; high up, a plane glinted in the rays of the still unseen sun, a

139

tear in the eye of the morning. A group of priests came down the narrow street from the Irish College, went past Kessler without a glance at him, and went on up towards Trinita dei Monti, where a special Mass was being said for the safe return of the Pope. Kessler looked after them, wondering how soon they would be coming down this street on their way to a Requiem Mass.

Then the shutters started going up on the shops, that slamming sound that is the European break of day. Kessler, chilled, tired but still ready to face another long day, moved a few paces down the hill to a bar-café. The proprietor, surprised to see a customer so early in the morning, sold him a coffee and a stale ham roll. Kessler came out to the doorway of the bar and stood there while he ate his breakfast and continued to watch the doorway up the street.

At eight-thirty the door opened and Kessler, once more back in the side street, straightened up, tired eyes suddenly alert behind his spectacles. But the person who came out of the doorway was not the little man; and he settled back against the wall. Then his eyes narrowed, straining to focus his gaze on the figure standing on the doorstep.

He turned quickly away as the man looked down towards him; he bent down and began to fiddle with the motor of the scooter. His head was throbbing as excitement gripped him and he could not resist the temptation to look back over his shoulder. There was no mistaking the figure now walking slowly up the hill.

Yesterday the same man had been walking across St Peter's Square with General della Porta, chief of the Carabinieri.

3

When McBride had got out of bed Toohey and Ryan were already up and dressed. Luciana was still sleeping and he had left her and gone out into the living-room. 'I have a maid comes in every day to rearrange the dust. You two had better stay out of sight till Luciana gets rid of her. You'll have to do without something to eat till Luciana goes out and gets some food.'

'I can go,' said Ryan.

'Better not. The other people in this building are used to seeing her around, but they don't know you. Just stay out of sight till I come back at lunchtime. If I can't get back I'll phone you from somewhere outside the Vatican.'

'Do they bug the phones in the Vatican?' said Toohey. 'You can't trust anyone these days.'

McBride said irritably, 'I don't want to make any calls from my office, that's all.'

'You sound to me like a bloke with divided loyalties. Have you got religion, mate?'

'Does being careful mean you've got religion?' McBride said sarcastically.

'That's the reason a lot of people are religious, ain't that right, Des?'

'Don't joke about it, Turk,' said Ryan. 'Me mam's religious. She'd be taking a bath in holy water if she knew who we've got out at the villa.'

'She probably has guessed by now,' said McBride, and Ryan nodded morosely.

McBride went back into the bedroom, closed the door and woke up Luciana. 'You're housekeeper today.'

She smiled up at him sleepily, still only half-awake. 'Do you always sleep with your housekeeper?'

She sounded like the old Luciana, but he glanced at her cautiously. 'None of that. I've just joined the celibacy corps.'

'The Pope will be glad to hear that.'

Then she blinked and was wide awake. She swung out of bed, her slip up round her hips. McBride caught a glimpse of hair and thigh, sniffed the warm sweet smell of her, and for a moment there was a surge of the old feeling in his loins. But he dampened it down at once, knowing it wouldn't last. He went into the tiny bathroom, shaved and showered, came out and dressed while Luciana showered. Again there was the odd feeling that they were an old married couple. On other mornings when she had stayed in the apartment she had called him into the shower, still hungry to touch him even after the gorging of the night.

When she came out of the shower, towel wrapped modestly

141

around her, she said, 'I'll help tonight with the collection of the money, if you want me to.'

He shook his head. 'No. You don't go out on any more limbs for me.'

She began to dress, her back turned to him: old married couples didn't do that, he told himself. She was establishing a whole new relationship between them and he was not yet sure of the form of it.

'You're out on a limb, darling. I can't leave you there alone.'

'You don't have to – ' He was torn between wanting her kept safe and knowing that tonight's operation would be helped if she were available.

She turned round, pulling up the zipper of her dress. 'We must get the money tonight, darling. And let Smith and Turk and Des get out of Rome, out of Italy, so that we shan't ever see them again.'

'You still think that the Pope is going to forget all about me when he's back in the Vatican?' He shook his head. 'I'll do my best to keep you out of it. But I think you better keep your Sundays free for visiting me.'

'Do you really expect to go to prison?'

He was silent for a moment, then he nodded. 'If the Pope stays alive – yes.'

'And if he doesn't stay alive?' She stood with one arm raised, her comb driven deep into her hair like a rack of needles.

'Don't think about that. The important thing is, he *must*.'

'I don't trust Smith. There's something – *psychopathic* about him.'

He nodded again. 'Sometimes I wonder why the IRA has tolerated him so long. He must be good in his job, that's all I can think.' He looked at her without really seeing her, his thoughts miles away at the villa with the man in the upstairs room. 'But if he harms the Pope – '

She came round the bed, kissed him gently, without passion. 'Don't look like that, darling. For a moment you looked like – like Smith. *Violent.*'

He blinked, then grinned, though with little real mirth. 'There must be more of my dad in me than I thought.' He

142

kissed her. 'Don't worry. I might get into a brawl with a guy, but I could never kill him.'

And now he was walking up the street to the garage. When he had come out of the front door of the building he had glanced around to see if the place was staked out; but there had been no obvious watchers, only a man in an overcoat trying to get his motor scooter started on the corner of the side street down the hill. He didn't give the man a second glance, but went on up towards the garage.

When he reached his office in the press building his secretary, a plump happy girl named Maria, was laying a file of newspaper clippings on his desk. Usually she wore bright colours that sometimes made her look like a walking arc of rainbow, but this morning she was in black.

'He's not dead yet, Maria,' he said gently.

'No, signore. But – ' She shrugged. 'The churches were full this morning at Mass.'

'We'll get him back unharmed, Maria. Just keep praying.'

The clippings were stories and editorials on the kidnapping. The Italian editorials were highly critical of Vatican security, ignoring the fact that the Pope appeared to have deliberately evaded his own Swiss Guards; the editorials adopted the stance that the national reputation was at stake, unconsciously underlining the *Roman* in the Roman Catholic Church. Editorials in newspapers in other countries, received by cable early this morning, were concerned for the security surrounding their own Heads of State; the guard had been doubled at Buckingham Palace, an extra detachment of marines was camped on the lawn of the White House, the President of France had cancelled a trip to Africa. The stories on the news pages were no more than a collection of guesses; with no hard facts to go on, the correspondents were building their own bricks. The one comforting note in the whole pile of clippings and cable forms was that the IRA was not mentioned. Everyone had his own guess as to who the kidnappers were, but no one had nominated the IRA.

McBride was still looking through the pile when O'Hara came in, bony face seemingly longer than it had been yesterday.

'I couldn't sleep. Jesus, Mary and Joseph, how can *anyone* sleep at a time like this?'

143

'Any more news come in?'

'None that I've heard of. Maybe they're sitting on something over in State. You know they never tell us Jesuits anything unless they have to. They talk to you more freely than they do to me.'

O'Hara couldn't sleep, but he also couldn't forget the intra-Vatican rivalry. McBride gestured at the pile on his desk. 'Have you seen these?'

O'Hara nodded. 'They're not all bad, Fergus. Don't lose your sense of perspective. When a reporter has nothing concrete to write about, it's easier to be critical than constructive. The thing is, everyone's condemned the kidnapping, even the Arabs. I wouldn't like to be in their shoes, I tell you.'

'Whose shoes?'

'The kidnappers. They've got nowhere to run to, nowhere at all. Nobody's going to give *them* asylum.'

'Time I was getting over to Cardinal Moroni,' said McBride, glad of somewhere to run to.

'I've got my appointment with the cops.' It had been the dream of O'Hara's boyhood to be a slum priest like Pat O'Brien, saving the likes of Jimmy Cagney from the dumb cops who didn't see the good in the little gangster; his memory was a fog of Thirties movies, the relic of a youth spent in village cinemas before he had gone into the seminary. But Cork had had no gangsters, just some pensioned-off IRA boys, and here in the Vatican the skulduggery was political and not criminal. 'They're interviewing every man-jack of us.'

McBride stopped at the door. 'Why?'

'Who knows? Maybe they're thinking it's an inside job.' He's genuinely worried and upset, McBride thought, but by God, he's almost enjoying it too. This is the biggest thing that's ever happened in all his life and when he goes back to Cork he'll spin it out into innumerable sermons. 'It'd be a dreadful thing if they were right! Glory be to God, it'd set us back four or five centuries!'

'Pat, don't get yourself steamed up. We've got to play this cool.' *With the sweat starting to moisten my palms and my legs feeling as if someone had sawn halfway through my knees.* 'We don't want the news guys blowing up rumours – '

144

'You're right, Fergus.' O'Hara took out his handkerchief and blew his nose; the trumpeting of his horn was a familiar sound around the office, the bugle note of his emotion. 'I'll pass the word no one is to talk to a reporter.'

'They won't all keep their mouths shut. Not eight or nine hundred of them. Are they interviewing *everyone* who works in the Vatican?'

'Everyone but the cardinals, I'm told. General della Porta is a very thorough man. He's been in Rome so long everyone's forgotten he's from the north, from Turin. They're a different breed up there.'

'I'll remember that,' said McBride, and tried to smile.

He left the office, had five minutes with Monsignor Lupi who made more sour remarks about not having his staff around him when they were most needed; then he went up the Via della Conciliazione to the papal palace. People stood about in the Square in groups, now and again glancing up at the windows of the palace as if expecting the Pope miraculously to appear there and give them his blessing. Some groups were on their knees praying: the voices wafted across the Square like the soughing of a winter wind. There was a noticeable lack of colour in the Square: everyone seemed to be dressed in black. They're already prepared for the worst, McBride thought, and was suddenly, irrationally angry at the despairing crowd.

In the palace he was checked at every door by security guards: they were a little late, but the stable door was not to be left unattended again. At least not till the old torpor set in once more.

The outer office to Cardinal Moroni's was as busy as an airline departure counter. Several clerics, including three bishops, sat on a line of chairs against one wall; a lieutenant and three other carabinieri were talking to two typists; four laymen, suspicious of both the clergy and the police, edged their way towards the inner door, afraid of losing their place in the queue. McBride, feeling an interloper, was admitted to Moroni's office as soon as his name was sent in.

'Signor McBride!' Moroni advanced from behind his smoke-screen, looking around for a place to deposit the ash from his fourth cigarette of the morning. He found an already full ashtray, then waved a hand at the other men in the room. 'You know their Eminences. We have been having a discussion on how much we should tell the newspapers and the other media.'

'Tell them as little as possible.' Cardinal Fellari was Prefect of the Sacred Congregation for the Doctrine of the Faith. One of the most powerful of the Curia cardinals, he was a septuagenarian who had arrived in the Vatican forty years ago and now considered himself its landlord. A tall thin man with a bald rock of head and face on which his eyebrows grew like weeds, he had saluted and buried three popes. He was within a few months of the recommended retiring age of seventy-five, but McBride knew he would treat that recommendation with the same contempt as he treated all other suggestions. McBride suspected that Fellari listened only to God and then only with reservations. 'No good ever comes of talking to people from the newspapers.'

Here we go again, thought McBride, reacting by instinct as an old newsman. 'I beg to differ, Eminence – '

Fellari made no reply, just gave McBride a look out of the sombre, heavy lidded eyes that stated that a layman's right to differ was a conceit he would not entertain.

Cardinal Victor, the plump Belgian whom Martin had only recently appointed to the Congregation of the Consistory, scattered oil on troubled waters as if he were drenching the room with holy water. 'I'm sure there are two sides to the question. Signor McBride understands his colleagues, Alfredo–'

'They do need a tight rein on them.' Cardinal De Luca was from the Congregation of the Council, a smooth financier who had got lost on the way to some bank and finished up in a seminary. He ran the Vatican's properties and revenues, indeed was McBride's own landlord, and it was he who had been given the task of collecting the ransom money. Like most bankers he did not believe in opening his books too widely. 'We can't suggest censorship – '

'I don't think it would have any effect if you did,' said McBride. He was as afraid as the cardinals of what the media might say, but for a different reason. He knew from experience that some newsmen could be better detectives than the official law men; a rumour was often the only spoor they needed to lead them to a definite clue. They had seen Toohey's arrest yesterday morning and they would know by now of his escape and the murder of the officer at Carabinieri Headquarters. They would be already building their stories on Toohey, and when they came looking for more bricks at the press conference they were not going to be put off by the bits of straw the cardinals wanted handed out. 'If we are honest with them, then I think we can ask for their co-operation. If we aren't, then they'll go their own way and God knows *what* they'll print.'

'Are you working for them or us?' Fellari said.

'Both, Eminence.' McBride suddenly saw a glimmer of daylight, perhaps he could be fired for disagreement with his bosses. But even as he saw the glimmering it faded: his real boss was out at the Villa Pericoli and his own fate had nothing to do with the men in this room. 'That's the job of a press relations man. His Holiness himself told me that,' he added, feeling hypocritical as he called on the man he had kidnapped as an ally. 'It was he who appointed me to this post, just because of the lack of co-operation in the past.'

'One of his mistakes,' said Fellari tartly, and looked at Moroni. 'So how much do we tell the Press?'

'There isn't so much to tell.' Moroni brushed ash from his soutane, reached for his silver cigarette case, then changed his mind. He had not slept well last night, realising for the first time that there would be a deep sad gap in his life if Martin did not emerge alive from this terrible event. 'We have the money – '

'The Deutschmarks have arrived?' McBride tried to keep his voice calm and objective.

'The German government and banks could not have been more co-operative,' said De Luca.

'He *is* German,' said Fellari, and McBride wondered how the Church managed to survive the closed minds of so many who ran it.

'The money is all ready to be paid over as soon as we hear from the kidnappers again.' Moroni had seen the look on McBride's face; he realised that he and his fellow cardinals, worried and exhausted, were letting their guard down too much in front of this lay staffer. He was glad of the interruption when the door opened and his secretary announced General della Porta. 'Ah, General! Any progress?'

'None at all.' Della Porta saluted the cardinals, nodded to McBride, took off his cap and sat down. He was wearing his best uniform today, the one that fitted him properly; but he looked thin and slumped in it, his face grey and strained. 'We are worse off than yesterday, much worse.'

'They've been in touch with *you*? His Holiness isn't – ?'

'Not the Pope, no.' Della Porta shook his head impatiently. The Premier had already been on the phone to him this morning, blistering him with an attack that was only a foretaste of what he could expect from the editorialists this evening and tomorrow morning. 'Two of my men have been murdered. The man we were holding for questioning yesterday – he shot one of my men and got away. That was in Headquarters itself,' he said, almost in self-disgust. 'He shot another of my men some distance away – the poor fellow was unarmed, was on his way home, going off duty.'

Victor gasped and the other cardinals shook their heads in disbelief. McBride said nothing till he saw della Porta was looking at him. 'You want me to say something, General?'

'I thought your natural instinct would be to ask questions.'

'I was deferring to their Eminences,' said McBride, recovering. *Two* carabinieri? Was there some nut in della Porta's force going around killing off his fellow cops and the chance for Toohey to escape had only been incidental? *But why is this son-of-a-bitch picking on me?* He added, still looking to be fired, 'I'm low man on the totem pole around here.'

But none of the cardinals was going to fire him while the Pope was still missing. Fellari ignoring him, said, 'What questions did you expect, General?'

Della Porta waved a hand, dismissing the need for questions now. He cast a sidelong glance at McBride, then he said, 'The man who shot my two men is a convicted criminal, a bank robber and a safe-breaker. His name is Toohey, he's an Australian and the Ulster police suspect that he murdered one of their officers back in 1970.'

'Ulster?' said Moroni. 'Is he one of those Irish revolutionaries? An IRA man?'

McBride felt the chill sweep through him. He looked at della Porta, but the Carabinieri chief shrugged off the question. 'They didn't mention any link.' Then he looked directly at McBride. 'This was the man you gave a press pass to, allowed to wander unhindered in and out of the Vatican.'

'I'm a press relations man, not a security officer.' Uneasy though he was, McBride managed a tone of controlled indignation. He was determined not to panic; all he had to do was remember the role he was playing. All he had to do was be himself of forty-eight hours ago. Split personality had never previously been one of his problems; yet now he felt split six or seven ways. Kidnapper, self-claimed peaceful revolutionary, press relations officer, ex-newsman, supposedly devout Catholic: he was a walking jigsaw, with several of the pieces dangerously loose. And if he came totally apart, della Porta would be the man to do it to him. 'It has taken your Headquarters twenty-four hours to find out who he is, and you have all the resources of Interpol. In that time he has killed two of your men – ' Then he heard what he had said. Jesus, he thought, now *I'm* putting the finger on Turk! 'You're sure he did the killings? How did he get a gun?'

It was della Porta's turn to be uncomfortable. 'We don't know how he obtained it.'

'Someone was lax, General,' said Moroni, reaching for his cigarette case again. He went back behind his desk, lit up and sank into his chair. His small, elderly, innocent face showed no expression as he said, 'I hope your men are more efficient from now on – '

'They will be,' said della Porta sharply. 'I don't need you to tell me how to run my force, Eminence. The rest of Italy have already started on that.'

Moroni was not a malicious man, not when a man could really be hurt; he relented, said more gently, 'When we hand the money over – '

'When is that to be?'

McBride glanced surreptitiously at his watch. Ryan would have sneaked out of the apartment by now, would be on his way to phone through the instructions; McBride hoped he would have got out of the building without being seen by the inquisitive widow on the second floor or the janitor on the ground floor. There would be no real danger if he were seen, no one would know who he was, but it had been agreed that the less any of them were identified with any of the others, the better it would be. Toohey had already been identified and pretty soon della Porta's men would be asking for a description of the other members of the Paragon film crew.

Suddenly McBride did not want to be here in this room when the call came. The original plan had been that he should remain as a close observer, calling the game play-by-play; it had seemed foolproof, a certain way of staying one jump ahead of the police efforts to trace the robbers of the Vatican treasures. But now he was no longer an observer. He was the man caught in a vortex whose glimpse of what is happening around him only adds to his panic.

He stood up; but Ryan, just over a mile away in a call-box in the Piazza di Popolo, trapped him. The phone rang and Moroni picked it up. He listened for a moment, then waved a hand to the others in the room. Della Porta was on his feet at once, moving with surprising swiftness to the door and opening it. He went out and McBride heard him telling the carabinieri lieutenant in the outer office to trace the call. Then he came back and moved over to stand close to Moroni, bending down to hear what was being said in the cardinal's ear.

'I understand,' said Moroni into the phone. 'We shall do exactly as you wish. But – how is His Holiness?'

He's all right, McBride told Moroni silently. But Ryan was evidently having trouble with his Italian; he had been given a three months' crash course, but he had no ear for languages. *Let him go!* McBride wanted to yell.

'Thank you,' said Moroni. 'Now I shall repeat your instructions to make sure there is no mistake. The money, fifteen million Deutschmarks – ' he was speaking more slowly than usual; he looked up at della Porta, who nodded approvingly ' – all of it to be in one suitcase, a plain dark brown imitation leather one with two straps – '

Des, for Christ's sake hang up! They're going to trace you before you get out of that box!

' – to be taken by Monsignor Arcadipane – does it have to be the monsignor? He's not a very strong man – '

Des, hang up! He could feel the sweat in his hands, under his arms, on his chest.

'All right, it will be Monsignor Arcadipane. We shall buy the suitcase where you say – it is in the window of the leather shop on the Via Nomentana near the Church of Corpus Christi – ' Moroni, making notes on a pad, glanced up at della Porta, who gestured to him to keep talking. 'Monsignor Arcadipane is to go to the Terminus Station at seven o'clock this evening – '

Des, for Christ's and everyone's sake, hang up! The goddam Irish never knew when to stop talking.

' – and wait outside the number 8 phone booth for a further call from you. Have I got it – ' Moroni put down the phone, looked up at della Porta. 'He has hung up, General.'

There was a knock on the door, it opened and the lieutenant stood there. 'We traced the call, General – it came from a call-box in the Piazza del Popolo. We got it just before he hung up – I doubt very much if we'll be in time to catch him. Cars are on their way there now – '

'Thank you, lieutenant.' The junior officer saluted and went out, and della Porta, knuckle at his moustache, shook his head at Moroni and the others. 'We shan't get him. We may get a description of some man who used the call-box in the last five minutes, but if six people saw him we'll get six different descriptions. Or we may get none.'

McBride wiped his palms against the sides of his trousers. It had been close, too close: another minute or two and Ryan might still have been in the call-box when the cops arrived.

'Why were they so precise about what sort of suitcase we must use?' asked Cardinal Victor.

'It's probably the sort that is sold by the thousands,' said della Porta; and McBride thought, You're on the ball, General. 'Once they've got it, they want to be lost in the crowd.'

'I don't like the idea of Arcadipane acting as courier,' said Fellari. 'He's too emotional. He could lose the money between here and the Terminus just as a result of nerves. Or he could have a heart-attack on the spot when they approach him.'

'Why did they choose him, I wonder?' said De Luca.

'He's readily identifiable to them, they've probably seen him a hundred times with His Holiness,' said della Porta. Good thinking, General, thought McBride. 'But it also suggests they know him well, very well. They've chosen him because he's exactly the type who won't act smart. They chose him because he's no stranger to them.'

Good thinking again, General, too goddam good. 'Will you – ' His voice sounded in his ears like that of a drowning man. He cleared his throat, tried for the objective tone that a good press relations officer should have in a situation like this. 'Will you have your men posted at the Terminus this evening?'

'Naturally,' said della Porta. He had begun to fill out his uniform; the grey, strained look had gone from his face. He was reacting as all good policemen do when they have got a lead, when the blank wall that has been facing them suddenly begins to show a crack or two. 'They'll be in plain clothes – I can lose fifty of them in the peak-hour crowd that will be there at that time.'

'You could lose the kidnappers too,' said Fellari. 'That's why they've chosen that time.'

There were other questions McBride wanted to ask, but he knew it would be dangerous to pursue them. Then Cardinal Victor asked one of them for him: 'You won't endanger the safe return of His Holiness, General? I mean, your men won't try to arrest the kidnappers before we know where His Holiness is being held?'

'That's a dilemma that faces all police in a kidnapping case. If I have the opportunity to pick up one of the kidnappers, why shouldn't I take it? With a little pressure we can get him to tell us where they are holding the Pope. But – '

'But – ?' said De Luca.

'But as Cardinal Victor says, perhaps that would endanger His Holiness's life. We have no guarantee these men intend to return him alive anyway. He may already be dead.'

McBride felt sick: he had never expected to be standing here and hear himself described as a possible murderer.

Della Porta said, 'My natural inclination is to grab whoever comes to collect the money. But he could turn out to be an innocent messenger, someone who doesn't know what's in the suitcase.'

Moroni then showed some of the authority that made him such a good Secretary of State. 'Then we shall solve your dilemma for you, General. The money will be paid over without tricks, without any attempt on the part of your men to arrest any of the kidnappers. His Holiness's life – if he is still alive, and we pray to God he is – his life is worth more than money, just as anyone's life is. It is also worth more than the capture and punishment of these criminals who have kidnapped him. I can't give you an order, General, but I can make a strong request. His Holiness belongs not just to us – the Vatican, Italy, even the Church – he belongs to the world. Pope Martin has proved himself a spokesman for humanity. In this particular circumstance I think his life is more important than justice and the processes of law.'

McBride covertly studied the reactions of Fellari and De Luca to the small speech by Moroni: they were two of Martin's most implacable opponents in the Curia and neither of them would ever see him in the same light as Moroni had just projected. They both nodded, but their faces were masks; only Victor showed an emotional response. The plump little Belgian clasped his hands and said in a thick, excited voice, 'He must come back safe and well, General! It will be a dreadful calamity if he doesn't!'

'He will.' Moroni was overcome by the words that had come out of him; he coughed hackingly and lay back in his chair. The others watched him silently, each remarking the change in the tiny man: he was now a devoted champion of the man who had defeated him for the papacy. 'We must trust in God.'

Della Porta harrumphed, as if mention of Divine intervention was no guarantee; he sometimes thought God was too often on the side of the devils. 'I shall come back this afternoon. I'll have my men at the Terminus this evening, but only in case of emergency. They will not interfere with Monsignor Arcadipane.'

'Will your men attempt to follow whoever picks up the money?' That was another question McBride wanted answered: Cardinal Fellari did him the favour of asking it.

'Yes.' Della Porta was emphatic; he meant to show these men his uniform meant as much as their red hats, that the law also meant something to humanity. 'I am not going to allow these men to get away unchallenged. If we do, who will be next on the list?'

'Who else is there?' said Cardinal Victor.

It may or may not have been an innocent question, but della Porta suddenly laughed, put on his cap and saluted the four cardinals. 'I wonder if the kidnappers knew just how much power and wrath they were taking on?'

'There is no wrath,' said Moroni sharply.

'Not now,' said della Porta with a glance at Fellari and De Luca. 'Good morning, gentlemen. Let's hope we have His Holiness back with us safe and sound by this time to-morrow.'

He went out, nodding curtly to McBride as he did so. The latter had a few final words with the cardinals, giving the Carabinieri chief time to leave the building. But when he got into the corridor beyond the outer office, della Porta was waiting for him. The general dismissed the aide who stood by him, curled a finger at McBride and fell into step beside the American. He seemed to have recovered all his bounce and confidence: his eyes gleamed and even the ribbons on his chest seemed to have taken on new colour.

'You're going to tell the Press nothing?'

'That's what the cardinals want, General. I presume you want the same?'

Della Porta ignored the elevator that stood waiting for them and kept on down towards the stairs. 'We'll walk down, Signor McBride.' It was a command, not a suggestion. 'Elevators are no place for a private conversation.'

'Is that what we're having?'

'I think that's what you may prefer to call it. You have probably heard we are questioning everyone who works in the Vatican?'

'I'd heard it. Are you personally going to question me, General? I'm honoured.' *But don't shake my hand or you'll feel the sweat on it.*

'Just convenience. I shouldn't want you disturbed by one of

my men while you're so busy – some of them stay too long, ask too many inconsequential questions.'

'What sort of questions are you asking?'

A Swiss Guard saluted them and della Porta, without taking his eyes from McBride, returned the salute. 'The other members of Paragon Films are also missing – Mr Lamington-Bass and a man named Jones to whom you also issued a pass. Do you remember him?'

'Jones? We could have given him a pass: I don't remember him. Where did you get your information?'

'From your office. They've been very co-operative while you've been so busy. Unfortunately, when we checked the addresses we were given, both Mr Lamington-Bass and Mr Jones had flown. Can you give me a description of them?'

'I can't remember Jones at all – there were dozens of men accredited to the Synod.' But he knew he would have to describe Lamington-Bass: it would be too suspicious if he said he did not remember him and any number of others who had worked around him could give a description. 'Lamington-Bass is tall, grey-haired, looks like an English colonel. Has a very clipped accent sometimes, other times he sounds like one of those "dear old boy" types.'

'You sound as if you didn't like him, Signor McBride.'

'I didn't,' said McBride truthfully. 'What little I saw of him.'

'He and Jones could have been the ones who engineered the escape of our man Johnston. It was so effective it could have been an army operation. Just like those English commando raids during the war. They could also have kidnapped the Pope,' della Porta added almost casually.

McBride showed the proper interest. 'Do you think they might have?'

'Wouldn't you suspect that they might have? If you were still working as a newsman, wouldn't you follow up such a story possibility?'

'Newsmen aren't policemen, General.'

'Oh? From their stories one would think they knew our job better than we do.' Della Porta's knuckle made a sharp jab at his moustache, then he said abruptly, 'I understand you could not be contacted the night before last – it was seven o'clock yesterday morning before your colleagues in the press bureau were able to get in touch with you. If it's not a rude question, as you Americans say, where were you?'

McBride managed a grin. 'Italians don't think questions are rude, do.they?'

'Neither do policemen – of any nationality,' said della Porta, returning the grin.

The stairways and corridors were not deserted; people passed the two men in a constant two-way stream. Yet McBride had the feeling della Porta had him staked out on a wide lonely plain. 'I spent the night with my girl-friend.'

'Her name?' The smile was still there on the lips below the thick moustache. 'Another rude question, I'm afraid.'

'Luciana Pericoli.' He had hesitated before implicating Luciana, but he knew he had no choice. 'She is the daughter of Count Augusto Pericoli.'

'An excellent family. You couldn't have better references. Does her father know you spent the night with her?'

'I couldn't tell you. You don't discuss those sort of arrangements with your girl-friend's father.'

'I wouldn't know. My youth, alas, was spent in less permissive days than we have now. Where can I find Signorina Pericoli?'

Again McBride hesitated, but again he had no choice: he gave Luciana's address, but didn't mention the villa out near Frascati. 'You may not find her there, General. We had – had a disagreement. She said she was going away for a few days to think about our – our relationship. I've tried to call her, but there's been no answer.'

'How very inconvenient – for you, I mean.' McBride looked puzzled and della Porta went on, 'At a time like this, when you're so busy and upset about the Pope, you're also having a romance problem. Women are never considerate in their timing, are they?'

'I wouldn't know, General. I'm a one-woman man.'

Della Porta acknowledged the point with a smile. He never boasted about the number of his own women but let it be assumed that a man as attractive as himself had never been lacking in them. 'I should have known. The Vatican has never

156

encouraged the libertine, has it? At least not since the popes gave up the practice.'

'I have the feeling, General, that you're anti the papacy.'

'Not the present pope.' Della Porta paused as they came to the outer doors; the banter went out of his voice. 'I am a very great admirer of Pope Martin. I am perhaps even more concerned for his safe return than a lot of other people. I agreed with every word that Cardinal Moroni said upstairs – but as a policeman I couldn't say them myself. But, believe me, I shall do everything I possibly can to see he comes back unharmed. And then, also believe me, I'll do everything I possibly can to bring his kidnappers to justice.'

(6)

Pope Martin walked slowly but steadily back and forth across the big bedroom. Once he had fallen asleep last night he had slept well; he had learned in Dachau the value of every minute of unconsciousness. He had long outlived the nightmares that had troubled him in the immediate years after his release; the nightmares, or daymares, now came when he was fully awake and almost as a self-flagellation. His life since the end of the war had been almost too rewarding, as if God were over-compensating; he had adopted the balancing attitude of re-minding himself of what Man, and he did not excuse himself from the category, could do to his fellows. He still remembered how, when he had felt certain of death in Dachau, when Kessler had told him their patience was finally exhausted and they were going to dispose of him, he had achieved a state of welcomed resignation, a calm waiting on God and eternity. Then they had come to tell him he was not going to be executed after all. He had gone into a paroxysm of rage, screaming that they should kill him; one of the benefits of solitary confinement, realised only later, was that no one heard him or, if they did, did not listen to him. But he still remembered with shame the weakness and fear that had gripped him as he was dragged back from the certainty of death, of how for a whole day he had doubted the wisdom and mercy of God. Every day since, his prayers had had the same theme: *I am a far from perfect man, Lord, make me better.*

For too long there had been no one to confide in but the Lord. His parents had died during the war, victims of a bomb-ing raid. His only brother, no Nazi but a good German who believed that the war, having been started, had to be won, had died on the Russian front. Before the war Stecher had been a friendly man, still looking for friends in the priesthood; but after Dachau he had found himself alone, both suspicious of friendship and yet suspected by those he tentatively approached. By the time he and his countrymen were sure of themselves again, putting the past behind them with either mixed feelings of guilt or stubborn insistence that they had been right, he had begun to rise in the Church. More outwardly friendly, he had become more withdrawn inside, disturbed by the opportunism that had gripped his fellow countrymen during the years of the so-called economic miracle. He had the native talent for organisation and administration, and those qualities, not piety or intellectual brilliance, were what his superiors looked for when they promoted men to the hierarchy; by the time he was Archbishop of Munich it was too late to make friends in whom he could confide his deepest doubts. Then they had made him a cardinal and the whispers had begun of his being a possible future pope. After that there were many who had wanted to be his friends, but he knew, more than ever, that it was much too late.

The door of the bedroom opened and Smith, wearing the friar's robe and cowl, came in with a tray of coffee and a sandwich roll of salami and cheese. 'We must keep you fed, Holiness. Although I suppose you feed a lot on prayer?'

'Just an occasional snack.' On those occasions when he had been allowed to mix with the other prisoners in the concentration camp he had met men like this, the unbelievers who had to attack; but scorn was a brittle weapon and he had learned how to cope with it. 'What is *your* main sustenance?'

'Myself,' said Smith complacently. He put the tray on the bed, moved across and sat down in one of the high-backed chairs. 'Ego, if you like.'

'Well, you're honest about that.' Martin lifted the paper napkin on the tray, found two boiled eggs beneath it.

'Oh, my dear chap, I'm honest about a lot of things.'

'What about your reasons for trying to steal the museum treasures? Were they honest?'

'To me, yes. We are not what you think, Holiness. There is more purpose to this operation than mere greed.' He smiled and held up a hand as the Pope looked at him. 'But don't expect me to confess it.'

Smith's mood was affable, but Martin knew the tall man

could not be trusted. There had been a time, when he was young, when he had believed there was good in all men; it had been one of the shattering disappointments of his life to realise that in some men there was nothing else but evil. He did not know this man well enough to know if such would be the case with him, but he was sure that the evil would outweigh the good in him. For one thing he did not value human life, Martin was certain of that. And Martin himself valued that above all else except his love for God.

'How are your eggs? Fortunately, though the electricity is cut off, the gas is still connected. If we had the ingredients I should like to cook you a *good* meal. I pride myself on my cooking. In other circumstances I like the good life.'

Martin heard the echoes of an earlier conversation and smiled at the irony of it. 'Rich food is the one indulgence I can't allow myself. I spent three years in a concentration camp – my stomach, unfortunately, has its memories.'

'Why did they send you to a camp?'

'I helped a Jewish doctor to escape and hide.'

'A Jew? Why did you bother? What did your Church ever owe them? The Pope of those years never did much to help them.'

He remembered bitterly his disappointment with Rome. There was another echo, of other conversations: 'My particular jailer, an SS man, used to ask me exactly the same question.'

'And what answer did you give him?'

'That Jews, too, are men.'

'An admirable statement. I don't know that I'd go as far as you evidently did to defend it.'

'You sound a bigoted anti-semite.'

'Oh, I'm anti a lot of things. Bigotry is one of my more consistent vices.'

Smith watched the other man for a while in silence. He had no curiosity at all about religion and a man's devotion to it; he had been fed atheism and anti-clericalism at an early age and had never rebelled against the diet. But he was fascinated by power and its uses and some day he hoped to be in a position to take advantage of it. And, he suddenly realised, he was sitting in the same room with one of the most powerful men in the world.

'When they made you Pope, how did you feel?'

Martin poured himself some coffee from the pot on the tray. 'Humbled. Afraid. When they told John he was to be Pope he said, "*Horrefactus sum*." It comes from the Book of Job and it means John was terrified, aghast at what faced him. I was so terrified I could say nothing at all.' He sipped his coffee, remembering that fateful night a year ago. 'When they come to you and tell you that you are their choice, you suddenly know how vulnerable the ego can be. Even yours might shrivel.'

'For the moment, perhaps. But controlling the destinies of millions would have its compensations.'

'Not controlling them – *guiding* them. I still have some of my humility left – if that isn't a vain thing to say.' He had prayed for Divine guidance, but had never been sure that he had responded in the way that God had intended. No man, he felt, should be judge of his own infallibility and it tortured him that some day he might be called upon to proclaim a decision on a matter of dogma. On that day he hoped he could be certain that God spoke through him. 'I learned a number of things in Dachau, one of them being that a priest should not expect too much of his flock, that even the example he may try to set can sometimes be an embarrassment to them.'

'I can understand that. Too much piety is an embarrassment.'

'In Dachau there were over 800 of us priests, of all denominations, who were isolated within the prison itself. It wasn't just that the SS men were afraid of what we might do – the other prisoners themselves wanted nothing to do with us. They were only concerned with survival and they were afraid we'd start preaching self-sacrifice. One hesitates to set an example in such circumstances.'

'Yet you did – you protected the Jew.'

'The man trusted me. He was my only concern all the time I was in there.' That sounded like a boast and he hastened to correct it. 'When they eventually found him and killed him, I almost gave up. I was ready to surrender, there seemed no point in defying them any further.'

'Did you?'

'They ignored me from then on, they never gave me the

opportunity to surrender. In the end I was like everyone else, intent only on survival.'

'As you are now, no doubt.'

'You'll kill me if you have to.' It was a flat statement, devoid of fear or heroics. Martin put down his cup and looked steadily at the man, shrouded and robed, who sat like a brown ghost in a darker corner of the room. *At least Kessler had a face, if I had died then I'd have known who my murderer was.*

Smith did not reply at once, then he said, 'There is no intention at present of killing you. But unlike you, Holiness, I am concerned only for myself – I've never troubled to set an example to anyone. If I am endangered, then all else goes by the board. It's a question of survival, too – only totally so.'

I am going to have to escape, Martin thought. Up till now the idea of escape had been no more than an idle consideration; the other imprisonment had conditioned him to acceptance of the circumstances. Then he had come to subscribe to the proverb of the concentration camps: *When things change, they change for the worse.* It had been a denial of God's possible help, but it had been a fact of one's thinking. But this situation was not so desperate. There was only one man here, not two or three hundred guards; there were no dogs, no machine-guns, no barbed wire. Just one smug man who, if caught off guard, might be hampered by the unaccustomed robe he wore.

Martin was calm and determined now that he had made up his mind. He was not afraid; the old acceptance of death came back. He knew that he could wait, could trust in God; but why should God be so concerned with him, why should popes not have to help themselves just as other people did? *Just give me the opportunity, Lord, that's all I ask.*

'I wish you hadn't brought up the subject,' said Smith. 'It spoils the atmosphere between us.'

'I'm sorry. But one finds it a little difficult to be ecumenical with one's kidnapper.'

'Well, we'll do our best to see you go home unharmed.' Smith stood up, moved towards the bed. 'It all depends on your flock – the sheep will give us no trouble, but one never knows with the goats. Did you enjoy your meal?'

'Just what I needed,' said Martin, lifted the tray and flung it at the cowled face.

Smith staggered back, cursing, one hand going to the pocket in the robe, the other trying to pull the pinned cowl away from his face so that he could see properly. Martin went after him, moving with the agility of the ex-athlete; he was slower and heavier, but his movements were co-ordinated. The fist he flung at Smith's head landed on the latter's cheekbone; Smith let out another curse. Martin kept at him, driving in with his shoulder; the two of them crashed to the floor, Smith underneath. There was a gasp from him and the hand that had clawed at Martin's neck relaxed for a moment; the Pope drew back, let go with his fist again into the opening in the cowl. Smith, struggling to get up, was in the worst position to take the blow; his head went back, cracked against the tiled floor, and abruptly he went limp. Martin, breathing heavily, slowly stood up.

He was trembling all through his body; not with fear of Smith but with fear of what he had done to the other man. He could not remember when he had last hit another person; perhaps as a child, but he couldn't remember anyone even then. Now he might have killed a man: *Lord, forgive me if I have.* He knelt down, unpinned the cowl and drew it back from the handsome face. It was the first time he had seen his captor; he was shocked at the surge of anger that swept through him as soon as the man became identifiable. But he bent down, put his ear against the man's breast, felt for the pulse in the wrist. Thank God, the man was still alive.

Martin got to his feet, still breathing heavily. He looked down at the unconscious man on the floor, imprinting the face on his memory; then he went out of the room and down the stairs, running softly in his bedroom slippers. He was certain there was no one else in the villa, but he was not going to throw caution to the winds: the winds had a habit of changing at the very last moment. One of the others might be returning, might already be about to open a door and come into the house.

He crossed the entrance hall, went down a narrow side hall-way to a door, its top half a partition of glass, that led into a conservatory. He slid back the bolts on the door, opened it and went out into a jungle of shrubs and plants. It seemed as if the foliage in the conservatory had not been attended to in years; he clawed his way through fronds and vines that slapped at and clung to him like live creatures. He came to the outer door, forced back the rusted bolts on it and stepped out into a gravelled yard. Opposite him was a low wooden door set in a high wall; he headed for it without a backward glance at the house. He had to run flatfooted to keep his slippers on his feet; the skirt of his soutane flapped around him and he almost fell as it caught in his knees. The gate was bolted, the bolts rusty from long disuse; he had to use all his strength to pull them back. Weeds had grown up at the bottom of the gate; again he had to use all his strength to drag it open against the hindrance of them. He was sweating, angrily impatient with the frustrating door; he swore at it in German, then at last it slid over the clump of weeds and came back hard against his instep. Hobbling now, he went through the gate, dragging it to after him.

He was in a narrow rutted lane between two low stone walls; on either side of him were groves of olive trees that soon petered out into open ploughed fields. Somewhere he could hear a tractor, but he couldn't see it. Then from far ahead of him, beyond a turn in the lane, there came the long drawn-out wail of a truck's horn. A main road, he guessed, must lie in that direction.

He ran on down the lane, shuffling and hobbling as his slippers threatened to slip off and the pain in his instep got worse. He had been cold in the villa, but now the running and the sun streaming down from the cloudless sky soon warmed him. He was sweating but it was from exertion now, not the sweat of impatience, anger and fear that had gripped him back in the villa's yard. He still could not see any people in the fields beyond the olive groves, but he could hear the faraway hum of traffic and he kept stumbling towards it.

The lane swung to the right, went down a slope and ran into another slightly wider lane. As Martin came to the bottom of the slope he heard the car coming up from his left. He leant against the rough stone wall, exhausted and aware of the increasing pain in his instep; but relief swept through him, swamping the exhaustion and pain, as the car came round the bend in the lane and coasted to a halt as he waved it down. He stepped out into the middle of the lane, thanking God fervently for the rescuer He had sent.

The car was an open one, an elderly model that the Pope had never seen before. Low slung and streamlined, its engine ticking over with a gentle throbbing note, it should have been driven by a young blade; instead, the man who sat behind the big steering wheel was white-haired and looked twice as old as the car. He frowned at the dusty dishevelled priest who limped up beside him.

'Yes, Father? What is it?' He had the impatient tone of the upper-class man who put village priests on the servant level.

'Signore, will you take me to the nearest police station? I am – ' Martin realised that it was the first time he had ever had to introduce himself in the identity that was his till death: 'I am Pope Martin.'

The old man's eyes opened wide and he leaned back in his seat, his mouth working; for a moment he looked as if he were about to have a stroke. Then he leaned forward, peered at the Pope and at last nodded emphatically. 'Yes, you are! My God, Holiness – get in, get in! We must get to the police – '

Martin hobbled around to the other side of the car, opened the door and sank gratefully on to the seat beside the elderly driver. 'Signore, you have been sent by the Lord – '

'The first time He has noticed me in years.' The old man turned his head on his thin, stiff neck and looked at the Pope. Then he took off one of the yellow string gloves he wore and put out his hand. 'Holiness, allow me to present myself – Count Augusto Pericoli.'

'I am in your debt, Count.' Martin shook the thin, weak hand.

'I was to have had an audience with you earlier this year, when my cousins were presented to you, but unfortunately I was ill. I have a heart condition – '

Let me be patient with him, Lord. Martin withdrew his hand as Pericoli bent his head. 'You are not wearing your ring, Holiness. Did they steal that from you?'

'No, no. I wasn't wearing it.' He remembered that it was probably still on his bedside table at the palace. He pressed the old man's arm. 'May we drive on, please? Just in case – '

'Of course, of course. Excuse me, Holiness. The shock – '
He let in the gears and the car went on up the lane, the throbbing note of its engine bouncing back from the stone walls on either side. 'I no longer drive fast because of my heart. When I was young, this car and I – ' The old man looked at the Pope, turning his head stiffly on his neck again. He seemed to forget what he was about to say and once more he looked forward. 'We are glad to be of service to you.'

'It is a beautiful car.' Martin could think of nothing else to say, was too exhausted for small talk.

'A Lancia – 1932. I cannot afford one of the new cars, not the sort a man in my position should have – ' The neck seemed to get a little stiffer. Martin, instep pulsing with pain now, lay back in the seat, closing his eyes. He knew what the old man meant: the Italian preoccupation with *bella figura*, the right image. *Dear God, let him talk, but have him get me quickly to safety.* 'Did they harm you at all, Holiness? The kidnappers, I mean.'

Martin opened his eyes. 'No. My foot is hurt, but that was not their fault. If you could hurry – where are we going?'

'To my house – it is up here at the end of the lane. I shall telephone the police from there – it will be quicker – '

They drove through a stone-posted gateway, the big rusted ornamental gates swung back, leaning drunkenly from their broken hinges; Martin saw an emblem in the grille-work of the gates that was faintly familiar. They were in the forecourt of a large dilapidated villa. Abruptly Pericoli took his foot off the accelerator, let the car slow.

'What am I thinking of? My memory is going. I am sorry, Holiness – we shall have to go back, try and find the police station. I have just remembered – the telephone is no longer connected to the villa.'

He was swinging the car round in a wide circle as he spoke. Martin sat up, remembering now where he had seen the emblem on the gates: on the worn blanket he had worn in the room where he had been held captive. He recognised the house, even though he had never seen it from this angle before; the recognition was not one of sight but of feel of its atmosphere.

He looked up, saw the skylight in the roof above the room on one corner, and felt sick with the pain, far worse than that in his foot, of betrayal. Why was the Lord so sardonic at times?

Then the tall man, minus his Franciscan's robes, came out of the front door of the villa. He ran across the forecourt, stood in front of the car as Pericoli brought it round to face the gates again, and aimed his gun at the old man's head.

2

As he drove across the Tiber in the lunchtime traffic, McBride had the temptation to keep going, to drive out of Rome, out of Italy, right up to Paris and a plane for home. But where was home, did any planes fly there? Boston was on the airlines' schedules, though not Cavanreagh; but neither of those was home. He was fighting for the Six Counties, but he knew in his heart that he had never belonged and never would belong to them. In a way he was no more than a mercenary with a blank cheque that he did not want to cash. Home, he guessed, was the memory of two people whom he had loved and memory was an unprofitable route for any public carrier.

The traffic screeched and honked its way past him, everyone wearing himself out in the effort to get home to relax for a couple of hours before beginning the return journey to their offices and stores. McBride pulled up at a red light and a man in a Fiat 600 slipped in beside him, squeezing his car in between the Alfa and a bus with only an inch to spare on either side. He was a thin-faced man with a frontier moustache and a look of utter defeat in his sunken bloodshot eyes; he glanced at McBride, took out a handkerchief and coughed into it. He looked at the handkerchief and shook his head, as if he had just coughed part of his life into it; then the light turned green and he shot the Fiat forward, tearing away as if he had to reach home before he died. Poor son-of-a-bitch, McBride thought, I wonder if he *is* dying? And, ashamed at himself for his reaction, suddenly felt better. *I complained because I had no shoes, till I met a man who had no feet*: his mother had spouted gems from the *Thesaurus of Quotations* that had stood beside the Bible on her bedside table, and his one-armed father, without bitterness, had laughed and said God only listened to complainers, otherwise why had prayers been invented? . . . McBride stamped on the accelerator of the Alfa, joined in the traffic battle, blew his horn, hated everyone.

After he had put the car in the garage he walked down the hill towards his apartment. Because the sun was warm and he wanted to remain in it as long as possible, he came down the street on the opposite side of the road from his apartment building. He was opposite his doorway, about to cross the road, when something registered in the corner of his eye. He turned his head and saw the tall thin man in the overcoat and glasses standing just up inside the side street. The man started as he saw McBride looking at him, then turned abruptly away and bent down over the motor scooter leaning against the wall behind him. Quick though the man had been, McBride recognised him: the guy had been there this morning, tinkering with his motor scooter, when he had come out of the building to go to his office.

Trying to be casually unhurried, McBride crossed the road and went into the apartment building. Once inside the door he did not wait for the elevator, which was somewhere on an upper floor; he went up the stairs two at a time, arrived at his front door breathless. He fumbled with his key, flung open the door and stepped quickly inside. Luciana, Toohey and Ryan, lunch laid out on the table before them, looked up as he came in.

'Turk, quick!' He crossed the room to a window, jerking his head for Toohey to follow him. 'That guy across the street there – has he been there all morning?'

Toohey, hidden behind one of the curtains, peered down into the street. 'I dunno, mate. He could've been – I've stayed away from the windows. Did you see him when you went out, Des?'

'I think he was there, but I'm not sure.' Ryan stood behind Toohey and gazed down into the street.

'Luciana?' said McBride. 'You went out shopping – '

'I didn't look. How would I know what a police spy looks like?'

McBride went into the bedroom, returned with a pair of

169

binoculars. Taking care to remain hidden behind the curtains, he focused the glasses on the man down in the street. 'I don't recognise him. Turk?'

Toohey took the glasses, stared steadily down into the street for almost a minute. Then he lowered the binoculars and said, 'I wouldn't bet on it, but I think it's the bloke who killed the demon last night. He ain't in uniform, but there's something familiar about him.'

McBride shook his head in puzzlement. 'Something's screwed up here. He's not a cop – '

'How do you know?'

'A second cop was killed last night – whoever murdered him stole his uniform. They think *we* did it, the kidnappers – but my money says it was that guy down there. Why the hell would he kill two cops just to let you escape and then follow you here? Why didn't he kill you too?'

'Maybe he wants to kill someone else,' said Ryan slowly. 'I don't know him, I don't think he wants to kill me.'

'He could've done me last night if he'd wanted to,' said Toohey.

McBride looked at Luciana. 'It wouldn't be you, honey. So it's either me or Smith he's after – assuming he knows Smith is in with us. Does Smith have any enemies in the organisation?'

'Some,' said Ryan, but said no more.

Luciana came and stood beside McBride, took his hand. 'Darling, let's finish with this, please! It's too dangerous – '

'Take it easy.' Toohey's tone was surprisingly gentle. 'We're not gunna let anything happen to Fergus. But we've gotta do something about that bugger across the street – we can't let him squat down there playing I Spy. Sooner or later someone else around here is gunna cotton on to him and maybe they'll report him to the demons. That's all we need, the street outside full of bloody coppers.'

'What do we do, then?' Luciana remarked the sympathetic note in Toohey's voice; she responded by controlling her growing panic. She knew now that, no matter how much she might dislike the three men with whom Fergus was involved, she was tied to them and him until the ransom was collected and the Pope returned unharmed to the Vatican. 'We can't ask him up here – '

'Why not?' said McBride.

'You out of your flaming head?' Toohey almost spat in disgust.

'I think Fergus is right,' said Ryan, still watching the man down in the street; this was not the first time he had been trapped in a house that had been staked out but he had always got away. 'We can't sit here on our arses. When I was fighting and I didn't know how the other feller was going to fight, I went after him, yes.'

'You lost more fights than you ever won, that's what you told me.' Toohey was unconvinced. 'We invite that joker down there to come up here, we could lose another fight. He could come in here and do the lot of us.'

'If he has a silencer, as you said he did, he could pick us off one by one as we came out of the door downstairs – they'd never hear it in the noise of the traffic.' McBride, his hand still in Luciana's, could feel the claw-like grip of her fingers. He was afraid, but he made a strenuous effort to steady himself. He knew he would have to force himself to go downstairs and cross the street to speak to the stranger; but he knew it would require more effort to stay up here in the apartment, trying to wait the man out. Patience, once a virtue, was now a luxury; 'We have to be out of here, on our way to the Terminus, by six o'clock. We can't afford to sit here and just hope he gives up and goes away.'

'I'll go down and see what he wants.'

Ryan made a move towards the door, but McBride put out a hand and stopped him. 'No, I'll go, Des.' He felt Luciana's fingers dig into him. 'If he did put a bullet into you, if you *were* the one he was waiting for, you'd be no use to us this evening. And you're necessary.'

'I'll take a chance – '

'No, I don't think you're the one he wants. How would he know you're here? He was out there this morning before you went out to make that phone call – he'd have got you then if you were the one he wanted. No, it's either me or Turk. Or Smith.'

'I've taken my chances. Like I said, he could've done me last night if he'd wanted to.' Toohey took out a cigarette, lit it. He was wondering if he should not just toss in the towel, forget the whole bloody schemozzle and head out of Rome while he was still free and on his feet. But even as he was debating the point, the practical side of his mind was telling him he was already in so deep he might as well, as the Yanks said, go for broke. He needed that ten thousand quid; you couldn't run very far on an IOU ticket. 'You've been saying all along this is your territory. You can go out there, mate, and prove it.'

McBride looked at the Australian, suddenly suspicious. 'He's not a friend of yours, is he?'

Toohey grinned. 'You think I'd go to all that trouble? I told you out there on the balcony, a coupla nights ago – if ever I decide to get rid of you I'll do it some time when you're least expecting it, when you won't know what's hit you.'

McBride felt Luciana's hand dig into him again: she hadn't known that Toohey might be an enemy as dangerous as Smith. 'Since you seem to be the safe one, what if I told you to go down there?'

'Nothing doing, mate. Des and I are just the workers around here. Isn't that what Dublin said?'

'Turk, I don't mind going down – '

'Shut up, Des. I'm the shop steward in this argument – I'm talking for both of us. You go, Fergus.'

'No!' Luciana's voice was harsh, a low scream of protest.

Toohey gazed steadily at McBride. 'It's up to you. There's no guarantee, like you said, that the bugger will move away from over there before we have to go down to the Terminus. If he doesn't go, then one of us will have to go out and hit him.'

'Hit him?' For a moment McBride didn't catch the full meaning of the term.

'Do him in. Kill him.'

'I'll do it if it's got to be done, yes,' said Ryan, and lifted the knife out of his pocket, then dropped it back in.

'I wouldn't walk straight up to him,' said Toohey as matter-of-factly as if he were discussing some sales approach to a prospective customer. 'If you go around the block, you can come at him from the back. Have you got a gun?'

'A gun?' McBride felt himself getting more and more out of step with the march of events. 'Do you think I'm going down there for some sort of shoot-out or something? Christ, I said there was to be no violence, and you're talking about guns and *hitting* him!'

Toohey sighed: *bloody amateurs, they never try to lay off their bets.* 'If you walk up behind him, put a gun in his back and suggest he come up here with you, chances are he'll do it without any fuss. But if you come up behind him and just tap him on the shoulder – ' He shrugged expressively.

'If you've got something in your pocket and he *thinks* it's a gun – ' said Ryan. 'I did it once. It worked.'

'Where?'

'At Ardmore, the picture studio back home. I had a small part in a picture, I was supposed to be an IRA gunman – ' His young battered face lit up with a smile.

'Oh, for Christ's sake!' McBride twisted and turned his head in frustration, as if looking for a way out of the situation. 'This isn't a goddam movie!'

'Fergus, it'll *work*, I tell you, yes. The feller in the picture, he was like me – he knew guns. He said it felt just like a real gun in his back – he used to laugh when he saw it in the pictures – '

'Just like I do – '

'What did you use?' asked Toohey.

'They gave me a piece of pipe, about that long – ' Ryan held his hands about nine inches apart. 'Wait a minute!'

He went through into the bathroom and McBride looked at Toohey. 'This is the craziest bit yet. Turk, the best way is to go straight across the street to him – '

'Fergus,' said Toohey patiently, 'do it our way.'

'If it's your way, then why the hell don't you do it?'

'Because I might, just might, have to kill the bugger. And you keep telling me you don't want any of that.'

Ryan came back with a piece of curved nickel-plated pipe. 'I made a mess in your bathroom. This is one of the brackets that held up your towel-rail – I had to pull it out of the wall.' He grasped the pipe as he would hold a gun, put his hand in his pocket, moved round behind McBride and shoved the end of the pipe into the latter's back. 'What does that feel like?'

'If you expect me to say a gun, forget it. I've never had a gun in my back.'

'Oh, come on, stop arsing about!' Toohey stubbed out his cigarette. 'Take the bloody pipe and get down there. Bring him up here and let's find out who he is and what he wants!'

McBride took the piece of pipe from Ryan, stared at Toohey. 'Who's talking as if he runs the territory now?'

Toohey said nothing and Luciana followed McBride as he went towards the door. 'Darling, be careful. I'll be watching from up here – I wouldn't want to see you – ' She blinked, shook her head. She knew what was driving him to take the risk of going down to the street. He was committing himself to protecting a growing list of men from violence: the Pope, the stranger downstairs. It was something she knew he had never envisaged, but she knew, too, that he would not, could not, turn back. He was a changed man from the aimless, gently cynical man she had fallen in love with. But she loved him more now. 'God be with you.'

'I'll go out on to the balcony,' said Ryan. 'I'll give you time to get up around the block, then I'll go out there. He'll be watching me, so you can come down that street behind him.'

'Thanks, Des,' said McBride, and looked scornfully at Toohey. 'I thought you might have volunteered, being the shop steward.'

'Not me, mate. Shop stewards never volunteer for anything – it's against union rules. Good luck.'

McBride kissed Luciana quickly on the cheek and went out. The elevator was on the floor above, but he ignored it and went on down the stairs. He was in no hurry to shove the piece of pipe into the back of the stranger across the road; he had to get himself into the frame of mind where *he* believed the pipe in his pocket was a gun.

Inside the front door he paused, gathering his courage in bits and pieces: the jigsaw image came back to his mind. Then he stepped out into the street, trying to appear unconcerned, and flinched immediately as a small boy, running down the street, almost cannoned into him. He fell back against the wall, looked after the running child; his eyes, like weights in his skull, wanted to swing towards the man across the road, but somehow he kept his gaze averted. He began to walk unhurriedly but stiffly up towards the Hotel Eden.

On the other side of the road, standing behind the corner of the narrow side street, Kessler watched McBride go up the hill. He was still puzzled as to what connection the man had with Toohey, the Australian. He had bought a copy of an early afternoon paper and learned the identity of the man he had followed last night; the newspaper story had said that Toohey was an international criminal who was vicious, dangerous and would shoot on sight. On another page of the newspaper there had been a story that Signor McBride, a Vatican press relations officer whose picture was shown, had not been very helpful with details about the kidnapping of His Holiness the Pope. Why was a Vatican press relations officer sheltering a vicious criminal in his apartment? Kessler closed his eyes, head aching with the mystery of it all.

He opened them again and caught the movement up on the balcony on the fourth floor. A man had stepped out there, a heavily built stranger. Kessler peered up at him, then suddenly recognised him. The man had come out of the building earlier this morning, had been away for half an hour, then returned. What was *he* doing in McBride's apartment? What was going on up there on the fourth floor?

The man had a pair of binoculars and was looking down towards the river. Towards the Vatican perhaps? There was a movement in the doorway behind the man and Kessler leaned away from the wall to get a better view. And heard the footstep behind him and felt the hard object dig into his back.

'This is a gun,' said the man behind him. He looked over his shoulder and blinked in surprise when he saw McBride. 'We're going up to my apartment. Don't try anything and you'll be okay.'

'I am pleased,' said Kessler in his stilted English.

They crossed the roadway, walking close together, Kessler calm and deliberate, McBride nervous and impatient to be up inside his apartment. They went into the shabby entrance hall of the building and someone in the elevator, about to close the doors, flung them open again.

'Signor McBride!' It was the plump widow from the second floor, all corset and curiosity; she oozed flesh and inquisitiveness. 'You may ride up with me! Be my guest!'

There was no avoiding her: McBride knew she would wait for him on the second floor to ask why he and his friend had bothered to walk up when she had offered them a free ride. He jabbed the pipe warningly into Kessler's back and the two men crowded in beside the widow. 'Thank you, Signora Ferragamo. Some day I'll spend ten lire on you.'

She shook like loose custard, one hundred and sixty pounds of merriment. 'Oh, the American sense of humour! Are you American too, signore?'

'No,' said Kessler, pressed hard up against McBride. 'German. We have a different sense of humour.'

Signora Ferragamo slowly subsided, drew her brows together as if she was not sure that the Germans had any sense of humour at all. 'I have never known any Germans. Except Il Papa – '

'You know the Pope?' Kessler said in surprise, looking sideways at McBride.

'Oh, not *know* him! Whoever knows a pope? No, I mean – '

'We understand,' said McBride, and opened the doors of the elevator as it wheezed to a stop at the second floor. 'I'll give His Holiness your greetings.'

'Oh, have they found him? I have been saying prayers – '

The elevator went on up: she disappeared inch by inch, pound by pound, beneath the third floor. Kessler looked at McBride, eyes alert. 'Have they found him?'

'No.' McBride felt more at ease now; he was beginning to believe the pipe *was* a gun. He opened the doors of the elevator, brought his hand up in his pocket just as they did in the movies. 'In there.'

Kessler stepped out of the elevator, stood listening: down on the second floor Signora Ferragamo was still trying to open her front door. Kessler put his hand in his pocket and at once McBride said, 'Don't try anything!'

Kessler stared at him, eyes unblinking behind the glasses. 'Will you shoot me, Herr McBride? Won't that bring that woman up here?' He took his gun out of his pocket. It was not fitted with the silencer and it looked brutal and deadly in his big bony hand. 'We shall kill each other, Herr McBride. I do not mind dying – do you?'

Christ, McBride thought; and fought against the weakness that rushed through him. What would the professionals inside have done? Would they have kept up the bluff? But he was the amateur, the one who had bungled it. There was a sick taste in his mouth; he licked his lips. Then he drew the piece of pipe from his own pocket, held it out with embarrassment. Kessler took it, smiled thinly, shook his head, then dropped the pipe into the open elevator and closed the doors. He nodded at the front door of McBride's apartment.

'Let us go in.'

Now he was actually facing the fact of the stranger's gun, was becoming used to it, McBride felt a little calmer; he was not unafraid, but his fear was not chopping him to pieces. There was still the sickening realisation that he had failed; but he was also puzzled, shocked by the chilling fatalism of the man with the gun. If he *had* had a gun instead of the piece of pipe, would he have shot the stranger? How was the German to have known that it was not a gun, that he would not have fired it? This was the sort of fanatical fatalism one read about in the newspapers, the recurring disease that still surprised whenever a new generation had to face it.

'Who are you? Why are you spying on me?'

Kessler ignored the question, gestured with his gun at the door. McBride, with fingers that he was surprised to see were trembling, put his key in the lock and swung open the door.

Ryan was the only one in the living-room; McBride noticed that the bedroom door was closed. Ryan's flattened face creased; he looked inquiringly at McBride as the latter came into the room ahead of Kessler. Then he saw the gun in the stranger's hand and he made a quick move forward. Kessler stepped round McBride, moving to one side, and pointed the gun at the Irishman.

'Do not attempt anything foolish!'

'Better not, Des,' said McBride through dry lips. 'I think he means it.'

Ryan stood poised on the balls of his feet, then sank back on his heels, a fighter who knew the bout was over. 'Jesus, man, how'd you let him get away with it? I saw you crossing the road – you *had* him – '

McBride shook his head: it was useless to explain that he hadn't had the guts to face down a killer as cold-blooded as this stranger appeared to be. He looked at the German and repeated his question: 'Why are you spying on me?'

'I am not spying on you, Herr McBride.' He spoke with precise diction, tonelessly, as in the voice of a deaf man; in the years before he had left the asylum he had learned English from another inmate, an ex-schoolmaster whose mind had broken when his heroes, the English, had declared war on the Führer. 'I have been waiting to see the man Toohey. Is he in there?'

McBride looked at the bedroom door, then nodded. 'Better come out, Turk.'

The door opened slowly, then Toohey came cautiously into the living-room, leaning forward as if ready to dive aside should Kessler start shooting at him. But the German just nodded to him, then stiffened and clicked his heels, bending his head, as Luciana, after a moment's hesitation, came quickly into the room and crossed to McBride's side.

'Good afternoon, Frau McBride.'

Luciana looked swiftly at McBride, then back at Kessler. 'No. I am – just a friend.'

Kessler nodded absently, as if he did not care whether she was wife, mistress or maid. He turned his head and the gun towards Toohey, who stood with his back pressed against the sideboard that ran along one wall. The Australian's thin face was expressionless, but his eyes never moved from the German.

'You are Herr Toohey.' It wasn't a question: Kessler spoke like a man laying all the facts out in proper order, the painstaking craftsman. 'I hope I did not shock you too much last night.'

'A bit.' Toohey's voice gave nothing of him away. 'What's the strength of all this?'

'Strength?' Kessler's English didn't run to Australian colloquialisms.

'What's the point, the meaning?' For a moment there was an

inflection in Toohey's voice; he had the non-linguist's impatience with the foreigner who couldn't speak his language. 'You kill two jokers – you did kill the second demon, didn't you? Two carabinieri?'

'Yes.' Kessler nodded calmly, another fact laid out. 'It was necessary.'

'What was the reason?' said Ryan, who himself had killed two policemen, Royal Ulster Constabulary men, for no other reason than that Dublin had ordered it.

'It was necessary,' Kessler repeated; he sounded like a walking phrase-book. 'You may sit down if you wish.'

But none of them felt relaxed enough to move. 'You haven't told us what you want,' said McBride. 'What brought you to us?'

'The Pope.' As they all looked at each other in puzzlement, Kessler went on, 'You have kidnapped him. Am I correct?'

They all exchanged glances again, then McBride said, 'We don't know what you're talking about.'

'I have read the newspapers. The police say they suspect Herr Toohey of being one of the kidnappers. I am sure he is.' He turned the gun in turn on each of the three men, as if nominating them; the last of them was Toohey and it remained pointed at him. 'Where is the Pope?'

'You tell me why you want him and maybe I'll give you an answer.' Toohey was still stiffly wary, but he was a long way from abject surrender to the gun.

'I want to kill him.'

Luciana let out a gasp and even Ryan made a sound like a stifled cough. Through the open doors to the balcony there came the laughter of some girls down in the street, the whine of a car as it accelerated up the hill, the bouncy rhythm of a James Last number from the radio in an apartment across the street: the sounds of the normal world that assassination never touched. Or so the world thought.

McBride said, 'You're mad!'

'Perhaps. I spent some years in an asylum. I would not argue with you. But I have a very sane reason for wanting to kill him.'

McBride was suddenly wary again, one eye on the gun: how

did you argue with a man who admitted he might be mad? 'There's no sane reason for killing anyone.' And heard the echo of an argument with his father.

'You are sentimental, Herr McBride. Vengeance is a sane reason – it is common here in Italy, for instance. The Pope killed my father – I am going to kill him.'

'The Pope killed – ? Ah, you're – '

'Mad? Crazy?' The barrel of the gun moved in McBride's direction, was raised an inch. 'Please do not continue with that talk. Where is the Pope?'

'What do you mean, he killed your father?' asked Toohey, not really curious but playing for time, waiting for the stranger's attention to be distracted just long enough for one of them to make a move.

'My father was in the SS, he was a Sturmbannführer – I think you call him a major. He was doing his duty to the Reich, that was all. But Kurt Stecher told lies about him and he was executed.'

'I remember that,' said McBride, certain facts springing into his mind as if a filing cabinet had just opened up in there. 'I had to prepare a biography of the Pope – or of Monsignor Kurt Stecher, if that's how you want to remember him – '

'I don't remember him at all,' said Kessler. 'I was in the asylum when it all happened. But he was Kurt Stecher when he told his lies at Nuremberg and it is Kurt Stecher I shall kill.'

'He is worth a lot of money to us,' said Toohey.

'Dead or alive?'

Toohey's eyebrows went up, his first real show of expression since he had come into the room. 'Alive, of course.'

'Not of course, Herr Toohey. If you get your ransom money, you will not care whether he is dead or alive. Correct?'

'Not correct,' McBride said. 'We didn't kidnap him to kill him. All we want is the money – nothing more!'

'You can collect your money – I do not want even a pfennig of that. But when you have collected it, you will hand the Pope over to me.'

'You can't kill him in cold blood like that.' McBride tried to keep his voice even, talking patiently as to a wayward child:

despite all his experience as a newsman he had never before conducted a dialogue with a madman. 'He is a good man, almost a saint to some people – '

'My father was a good man – ' Behind the cheap glasses the pale blue eyes glistened for a moment with tears held back; the gaunt bony face tightened with pain. 'I loved him.'

'Perhaps your father was a good man – I don't know.'

McBride scraped his memory for some more facts of what Kurt Stecher had said and done at Nuremberg; but the biographical material had been skimpy. Pope Martin himself had asked that that period be underplayed. *Had* Martin lied at Nuremberg, was there something there in his past life of which he was ashamed? But even as he raised the doubt in his own mind, McBride couldn't bring himself to believe that Martin would have lied to send another man to his death.

'But he must have done something wrong – there were no innocent men sentenced at Nuremberg – '

Kessler took the silencer out of his pocket and fitted it to the gun, stepping back as he did so, opening up the space between himself and the others. 'Continue talking like that, Herr McBride, and I shall kill you. It is not necessary that you remain alive – or you.' He nodded at Toohey and Ryan. 'I need only one of you to take me to where the Pope is hidden. I shall take you, Fräulein.'

Luciana shook her head dumbly, clung fiercely to McBride's arm. The latter freed his arm from her grasp and put it around her shoulders. 'You're not taking her – I'll go with you – '

'You would be too much difficulty, Herr McBride.'

McBride looked at Toohey and Ryan, then back at Kessler. 'He is out at – '

'Shut up!' said Toohey. 'Let the bugger find out.'

'I shall find out, Herr Toohey.' Kessler raised the gun and aimed it at Toohey's head. '*You* tell me.'

Toohey sucked in his breath as he saw the bony finger tighten on the trigger, seemed to shrink back against the sideboard behind him. He didn't look at McBride or Ryan as he said, 'He's out at the Villa Pericoli.'

'Where is that?'

'Out on the road to Frascati,' said McBride, and looked

at Toohey. 'Okay for me to tell him that, shop steward?'

Toohey didn't move his head, just kept staring at the gun still pointed at him. Then Ryan said, 'We can't let him kill His Holiness, Fergus – '

'It does not matter what you say – Stecher dies,' said Kessler. 'The fräulein is coming with me. Let her go, Herr McBride.'

The gun came round to point at McBride. Down in the street a car backfired and a girl screamed; then there was a burst of laughter and the toot of a horn. Across the street the blaring radio was giving another news bulletin: *There is no further news on the kidnapping of His Holiness* . . . Luciana pulled away from McBride's protective arm, moved away from him. 'I shall go with you. But you must promise not to harm Signor McBride.'

'I shall not harm anyone if they behave themselves,' said Kessler. 'But if you do not behave, Fräulein, when we are outside in the street – ' He gestured with the gun.

McBride heard himself say, 'You harm her and I'll find you and kill *you*.'

Luciana looked at him, shocked; but the threat did not seem to worry Kessler. 'When I have done what I came to Rome to do, I shall not care what happens to me. Do you have a car?'

'Yes.'

'What sort is it?'

'An Alfa Romeo.'

'Is it parked down in the street?'

'No, it's in a garage up on the Via Lombardia.'

Kessler looked disappointed for a moment. 'A pity. Your keys, please.'

McBride hesitated, then reluctantly handed over his key-ring. 'Let the Pope go and you can have the ransom money – '

Kessler shook his head; his face creased, he almost smiled. 'I am not interested in money. In the asylum you learn it means nothing, except that it can be another cause of insanity.'

McBride nodded bitterly. 'You may be right.'

'You can still collect your ransom. What I am about to do will not interfere with that – by the time they know what has happened to him, you will have the money and be gone. Come, Fräulein.'

He opened the door, pushed Luciana through it and followed

her. McBride heard the key being turned in the lock on the outside, then there was the clacking of heels going down the marble stairs.

Ryan went out on to the balcony and Toohey moved quickly to the phone. 'What's the number out at the villa? Smithy can find somewhere else to take him!'

'The phone's cut off out there,' McBride told him. 'Can you pick that lock?'

Toohey banged down the phone. 'Don't you have a spare set?'

'All I have is a spare car key – wait a minute!' He went into the bedroom, came out with Luciana's handbag, up-ended it over the table. Everything fell out, the small mysteries of a woman's handbag that no man understands: but he understood the key-ring that lay among the little mess and he grabbed it. 'Okay, let's go!'

But Kessler had left the original key on the outside of the door and Luciana's key would not fit into the lock. Then Ryan came in from the balcony. 'He's just grabbed a taxi – we'll have to be quick!'

'Phone the caretaker,' said Toohey. 'Get him to come up and open the door for us.'

'The janitor doesn't have a phone – ' McBride, cursing, feverish with anxiety for Luciana, stepped back from the door. 'You're the professional – get that key out of there!'

With a piece of wire unwound from the handle of a kitchen brush it took Toohey three minutes to release the outside key from the lock. He grabbed his hat, shoving it on his head as if he would be naked to go out in public without it, and the three of them went down the stairs in a rush, ignoring Signora Ferragamo as she opened her door and called after them.

'Signor McBride! A moment – '

When they reached the street there was no sign of Kessler and Luciana; their taxi had disappeared. But across the road, on the corner of the narrow side street, two carabinieri on motor cycles had just pulled up beside Kessler's stolen motor scooter. One of them dismounted and bent down to examine the machine.

'Take it easy,' said McBride, struggling to control his own

growing panic. 'We'll go up and get my car, go out to the villa.'

They walked up the hill, careful not to hurry, ears strained for the hailing shout from the carabinieri. On the corner near the Hotel Eden they had to pass a policeman, but he barely gave them a glance. By the time McBride had got his car out of the crowded garage, Kessler had a start of fifteen minutes on them.

3

As Kessler and Luciana came to the corner of Francesco Crispi and the Via Sistina the taxi drew up at the lights. Kessler, the gun now in his pocket, pushed Luciana into the taxi and nodded to her as the driver looked over his shoulder for instructions.

Luciana wanted to cry out for help, but she knew she would be dead before the driver could do anything; and the driver, too, might be dead. Her voice just a hoarse whisper, she said, 'The main road to Frascati – '

The driver was a beefy man in a peaked cap and a bright red sweater. 'Excuse me, signorina – where? I didn't hear you.'

She cleared her throat. 'The main road to Frascati – I'll tell you where to turn off. We want to go to the Villa Pericoli.'

The driver turned forward again, glanced at both of them in his driving mirror, flicked on his meter and set the taxi moving. Luciana sat back in the seat, every muscle stiff as a bone in her body; she was terrified, ready to be sick. Kessler sat in the corner of the seat half-turned towards her, the occasional glint of reflected light on his glasses the only sign of movement on his impassive face. She looked down at the pocket of his overcoat and, catching her glance, he moved his hand in the pocket. She saw the hard shape of the gun barrel, no less threatening because it was hidden by the threadbare wool.

'Please – ' she whispered.

'I do not want to talk,' said Kessler just as softly.

Despite his cool exterior Kessler was trembling inside with excitement. Soon he would be meeting the man who had sent his father to his death; he could taste the sweetness of vengeance, like the memory of a childhood treat. Eyes blind for a moment to the present, he saw his father smiling at him, faint as a dream at the periphery of his consciousness. His head began to throb, his mind stopped comprehending the reality of stone and steel and wood through which they were passing; he was lost in the past entirely, two shadows hand in hand in the Englischer Garten. Without knowing what it was, he felt the unutterable loneliness of madness, the desolation inhabited only by himself and the memories that tortured him. His hand tightened on the gun, but fortunately his finger was not on the trigger.

Luciana, out of the corner of her eye, saw the glazed look behind the glasses: the cold look of statues' eyes, the callousness of marble. She shuddered, a spasm of terror that ravaged her face for a moment; but the taxi driver, halted at a traffic light, watching them both in his driving mirror, saw it. He turned round.

'Are you all right, signorina? What's going on here?'

Kessler snapped back into the present, body jerking forward like a puppet. He took the gun out of his pocket and held it just below the level of the back seat, so that the two people in the car standing beside the taxi at the traffic light could not see it. The driver twisted his head still farther, staring down at the gun as if wishing he had minded his own business.

'Turn into the next street,' said Kessler. 'Do what I tell you or I shall kill you.'

The driver looked at Luciana and she nodded, her face reflecting his own terror. 'Please do what he says. I don't want you hurt – '

The light turned green and the traffic on either side moved forward. The taxi driver couldn't find the right gear; cars behind him hooted at him to get moving. The taxi jerked forward, slid round a corner fifty yards farther on. As it came to a stop and the driver pulled on the hand brake, Kessler hit him hard across the back of the head with the gun. Luciana let out a muffled scream as the man slumped sideways in the front seat.

'Can you drive?'

Too frightened to lie, Luciana nodded dumbly. Kessler got out of the taxi, glancing quickly around to see if he was being observed. But the street, a quiet residential one, appeared deserted. He dragged the driver out of the taxi and in between two parked cars. Then he gestured for Luciana to get into the front seat while he got back into the rear of the taxi.

'Now drive to our destination. And hurry, Fräulein!'

Luciana was a good driver, but not today. She could not get the feel of the clutch, she clashed the gears, when she turned the corner at the end of the street she over-steered and only just managed to miss a car parked at the kerb. Desperately she tried to calm herself, wondering if she had the nerve to drive, not out to the villa, but to the nearest police station. But the thought made her even more nervous and she put it out of her mind before she finished up crashing the taxi. She was no heroine, she admitted to herself; again she fell back on the crutch of the hopeless, praying for a miracle.

In the rear seat Kessler sat back, gun in his lap, face expressionless, a businessman on his way to a long-awaited appointment.

4

'Drive your car into the stables.' Smith stood on the running-board of the Lancia, his gun held against Count Pericoli's head. 'Just do as you are told and you will be all right.'

He jumped down from the car as it came round the back of the villa, swung back the doors of the stable, his gun still pointed at the car, and stood aside as Pericoli drove it into the big dark cavern. The old man turned off the engine, then sat unmoving behind the wheel, looking at the Pope with a mixture of pain and shock on his thin pale face.

'I do not feel well, Holiness – '

Smith came into the stable. 'What's going on? Get out of there!'

'Count Pericoli is ill,' said Martin. 'I think it is his heart.'

Smith hid his surprise at the name Pericoli, and his chagrin: Christ Almighty, what else could go wrong! He remembered the other abortive operations he had been involved in, that had gone wrong because someone had not checked every detail; he had argued for promotion, to be allowed to show them how a *professional* soldier could make every operation a successful one. But always there had been someone at GHQ who had vetoed giving him more authority; there would always be the diehards who would always suspect the English blood in him. He had argued to be allowed to run *this* show, knowing he could have done it ruthlessly and without fuss; perhaps a security guard or two would have died, but if the identity of the raiders had been kept secret, if it had never been known that the IRA had collected the money for the ransomed treasures, no harm would have been done. Instead of which authority had been given to the pussyfooting amateur, McBride, and nothing had gone right from the beginning.

'I'm afraid the Count will have to suffer a little more – we can't stay here. Please get out.'

Martin got out of the car, went round and helped Pericoli down from the front seat. The old man was breathing heavily, but he made a conscious effort to straighten up as the Pope put a hand under his arm. 'I am sorry to be such a burden, Holiness. I don't know what came over me – '

'A gun at one's head would shock anyone.' Martin knew, as surely as if the words had been written on the stable wall in front of him, that he was once again responsible for another man's life. He felt the burden of it, almost as if Pericoli had been physically laid across his shoulders: Oh, God, he thought, when does my testing end? He looked at Smith, a sudden anger at the tall man flushing his face. 'You didn't have to be so brutal! This is an innocent man – '

'Blame yourself. If you hadn't got away for those few minutes, the Count wouldn't be in this predicament.'

'I was coming here in any case.' Pericoli's breathing was easing and he was trying not to lean on the Pope. He was not the sort of vain man who had no real pride; his courage had a solider base than the mere desire not to appear a coward in front of other men. He stared at Smith, ignoring the gun, and said, 'You would have been encumbered with me just the same.'

'Did anyone know you were coming here?'

Pericoli remarked the suspicious concern in Smith's voice; and so did Martin. The two men looked at each other, then Pericoli looked back at Smith. 'That is for you to worry about.'

Smith's handsome face stiffened; and so did his finger on the trigger. These arrogant no-account Dago aristocrats with their titles that meant nothing: one of them would never be missed if he were killed. Then his control came back and he motioned the two men out of the stable, waving the gun at them. He closed the stable doors, then pushed Martin and Pericoli down the driveway beside the house towards the forecourt. Pericoli walked slowly, with faltering steps, and the Pope, though hobbling with the pain of his swollen instep, took the older man's arm again. *Don't let this man die because of me, Lord.* But he knew Pericoli's life was in his own hands, not God's; the spectre of the Jew walked down the driveway beside them, another shadow. *Why me, Lord?* he wanted to cry out; but he knew no man ever knew the reason for such a price till he heard it in the echo chamber of his dead skull. In the meantime he was still living and he had to keep this frail, sick man beside him living too.

He discarded any further thought of escape. His only chance of that would be to attempt to catch the tall man off guard again, and even if he were so fortunate it would not be enough just to stun him. To give them time to flee, with Pericoli as handicapped as he was, the tall man would have to be killed, or at best seriously crippled so that he could not chase them. And Martin could not bring himself to contemplate such an act against another human being. He would willingly die rather than kill another man to prevent his own death. But – and the thought burned in his brain like a cinder – would he kill to prevent the death of Pericoli? How blind could the eye be above the cheek that was turned?

Smith moved ahead of them, watching them carefully, pointed through an archway in the forecourt wall down towards a small, vine-covered structure beyond a grove of olive trees at the distant end of a long field. 'What's that?'

'It is the Chiesetta Sant' Augusto,' said Pericoli, glad to stand still for a moment. 'It used to be my family's own private church, but we have not used it for several generations.' He looked apologetically at Martin. 'We have not been as good as we might have been, Holiness – '

'Who has?' said Martin, and smiled comfortingly; he knew

the measure of his own failings. 'I don't think you should ask Count Pericoli to walk all the way down there, Mr – ?'

'Brown, if you must call me anything,' said Smith. 'And I'm afraid the Count *will* have to walk down there. We'll take it easily – make it just an afternoon stroll.'

They went through the archway and out into the roughly ploughed field, skirting it and keeping close to the weed-encrusted stone wall that ran down the far side of it from the approach lane. They came to the grove of olive trees and moved into the pattern of its shadows, effectively camouflaged now from any observer who might be watching them. Pericoli stopped, put out a hand and leaned against a tree; the twisted trunks, the tree's and the old man's, seemed to match each other in their impression of pain. Smith, impatient and nervous, looked all about him, through the trees and up across the wide fields stretching away in mottled corduroy to a distant ridge. But he said nothing and waited while Martin ministered to the ailing older man. Pericoli managed a caricature of a smile.

'In my pocket – a flask. Forgive me – it sustains me better than prayer.'

Martin took the flask from the Count's pocket, uncorked it and held it to his mouth. A little of the brandy trickled down over the trembling chin and Martin took the silk handkerchief from the old man's breast pocket and wiped his mouth. Pericoli coughed once, closed his eyes and leaned back against the tree.

Martin looked angrily at Smith. 'You don't have to do this to him!'

'What alternative is there?' Smith was not incapable of pity, though it was a virtue that had to be squeezed out of him; but now he was sorry for this old man, the father of the stupid Luciana. 'I can't leave him here.'

'Why not? You and I can go back to the villa, take the car – we'll go anywhere you wish. But don't subject Count Pericoli to any more of this agony!'

'A car as conspicuous as his?' Smith shook his head. 'We'd be picked up before we'd gone ten miles. I'm sorry, dear chap – ' He looked solicitously at Pericoli. 'I'm afraid you'll have to bear with me a little farther.'

Pericoli, revived a little under the influence of the brandy, straightened up, bowed his head. 'Whatever you say, sir.'

'Thank you,' said Smith. 'You're obviously a gentleman. I knew you'd understand.'

On the still afternoon air there came the sounds of the everyday world that Martin, hearing them again, felt as if he were hearing for the first time: the hum of traffic on a distant highway, the muttering of a tractor somewhere over the brow of a hill, the scream of a jet heading down towards Fiumicino in the west. But he could hear no voices: no one was close enough to help them.

At last they came to the tiny church. From a distance it might have been mistaken for no more than a brush-covered hillock; vines, weeds and shrubs grew out of the brickwork and one side of the building was hidden by a sloping, weed-tangled mound. Through the camouflage of vines and shrubs one could see glimpses of the brick- and stone-work; thick iron rods, like rusted ribs, shored up three of the walls. Above the climbing vines, like a struggling symbol of what the building had once been, a broken dome pointed a jagged edge at the sky.

'It began life as a Roman temple.' Pericoli sat down on a block of masonry near the narrow door. 'It has been badly neglected.'

'You are all too careless of the past,' Martin chided gently.

'How true. But antiquity – ' He breathed deeply, sucking in the air loudly. 'Too many of us have to struggle too hard with the present.'

Smith was carefully pulling the vines back from the door of the tiny church. The door itself was iron, rusted where it had been exposed to the elements, green with mould where the vines had lain against it. He slid back the rusted bolt, then grasped the big ornamental handle. It took all his strength to shift the door, but then it gave and opened inwards, the hinges whining in protest. There was a flutter of wings from inside and a bird suddenly spurted up through the hole in the domed roof.

Dank air wafted out, and Smith wrinkled his nose; but it was not as bad as the air in the Vatican grotto had been and it was soon dissipated. 'This will do us. We have only a few more hours to wait.'

'You sound confident.' Martin helped Pericoli to his feet. 'You'd do well to feel the same,' said Smith. 'After all, we are both depending on the good sense of your underlings.'

'Underlings? My colleagues wouldn't like that.' Martin smiled, trying to lighten the mood; he had felt the tension in the thin bony arm in his hand. 'You are a Roman, Count Pericoli. Do Romans ever think of themselves as underlings?'

Pericoli tried to smile, but his mouth was still too busy gasping for air. 'I – I have never noticed it.'

Smith ushered the two men into the dank gloomy interior of the church; light straggled in through the hole in the dome but it was not sufficient to illuminate all the corners. Smith half-closed the door and sat down on a marble plinth just inside the doorway. A statue of a former Pericoli had stood on the plinth but it was now gone the way of the man it had honoured. 'Make yourselves comfortable. We just sit and wait now.'

The tiny church would have had room for no more than a dozen pews; but they had long been removed for firewood by the local peasants. The broken tiled floor was a mess of earth, rubbish and shattered pieces of masonry and statuary. Four steps, the width of the interior, led up to where the altar had stood; but there was no altar now, only the spectral profile of it outlined against the back wall by the light from the dome. To one side, dimly visible in the gloom, half a dozen wine casks were clustered in a corner, one of them with its timbers splayed out so that it looked like some huge evil man-eating bush. Vines had penetrated cracks in the walls and hung down like shredded tapestries; weeds grew, mocking harvest offerings, out of the altar steps. When Martin looked up he saw, dirty and half-obscured though it was, a repeated pattern on the inside of the dome: a bunch of grapes wrapped round a key.

'The Pericoli family emblem.' Pericoli had stiffly lowered himself to sit down on the altar steps; Martin dragged across one of the wine casks, disturbing some rats, and the old man leaned back against it. 'Wine is the key to life. My ancestors, I'm afraid, worshipped Bacchus more than they should have.'

'It is a beautiful church. You should be ashamed to have let it be neglected like this.'

Pericoli nodded. 'Money was the problem – but perhaps that

191

will all be solved now.' His voice was softer, weaker; but his breathing sounded easier. 'I am selling the villa. That is why I came out here today, a sentimental journey if you like. It was not an easy decision to sell something that has been in the family for so long. Some Americans are buying it – they want to build houses in the fields and some offices. Perhaps they will restore the church. Americans have a regard for the past, having so little of their own.'

'If you own so much land,' said Smith, who had no regard for any past that did not directly touch his own life, 'you must have had enough money to restore this, surely?'

'Debts, mortgages – ' Pericoli looked at Martin, who was moving aimlessly about the church, scraping dirt off the walls to peer at the blotched and faded frescoes beneath. 'I hope they will include me in your ransom price, Holiness.'

'I'm sure they will,' said Martin, and looked at Smith.

The latter nodded, then stood up and moved to the door, opening it a little wider to stare out at something coming up the lane on the other side of the olive grove. Martin, still discovering the neglected beauties of the church, turned away from Smith and moved across towards the wine casks. Then he stopped, gently rocking himself back and forth on a loose slab in the floor.

Pericoli, watching him, said, 'There's a vault beneath there. The family was buried there till about three or four generations ago.'

'Just a vault? Nothing else?'

'Catacombs,' said Pericoli with the same careless regard for history. 'I found them when I was a young man – they had been closed up for years. My father never said anything to anyone about them – he was afraid Mussolini would open them up as a tourist attraction. And I – ' he sucked in his breath again as another spasm of pain bit him ' – I just forgot them.'

Smith, halfway out of the door now, saw the taxi drive slowly up the lane towards the villa. It was too far away for him to recognise who was in it, but he knew none of the other four would be foolish enough to hire a taxi to bring them out here. He stayed behind the tangle of vines, watching the car disappear through the gates into the villa forecourt. Then he heard the noise behind him and he ducked back into the church.

'What are you doing?'

'Keeping myself occupied,' said Martin, puffing with the effort of having moved the slab. 'There is a vault down here.'

'Dammit,' said Smith irritably; *what the hell was going on up at the villa?* 'Are you always so damned restless?'

'I'm afraid I am,' said Martin, watching the tall man carefully. 'One is always counting the minutes one might waste – I lost so many when I was in the concentration camp. You sound nervous, Mr Brown.'

Smith said nothing, but went back to the door. He continued to watch the gates of the villa; then the taxi appeared again. It was halfway down the lane when there came the sound of a siren. The taxi pulled up abruptly, swerving to one side and slamming against the wall, as if someone had grabbed the wheel from the driver and tried to take over. The back door opened and a man in an overcoat got out and wrenched open the front door, pulling out Luciana. The siren got closer, then Smith saw the police car coming up the lane at speed. Puzzled, all his reflexes gone, he stood stockstill behind the vines, staring across at the scene that, though remote as something seen through the wrong end of a telescope, yet had a personal immediacy that shocked him. His hand tightened on the gun. But what was there to shoot at from this distance?

Then he saw the man break away from Luciana and scramble over the wall. He came running through the olive grove as the police car skidded to a stop and two carabinieri and a man in a red sweater jumped out. One of the carabinieri went to Luciana and the other vaulted the wall and came after the fleeing stranger. Smith stayed only long enough to see that the man, whoever he was, was gaining ground on the carabinieri; then he moved quickly back into the church, pulling the door closed behind him, and in the pale gloom waved his gun at Martin and Pericoli. 'Not a sound from either of you!'

From outside there came a sharp crack, then another: the carabinieri was shooting at the stranger. Smith moved swiftly and silently up on to the altar steps, took out his cigarette lighter and flicked it on, peered by its yellow glow down the steps that led into the vault. Then he gestured with his gun at the other two men. Pericoli, gasping for breath again, stood up; Martin limped to him and took his arm. They groped their way down the steps, the older man leaning heavily on the Pope; Smith followed them, dragging the slab across the opening above his head but not fitting it exactly into position. He would have to trust to luck, if anyone came in here, that they would not notice that the slab had been only recently moved.

He glanced quickly around the vault. It was like any other vault: he was becoming familiar with the neighbourhood of death. The long-buried Pericolis were stacked one above the other behind marble panels; the end of one of the tombs was broken and the skull of a dead Pericoli grinned out at them mockingly. Smith flicked off the lighter and the three of them stood in absolute blackness.

'The colour of eternity, eh?' he whispered.

'Not if you believe,' said Martin, also whispering; then put out a hand, groped for Pericoli. 'Are you all right, my friend?'

Pericoli gave no answer but a strangled whimper; in the darkness Martin felt the old man's hand feebly grasping at his own. Smith, crouched at the bottom of the steps, heard the scrape of iron against stone as the door of the church was opened; he brought his gun up, aiming it in the darkness at where he guessed the slab was. There was the sound of footsteps on the tiled floor above their heads; they came to the altar steps, then stopped. A boot rasped on some grit; then the footsteps went quickly back to the door and were gone. Smith let out a sigh of relief that was almost as loud as the gasping of Pericoli.

'Stay here!'

He felt his way up the steps, cautiously heaved against the slab and pushed it out of the way. He hesitated, gun held ready, then he stepped up into the church and crossed to the door. When he looked out into the afternoon sun, after the blackness of the vault and then the gloom of the church, he saw nothing for a moment. Then his eyes quickly adjusted to the light and he saw the carabinieri going back through the olive grove. The policeman clambered over the stone wall, conferred for a moment with his colleague, who stood holding Luciana by the arm. Both policemen looked back through the olive grove, then said something to the man in the red sweater. The man got into the taxi and the two carabinieri led Luciana to the police car. Then the car, followed by the taxi, backed down the lane and in a moment both were gone from view. A small group of farm workers, who had appeared out of nowhere like a flock of crows, stood watching the departing cars, then they, too, went down the lane out of sight.

Smith, puzzled but relieved, stepped out from the church and looked around. There was no sign of the stranger; he had disappeared completely. Smith shrugged, turned and went back into the church. The Pope, looking in the gloom like a legless man, his trunk chopped off at the waist, stood on the steps of the vault, one hand resting on the floor of the altar.

'You can come up,' Smith said, relief making him sound sympathetic.

'I'm afraid Count Pericoli can't,' said Martin. 'He is dead.'

7

McBride drove fast: in Rome slow drivers got more attention from the police than speedsters. Ryan sat beside him and Toohey lolled low in the back seat. Traffic was thin, everyone now at home for the lunchtime break, and McBride hoped they could reach the villa before the stranger had time to kill the Pope.

'What do we do if he does kill him?' Ryan asked.

'I don't know.' The thought was too horrifying, his mind refused to go beyond it.

'Maybe Smithy can stop him,' said Toohey.

'Yes, but if he doesn't – ?' Ryan swung his head, looking out of both sides of the car, like a man trapped. 'We'd better forget the money, forget the whole thing and just go home, yes.'

'Except me,' said Toohey, sitting up now they were out on the open road to Frascati. 'The demons ain't gunna forget me. You bastards are still in the clear. But me – ' He looked bitterly out at a village church as they passed it. He was becoming superstitious, convinced that the bloody God-botherers had pointed the bone at him just like the blacks did back home in Aussie. 'Don't they call the Pope the Fisherman or something? No fisherman ever had my luck. A wet arse, no fish and a hole in the bloody boat.'

Then they heard the siren behind them. McBride glanced in the driving mirror, saw the police car barrelling up the road behind them, lights flashing, siren wailing; his foot instinctively pressed down on the accelerator, panic prompted him to try and flee, then all the old instincts of respectability came back. He pulled over to one side, began to slow down.

'Slide out quick, Fergus.' Toohey grasped the back of the driver's seat, ready to push it forward as soon as McBride vacated it. 'I'm gunna make a run for it!'

'Hold it!'

McBride, still looking in the driving mirror, saw that the police car was going too fast to pull up. It went by them with a deafening whine of its siren, was gone out of sight round a bend in the road before McBride had brought the Alfa to a halt. They heard the siren receding into the distance, the police car still obviously travelling as fast as when it had passed them.

Ryan looked inquiringly at McBride and the latter, feeling sick, said, 'We could be too late. Maybe the shooting's already over.'

'Bugger!' said Toohey, and slumped back in his seat.

'What does that mean?'

Toohey stared at McBride as the latter turned around. 'It means I'm crooked on the whole bloody schemozzle – and it's been nothing but a schemozzle ever since the word Go. If His Nibs has copped it, I'm sorry. But I'm sorrier for m'self. If that Hun bastard has got away and they haven't seen him, I'm Public Enemy Number One anywhere in the whole bloody world!'

McBride, already accepting that the worst had happened to the Pope, nodded slowly. But he was too far gone in sudden despair to feel any immediate sympathy for Toohey. 'Do you want me to say I'm sorry for you?'

'I couldn't care less, mate.' Toohey took out a cigarette, lit it. 'I found out a long time ago – pity only makes the *other* bloke feel good. You feel all the pity you want. It ain't gunna help me.'

Ryan said, 'What do we do? Go on out and see what's happened?'

'I've got to,' said McBride simply. 'You guys please yourselves.'

Ryan looked at Toohey and after a moment the Australian nodded. 'Just don't get too close, that's all. Give me room to run.'

McBride drove sedately the rest of the way: at one moment the image came to his mind that he could be in an invisible funeral procession. At last he came to the lane that ran up to the Villa Pericoli, but he went on past it when he saw the half a dozen farm workers running up towards the police car and the taxi stopped halfway up the lane. Two hundred yards up the road he turned off into another lane and pulled up. The three men got out, crossed the road, clambered over a stone wall and moved into a small grove of olive trees. Beyond the grove an open field ran down to the wall that bordered the lane. From the shelter of the trees McBride and the other two had a clear view of what was happening.

'There's a cop down there with Luciana and some guy in a red sweater,' said McBride. 'Where's the other cop? There were two in that police car, maybe more.'

'He's coming back through those trees on the other side of the lane,' said Ryan.

'Where's the Hun?' Toohey, a man for tunnels, didn't have the long sight of the other two.

'Can't see him. I wonder – ' McBride felt a lift of hope. 'The taxi is pointed *down* the lane, so they must have been up to the villa – you have to go right up to it before you can turn around. I wonder if he heard the cops coming and tried to get away before he got to Smith and the Pope?'

'If Smith's still up in the villa,' said Toohey, 'he'll be crapping himself.'

'The German could be with him. Have you thought of that?'

'If the Hun's up there,' said Toohey, colder-eyed than McBride, 'your girl would have told the cops by now. She's not gunna let the Holy Dad have his head blown off – she already sees herself in hell for what she's already done.'

McBride looked curiously at the little Australian. 'You're a whole bunch of surprises.'

Toohey made no reply and Ryan, still staring down towards the lane, said, 'The other cop's back there now. I think maybe he was chasing the German through those trees and he's got away. Doesn't look as if they are going up to the villa after all.'

'Luci must've kept her mouth shut,' said Toohey. 'You never know with women.'

McBride ignored that, just watched Luciana be put into the police car, then saw both the car and the taxi go down the lane, the police driver backing down at some speed as if in a hurry to get somewhere else. The small group of farm workers stood for a moment talking among themselves, then went back down the lane. McBride and the other two men remained in the shadows of the olive grove till the lane was deserted.

'I'm going over to the villa. You guys can stay here if you want to.'

'I wonder what they're going to do to Luciana?'

McBride had watched, with a hollow feeling of helplessness, as Luciana had been put in the police car and driven away. 'If she tells them nothing but that the German kidnapped her,' he said without much hope (why should she be loyal to him? He had reached a stage where he was whipping himself with guilt: the Jesuits still had him, goddam them), 'they'll let her go. Why would they want to hold her?'

'You reckon she'll tell 'em he wants to kill the Pope?'

'If she tells them that, we're done for. They'll want to know why he picked her to lead him to the Pope.'

'Why would he have kidnapped her anyway? She's gunna have to do some fancy talking. I hate to say it, mate, but there's no guarantee she's gunna look after anyone but herself.'

'We'll see,' said McBride, and hoped that Luciana might find a story that would enable her to walk away from the carabinieri without their suspecting her of being anyone but an unfortunate girl picked up at random by a strange madman. But even as he hoped he knew the situation would not end as simply as that: sooner or later the shadow of della Porta would loom up again.

'Let's go and see what's happened up at the villa,' said Ryan.

The villa was empty. McBride felt no surprise at the fact, only relief: at least they had not been confronted by the dead body of the Pope. In the bedroom where Martin had been kept prisoner they found the upset tray on the floor.

By the door Toohey picked up the friar's robe, pointed to the coffee stains down the front of it. 'Looks like there might've been a bit of a donnybrook. You think the Pope might've clocked Smithy and done a bunk before the Hun got here with Luci?'

McBride shook his head, shutting his mind against further thoughts. 'Let's look around. Des, while Turk and I are doing that, you clean up everything we brought out here – those friars' robes, the food, everything. If the cops come back and search the place, we don't want them to find anything that will link the kidnapping to the villa. We owe that to Luciana, just in case she manages to stay in the clear.'

'Be careful with that drill of mine,' said Toohey.

'You think you'll ever get the chance to use it again?' said Ryan.

'You never know.' Toohey grinned sourly. 'I might use it to tunnel my way outa whatever jail they sling me into.'

McBride and Toohey went through every room in the villa, then crossed the yard to the stables. When Toohey swung back the doors McBride could hardly believe what he saw.

'Who owns the chariot?' Toohey said.

'Luciana's old man. What the hell brought him out here?' He looked wildly around, as if expecting Count Pericoli to step suddenly on the scene like some practical joker. 'Where the hell is he?'

'I don't like it.' Ryan had come out to join them when he had looked through a rear window of the villa and seen the car in the stables. He knew suddenly, deep in his Irish bones, that their whole operation was doomed. Better to go back to Dublin and wait for another day. 'Let's pack up and go home.'

'What about Smith?'

'I don't care about him,' said Ryan flatly, all at once knowing it was the truth. He had never had much time for the tall man who neither looked nor spoke like an Irishman, who was always critical of GHQ. 'Let him look after himself. If he's okay, he'll phone you at your apartment.'

'No, wait a minute – ' McBride, anxious, puzzled, but knowing he could not leave here till he had some clue as to what had happened, walked down the side of the house to the forecourt. The other two followed him, cautious, alert, like men waiting to be ambushed. 'Three guys are missing – Smith, the Pope and Luciana's old man.'

'And the Hun,' said Toohey.

McBride nodded. 'Wherever they've gone, they must have gone on foot. Why would they have left the car in the stables?'

'Don't start playing bloody detective,' said Toohey. 'Let Smithy look out for himself, like Des said.'

'I want to find out what's happened to the Pope. And Luciana's father.' He looked around him, not really knowing what he was searching for; then he saw the mess of footprints in the soft earth beneath the archway in the wall. He went through the archway, alert now for the signs he was looking for, and saw the newly trodden path through the damp weeds and wild grass at the side of the field in which he now stood. He looked down towards the olive grove, saw the ruined church beyond it, and suddenly shouted, 'He's down there, I'll bet!'

'There's someone just come out of the door of the church!'

They ran down the side of the field and through the olive grove, slowing when they came within fifty yards of the church. Smith was standing with his back to them, staring across towards the lane; but he spun round, gun up, when McBride called to him, 'Is everything okay? Anyone with you?'

Smith motioned them to come on and they stepped out of the grove and hurried across towards the church. Smith stepped back inside the door and the others followed him.

I'm back in goddam shadows, thought McBride as he peered about in the gloom. 'Something's wrong. What is it? Where's the Pope?'

'Here.' Martin limped slowly up the steps from the vault, stood in the pool of grey light from the hole in the dome. 'Have you told them yet?'

'Not yet,' said Smith, and the three newcomers sensed the change in him; in the gloom in which he stood, his silver hair dulled for want of light, he looked an old man. 'Luciana's father is down there. He's dead – a heart attack.'

Toohey let out a curse and Ryan, voice thick with brogue, said, 'Holy Mother of God!' The Pope looked at him, then turned his head towards McBride. The latter had no curses or prayers left: he was dried out and empty, a ready receptacle for the worst. He moved stiffly across the church to the vault steps; as he went past Martin the latter held out Smith's lighter to him and he took it. He went down the steps, flicked on the lighter and stared at Augusto Pericoli lying among the bones of his ancestors, his thin pale face already with that look of the dead that somehow at once makes them part of the past. He had never been close to the Count, suspecting that Pericoli had hoped his daughter would marry someone better than an American ex-newsman working for the Vatican; but he knew how much Luciana loved her father and he wondered how he was going to break the news to her. She would blame him for her father's death and he would accept that blame: the scourge was at work again. He flicked out the lighter, put it in his pocket and went back up the steps.

Toohey, still standing in the shadows behind the door, said, 'What are you doing, parading around in front of *him*?'

'It doesn't matter,' said McBride. 'He recognised me last night.'

'You didn't tell us – '

'Would it have made you any happier if I had?'

'No,' said Ryan, and neither Toohey nor Smith contradicted him.

'None of you seems concerned about the death of Count Pericoli,' said the Pope. 'How is your conscience, Mr McBride? One innocent man dead – '

'Three,' said McBride, standing on the altar plinth; this was the place to talk of death. 'Two carabinieri are dead. I have a conscience about them, Holiness – you don't have to remind me. How did Count Pericoli die? What was he doing out here?'

Smith said nothing and Martin took it upon himself to explain the circumstances. Then he said, 'The carabinieri – how did they die?'

'They were murdered.' McBride looked at Smith. 'Did you see the guy who brought Luciana out here?'

'Only at a distance. We were down here when the taxi drove up the lane. I saw the chap run by here when he got away from the police. He was a stranger, I've never seen him before.'

'He's a stranger to us, too – though Turk saw him last night.' McBride briefly related the events of the past twelve hours at Carabinieri headquarters and at his apartment. Then he looked back at Martin. 'He's a German. He's come to Rome to kill you.'

'Me?' Martin's broad handsome face creased, he looked at McBride as if the latter had accused *him* of wanting to kill someone. 'Kill me? Why?'

'He said you murdered his father. He was in the SS, his father, I mean, a Sturmbannführer. You're supposed to have told lies – given evidence, I guess – and his father was executed. Would it have been at Nuremberg?'

Martin stood absolutely still for a long moment. Then slowly he nodded, trying to comprehend the complexities of time: the past and the present brought together here in this tiny church? Try as he might, would he ever really understand the ways of God? But he pleaded for forgiveness even as the doubt nibbled at his mind. Faith was his only strength.

'A man named Kessler, Wolfgang Kessler.' He glanced at Smith. 'The one I told you about.'

'The one who wanted the Jew?'

'Yes.' He shook his head dazedly. 'But I never knew he had a son. None of his family came to the trial – ' He put his hand up to his eyes; he wondered when his punishment was to stop for his lack of charity. *Forgive thine enemies* . . . But Kessler had been the Jew's enemy, that was what he had told himself at Nuremberg. 'Why has he waited so long?' He meant God, but the question included His instrument, Wolfgang Kessler's son.

'Are you afraid of him, Holiness?' asked Ryan.

Martin looked again at the Irishman, almost as if he were studying him. 'No. Not afraid of what he might do to me. But another death – mine, anyone's – does it help? They'll probably kill him too, when they catch him.'

'He didn't seem to care if they did,' said McBride.

'He's mad,' said Toohey, coming forward into the pool of light; it was no longer necessary to keep their identity hidden, they had all suddenly become victims of the same dilemma. 'He said he'd spent quite a while in the nut-house. Jesus, you're a real bloody complication, you know what I mean?'

'Take me back,' Martin said simply but without pleading: he wanted only to relieve them of the burden of himself.

McBride nodded, but the other three looked at each other. Then Smith said, 'No, we have to go through with it. They told us the money is still needed – '

'Who are *they*?' said the Pope. 'The IRA?'

Everyone's gaze snapped back to him; Ryan hissed in through his teeth. McBride said, 'You're guessing, Holiness.'

'Admittedly.' Martin knew he had hit the target. He sat down on one of the smaller wine casks, taking the weight off his swollen instep. 'I've suspected all along that there is someone other than just the four of you behind this whole thing. You are not a criminal, Mr McBride – you are a disappointment to me,

204

but you are not a criminal, you arc not in this for your own ends. So you must have some cause you believe in. You are a mixed lot – an American, an Australian, an Englishman – '

'You are wrong there!' Smith was unable to prevent the denial bursting out of him.

'You're not? Then why do you imitate an Englishman so much?' Though none of them, not even Martin himself, realised it, the Pope was in command: it was almost as if he were holding an audience.

Smith did not reply, because he had no other answer than that it was egotism, it set him apart from those he dealt with. Ryan looked at him and grinned, a mocking smile that made Smith want to smash his fist into the ex-boxer's already battered face.

'And an Irishman,' said Martin, and looked at Ryan. 'Are you the only true member of the IRA and the others were just hired for the occasion?'

'With all respect, Holiness,' said McBride, 'I think we had better not pursue the subject.'

'I think we should, Mr McBride. If you don't tell me the truth about yourselves, when you release me I shall offer the guess, as you call it, that I was kidnapped by an IRA gang.'

Smith had recovered his poise: he laughed, shook his head. 'All papal minds have something Machiavellian in them. But what if we decided to kill you?'

'That proves my guess was correct,' said Martin. 'What was the IRA intending to do with all that money?'

There was silence among the four men for a long moment. Then McBride said, 'You won't believe it, but it was intended to buy peace.'

'My life is a testament to believing the unprovable,' Martin said with a tired smile. 'Tell me about it, Mr McBride.'

McBride looked at the others and Smith said, 'What do we have to lose now?'

As briefly as possible McBride explained the strategy behind the attempt to steal the Vatican treasures. 'If things had gone as we had planned – '

'One might suspect the Lord's hand was involved in what

has gone wrong. But that would mean He had a reason for my being here.'

'Could we use you to help us get the money?' said Smith.

'*That* is a Machiavellian thought, Mr Brown.' The others glanced at Smith but made no comment on the name he had given the Pope. Martin saw the glances but he, too, refrained from any comment on the obvious pseudonym. 'Like any sane man, I pray for peace in Northern Ireland. But I can't take sides – a great deal of the feeling in that unhappy country stems from the hatred of the Papacy. Who is not to say that someone on the Protestant side would try to link me with the IRA, that it was not all a conspiracy on the part of Rome? That the kidnapping was not just a camouflage to hide a massive contribution by the Vatican to the IRA cause?' McBride shook his head and Martin said, 'Too bizarre, is that what you are thinking, Mr McBride? Nothing is bizarre if you look at history or even at today's headlines. We just go through a generation or two of peaceful dullness and we are lulled into thinking that is the norm. But it isn't, Mr McBride. Man, I'm afraid, does his best to travel the road to hell.'

'If we do get the money and we let you go unharmed,' said Ryan, 'will you let the world know where we came from?'

'You present me with a dilemma – '

'You should be used to those,' said Smith.

'I am, Mr Brown, indeed I am.' Martin smiled, but he looked suddenly exhausted. 'Even if the Protestants did not trumpet there had been a conspiracy between us, what would be the effect on the Church in Eire? You have support there, I don't doubt. But even the most ardent IRA priest must be troubled if he knew that you have gone to such lengths as to kidnap me. But again, if I am questioned by the police, do I lie about what I know?'

'The truth can always be bent, Holiness,' said McBride. 'The Church itself has been guilty of it in the past.'

'Don't remind us of our sins, Mr McBride. You will have to trust to my conscience when the moment comes. That's all I can promise you.'

McBride did not bother to look at the other three. 'That is good enough for me, Holiness.'

There was silence for a moment, then Ryan said, 'Me, too.'

McBride turned his head, looked at the other two. Toohey hesitated then nodded. McBride said, 'The majority gets it.'

'If he doublecrosses us,' said Smith, 'I want it on the record that my vote was against him.'

'I'll see there is a special press release,' said McBride with sour dryness. 'In the meantime we've got to get back to town, see how we collect the money this evening. It's not going to be easy, the Terminus is going to be crawling with cops.'

'What do we do with him downstairs?' Toohey nodded towards the vault.

'Another day down there won't harm him,' said Smith. 'He is with family.'

'You'd better not go back up to the villa,' said Ryan. 'Just in case the cops come back.'

'If Luciana is still with the police,' Smith said, 'we need someone else to collect the money.'

'Count me out,' said Toohey as the tall man looked at him. 'Every demon in Italy must be looking for me now.'

'And the Mafia and the Communists.' McBride had been amazed at what some of the newsmen had told him this morning when they had come individually to see him; as one of them had said sardonically, there were more stories on the kidnapping of the Pope coming from outside the Vatican than from in it. 'Everyone's trying to prove he didn't do it. Even the Black September gang have issued a denial.'

Toohey sagged under the invisible weight of those pursuing him. 'I'm dead, then.'

'Not necessarily,' said McBride, trying to be the leader again; somehow he had to keep hold of the reins or Christ knew what would happen. Only Christ knew what would happen anyway, he guessed. 'Seamus can come in with us – '

'Don't *nominate* me,' Smith interrupted: he recognised the challenge. 'I was just about to volunteer.'

'I'll need your gun if I'm gunna stay here,' said Toohey, and glanced at the Pope. 'I don't suppose I can trust you, can I?'

'That's up to you,' said Martin.

Toohey shook his head. 'It's too late for me to start trusting anyone now.'

'It'll be dark by the time we're back.' Ryan was accustomed to being left out of decisions; he occupied his mind with small matters. 'I'll go up to the villa and get some candles and food.'

'Better bring down everything you can,' said McBride. 'And be careful. Just in case that guy – Kessler? – comes back.'

'Do you want the gun?' Smith held it out.

Ryan hesitated, then shook his head. 'I'll take my chances. I agree with His Holiness – there's been enough killing. Yes.'

'He could kill you.'

'I'll take my chances,' Ryan repeated stubbornly; in the gloom his battered face looked bruised and pained. 'So far on this job I've killed nobody. If the police catch me, maybe they'll take that into account.'

'There is far too much pessimism around here,' said Smith.

McBride looked up and around the ruined church, down at the steps leading into the vault. 'It's the right atmosphere for it, isn't it? What else did you expect?'

'My dear chap – ' Smith was himself again. If this second phase of the operation should fail he was not going to concern himself with anyone else's fate: he would look out only for himself, was certain that he could dodge the Italian police and escape. He would go back to Eire, form his own group: it had been done before by others, there were always enough who believed in the truth of the gun and the bomb. Behind the languid façade ambition shook him for a moment: he saw himself as the new Leader: he suddenly wished for an Irish name, something to be in key with the music of names such as Rory O'Conner, Cathal Brugha. Smith was so mundane, so inescapably *English*. 'My dear chap, let's wait and see if the worst is going to happen. Don't let's talk ourselves into it. Let's borrow some of His Holiness's faith in the impossible. Perhaps he might even say a prayer that we can bring it off without anyone else getting hurt?'

'I shall pray for that,' said Martin.

Ryan nodded gratefully to the Pope. 'Thank you, Holiness,' he said, and went quickly out of the church.

He was back within ten minutes, loaded down like a pack mule. 'I brought everything like you said, just in case the cops do come back. There's your drill, Turk.'

'Thanks, mate.' The relationship between the Australian and the Irishman seemed suddenly to become something special; they talked to each other as if McBride and Smith were strangers to be ignored. 'You be careful when you go to get that dough this evening.'

Ryan smiled, stoking up his own morale. 'Everything will be all right, yes.'

For the past ten minutes McBride had been sitting on the top of the vault steps. He was staring down into the darkness there when he became aware of the Pope studying him. He looked up.

'Should I leave him down there?'

'If there are any thoughts after death, he is satisfied,' said Martin. He had said a prayer for the Count's soul, the verbal *viaticum* that one always hoped would be heard; Pericoli's sins, repented or not, were behind him and Martin prayed that the old man had found salvation. 'You must take care of his daughter.'

'He told you about her?' McBride couldn't keep the surprise out of his voice; he saw Smith turn, stand very still. 'Why did he mention her?'

'He didn't. But I put two and two together – your girl-friend *belongs* to that house, she knew all about it. She is his daughter, isn't she?'

'You seem to be getting to know all of us,' said Smith quietly.

'Perhaps not all your real names. But yes – I know you now.'

'Don't get any ideas, Smithy,' said Toohey. 'We're trusting him. You better do likewise.'

Smith held out the gun to him. 'You said it was too late for you to trust anyone.'

Toohey took the gun, looked at the Pope. 'Don't make me prove him right.'

'I promise,' said Martin; then, as McBride, Smith and Ryan prepared to leave, 'Good luck.'

McBride marvelled at the fantasy, or the nightmare, in which they were all involved; but he just nodded matter-of-factly. 'You should be back in the Vatican by nine o'clock at the latest.'

'I shall look forward to it.' Martin suddenly raised his hand, held it in front of his face for a moment as if debating whether to go ahead with the thought in his mind, then he gave them a blessing. He saw the looks on the faces of the three men at the door. 'That is not a satirical gesture.'

'It never crossed my mind that it might be.' McBride paused as he was about to go out the door, looked back at Toohey. 'If that guy Kessler comes back – '

'Don't worry, mate. I'll use the gun on *him*, no risk.' Toohey looked at Martin. 'You'll have to let *my* conscience worry about that.'

2

General della Porta was in one of his moods that were famous and feared in headquarters. The first editions of the afternoon papers had arrived and his subordinates had not been able to keep them from him. The editorials, he thought, all read as if they had been written by Communists or underground radicals from the universities; another Mussolini was needed to keep these character assassins in their place. The editorial writers, smug and safe in their office chairs, ensconced behind the barricades of their typewriters, all but blamed him personally for having allowed the Pope to be kidnapped. He was *not* symptomatic of the decay in Italian bureaucracy and when this business was over he would look for ways of suing the newspapers and their hatchet men.

It was his fiery mood that prompted him to send for Luciana Pericoli when the hourly report, brought in by his secretary, told him she had been picked up by two carabinieri after being kidnapped. Normally he would never have bothered with such a matter; this afternoon he trusted no one else to do a job properly. There was also the hope that through her he might get some insight into Fergus McBride. There was something about the American that wasn't quite right, an attitude towards the kidnapping of the Pope that was not as clear-cut as one would have expected from a man in his position. He did not suspect McBride of being involved with the kidnapping, but there was something about the man that hinted he knew more than he was telling. Though that, of course, might only be part of the Vatican mentality.

When Luciana was brought into his office he was surprised at the beauty of her; at once his mood became a little more agreeable. She was still pale and strained from her experience with Kessler, but she had the sort of looks that were rarely seen around Carabinieri headquarters. She sat down in the chair that della Porta's aide offered her; and the General, a secret monarchist, found himself admiring her aristocratic composure. He was not to know that Luciana, frightened, bewildered, had unconsciously fallen into an imitation of her father, who had always made a conscious effort to appear an aristocrat.

'That will be all, Alfredo. Wait outside.'

'But, General, I thought I'd take notes – ' The aide, too, wanted to savour the presence of this beautiful girl; but he recognised the warning flush in the General's face. 'Yes, sir. Call me when you need me.'

When the door closed on his aide's back, della Porta smiled. 'You have had quite an effect on my young lieutenant, Signorina Pericoli. Signor McBride is a very lucky man.'

Luciana's voice was low, coming out of a throat almost paralysed by apprehension. 'How do you know – ?'

'I talked with him this morning. I understand he – forgive my bluntness, signorina – spent the night with you the night before last.'

'Yes.' She was wary: how much did the General know, what had Fergus told him?

'Last night, too?'

Still frightened, she decided to attack: 'Am I here on some sort of morals charge, General?'

'No, no. Forgive me – ' He stroked his moustache with his knuckle, glanced at the one-page file to which the report on the kidnapping was clipped. The girl had him puzzled. She was obviously still upset from her experience with the man who had kidnapped her; but she was also afraid of *him*. A girl in her position, of her background, normally would be arrogantly indifferent towards a policeman, even someone of his own rank. Particularly a girl who, according to the file, had been arrested for radical demonstrations at the university. 'We shouldn't be talking at all about Signor McBride. This other man, the one who kidnapped you – who was he?'

'I had never seen him before.'

'What did he look like?'

He was imprinted indelibly on her memory; yet the details of him were blurred. 'Tall. Thin. I don't know – sort of nondescript, sad-looking. He wore gold-rimmed glasses and a cheap old overcoat.'

'It could be a dozen men. But you'd recognise him if you saw him again?'

'Of course.' She was sure of that: the *atmosphere* of him would always be recognisable.

'Where did he abduct you?'

'Abduct?' It was a word that puzzled her for a moment; was it not only children who were abducted? She was still trying to force the events of the last hour and a half into a framework of reality; her mind was a jumble of refracted impressions, like a broken mirror. 'You mean where did he pick me up?'

'Yes.' Della Porta sounded as if he was trying to put her at ease; but he was watching her closely. 'I hesitated to use that phrase – it suggests immorality to an older man such as myself.'

She was not so afraid that she missed the small point he was trying to score; his needling somehow gave her a little confidence. She liked men; but not those who tried to score off her. 'He picked me up just outside the entrance to Signor McBride's apartment building. He – he was standing in the entrance hall as I went to go in.'

'Did he tell you why he was there?'

'We – we hardly spoke. He was a German – he didn't seem to have any Italian.' She was suffering from having been too truthful all her life; she had no experience of how one lie led to the next; she groped her way down a path of invention like a blind girl. 'I – I know nothing about him, General, nothing!'

'Please – don't be upset.' Della Porta poured a glass of water from the decanter on his desk, handed it across to her. 'I am only trying to help – not just you but perhaps some other young girls. Who knows? The man may already be looking for another girl like yourself. Forgive me asking – but did he try to molest you?'

She drank from the glass, put it back on the desk. 'No.'

'Were you going to see Signor McBride?'

'Yes.'

'To tell him what you had decided?'

She stared at him, hardly seeing him. What did he mean by that question? Suddenly cunning, she said, 'Yes.'

'What did you tell him?'

'I didn't get to see him, General. The German prevented that.'

Your point, della Porta conceded: this girl is shrewd. 'You didn't spend last night with Signor McBride?'

'I'm afraid that is between him and me. I repeat, General – am I here on some morals charge?'

Della Porta ignored the question, glad that he had dismissed his aide from the room. He got up, pulling his tunic down around his hips, began to walk slowly about the room. Perhaps he should do more exercise; he would start a programme as soon as he had the Pope back in the Vatican. 'You said the man who kidnapped you was a German. Did he say anything about the Pope?'

What was she to tell him? If she told him of the German's intention, could they catch him before he killed the Pope? But would that lead them to the Pope and then to Fergus? Her head ached with the effort to stay alert, to be ready for every pitfall her own words could lead her into. Lying was such hard work, she couldn't understand why some people made a career of it.

'I told you, General – we hardly spoke.'

'We have tried to get in touch with your father.' He was moving around, physically and verbally, trying to catch her off-balance; she was hiding something, she knew more about the man who had kidnapped her than she was admitting. 'To tell him of your terrible experience. But he isn't at home.'

'Perhaps he has just gone for a walk – he sometimes does so in the afternoons.'

Della Porta shook his head, came round in front of her. 'He went out just before lunch, your housekeeper told my men. He said nothing to her, just walked out of the apartment, as if

213

on the spur of the moment. Does he often act that way?'

Puzzled, suddenly worried for no reason she could name, she said, 'No, that's not like Papa. He is a very deliberate man. Unless it was some unexpected business – he had some Americans to dinner last night – no, not last night – ' She had lost track of time. Abruptly she was as worried for her father as she was for Fergus. Surely he, too, wasn't somehow connected with this terrible mess? 'The night before.'

'The night Signor McBride spent at your place?'

He had made a mistake there, because she said at once, 'Why do you keep going back to that? You should be concerned with the German – he may be out now trying to abduct another girl.'

'Of course.' He had to admire her; she was almost as good as a professional witness. He was enjoying the questioning, as a professional; it was almost like the old days as a captain, when there had been none better than himself at getting information from a suspect. 'Before the German put you in a taxi, did he take you across the street to look at a motor scooter?'

'Why should he do that?'

He decided to lay a card or two on the table: 'Two of our officers were shot last night, one of them right here in headquarters, the other not more than two hundred metres down from the square outside. A motor scooter was stolen from outside an apartment building near here and it was found this afternoon in a street just across from Signor McBride's apartment.'

'I don't see the connection – '

'There may be none. But coincidences are often a policeman's only aid. Two of my men are shot here, a motor scooter is stolen from across the street, the same scooter turns up opposite Signor McBride's apartment, a strange German kidnaps you in the entrance hall to the apartment building – '

'Are you suggesting the man has something to do with Signor McBride?'

'I am suggesting – ' The thought had only just occurred to him; to her he looked confident, but he was grasping at any random clue that presented itself. 'I am suggesting that perhaps the German was after Signor McBride, but for some reason took you instead.'

214

'Why should he want Fergus?' She was losing control now: she used McBride's given name, made this interrogation too personal. 'A perfect stranger – ?'

'He has been working with the Pope, he is the one who has been conducting the press conferences on *that* kidnapping – ' He had to keep the excitement out of his voice; he was still blundering blindly but he could see a gleam of light. 'The German could have the Pope, he could want Signor McBride to be the go-between – '

He suddenly shut up: excitement was making his tongue too loose. He walked to the window, looked down into the street for a moment's distraction while he calmed himself. A carabiniere, helmet off, straddled a motor cycle at the opposite kerb, flirting with a young girl; he'd have the fellow up before one of the disciplinary officers tomorrow. He turned back into the room, saw the girl was watching him carefully, poised on the edge of her chair as if ready to run. Run where? 'Why did you go out to the Villa Pericoli? The taxi driver said *you* gave the directions, not the German.' He looked at the report again: the sergeant who had interviewed the driver had been thorough. 'The driver said that the German did not speak at all.'

She was fencing herself in with a picket of lies. Honesty *was* the best policy; but she realised now that whoever had said that must have been some hypocrite who had made a profit out of honesty. She wasn't looking for a profit: to go back to the circumstances of a week or two ago was all that she wanted for Fergus and herself. 'It – it was the first place I thought of. He said we had – had to get out of Rome. Somewhere quiet, where no one would find us.' The lies came easily once she had started; invention lay on her tongue like another language. 'I hoped I could give a message to the taxi driver before he dropped us off, that he would come back and tell the police – '

She is lying: he was too familiar with the country of deceit not to recognise the landmarks. He had already given orders that the Villa Pericoli was to be searched, though he had no idea what, if anything, might be found there. But all he said was, 'You were fortunate he was able to get in touch with my men so soon. Someone saw him lying in the gutter just after the taxi was driven away – they rang the police – ' He went back behind his desk, pressed a buzzer and at once the aide opened the door from the outer office. 'Telephone Signor McBride and ask him to come and pick up – ' he smiled apologetically at Luciana ' – Signorina Pericoli. Try his apartment first. If he is not there, try his office.'

The aide went out and Luciana stood up hurriedly. 'Please, there is no need to bother him. He will be busy – I can go home on my own – '

'Signor McBride would never forgive me for not calling him. He is very considerate of you, signorina. He paid you the highest compliment – he said he was a one-woman man. When a man feels like that, he would *want* to be here with you after the experience you have been through.'

She hesitated, then sat down again. 'He is a very good man. We are going to be married.'

'Was that the decision you had made when you were on your way to see him?'

Another lie: but no, it would be the truth when she next saw Fergus. 'Yes.'

'I repeat, he is a very fortunate man. I must congratulate him when he comes. Are you still interested in radical politics?'

The question was so unexpected that at first she wasn't sure he had asked it. 'I don't understand, General – '

'You were arrested while you were at university – ' He flipped open the file, flipped it shut again; his interest seemed only casual, almost as if he was just making conversation. 'I see no charges were pressed.'

'My father intervened.' She had recovered a little. 'No, I am no longer interested in politics. I gave up the struggle – Italian men don't think women should move out of the home.'

'And American men?'

'Signor McBride and I never discuss politics.'

They said nothing further, just sat and watched each other with cautious politeness, like enemies who knew they must keep up appearances because, for better or worse, they were on the same side. Then the aide came back.

'I am sorry, General. There is no answer from Signor McBride's apartment. And his office says they expected him back there half an hour ago, but so far he hasn't appeared.'

Della Porta looked at Luciana. 'Perhaps I had better send some men to the apartment, just in case.'

'Just in case what?' But already the picture was forming in her mind, she felt sick and wondered if she was about to faint.

He said with gentle ruthlessness, watching her carefully, 'In case the German has already paid a return visit.'

3

As the elevator lurched to a halt on the fourth floor McBride heard the phone ringing in his apartment. He wrenched open the elevator doors, but by the time he had opened the apartment front door the phone had stopped ringing.

'There is nothing so annoying as the phone that stops ringing just as you are within sight of it,' said Smith.

'It should never have been invented,' said Ryan, but did not have time to give his reasons.

'Signor McBride!' Signora Ferragamo came rolling up the stairs. 'A moment, signore – '

McBride jerked his head and Smith and Ryan slipped quickly into the apartment. 'Can't it wait, signora? I have business – '

'Only a moment, signore!' She arrived on the fourth floor, leaned against the wall. She fanned her face with a sheet of paper, then held it out. 'A petition. To the police.'

'The police?' Behind him he thought he heard Smith laugh.

'Yes, signore. We want the prostitutes moved from our doorstep.'

'Signora, the girls do no harm – '

The phone rang again, kept ringing. Signora Ferragamo cocked an ear, tried to squint past him into the apartment. 'Your telephone, signore – why don't your friends answer it?'

'They don't speak Italian,' said McBride, and stepped into the apartment. 'I'll have a word with the girls, signora. But no petition. We must show Christian charity.'

He closed the door in her face, moved across to the phone. It was O'Hara. 'Fergus? Where the hell have you been, man? Everyone is looking for you – the police, Monsignor Lupi, half a dozen bishops from the Synod, McEvoy from *The Times*. Where the hell have you been, man?'

'Sorry. I – I've been trying to get in touch with my girl. We've had a little trouble – '

'Join the priesthood, Fergus – it saves you all that wear and tear.' O'Hara was a man who could do without women, a true misogynist: nuns were a bane, the canonisation of women an aberration on the part of the Church, and it took a conscious effort for him to remember the Virgin Mary in his prayers. 'When will you be coming back to the office?'

'I'll be there in half an hour. Pat – ?' He was almost afraid to ask the question. 'What did the police want?'

'I don't know. But the call came from the top man's office – he said he was General della Porta's aide. You're in demand.'

McBride hung up, turned to Smith and Ryan. 'Della Porta himself must be questioning Luciana.'

Ryan punched a fist into an open palm, then reversed the hands and did it again; he was like a nervous boxer just before a bout was to begin, one he was afraid of losing. 'God knows what she is telling them!'

'There's no reason to suppose she's telling them any more than Turk did!' McBride felt a sudden fierce loyalty to Luciana; and, he realised, a deeper love for her than he had felt at any time since they had met. 'If she had told them anything, they wouldn't be phoning me – they'd be here to pick me up!'

'A point,' Smith conceded. 'Nevertheless, I have no faith in the ability of women to keep a secret.'

'Another misogynist. You should join O'Hara in the Jesuits.' Smith raised an eyebrow at the suggestion, but made no comment. McBride went on, 'The real point is – do we go through with the plan to pick up the money? If della Porta is going to have the Terminus packed this evening with plain-clothes cops, our chances are going to be about one in a hundred of getting away with it.'

'We always knew the odds would be against us,' said Smith.

'Sure – but not like this. The idea was to threaten to destroy those treasures if the Vatican told the cops – and I think they'd have kept quiet, just to get them back.'

'Maybe we should ring Dublin,' said Ryan.

'No.' It was the first time that Smith and McBride had agreed at once on anything; they looked at each other almost in surprise. Then McBride said, 'They're too far away to make the decision for us.'

'Why should we keep running to them all the time?' said Smith. 'If the money is going to be there this evening to be collected, then I am certainly going to be there to pick it up. I shall have to dye my hair – ' He looked at himself in the mirror on the wall. 'A pity. It may take *months* to grow out.'

'Des can go out and buy you a wig – there's a shop down the Via Sistina. And you can wear your glasses,' McBride added maliciously; he knew that Smith needed glasses but never wore them in public. 'Nobody is going to be looking at you this evening.'

'One hopes not. So Des and I go ahead as planned, only I take the place of the women, the Fitzgibbon woman or your girl-friend.' He added his own touch of malice: 'We never really needed her in the first place.'

The phone rang again. Apprehensive, McBride picked it up. 'Yes?'

'Herr McBride?'

'Kessler?'

There was a moment's silence, then. 'Where did you get that name?'

Smith had gone through into the bedroom, picked up the extension there. Through the doorway McBride could see the tall man shaking his head at the stupid mention of Kessler's name. Awkwardly, he hedged: 'I did a check on you – '

'I do not believe that, Herr McBride. You have seen the Pope since I saw you – *he* gave you my name.'

'How would he know who you are?'

'His conscience wouldn't allow him to forget my father's name. He is an intelligent man – when you told him that I am going to kill him, he would have guessed who I am – '

'He didn't even know you existed.' There was no point in denying that he had seen the Pope. 'What the hell do you want now, Kessler? My girl is still with the police – she will be telling them all about you – '

219

'I doubt it. If she tells them all about me, she will have to tell them all about you.'

Crazy, like a fox. 'Okay, what do you want?'

'I want Kurt Stecher. You will take me to him or deliver him to me by ten o'clock tonight, or I shall kill all of you. Beginning with Signorina Pericoli.'

McBride, weightless, head aching, abruptly adrift again in the nightmare that was recurring too frequently now, looked through the bedroom doorway at Smith. The latter stared at him for a moment, then spoke into the extension. 'You will have the Pope, Herr Kessler. How shall we contact you?'

'I do not know who you are, but you sound a sensible man. Do not worry, I shall be in touch with you. *Auf wiedersehn.*'

The phone went dead and McBride, stiff as a puppet, put it back in its cradle. Smith came through from the bedroom. 'No one is going to be killed if we can possibly avoid it. Especially none of us.'

'How do we avoid it?' asked McBride as Ryan looked uncomprehendingly at both of them.

'As soon as we collect the money this evening we take the Pope and we all head north. We'll need a large car, so Des can rent one. We'll stay off the autostrada, leave the car in Milan, rent another to take across into France.'

'Will you be with Des? Because I'm not going – I have to stay here. For appearances' sake.' And for Luciana's sake: he wasn't going to leave her alone to be murdered by Kessler.

'I'll have to leave Des and Toohey at Milan. Once we have the money, then it becomes my only concern, to get it to Beirut. Des and Toohey can leave the Pope tied up somewhere where he won't be found till they've phoned the police and told them. It will be up to them to choose their own spot for that.'

'What about Kessler?' asked Ryan. 'Is he trying to kill *us*?'

McBride nodded. 'All of us, beginning with Luciana.'

'She's your concern, I'm afraid,' said Smith off-handedly, and went back into the bedroom. He returned with a medium-sized suitcase. 'You're sure this is an exact match for the one Arcadipane will be carrying?'

'I bought it in the same store – they sell them by the dozen.' McBride was taking time to recover from Kessler's phone call; he was half-buried in an avalanche of exhaustion. 'It will be the same as Arcadipane will have.'

Smith went to the sideboard, opened it and began to take out the stacks of small cosmetic boxes that were on the shelves. He packed them into the suitcase, closed it and lifted it. 'Won't the money weigh more than this?'

'Just a pound or two. If they do as we've told them, bring the money in thousand-mark bills, there'll be fifteen thousand bills. They'll fit in there and weigh roughly twelve kilos.'

'I hope Arcadipane can carry his bag,' said Ryan. 'He doesn't look strong enough to piss downwind without wetting his shoes.'

'Perhaps we should have chosen another go-between,' said Smith. 'One of the cardinals?'

'If it means getting his Pope back,' said McBride tartly, 'Arcadipane will carry two or three times that weight.'

'Perhaps we should have raised the stakes,' said Smith. 'Enough to have outfitted an army in case our peace policy doesn't work.'

Then the doorbell rang. The three men looked at each other; then Smith, carrying the suitcase, and Ryan went quickly into the bedroom and closed the door. McBride, ready to face Signora Ferragamo again, crossed to the front door and opened it. Two carabinieri stood there.

'Signor McBride? General della Porta's compliments and he wishes you to accompany us to headquarters.'

4

'Signor McBride, I am relieved to see you are safe. Signorina Pericoli and I have been worried – '

McBride embraced Luciana, kissed her cheek, tried to tell her without words that he loved her more now than ever before. But the circumstances kept his mouth shut, which was just as well: he wasn't sure that any woman wanted to be told that at one time she might have been only half-loved. 'You're okay? The carabinieri told me what happened. He didn't hurt you?'

Luciana shook her head, buried her face against his chest and began to weep, letting go all the fear and tension of the past two hours in a flood of relief. He pressed her shoulders, gave her his handkerchief, looked over her head at della Porta. 'May I take her home now, General?'

'Just a few minutes, please.' Della Porta pushed forward two chairs, sent his aide out for coffee. He waited till McBride and Luciana, their chairs close together, were seated. 'I shan't keep you longer than I have to, signore. The signorina has some good news for you.'

Even Luciana, drying her eyes, looked up in puzzlement. McBride, convinced there was no good news left in the world, said, 'What's that, General?'

'Tell him,' said della Porta, beaming at Luciana like a uniformed official uncle. 'Tell him your decision.'

'Here?' Luciana had recovered; she folded McBride's handkerchief and gave it back to him. 'Thank you, General, but I think that is something to tell him in private.'

The tone of her voice, the confidence in it, all at once told McBride that she had held her own in this office with della Porta. He looked at the Carabinieri chief and saw that the latter, with a slight smile, acknowledged a worthy opponent. But he didn't like the sight of the General's knuckle stroking his moustache.

The aide came back with three cups of coffee; della Porta almost succeeded in turning the interview into a social occasion. He went back behind his desk, sipped his coffee, nodded appreciatively and said, 'Signore, has it occurred to you that the German who kidnapped the signorina might have been looking for you as a go-between in the kidnapping of the Pope?'

'No.' McBride sipped his own coffee, only reminded now that he had had nothing today but just another cup of coffee at his office first thing this morning. His stomach was tight with nerves, but pretty soon he was going to have to eat something. 'But it could be.'

'Then you agree it is possible?' Della Porta nodded as if it would have made no difference to him whether McBride agreed with him or not. 'All along I have thought the kidnapping was planned by someone with a working knowledge of the Vatican – an inside job. Signorina Pericoli's German could be a German-speaking Swiss, an ex-member of the Guards – such a man would know exactly the routine of the palace. There have been one or two malcontents in the Guards in the past – several years ago one of them who had been dismissed came back and tried to murder the commander.'

'That could be.' McBride was cautious; would this offer some sort of way out? 'But why would he choose me as go-between? If he had worked at the Vatican, wouldn't he be afraid that I'd recognise him?'

'Possibly.' It was a point della Porta had failed to think of; he, too, was almost exhausted. But no concession showed in his face; his façade was as durable as that of the building in which he sat. 'But perhaps he had no intention of showing himself to you. He took Signorina Pericoli – she was very fortunate that my men rescued her from him – as his insurance that you would do whatever he asked. He could come back to you – which is what the signorina and I were afraid of.'

He's already been back, at least by phone. 'What do you want me to do?'

'Do whatever he asks. But let me know at once. We shall take it from there.'

'Do I let the cardinals know too?'

'Naturally,' said della Porta, but without any enthusiasm; it was obvious he thought clerics were better left out of police affairs. 'But talk to me first.'

'Naturally,' said McBride, and stood up. 'Now I'll take Signorina Pericoli home.'

'I'll post a guard on her apartment, just in case.'

'For how long?' Luciana had taken McBride's hand; he could feel her fingers clutching at his. 'It will upset my father.'

'Only till this whole dreadful business is over.' Della Porta's eyes had flickered to the clasped hands for just an instant: what was worrying these two? 'Till we have the Pope safely back in the Vatican and we have captured the gangsters who have taken him. And, of course, the German.'

A police car took them back to the Pericoli apartment. McBride, faced now with the task of telling her of her father's death, sat silently beside Luciana in the back seat, still holding her hand and just nodding when she made any comment. After a while she noticed his silence and said no more.

A carabiniere, a middle-aged man with coarse blunt features and a crisp no-nonsense air about him, accompanied them up to the apartment. He asked for a chair, set it down outside the front door as if planting a standard, took off his cap and sat down. 'You will be safe, signorina. I promise.'

'I'm sure I shall,' said Luciana, closed the door and turned to McBride. 'Darling, what is it? You are so quiet – '

McBride let her farther into the apartment. Fortunately the cook-housekeeper was out somewhere; they had the place to themselves. He took her into the shabby, high-ceilinged salon that still had echoes of the past grandeur of the family: the big shield with its coat of arms hung on one wall; the heavy velvet drapes that looked like sculptured dust; the huge gilt-framed mirrors that stared at each other across the room, each reflecting the other into infinity, like a view down a long corridor into a past that no longer had any meaning. They sat down on a couch, the velvet dry and irritating beneath them, and she gazed steadily at him, knowing his news was going to be bad.

But she was still not prepared for what he told her. She stared at him in frozen disbelief, then she began slowly to shake her head like a clockwork doll whose motor could not be stopped. McBride was not an unsympathetic man but he had no way of dealing with grief; he remembered how helpless he had been when his mother had learned of his father's death. He put out an awkward hand, but he could have been warding off something as much as trying to comfort.

'I'm sorry, honey. I don't know why he was out there at the villa – '

'We are being punished for our sins.' Her voice, too, was that of a clockwork doll: flat, thin and harsh.

He nodded: the old sense of guilt linked them like a wedding ring. 'It will all be over in a few hours.'

She shook her head, emphatically this time. 'It will never be over. Those men will come and ask you again to help them.'

'No!' His own shake of the head was just as emphatic.

224

She got up, began to walk about the room, stiff-leggedly, aimlessly. She touched pieces of furniture, as if looking for some sign of her father; she looked into one of the mirrors, searching for the ghost of him, but he was already gone from her down that long corridor of the past. 'I want him brought back here.'

'Not yet,' he said gently. 'It isn't possible.'

'Does the Pope know who he is? Who we all are?'

'He knows who your father was. And who we are – not all our names, but he knows we're working for the IRA.'

'The Pope is with him?' She seemed unconcerned at the news of their identification. McBride nodded in answer to her question and she seemed satisfied, as if that were the final guarantee that no more harm could come to her father. 'All right. I shall stay here. Bring him back with you tonight.'

'Don't say anything to Isolina.' The cook would have the news all through the other apartments within minutes.

'You are safe from now on?'

He wondered at that, but all he said was, 'Yes. At least till we bring the Pope back. There is nothing more I have to do. Smith and Des are picking up the money.'

'I am still praying for a miracle.'

'Do that.' He kissed her and left her, letting himself out of the apartment, telling the carabiniere not to disturb her.

'She will be safe, signore.'

He took his time about going across the river to his office. He walked through the city, needing to be alone to adjust himself to the hours that lay ahead. He was no longer interested in the original game; he would never see the money and he never wanted to see or hear from the men in Dublin again. But the safe return of the Pope had to be accomplished: that had become, if you liked, his vocation. But tomorrow? Tomorrow was gone from the calendar of his life. Like Luciana, he wanted to pray for a miracle of some sort, but he was devoid of faith.

He crossed the river, skirted the Castel Sant' Angelo. Maybe he should go in there, lock himself in: it was an ideal place for a siege. Cagliostro had been imprisoned there and maybe the ghost of the alchemist could conjure up some potion that would solve everything. With the wryness of the utterly despairing man, he raised his hand and saluted the dead necromancer; a passing priest, mistaking the gesture, nodded in reply and said, 'Thank you, my son.' McBride grinned, suddenly feeling better for no other reason than that he couldn't feel worse.

When he reached the Porta di Santa Anna two security guards barred his way until they recognised him; then they waved him through perfunctorily, as if disappointed that he was friend and not foe. He was aware of the changed atmosphere in the courtyards: no one laughed, everyone had an air of urgency about him, almost of desperation. Though no one had yet confessed it, the thought was beginning to take hold that perhaps God was not going to guarantee the safe return of His Vicar.

As McBride went into his office O'Hara came in after him. 'The D-G has called me a couple of times to ask if you're still working here – he's in one of his Italian moods.'

'It figures,' said McBride. 'He's Italian.'

O'Hara made no apology for his prejudice. 'Where have you been?'

'With the police. My girl was kidnapped today.'

'You're joking! Fergus, this is no time – ' Then he stopped and looked carefully at the American. 'No, you're not joking. Holy God, what's the world coming to?'

McBride told him the bald facts of Luciana's kidnapping, careful not to let drop any more than he was supposed to have been told himself. 'But she's safe now. Any more on the Pope?'

'Nothing.' O'Hara slumped in a chair. 'I handled some Synod inquiries for you while you were out. They're going on with their meetings. A sense of continuity, all that sort of stuff – they've got to set an example, one of them told me. That's all very well, but in the meantime I'm only thinking of Martin. Jesus, I never realised how much I love that man! He's got to come back – we need him!'

'He will, Pat. Just keep praying.' He looked at his watch: the hours had to be filled in till it was time to drive out and collect Martin. 'What work is there?'

O'Hara, sunk in depression, roused himself. 'It's all there

on your desk – about three dozen requests for interviews with yourself. They've just discovered the Pope called you in for a special meeting with him the evening before last and they want to know what it was all about.'

'I'm too bushed to face them all, Pat. Put them off till tomorrow, if you can.'

O'Hara, on his feet, paused. 'What *did* he want to see you about, Fergus?'

'He wanted to know if I'd accept a papal knighthood.'

'Bull,' said O'Hara. 'You'll tell me in your own good time, is that what you mean?'

'When the Pope comes back.'

O'Hara was still stiffly poised, as if reluctant to go. 'Do you think he *will* come back?'

'Yes.'

'I've racked my brains trying to think who would do a thing like this. It's got to be some gang of heretical scoundrels, in it just for the money. All the political groups have denied anything to do with it.'

'All of them?'

'Every last one of them, even groups I'd never heard of. The latest one to come out is the IRA, though I don't think anyone would ever have suspected them. Holy Jesus, I'd renounce my Irish citizenship if it was them! Even the fanatics in the Six Counties wouldn't try something like this. No, it's got to be some black-hearted buggers just like those old-time pirates. And if it's them, we've got to be prepared for the worst!'

O'Hara went out and McBride turned his attention to what lay on his desk. Memos, letters, clippings were scattered like a drift of leaves; Maria, his secretary, was a girl who had only contempt for neatness. Today he didn't mind; sorting out the papers gave him something to do. He scrawled answers to some of the letters, read the clippings, initialled the memos. Somehow the time went by, crawling slowly round the dial on his watch like a dying insect. His phone rang several times and he answered it automatically: this phone was not dangerous, not like the one in the apartment, which had become wired only for bad news.

Then at six o'clock the phone rang again. He reached for it, wondering which newsman it would be this time: some of the questions he had been asked in the past hour made him wonder if Vatican correspondents ever bothered to do any of their own legwork. Weariness and worry had made him irritable and he snapped into the phone, 'Yes? What is it?'

Cardinal Moroni, coughing his lungs out over the line, said, 'Signor McBride? Could you come over to my office at once, without delay. There has been a change of plans in the delivery of the ransom money.'

5

Heinrich Kessler sat in the café bar on the Piazza del Popolo, drinking his third cup of coffee and eating his third salami roll. Hunger normally never troubled him, his stomach had long ago stopped making demands on him; he could still subsist on rations no greater than those they had given him in the asylum during and just after the war. But the excitement of the day had drained him of the nervous energy that usually kept him going. He ate and drank ravenously now, knowing the excitement for the day was not yet over. He sat in the back of the bar, oblivious of the mid-afternoon loafers arguing lethargically over their *Espressi*, and munched away determinedly. The waiter looked at him curiously when he brought him his third order, but Kessler was oblivious of him too.

He was disappointed he had not caught up with Kurt Stecher; but he knew the meeting was inevitable. He had been surprised at how he had felt when he had finally pulled up after evading the carabinieri who had chased him across the fields; he had not felt such exhilaration since he had been a child. The thrill had been almost sexual; he felt ashamed that he was beginning to enjoy this part of the search for Stecher. Somehow it cheapened the purpose of his trip to Rome.

He paid for his meal, went out and stood in the sunlight in the square. The waiter came to the door of the bar and looked after him; for the first time he noticed the waiter's interest in himself. He looked down, wondering what made him conspicuous. The shabby overcoat, streaked with mud where he had fallen when running across the fields? He had no interest in clothes, wore them only because they were necessary for warmth and modesty. But now he recognised that they could also be a disguise.

He walked back towards the centre of the city, looking at the men he passed, trying to see himself among them. He passed a cheap leathergoods store and when something in the window caught his eye he went in and bought it: an imitation-leather briefcase. He came out of the store, moved into a doorway and transferred the gun, silencer and the box of bullets from his overcoat pockets to the briefcase. He took off his overcoat, rolled it in a bundle and dropped it behind the door of the entry where he stood. Then he went on, found a menswear store and turned in. He bought a cheap dark raincoat and a hat, put them on and wore them out of the shop.

He paused in the doorway and looked at himself in a mirror; he smiled with innocent pleasure at his reflection, hardly recognising himself. He took off his gold-rimmed glasses and put them in his pocket. He had to squint to see anything at a distance, but when he looked into the mirror again the man he saw there was a stranger.

He went on along the street, anonymous now in the crowd coming out for its afternoon shopping, the instrument of death bulging slightly in the briefcase tucked under his arm. His step was lighter, almost jaunty, and he was smiling quietly to himself. He looked like a minor bureaucrat who had just been told of a promotion.

6

At 5.48 p.m. Greenwich time, 6.48 p.m. Rome time on that evening a message was received in London. It read:

To: Head of Special Branch, Scotland Yard.

From: Superintendent Laurie, Belfast.

Message: Following your instructions have checked all movements of all known IRA personnel in Ulster stop Only IRA person apprehended exiting Ulster is Mrs Maire Fitzgibbon held crossing border into Eire stop

Refuses answer questions stop However Roman Catholic priest name withheld by request informs recent rumours something big to be attempted on Continent no exact location known stop Priest previously sympathetic to IRA suggests IRA could be involved Pope kidnapping stop Checking now further contacts stop Significant coincidence American citizen Fergus McBride Vatican press officer son of Joseph McBride IRA agent killed in Dunlaven power station raid November 1956 stop No record Fergus McBride IRA sympathies or activities but male relatives United States Boston area known members of Clan na Gael stop Suggest contact Rome police check Fergus McBride message ends

The message landed on the desk of the duty Superintendent at 5.57 p.m. He studied it for several minutes, then rang the office of the Assistant Commissioner in charge of Special Branch.

'I'm sorry, Superintendent,' said the A.C's secretary. 'He is with the Commissioner. I'll have him ring you back.'

At 6.18 p.m. the Assistant Commissioner phoned. 'What's the trouble, Innes?'

The Superintendent read out the message. 'It might be the IRA who have pulled this job, sir. But it could also be the Loyalist bunch – it wouldn't be the first time each has tried to frame the other.'

'I hope it's neither of them. We – I mean the Government – are having enough trouble trying to handle things in Ulster. If either side has kidnapped the Pope, we're sure of getting at least fifty per cent of world opinion against us for not solving the Ulster problem. There are always going to be two losers in Northern Ireland and we have to be one of them, no matter who wins.'

'I think we must take the risk, sir. There may be no connection at all between this man McBride and the IRA.'

'I was only thinking out aloud – I wasn't suggesting the information shouldn't be passed on.'

'Sorry, sir. It's a ticklish one.'

'A nice understatement. I sometimes think you Scots are worse than we Sassenachs when you've been south of the border a few years. Send the information on to the Italians and let us pray the IRA have nothing to do with this business.'

A message regarding Fergus McBride went off to Rome at 6.28 p.m. Greenwich time. It was in English, translation being left to the foreigners at the receiving end.

8

'I am truly sorry,' said Monsignor Arcadipane. 'But I am sick –
I have been vomiting all day. Nerves.'

'We understand,' said Cardinal Moroni.

'I am letting His Holiness down, I shall never forgive
myself. But I know I should not be able to follow all the
instructions once I got to the Terminus. I didn't sleep at all
last night – ' Arcadipane beat his breast, dropped his head. 'I
am truly sorry, Eminence.'

'We understand,' said Moroni, and looked at the other three
cardinals and della Porta. 'One of us must take the money.'

'With all respect,' said della Porta, 'how are we to know
that the kidnappers will recognise any of you? If it is an inside
job, certainly they will know you. But if it is not – '

'Whom do you suggest, then?' Cardinal Fellari had no wish
to be the courier.

'Signor McBride,' said della Porta, and turned to McBride.
'You are known to the German – you may be doing exactly
what he was intending to ask you when he kidnapped Signorina
Pericoli.'

'That's just a wild guess! You don't even know the German
has anything to do with the Pope's kidnapping!' McBride's
voice sounded too loud in his own ears, as if it were being
amplified by the corner into which he had been suddenly
backed. Profanity escaped him: 'Christ Almighty, General – '

'Christ Almighty is on our side – I think. This is the opportunity we have been waiting for. Please, Eminence – ' He held
up a hand as Moroni tried to interrupt him. 'Let me explain.
We have no guarantee that His Holiness is still alive – do you
accept that?'

'We have faith in God's care of him,' said Cardinal Victor.

'I have no faith at all in criminals. Life doesn't mean much
any more to animals like these – we are back in the Dark Ages.

Somewhere along the way influences such as ours, the law and religion, have failed – '

'That's not true,' said Cardinal De Luca, but his protest held no conviction. 'The great majority – '

'The great majority will always respect us, Eminence, but in an apathetic sort of way and only while we do our job success-fully. The great majority have never been criminals or heathens. Perhaps they break the law in lots of small ways and perhaps they don't practise religion as you would wish them to – they just do their best to live and let live. Sometimes it is not enough, but most of the time I find it hard to criticise their attitude. But we are not dealing with men like the great majority – these criminals place no value on other people's lives. My two dead men prove that.'

'What are you proposing then?' Moroni asked.

'That Signor McBride should take the money to the Terminus. He can explain the reason for the change of courier when he takes the phone call at Number 8 booth.'

'That's not all you want me to do.' McBride could feel della Porta tightening the screws of the rack.

'When you take the phone call, you are to tell them that you will not just leave the money unattended anywhere, that you insist you have to hand it over personally – '

'They'll never agree to that!'

'My experience is that if the amount is large enough, criminals will do anything. For fifteen million Deutschmarks they will take the added risk. If they are political terrorists – and I'm not ruling out the possibility – they seem to *enjoy* coming out into the open. The Black September group did it in Munich and again in Khartoum – '

The nightmare is getting worse: in a moment I'm going to wake up screaming, as mad as Kessler. 'What do I do if they agree to meet me?'

'We want you to hold the man who meets you. We'll give you a gun – '

'You're out of your head, General!' *We'll give you a gun:* Jesus, wasn't that why he was in this whole goddam mess, to eliminate the gun? 'Eminence, for God's sake tell him you'll have nothing to do with this!'

All three of the other cardinals rose up in protest, but Moroni sat still. Della Porta had no respect for the red hat, not when it came to *his* law, and he said, 'I am trying to make sure we get the Pope back safely! We shall do a little kidnapping of our own. We'll exchange their man, plus the money, for His Holiness, and we'll do it without further tricks. But I am not going to let them hold all the cards!'

'General,' said Fellari, 'if they kill His Holiness, do you realise how you will stand in the eyes of the world?'

'Monsignor Arcadipane is not the only one who did not sleep last night.'

Della Porta suddenly sat down in the seat behind him. He reached for his moustache, pulled at the end of it with scrabbling fingers. Doubt rose up behind the dark eyes; he would have to resign if the Pope was murdered. The resignation would be bad enough, an ignominious end to an honourable career, but it would not be the worst: there would always be someone who would never let him forget what he had done. Some fanatic would always threaten revenge . . . But he knew in his heart that he was right, that he could not let the kidnappers hold all the cards. He had no faith, as these prelates understood it; human nature had taught him that suspicion was the only true belief. Trust always lost the battle against evil; he also knew in his heart that Hell had already won, the Devil would have equal rights on Judgment Day. All one could do in the meantime was play the game the Devil's way.

'It may be dangerous for you, Signor McBride,' he said, 'but that is a risk I have to ask you to take. I'd go myself, or have one of my men carry the money, but then, I think, the kidnappers would *not* respond. I am banking on their deciding to trust someone they know is from the Vatican.'

'What am I supposed to do if they produce a gun? Shoot it out with them?' But Smith, he now remembered, had left his gun with Toohey. He got off the rack: the nightmare began to fade: his mind started to work, to look for advantages in what della Porta was proposing. Just like a criminal's mind, he thought.

'No, no shooting. If it looks like any fight at all, you give them the money and retreat at once. If you can't take the man without a fight, forget it.'

'You are asking a lot of Signor McBride.' Moroni spoke at last.

'A lot is at stake,' said della Porta, and looked back at McBride. 'Well?'

There was no way out. He lifted his hand, wiped the back of it wearily across his face: his watch showed 6.28. Smith and Ryan would have to take their chances. There was no way of warning them of the change in plans; they would already have left the apartment for the Terminus. The first they would know of the substitution would be when Ryan spoke to him on the phone in Number 8 booth. The line would be tapped, for sure, and he just hoped that Ryan, in his shock, would not give the game away.

'Okay, I'll do it. But I'm not happy about it, General – I'll tell everyone that when it's over, if something goes wrong.'

'I'll take the full responsibility.' Della Porta stood up, pulled his tunic down over his hips, stroked his moustache with his knuckle; he donned confidence like a clean shirt, became brisk and authoritative again. 'I am certain this is the best way of assuring that we get His Holiness back safely.'

He went to the door, called in his aide. The latter came in with a suitcase and a small flat pistol. 'It is a Beretta .25, signore. It is sometimes called a ladies' gun, but since we hope you don't have to use it, that doesn't matter. The beauty of it is that it is fairly easy to conceal. Do you know how to handle a gun?'

'No.'

'No? I thought Americans were given guns as toys.' Della Porta looked curiously at McBride. 'Well, no matter. It is only a bluff, anyway. You produce it and if the man doesn't respond – ' He shrugged.

Goddam Italians, McBride thought: the shrug is their answer to everything. 'What about the money? Is it there in that suitcase?'

He recognised the suitcase, an exact match for the one he had bought for Smith. At least the cardinals had followed instructions so far: things had only become bitched up when della Porta took over.

'No tricks there – we play that part of the game honestly.' Della Porta nodded to his aide and the latter hoisted the case on to Moroni's desk and opened it. 'Fifteen million Deutschmarks in used notes, as directed.'

'Our German friends had a little difficulty in raising the amount in *used* thousand-mark notes,' said Moroni. 'There are fifteen thousand of them there. One wonders where they will get rid of such large notes.'

'There are banks in various parts of the world, Eminence, that never ask questions of their depositors,' said della Porta.

There were several banks in Beirut, McBride had been told, that had already been used by the IRA. The large-denomination notes would be distributed by those banks; by the time the notes arrived back in Germany it would be almost impossible to trace the original depositor. Smith was the money man and though he had his faults, the men in Dublin trusted him in those matters.

'Satisfied, Signor McBride?' Della Porta gestured at the open suitcase.

'Satisfied,' said McBride, and looked at the fortune and wondered if it really would buy peace in the Six Counties.

Della Porta looked at his watch. 'Time we were leaving.'

Cardinal Fellari looked at the General's uniform. 'You are not putting in an appearance at the Terminus, are you, General?'

'Yes.' Della Porta gave the cardinal a thin smile; there was no concordat between these two. 'But I shall call in at my office on the way and change. Hiding one's light under a bushel occasionally does wonders for one's soul.'

'I must remember that,' said Fellari with an even thinner smile. 'It sounds original.'

McBride took the gun from the aide and picked up the suitcase. The weight seemed, to his memory, to be much the same as the case with its contents of cosmetics.

'How do I get to the Terminus?'

'You'll travel in one of the Vatican Mercedes,' said della Porta. 'With one of my men in plain clothes as your driver. You

237

know the instructions they gave us – just follow them to the letter until you take the phone call.'

'Will Number 8 phone be tapped?'

'We have had a tap on it since midday, just in case they called in and brought the time forward.'

'God bless you,' said Moroni, and put out his hand to McBride. 'We shall pray for your and His Holiness's safe return.'

'Thank you, Eminence.' He didn't bother to kiss the episcopal ring on the extended hand: sacrificial lambs weren't expected to be respectful. 'I'll do my best.'

Fellari and De Luca wished him luck; Victor shook his hand with warm sympathy. Then Arcadipane came tentatively forward. 'I am sorry, signore. I shall never forgive myself, failing His Holiness like this – '

And me. But McBride suddenly felt sorry for the little man, and ashamed: he was the one who had put Arcadipane in this situation. The Lord works in mysterious ways, His wonders to perform. Amen, brother, amen. 'I understand. And I'm sure His Holiness will.'

Then he went quickly out of the office, eager to escape. All at once he wanted to reach the climax of the last two days as quickly as possible: even disaster, if it finished everything, would be a relief. He went down in the elevator with della Porta and his aide, out to the car already waiting for him outside the private entrance to the palace. He got in, put the suitcase on the seat beside him and looked out at della Porta.

'If this goes wrong, General, God help you.'

The Carabinieri chief looked up at the dome of St Peter's, shining faintly in the light of the moon. 'If one can't get His help here, where else can one expect it?' He looked back at McBride. 'Good luck. At one time, you know, you were on my list of suspects.'

It was difficult to read the General's smile: was the son-of-a-bitch tightening those screws again? 'But not now?'

Della Porta shrugged. 'If you come back with His Holiness, what answer can I give you?'

The goddam shrug again, no answer at all. McBride sat back in the car as it drove slowly through the gateway. He tried to relax, but the gun in his pocket was like an iron abscess on his hip. They made their way down through the peak-hour traffic; it flowed around them, the moving contours of the city. The driver drove into the steel glacier wedged below the white mountain of the Victor Emmanuel II monument. A bus pulled up beside the Mercedes; the passengers, crammed together like hostages, looked down enviously at the solitary passenger in the big limousine: some of those Vatican bastards had all the luck. He could read their thoughts as they would see the Vatican number plate and mutter the old Roman joke to each other: SCV, which they translated into the initials for Se Cristo Venisse: If Christ were to return . . .

Aware of their stares he turned his head away, looked into the car on the other side of him where the driver and his girl, warming up for the evening that lay ahead of them, were kissing each other passionately, giving the green light to each other while they waited for the traffic lights to change.

As he waited, imprisoned in the stalled car, he felt the urge to tell the driver to head back to the Vatican. Superstition now wrapped him like a rash; this hold-up in the traffic could itself be a (Divine?) warning. Too much had gone wrong: the whole venture had been meant to fail from the beginning: *this* was the luck of the Irish. He wanted to go back to Moroni's office, hand over the money and the gun, tell them exactly what the situation was and lead them out to the Chiesetta Sant' Augusto.

'We're moving now, signore,' said the driver, and slowly the car moved forward.

It's too late to back out now, McBride told himself; but he was not thinking about being trapped in the car. The trap was far wider than that. To go out to the Chiesetta Sant' Augusto would mean betraying Toohey, Ryan and Smith: it would mean betraying the IRA. But beyond them there was Luciana: she was in the clear now, but she would not be if the others were caught. Smith would implicate her, as revenge for the betrayal of them: McBride was sure of that. He sat back again as the car picked up speed and headed up the Via Nazionale. He began to pray, then stopped. In the circumstances that would be the final hypocrisy.

The car pulled in before the main entrance to the station.

The huge building blazed with light, a secular cathedral; when it had been first built it had been the pride of the Romans, but now they took it for granted with all their other treasures. As McBride got out of the car a boy rushed forward to take his suitcase, but he brushed him away; his rebuke was too sharp and he wanted to apologise, but the boy had already gone on to another approaching car. McBride thanked the driver, picked up the suitcase and allowed the tide of commuters to carry him forward into the main hall of the station.

Hampered by the suitcase, he had to struggle across the current towards the line of phone booths. He stopped for a moment, put down the suitcase while he tried to overcome the nervousness that was weakening him. He looked around for anyone who might resemble a plainclothes policeman; but what did a cop out of uniform look like? He saw at least a dozen men who could have been della Porta's men; but while he looked at the most obvious of them, a beefy young man reading a newspaper, another, slender young man came up, took the burly one by the hand and they walked off, oblivious of everyone but themselves. He looked around for della Porta, but if the General had arrived he couldn't see him. Maybe the Carabinieri chief was unrecognisable in civilian clothes.

He picked up the suitcase again, moved through the crowd towards the phone booths. Number 8 was occupied; a girl stood there, leaning negligently against the bench, seemingly ensconced for the evening. She stared out of the plastic bubble at the passing parade, head turning as she caught sight of someone interesting, describing the passer-by to her unseen listener. McBride looked at his watch: the train he knew he had to catch left in five minutes. Why the hell hadn't they thought to instruct the Vatican to have someone keep the booth clear?

He stared at the girl and after a moment she caught his eye; she returned his glare, made some comment to her listener. He moved in closer to her.

'If you don't move,' he said, 'I'll have to take you in for soliciting. You can't run your game from a phone booth – '

The girl smiled at him. 'I've been holding it for you, Signor McBride. It's all yours.'

She moved out of the booth and disappeared into the crowd with a twitch of her hips. Jesus, della Porta had thought of *everything*! Even though he was standing immediately in front of the booth he had to move quickly, swinging the suitcase as a weapon, to beat two men and a woman for it. He waited for the phone to ring while the men and the woman stared at him, waiting for him to pick it up and dial. *Come on, Des, for Christ's sake come on!* He looked at his watch: four minutes and he still had to buy his ticket. The phone rang and he snatched at it.

'Monsignor Arcadipane?' Ryan was phoning from outside in the square: they had figured Number 8 booth would be tapped, that it would be too dangerous to phone from one of the phones in the station.

'No, this is Signor McBride.' McBride hurried on before Ryan could give himself away over the line: 'Arcadipane is ill. You will have to accept me as his stand-in – I think you will recognise me. What am I to do?' *Come on, Des!* He looked at his watch again, then out at the big station clock. His watch was a minute slow.

Ryan responded: all of his reflexes hadn't been thumped out of him in the ring. 'Okay, you'll do. There is a screwed-up piece of yellow paper on the floor of the booth in the right-hand corner. Got it? Your instructions are on it. And you'd better hurry.'

McBride bent down, picked up the ball of paper, opened it and made a pretence of reading it. He knew the message by heart: *Catch the 7.12 express for Frascati, ride in the third car from the front, Compartment D. Do not stop to pass this information to anyone or the exchange is off.* He came out of the booth, almost being knocked over by the two men and the woman as they fought to take his place; he looked up at the station clock, seeing the quivering hand as it settled on 7.11. There was no time to buy a ticket or go through the usual gate. He had scouted the station till he knew it as well as he knew the Vatican. He hurried across the big hall, passing the departures board and remembering to look up at it, going through all the motions of a man who up till a moment ago had had no idea of where he was supposed to go. He found the gate he was looking for, slid it back, went through and turned back towards the

241

platform where he knew the Frascati train would be standing.

He made it with barely seconds to spare. The train was pulling out as he swung aboard, heaving the suitcase in ahead of him and causing angry abuse as it hit a man in the belly. He was aware of someone else crowding into the car after him, but he didn't look over his shoulder. He pushed his way down the crowded corridor, using the suitcase as a battering ram; people snarled at him but gave way under his dogged progress. He came to Compartment D, but there was no hope of forcing his way in there. He managed to wedge himself in the doorway, which was all that would be needed. He put down the suitcase and looked into the eyes of the black-haired man with horn-rimmed glasses who lowered his newspaper as the suitcase bumped his knees.

'Pardon me, signore,' said McBride.

Smith stared at him, face expressionless: nothing, it seemed, ever surprised him. He nodded and went back to his newspaper. McBride, feeling like a runner only halfway through a marathon, leaned back against the door. He looked around the compartment, but it was too crowded for him to see everyone. A short fat man stood next to him, swaying with the motion of the train, eyes closed, the strain of a long day causing shadows in his cheeks that no amount of dieting would have achieved. Beyond the fat man were two girls, leaning against each other, eyes watchful for the possible exploring hand in the crowded space. Seated opposite Smith was a man in a dark raincoat and a hat with the brim turned down all round; standing above him McBride couldn't see the man's face but he appeared to be short-sighted, judging by the way he held his newspaper close to him. At least he wasn't one of della Porta's men: they would not have known what train he was to board and certainly not what compartment he was to enter. McBride turned his attention to the corridor.

He was sure the man who had followed him on to the train was one of the plainclothes men. He looked down the packed line of commuters, but any one of half a dozen men could have been the policeman. He twisted his head, looked in the other direction, at once saw Ryan standing outside Compartment A. He had no idea how the Irishman had managed to make the train, but he was there and that was all that counted. So far everything was going according to plan.

But for one thing: when he got off this train at Frascati he would have to have someone with him whom he could accuse of being one of the kidnappers. He looked up and down the corridor for a likely victim. How did you choose a man who would fit the imagined picture of a kidnapper? Kidnappers wore no uniform . . . *And neither did plainclothes cops.* What if he should shove the gun into the side of della Porta's man and accuse him of being the pick-up man? The corridor was out: any man in it, with the exception of Ryan, could be the cop.

He turned his head and looked back into Compartment D. The train lurched round a curve and he lost his balance, falling against the fat man. His elbow dug into a pillow of fat and the man opened his eyes in anguish, glared at McBride as if he had been shot.

'Watch what you're doing!'

'Pardon me,' said McBride, and added silently, *You've just volunteered, buster.* He leaned back against the door, turning his head away but watching the fat man out of the corner of his eye. The stranger, tired, irritable and innocent, was still wincing with the pain of the jab from McBride's elbow. His red-rimmed eyes stared at McBride, looking for a focus for the accumulation of the day's irritations; but the effort was too much and after a moment the eyes closed and the man went back to rocking back and forth with the train's motion. Poor son-of-a-bitch, McBride thought, your day's not over yet.

He looked at his watch: not long now. He nudged the suitcase with his knees, pushing it against Smith's legs; the latter didn't raise his head, went on reading his newspaper. But McBride felt the answering nudge on the other side of the suitcase.

Then the train, hurtling along as if its driver was just as impatient as his passengers to get home, began swaying as it hit another curve. McBride braced himself, knowing this was the place and the time. Originally Luciana was to have started the commotion, accusing someone of pinching her; in the ensuing confusion Ryan was to have switched his own for Arcadipane's suitcase. Now Ryan had Luciana's role, without the ass-pinching, and Smith was in Ryan's seat. The commotion started down the corridor; Des was doing his job, yes. The noise of the argument rose above the whirring rattle of the train; everyone craned their necks to see what was going on. The train plunged into the curve, swaying dangerously; every night the train's drivers provided its jaded travellers with this excitement. McBride, watching the argument between Ryan and the man next to him (how had Ryan decided on *his* victim?), saw the Irishman suddenly topple backwards, cannoning into the man behind him. The movement turned into a chain fall: people fell against each other, grabbing wildly at the person next to them, all shouting hilariously. McBride had made this run six times, five times with Ryan and once with Luciana, never rehearsing the commotion but always trying the chain fall: on this particular curve it had always worked. A man and a woman fell against McBride and he let himself go, slumping into the fat man. He felt the suitcase slide out from between his legs as Smith reached for it, felt the substitute case bump his knee.

Then the fat man, eyes wide open again a red-rimmed glare, grabbed at McBride as if trying to wrestle with him.

'Get your hands off me!' McBride snarled loudly: he might need a witness, someone who had heard his warning to the fat man.

But the fat man paid no heed to McBride. His legs suddenly buckled under him and he sat down, sprawling against Smith. The two suitcases fell under him; he covered them like a small waterbed. He flopped about on the suitcases, trying to get to his feet again; he clawed his way up McBride, gasping apologies. Somehow he reached down, picked up the two suitcases, pushed one at Smith and the other at McBride.

'Excuse me, signori, excuse me!'

A suitcase was shoved between McBride's knees again; he looked down at the upturned face of Smith. The tall man's eyes blazed behind his horn-rimmed glasses; but all McBride could do was give a slight shrug and turn away. The shrug: the answer that was no answer. *Christ, which suitcase had the money in it?*

Everyone was trying to regain his balance as the train came

out of the curve. The corridor was a babble of voices; some people were still laughing, but McBride could hear an angry voice and Ryan trying to offer an apology. He straightened up in the doorway, looked in the opposite direction from Ryan and saw the plainclothes cop: a medium-sized, thin-faced man born to be lost in a crowd. The man looked at McBride, one eyebrow raised, and McBride, after a moment's hesitation, nodded. He had to go through with the act, hope that Smith had got the right suitcase.

The train was slowing down, its swaying decreasing; it rolled into Frascati as sedately as a State coach. Newspapers were folded, briefcases and bags reached for. Those who were seated stood up in the compartment, taking their places for the stampede to get off the train, to get home to the evening meal, the television set, the hours of parole till the pattern started again tomorrow morning. McBride bent down, took a quick look at the suitcase between his legs: was it the one he had brought or was it the one Smith had carried on to the train? He glanced at Smith, but all he got was the hard angry glare over the top of the newspaper. Something else had gone wrong. God in His Heaven must be busting His guts out with laughter.

McBride picked up the suitcase, took the gun out of his pocket and put it in the belly of the fat man. 'You will accompany me to the police.'

For a moment he thought the fat man was going to faint. The thick-lipped mouth opened like a fish's in the triple-chinned face; his eyes rolled downwards, but his own belly hid the gun that was poked into it. He shook his head, loosening the hat he wore; it wobbled dangerously on his pumpkin head. The girls behind the man stared curiously at him and McBride; they had heard only the word *police* and they could not see the gun. Then the other passengers, who had heard nothing, began to push their way out. McBride went backwards out into the corridor, the fat man following him as the others behind him shoved him up against the gun. His mouth was still open and his eyes had a pained, incredulous look. I know how you feel, McBride thought, that this can't be happening to you. As McBride went backwards down the corridor he saw the policeman pushing his way through the crowd. As they got to the door and stepped down on to the platform the policeman reached them, grabbed the fat man by the arm.

'I'm Sergeant Castelli. This the one we want?'

McBride nodded. 'He's the one. Let's get him out of here.'

The fat man started to protest incoherently, still unable to believe what was happening to him. Some of the crowd, attracted by the argument, paused to see what was going on; the fat man looked around wildly, appealing to them, but nobody seemed to want to interfere.

The carabinieri sergeant tightened his grip on the plump arm. 'I'd come quietly if I were you. If we tell these people why we are arresting you, they might tear you apart.'

The fat man looked at him in terror, puzzlement taken to an extreme now where it threatened to give him a brainstorm. His hat fell off, but he didn't notice it was gone; the fight went out of him and he seemed to fold inwards, a waterbed of a man in whom the outlet cock had been turned on. He went down the platform between McBride and the sergeant, head bent, already looking a figure of guilt. He couldn't be acting the part better, McBride thought; and hated himself for casting the man in the role. He did not look back, knowing Smith would not be following them. He was to stay in the train until the platform was almost cleared, then leave the car, cross the tracks and go out by another exit.

'The local carabinieri should be waiting for us,' said Sergeant Castelli. 'They would have phoned ahead from Rome what train we were on.'

'I'm glad it's over,' said McBride. He saw Ryan going out the gate ahead of them, not looking back, hurrying to the rendezvous with Smith and the money. McBride hefted the suitcase in his hand, but there was no way of knowing what was in it. God, he prayed, let Smith have the right suitcase, the one with the money in it, because only You know what he will do to the Pope. It did not occur to him that the prayer came as naturally to him as if he had been praying all his life.

'It's not over yet, signore,' said Castelli. 'We still have to get His Holiness back.'

The fat man's head jerked up. 'The Pope? What have I got to do with the Pope?'

'Quiet!' snapped Castelli. 'Do you want these people to know what you've done?'

'But I haven't done anything! I'm – '

They were through the gate and three carabinieri descended on them, faces stern and determined as if they were about to plunge in to stop a riot. McBride could see other carabinieri in the background: della Porta had left nothing to chance. The lieutenant in charge looked at McBride and the suitcase, then at the fat man, finally at Castelli.

'Sergeant Castelli? I am Lieutenant Moro. What are you doing with Doctor Clari?'

'You know him?' The sergeant's thin face seemed to broaden with shock.

'Of course. Doctor Clari is among other things the police coroner – '

'I have been trying to tell them!' Recognition filled out the fat man again; his thin voice suddenly was a booming bass. 'They are accusing me of having something to do with the kidnapping of His Holiness! I have been down in Rome on the Scarpelli case – '

'I know, Doctor,' said the lieutenant. 'I talked to you yesterday about it – '

But Castelli wasn't listening to him. He looked at McBride, his face thin and sharp again with annoyance. 'You've let them get away, signore!'

'How was I to know?' McBride, from the moment he had chosen the fat man as his victim, had had a quick rehearsal of what he would say when his mistake was exposed; but the exposure had come quicker than he had expected, there was the chance that Smith was not yet safely out of the station. 'The doctor bumped into me when someone caused that argument on the train, he grabbed me and he handled the suitcase – '

'It is fortunate they didn't get it,' said Castelli, but his tone implied that only good fortune, and not McBride, had prevented the kidnappers getting away with the money. He looked at Dr Clari, clicked his heels and saluted. 'I apologise most humbly, Doctor.'

'What about my reputation? In front of the people of Frascati you treat me like a common criminal – '

247

'It was my fault, not Sergeant Castelli's.' McBride kept talking, trying to gain a few more minutes for Smith and Ryan. The latter should be up at the garage now, getting the rented car that had been ordered by phone this afternoon; Smith should be on his way down to the junction with the minor road that went from Frascati back through several villages towards the Villa Pericoli. Somehow he had to gain another ten minutes for them, before he was asked to open the suitcase and the substitution would be revealed. Or he hoped it would be revealed. 'If you would care to accompany me to Lieutenant Moro's office I'll dictate a statement, a public apology that you can have printed in the newspapers.'

'To be accused of such a heinous thing! Every morning I have been at Mass praying for the safe return of His Holiness –'

Keep talking: you're helping us more than you know. 'Doctor, please – I couldn't be more distressed at my stupid mistake!'

He had put down the suitcase. Now he picked it up again, hefting it gently; it was still impossible to tell what it contained; they had been too meticulous in balancing the weight of the two cases. Castelli took the doctor by the arm and began to lead him gently out of the station. A small crowd of commuters had stayed to see what was going on, but now they too began to move off; obviously it was nothing serious, not worth the bother of being late for supper.

One of the carabinieri, a youngster who looked as if he might go in for muscle-building, touched McBride's arm. 'Allow me to carry it for you, signore. It looks heavy.'

Not really, thought McBride: you just don't know how weak I am. He gave the carabinieri the case. 'It gets heavier by the minute.'

The youngster nodded. 'They say money is a burden. Too much of it, I mean. We should all have such a burden –'

They were outside the station, approaching the four police cars lined up at the kerb. Then they heard the sound of running feet and the carabinieri, still on the alert, swung round, their hands going to their guns. A porter, elderly and arthritic, was galloping after them.

'Lieutenant Moro! A man in the train – dead!'

Moro and one of the carabinieri went running back towards the gate leading to the platform. The youngster handed the suitcase to McBride and took off after his colleagues. Dr Clari put a hand on top of his head, realised for the first time that he had lost his hat, said, 'I had better go with them!' and ran after the carabinieri.

Castelli looked at McBride. 'I think we had better go too.'

There was a screech of tires and three police cars swung into the forecourt of the station and juddered to a halt at the kerb. Della Porta, unrecognisable at first in a grey suit and hat, got out of the first car, pulled up sharply when he saw McBride and Castelli were alone, then came on to them.

'Weren't they on the train?'

'They could have been, General.' Castelli had snapped to attention, gave a smart salute, which della Porta returned; in their civilian suits they looked like actors rehearsing for some military drama. 'There was a mix-up. But now they have found a dead man on the train – '

Della Porta wasted no time with further questions. 'You had better come with us, Signor McBride. Give the suitcase to my men – they will look after it.'

McBride followed della Porta back towards the platform gate. Castelli and three other carabinieri, all in plain clothes, fell in behind, matching their step to the General's. Della Porta hurried, but did not run; he knew the age and weight at which a running man lost his dignity. McBride felt as if his own legs were just lengths of wood, connected at the joints with rusty pins; he could no more have run than he could have flown, he could not even have kept up with the arthritic old porter who had discovered the dead man in the train. They reached the car he had alighted from five minutes before, got into it, went down the corridor to Compartment D.

'He's been shot, General,' said Lieutenant Moro, recognising his chief and giving a cramped salute in the crowded compartment. He put his hand under the chin of the dead man and lifted the long handsome face, taking off the horn-rimmed glasses as he did so and pushing back the disarranged wig. 'He could be one of the men we were looking for.'

McBride, looking into the compartment over the shoulder

249

of della Porta, felt sick and faint as Smith's dead eyes stared up at him, arrogant and accusing even in their blankness.

2

Kessler had not intended killing the black-haired man.

After he had bought his raincoat, hat and briefcase he had walked back through the city and up the hill of the Via Vittorio Veneto. He had turned off it, disgusted by the loafers sipping their *Espressi* and Cinzanos in the enclosed sidewalk cafés; he wondered why so many Italians had no sense of purpose, were content to spend their days watching life go by. He walked down the Via Ludovisi, almost smug with his own sense of purpose; he squeezed the briefcase under his arm, feeling the bulge of the gun. He came to the end of Ludovisi, crossed Via di Porta Pinciana where it ran into Francesco Crispi, and paused beneath the high wall that bordered this end of the Borghese Gardens. He moved down the hill a few yards, finally took up his position near the print shop that was the first of the row of stores that ran down to the entrance to McBride's apartment building. He had bought a newspaper and he opened it and leaned his shoulder-blades back against the wall that had soon chilled as the sun had crept above it and moved on over the Gardens. The kidnapping of the Pope was still front-page headlines; the other main story was of the killing of the two carabinieri and the disappearance of the Australian bank robber, Michael Turk Toohey. War, disaster, politics, were all relegated to the inner pages, which Kessler did not bother to open; all that belonged to another world that meant nothing to him. He did not have enough Italian to read all the front page, but that did not matter. The newspaper was only a blind behind which he could wait.

He did not have long to wait. He saw the two men come out of the entrance down the street and he recognised one of them at once: the big Irishman whom McBride had called Des. He had put on his glasses, but as he saw the men come up the hill towards him he took them off again, folded up the newspaper and walked across to stand in front of the Hotel Eden.

The Irishman was carrying a suitcase, leaning slightly to one

250

side against the weight of it, though it did not look heavy. The tall man with him, black-haired and wearing horn-rimmed glasses, was a stranger: Kessler had never seen him before. There was an air about him that suggested he was Des's superior; while the two of them were together, *he* would never carry the suitcase. Several taxis were lined up outside the hotel; the two men went to the taxi at the head of the rank, gave directions to the driver and got into the taxi. Kessler heard them give their destination and as the first taxi moved off he walked quickly across and got into the next on the rank.

'The Terminus Station.'

Leaning forward in the back seat he kept a constant eye on the taxi up front. As they came down to the square in front of the station he saw that the other taxi was not heading for the main entrance. He tapped the driver on the shoulder.

'Follow that other taxi. My friends are in it.'

The driver looked over his shoulder, shrugged and swung his taxi down towards a side entrance. 'Here will do,' Kessler said suddenly, and already had the door open as the driver pulled into the kerb. He thrust money at the man, careless of whether it was enough or too much, scrambled out and hurried jerk-legged down to the entrance through which he had seen Des and the other man disappear when they had got out of their taxi.

He lost them for a moment and he panicked; then he saw the tall black-haired man. He was alone now and carrying the suitcase; there was no sign of Des. Kessler stood irresolute for a second or two: he could be looking for Des or he could follow the tall man. He chose the latter, hurrying after him as he went down towards a closed, unattended gate. The gate was not locked and the tall man pulled it open, went through and closed it behind him. He seemed in no hurry, making his way down behind the barrier to a far platform. Kessler, standing outside the gate, watched him till he stopped, put down the suitcase and opened the newspaper he had been carrying. Then Kessler went through the gateway, closing the gate carefully behind him, and just as unhurriedly walked down towards the far platform. By the time he reached it it was filling up with commuters waiting for the train to pull in.

He took up a position near the tall man, opened his own newspaper. He had been there only a minute when over the top of his paper he saw the two carabinieri approaching him. Again he felt the chill of panic; they couldn't arrest him before he had completed his task! He put his hand into the briefcase, took hold of the gun as the two policemen came abreast of him; but they did not look at him, went past and stopped by the tall man. They said something that Kessler did not catch, but he did catch the tall man's look of indignant surprise.

The tall man bent down, opened his suitcase: it was packed with what looked like boxes of cosmetics. One of the carabinieri bent down, perfunctorily examined the contents of the case; then gestured for the tall man to close it. They said something further to him and he took a business card from his wallet and showed it to them. They looked at it, then one of the carabinieri put it in his own pocket. They saluted and marched off. The tall man looked after them, then glanced around at the curious bystanders; he gave them a withering stare that turned their curiosity to embarrassment, a feat with Romans that Kessler did not appreciate, and went back to reading his newspaper. Further up the platform the two carabinieri had stopped to speak to another man with a suitcase.

Kessler watched the tall man covertly, wondering if he had chosen to follow the wrong man. But Des was lost now and the tall man was the only scent, faint though it was, on the trail to Kurt Stecher. He could not risk going back to trail McBride: the American would be too watchful now.

The train backed into the platform and the crowd surged forward. Kessler let them carry him up behind the tall man; they went into a car and down the corridor one behind the other. As the tall man went into Compartment D, Kessler followed him and sat down opposite him. A moment later the compartment was crowded, bodies thrown up as a barrier between the two men. All Kessler could see of the tall man was occasional glimpses of a newspaper and, pushed beneath the seat behind the man's legs, the suitcase.

The train had just begun to move when there were some angry mutterings in the corridor and a man carrying a suitcase pushed his way into the doorway of the compartment. Kessler saw the suitcase first as it was put down on the floor between the newcomer's legs; he felt a shock of excitement as he recognised it was a replica of the one under the opposite seat. He glanced up quickly, then just as quickly looked down again, raising the newspaper close to his face. He could feel the trembling in his hands and he tried to keep the newspaper from shaking. God was good to him, meant him to kill Kurt Stecher. Or why else would He have brought McBride on to this train? The American and the tall man opposite must be on their way to collect the ransom and then release Stecher. He closed his eyes, cursing the excitement that was making his head throb.

The journey to Frascati seemed interminable to him. He heard the first small altercation between McBride and the fat man next to him, but he didn't look up; it was none of his business, the fat man was not involved. Even when the commotion started in the corridor outside he paid no attention; then the train swept round a curve and McBride and the fat man almost fell on him. Then, head still bent, he saw the attempted exchange of the suitcases. And in that moment the fat man fell over. He bumped against Kessler, dragging the latter's newspaper down; the German almost hit him in panic, afraid that McBride above him would recognise him. The fat man sprawled on the suitcases, then slowly crawled to his feet, working his way up McBride. He straightened the suitcases, pushing one at the tall man's legs, the other at McBride's. Kessler caught a glimpse of the tall man's face: something had gone badly wrong. Kessler sat back, lifting the newspaper again: the next move was with McBride.

The train began to slow, pulled into Frascati. The passengers gathered their belongings and themselves; Kessler sat patiently, like a long-time commuter who saw no point in turning homecoming into a race. Then the fat man above him jerked and, on a level with his own eyes, Kessler saw the gun go into the big belly. He resisted the temptation to look up at McBride; he felt the conscious strain of his neck muscles keeping his head down. He heard the word *police*, then McBride was backing out of the compartment, the fat man was following him and the other passengers were pushing by. Kessler continued to sit, folding his newspaper carefully and putting it in his briefcase.

253

With his hands still in the briefcase he fitted the silencer to the gun. He hoped he would not have to use it, but one never knew.

People continued to push by in the corridor outside, but Kessler made no attempt to follow them. McBride was not the man to follow, not with that gun shoved into the belly of the innocent fat man. Then abruptly the corridor and the car were empty. The tall man looked across at Kessler, his handsome face suddenly taut with suspicion. He stared at the German, then he bent down and pulled the suitcase from beneath the seat.

Kessler said, 'Does it contain the ransom money?'

Smith jerked up straight, but didn't rise from his seat. 'Who are you? Are you the police?'

Kessler shook his head, smiling. He had begun to see glimpses of humour in certain things: the world was opening up to him: perhaps he might even begin to enjoy life in the future. For the first time he thought beyond the killing of Kurt Stecher; he would even try to escape, to get back to Germany. He might even take some of the money that was in the suitcase.

'I believe I spoke to you on the telephone this afternoon.' His right hand was still inside the briefcase; with his other hand he took out his glasses and put them on. His eyes were beginning to ache from the strain of being without the glasses; from now on he would need the full strength of all his senses. 'I recognise your voice.'

'You're Kessler?' Smith had lifted the suitcase on to the seat beside him; he gripped the handle of it tightly. 'What do you want?'

'Kurt Stecher. The Pope. That is the ransom money for him, isn't it?'

Smith hesitated, looked at the suitcase. *Jesus Christ, why hadn't they put a distinguishing mark on it!* He wanted to curse aloud; but this German opposite him wouldn't understand the reason, might panic and shoot him. He was certain that the hand hidden in the briefcase held a gun.

'Yes, dear chap.' In his own ears his voice sounded phoney; all the affectation of years was a sham that anyone, even the German, must see through. 'But you don't want that, do you?'

'Money doesn't interest me. I shall let you keep it – perhaps

254

I shall borrow just a little of it. But you must give me Stecher.'

'Let me go with this.' Smith patted the suitcase. Even if this suitcase didn't contain the money, it didn't matter. He would make his way back to Eire, gather the young impatient ones about him, lead them on his own crusade. The gun was the only solution, the man opposite him knew that. 'I'll tell you where you can find the Pope.'

Kessler looked at him shrewdly and with disgust. Why were so many people completely amoral? Was there no trust left in the world? 'You want to betray your friends, take all the money for yourself? If you would do that to friends, why should I trust you?'

'I give you my word – ' said Smith, and heaved the suitcase up. But the weight of the case, money or cosmetics, was too much for a forearm with no proper leverage. The suitcase slid off the seat in a futile swipe at Kessler as the latter brought his hand out of the briefcase and fired the silenced gun. Smith leaned back as if he had changed his mind about attacking, his head falling into the angle of the seat. The black wig slid forward, giving him a low forehead; the man of arrogant intelligence died with a slightly moronic look on his handsome face. Blood seeped from the hole in his chest, staining his otherwise spotless shirt. Kessler, a poor shot, had found Smith's heart, something no one had ever succeeded in doing while he lived.

Kessler stood up, put the gun back in the briefcase, picked up the suitcase. He heard a door slam at the far end of the car; he went out of the compartment and headed for the opposite end of the corridor, struggling with the suitcase in the narrow aisle. He felt weak with disappointment: God was laughing at him, Kurt Stecher was as far away as ever. He swung down from the car, ran across the platform and scrambled aboard the train that was pulling out from the opposite side. As he sat back in the empty compartment, the suitcase on the seat beside him, he realised for the first time how exhausted he was.

He closed his eyes, leaned his head back against the seat, rode back to Rome drained of all feeling, even the urge for revenge. He began to pray, asking for the strength to go on.

'You're certain he was Lamington-Bass?' said della Porta, knuckle at his moustache.

'Yes.' McBride no longer felt he owed any loyalty to Smith. The dead never asked for it, they knew better than anyone that it was every man for himself. 'I'd have recognised him anywhere. Without that wig, I mean.'

'I wonder who he really was? His suit was custom-made in Dublin. The name on the tag in the inside pocket was Smith. Smith and Lamington-Bass – both of them obvious aliases. Which one shall we bury him under?'

'What was the name on his passport?'

'Lamington-Bass. It was a British passport. His business cards had no name on them, just said he was the representative of some Swiss cosmetics firm. He seems to have been a man of many parts. I wonder if we'll ever really know who he was?'

'I wonder,' said McBride, who had certainly never known Smith while he lived. Or had not known what made him tick.

They were riding back from Frascati in the police car. Up front the driver and della Porta's aide were silhouetted against the glow of the headlamps; the General and McBride sat in darkness in the back, the suitcase on the seat between them. The countryside slid past, a dark graveyard of past triumphs no longer remembered; a headless statue flashed by, a mindless sentry careless of who went where. Cicero had ridden this road coming back from Tusculum, returning to an oration in tomorrow's Senate. I wonder what advice he would have had for me, McBride thought. *Any man can make mistakes, but only an idiot persists in his error?* And there was another one: *What is dignity without honesty?* Both unarguable statements: all the sages and the idiots had probably nodded their heads in agreement when he had first made them. But here in the back seat of a police car McBride looked for comfort, not reproach. He stared out of the window, but the night outside told him nothing: darkness and time had obliterated the inscriptions from the ruined statues.

'Why would his partners kill him?' della Porta mused. 'If they had taken the money from you, I could understand it.

One man kills another out of greed . . . He made no effort to communicate with you at all?'

'None. I think I fell on him once when I lost my balance, but I can't be sure.' He had to establish the moment when the suitcases had been switched. *If* they'd been switched. His fingers clawed at the imitation leather beside him, trying to feel what was inside it.

'Who was sitting in the seat opposite him?'

'I don't think I even looked at him – ' As soon as he said it he knew he had made a mistake.

'Why not? How were you to know whom you were looking for?'

'I was waiting for them to let me know who they were.' He was glad of the darkness in the rear of the car; his hasty invention would be as plain as sunburn on his face. 'The compartment was crowded – I couldn't see half the people in it – '

Della Porta seemed to accept the explanation. 'A pity you had to pick Dr Clari. If the newspapers get to hear of this – '

'I'm sorry, General. We all make mistakes.' *But only an idiot* . . . No, he wasn't going to make any confession, not yet.

The Carabinieri chief nodded morosely. 'If only we could have just *one* stroke of luck – I'm beginning to wonder what sort of prayers they are saying over there at the Vatican.'

'Don't give up, General,' said the aide from the front seat.

'I wasn't intending to,' said della Porta raspingly; he did not employ an aide to give him facetious comfort. He put his hand on the suitcase. 'They'll still want this, so they'll come back to us. The point is, was the German on the train tonight?'

McBride had to restrain the involuntary urge to nod. As soon as he had seen the dead Smith, he had known who had murdered him. He had stepped back into the corridor, waited there while the police made their quick preliminary examination of the compartment. He saw them stretch the body out, slipping off the wig as if scalping Smith; someone had closed the eyes and the handsome face was no longer arrogant, just surprisingly resigned-looking. Lieutenant Moro had picked up the newspaper Smith had dropped, but there was nothing else in the compartment; the other suitcase had disappeared. McBride had known then that Kessler had been on the train.

'Do you think he will come back? Three murders – they must know their luck is going to run out soon.' He had to keep remembering that Toohey was still suspected of having killed the two carabinieri. His brain ached: again he had the urge to confess.

'After their second murder most killers don't count the odds. They can only be hung once.'

'Not if there is no death penalty.'

'A figure of speech. There are some men who would rather die than spend the rest of their lives in prison.'

Including this one. But he pushed the thought to the back of his mind. The only thought that could occupy his mind now was getting the Pope safely back to the Vatican. But where was Kessler, what information had he gouged out of Smith before he had killed him?

He lifted his wrist into the flash of a passing street lamp: his watch showed 8.40. The time meant nothing: he realised that as soon as he looked at his watch. But several miles away, unknown to him, a message from Special Branch at Scotland Yard had been translated and was being read by a senior officer at Carabinieri headquarters.

McBride sat back in the car, trying to relax, as they came into the city. His arm rested almost gingerly on the suitcase; he was like a revolutionary on his first bomb mission. Was this how his father had felt on his way to the power station at Dunlaven? No, Joe McBride would not have been nervous: McBride knew that as surely as if he had accompanied his father on the raid.

He was relieved that so far he had not had to open the suitcase in front of della Porta. If this was the case full of cosmetics, somehow it would be easier to face the cardinals first, although he had no illusions that they would be naïvely resigned to the loss of the money. He would have to convince them all that the only thing to do was wait for the Pope to be returned, that now the kidnappers had their ransom they would honour their bargain. It could be difficult; it might be more difficult to convince Toohey and Ryan (or anyway Ryan: Toohey had never had any dedication to the job) that the game was lost, that the Pope should be returned and everything written off.

It would be useless calling Dublin; they would ask for time to call a meeting. And in the meantime Kessler could have found the Pope . . . He began to pray again, that the suitcase beside him contained the money, that he could leave it with Moroni and somehow get away to go back to the Chiesetta Sant' Augusto before Kessler got there.

When they got out of the car in the courtyard of the Papal palace, della Porta waited while his aide put through a call on the car radio to headquarters. McBride stood to one side, holding the suitcase, aware of the curious stares of the security guards who had formed a ring round them.

The aide turned to della Porta. 'There is a message from London, sir. Headquarters says it is highly confidential and they would rather not read it over the air.'

'Have a dispatch man bring it to me here,' said della Porta. 'Shall we go up to the cardinals, Signor McBride, and confess our failure?'

As they went up to Moroni's office McBride's mind sloshed with quicksilver thoughts. When the door into Moroni's office was opened he turned and handed the suitcase to the senior security guard who had accompanied them. The latter took it and looked at Moroni for instructions.

'I think it should be kept in a safe place,' said McBride, looking glad to be relieved of it, the impersonation required little effort. 'But readily available, in case they contact us again and I have to meet them in a hurry.'

'I'll go over with the guard.' De Luca rose from his chair, glad to escape from this room after hours of his fellow cardinals' company; collegiality had its limitations, he wanted time and solitude to think, to adjust himself to the dreadful possibility that perhaps now Martin would not be returned alive. 'The money is my responsibility again.'

Just don't feel so responsible for the money that you have to open the case and check it. But perhaps recklessness was the best insurance: he heard himself say, 'Shall we open it and count it, Eminence?'

'I don't think there is any necessity for that.' De Luca's voice was as cold as an inquisitor's; he wished the whole matter had been left to the Curia, that the police and this layman had not been called in. 'This is no time for levity, signore.'

'I know that,' said McBride, not needing to be reminded. He was on the verge of hysterical exhaustion: the giggle and the tear were never far apart. He tried for appeasement: 'But I'm like you, Eminence – worn out. The tongue makes a slip – '

De Luca nodded, warming for a moment; but he still gave the impression of giving absolution. 'We must not let ourselves weaken. I shall be in my office if I'm needed.'

'Before you go, Eminence,' said della Porta, 'I think we should open the suitcase. One should not treat so much money with any carelessness.'

'What could have happened to it?' said Moroni, chewing on a peppermint, coughing as he spoke. He had given up cigarettes for the day, had called in his secretary to clear the overflowing ashtray on his desk. It was as if he felt he was dying, would not last till the Pope came back. 'It hasn't left Signor McBride's possession – '

'Just a precaution,' said della Porta. 'It is the way I work.'

McBride, paralysed, watched as De Luca nodded and the guard brought the suitcase back and put it on Moroni's desk. He seemed to have lost all his senses but that of sight; his eyes, deprived of the support of the other organs, became magnifying glasses. He saw the big hands, scabbed by sun cancers, of the guard loosen the straps; one strap, he noticed, was lighter in colour than the other, a mark of identification of this particular case. But who had noticed that when the information would have been valuable? A hand, a broken nail on the second finger, opened the lock. Then both hands took hold of the double handle, one to each side of the case, and pulled them apart. McBride shut his eyes, all senses gone now: he knew he was about to faint.

Then one sense came back: he heard Moroni say, 'Satisfied, General?'

He opened his eyes, felt a rush of awareness that made him dizzy. He planted his feet firmly in the carpet, looked at the money in the suitcase and said, 'The General was right, Eminence. There was some confusion in the train – I *could* have had the case switched on me without my knowing.'

De Luca nodded to the guard, who shut the suitcase and

picked it up. He followed De Luca out of the room, the cardinal making no further comment.

'We should have insisted Arcadipane took the money,' said Cardinal Fellari. 'As soon as they saw you, signore, they panicked and fled.'

'Not quite,' said della Porta. 'There was the dead man on the train. He was one of them.'

Moroni nodded, too tired to listen to argument. All day phone calls and cables had been coming in from all over the world, not all of them from outposts of the Church; there had been messages from the White House, Buckingham Palace, from Moscow, from Delhi, Cairo, Tel Aviv; the spirit of ecumenism had never been so strong. But even as he had been moved by it, he had wondered how long it would last. Even the death of Martin (he had shivered at the thought) would only mean a temporary prolongation. When the fate of Martin was known, when he came back unharmed or was found dead, all the callers would go back to their own problems, their own interests, their own hates. Moroni had long ago given up believing in the essential goodness of Man; there were good *men* in the world, but they never made a whole. I'd have made a terrible pope, he thought.

'We can't give up hope,' said Cardinal Victor, and Moroni looked up, afraid for a moment that he had just spoken his thoughts aloud. The Belgian had lost his pink healthy look and his hands crawled over each other like grey mud crabs. 'But if we don't hear from them again by tomorrow morning – ' He shook his head, already surrendering hope.

'They don't have the money,' said della Porta. 'We shall hear from them again.'

'If I can be excused for an hour or so?' McBride said. He had a new lease of life: at least one prayer had been answered. 'I'd like to see how Signorina Pericoli is. She must still be suffering from the shock of what happened to her today.'

'Of course,' said Moroni. 'We are so preoccupied with His Holiness – I know *he* would be concerned for Signorina Pericoli. And for the families of the two carabinieri who were shot.'

McBride tried not to look in too much of a hurry to be gone.

261

'I can be back here within ten minutes of your calling me, if I'm wanted. I'll go home first, but I'll call you as soon as I reach her apartment.'

'I'll go back to my office,' said della Porta. 'Good night, Eminences. Call me as soon as they contact you again.'

'You're sure they will?' said Fellari.

'I have faith in the greed of criminals,' said della Porta.

When they reached the courtyard della Porta said, 'Do you want a lift to your apartment, Signor McBride?'

'I have my car,' said McBride. 'Let's hope we hear from them soon, General.'

'Give my respects to Signorina Pericoli and I hope she has recovered from her ordeal.'

McBride walked away and della Porta moved across to join his aide by the car. 'Has that message arrived yet?'

'Not yet, General.'

'The dispatch section needs to be smartened up. Remind me to speak to Administration about it.'

'Yes, sir,' said the aide, and opened the door of the car. Then he turned as a motor cycle swung in the gate. 'Here he is now, sir!'

Della Porta took the message, read it and swore. Then he snapped, 'Find out where the staff car park is. Pick up Signor McBride. Hurry!'

4

McBride had turned instinctively towards the small cul-de-sac where he usually parked his car during the day. Then he remembered his car was still in the garage on the other side of the river; a police car had brought him here this evening. He walked down to one of the side gates, nodded good night to the guard and went out into the street and at once hailed a passing taxi. He had no intention of going to see Luciana tonight; she was out of it all now and she had to be kept out. He gave his own address and sat back in the taxi.

He had a thousand dollars in cash in the apartment, money that had been given to him by the Dublin men for his own escape if something went wrong with the original plan. He would give it to Toohey and Ryan, it would be enough to get them out of Italy and after that they, or Dublin, could look after themselves. He would bring the Pope back to Rome, drop him as close to the Vatican as he dared and ask him not to put the finger on Luciana. Then he would take his own chances on getting out of the country. If he made it to Zurich he would draw money from the account he had established there some years ago when he had been freelancing; there wasn't much, probably no more than plane fare, but it would get him to Brazil, Australia, wherever. He would write Luciana from there, hope that she might still love him enough to join him.

The taxi pulled up at the red light at the intersection of Sistina and Francesco Crispi, waiting to turn right. He glanced out and saw the police car parked outside the entrance to his apartment building. Then he heard the car roaring up the street behind the taxi. It went by them, through the red light, and with a squeal of tyres swung right and went up Francesco Crispi to jerk to a halt in front of the other police car. He recognised the car, saw della Porta and his aide jump out.

He was surprised at how calmly he acted. He took money from his wallet, pushed it at the taxi driver as the light turned green. 'I'll get out here, see what's happening. You can go straight on.'

'Goddam gazelles,' said the driver. 'Red lights mean nothing to them.'

McBride slipped out of the taxi, crossed the sidewalk and stepped close to the corner. And at once Rosanna stepped out of a doorway behind him.

'Oh, it's you, signore! I thought – '

'Sorry, Rosanna. How's business?' The question was automatic, he was watching the entrance to his apartment building.

'This time of year I can almost remember what it was like to be a virgin.' He went to move past her, but she put a hand on his arm. 'Signore, the police are up there.'

'I can see them. What do they want?'

'They are after you, signore.' He turned and looked at her. 'That first car was there this evening when I came to work. They asked me questions.'

'What about?'

'You, signore. I didn't know what it was all about. They said something about a stolen motor scooter, but I knew you would have nothing to do with that. They asked me about your movements and I let slip – I'm sorry, signore, if I did the wrong thing – I told them you went out the night before last, that you'd gone out to dump rubbish. They got very interested, asked me what time it was, what time you got back. I said I couldn't tell them – I woke up then, they were asking too many questions, I told them to ask you. Are you in trouble, signore?'

'No, it's just routine,' he said, knowing it was anything but that. 'They are asking questions about everyone who works at the Vatican. Did they ask you anything else?'

'Not me. But they went upstairs, asking questions of everyone who lives over there. I stood in the hallway – I could hear them down the stairwell.'

'What did you hear?'

'I heard the fat bitch, the widow, tell them you had a German visitor this afternoon. That seemed to interest them. They got the janitor to open your door – they're in your apartment now. And now this second lot has arrived.'

'Do they know you're still around here?'

'No. The first bastards told me to get lost, said they'd run me in if I didn't disappear. But I stayed – I thought you should know, signore – '

McBride, the whores' friend: he was glad now that he had refused to sign Signora Ferragamo's petition. He pressed Rosanna's arm, the first time he had ever touched her.

'I don't feel like facing any cops tonight. I'll go see them tomorrow.'

He moved off down the Via Sistina and she fell in beside him. 'Do you mind me walking with you? I'll try the Via Veneto for a change.'

'Won't the girls up there resent you moving in on them?'

'I'll see the pimp, tell him about the cops down here. The girls will back me up – there is a lot of worker solidarity among us girls.' They passed under a street lamp and she saw him grin. 'Well, sometimes.'

They walked up back streets to the Via Lombardia and he left her outside the garage. He would never see her again, but

264

he couldn't say goodbye to her; he suddenly realised she was an old friend, someone he could trust. 'Rosanna, if the cops come back tomorrow night, don't say you saw me tonight. I think the less they bother you, the better.'

'You sound – worried?'

'Only for you, Rosanna. Love and let love, that's my motto.'

'I wish it were true.' She smiled sadly, touched his arm shyly. 'Is there any more news on His Holiness?'

'None. But we're still hoping.'

'I do that every night,' she said, but went off without telling him what she hoped for. He watched her go, walking slackly at first; then her hips began to sway professionally as she realised he was looking after her. She looked back over her shoulder at him before she turned the corner at the end of the block. 'Ciao.'

He walked down the incline into the garage. The old man in the office came out, grumbling to himself at having to leave the comic-strip memories of his youth. Ovid, Vergil, Horace: they had all been reduced to the one common denominator, the comic book. The old man moved cars back and forth in the garage in what could have been a fury of sexual frustration; at last the Alfa was free to be driven out. McBride tipped the old man, who just grunted and stamped back to his balloon-breasted heroines. I hope your prostate kills you, thought McBride, suddenly as sour as the old man.

He got into the Alfa, sliding into the seat as Kessler, gun in hand, sat up on the cramped back seat.

'Now we shall go and meet Kurt Stecher, Herr McBride.'

(9)

Somewhere along the way I have failed, thought Pope Martin, and this is His way of telling me. When they had crowned him with the Triple Tiara he had recognised, in all humility, that the Church was hoping for a pope who would throw new light on an old road, who would broaden the horizons on either side without deviating from the True Path. He was not the revolutionary some of the more radical had expected him to be; he knew there were many who were disappointed in him, from both sides. Like all men who ascended to power he had soon come to appreciate that, unless one was a tyrant, power had woven into it many unrecognised skeins of compromise.

He had experienced the outside world as his predecessor, who had been only an occasional visitor to it, never had; he had suffered, for his charity if not for his religion, as no pope in recent times had. He knew the aching need of the intelligent believers in the Church, the wish for identity as an individual within the impersonal monolith that Rome had built; he had heard the cry of women protesting against laws made for them by celibate men, listened to the pleas of missionary priests who asked for the comfort and support of a woman in their lonely fields; he had considered the arguments of non-Italian clerics and laymen who wanted the autocracy of the Curia diminished. He had already made certain decisions in his mind but had not announced them yet: one did not wipe off the barnacle-encrusted traditions of two thousand years with a stroke of the pen. The decisions he *had* announced, the allowing of contraception to be a matter of conscience for married couples, the revival and encouragement of the worker-priest movement, had exposed him to savage attack from the conservatives. So savage that, fearing for the fabric of the Church, he had delayed his other major decision, that to open up the election of the next pope to all the bishops instead of just to the College of Cardinals. The Church was as torn now as it had been under his predecessor; he had widened the horizons and found that too many did not like the view. There were some, he knew, who would see his kidnapping as the natural result of his concern for the individual conscience. Perhaps he had been wrong: perhaps God knew that a man could not be trusted with his own salvation.

'Do you believe in the hereafter, Turk?'

'I don't know, Dad – '

'Don't call me Dad.' There was a touch of the authoritarian in his voice; patience and humility had their limits. 'If my title or the mode of address worries you, call me Stecher – it was my name once. But don't mock the papacy.'

'Sorry. Dad is a bloody cheap joke anyway – kid stuff.'

Toohey looked across at the older man sitting on a tomb in the vault. When darkness had fallen he had brought the Pope down here, afraid that the glow of the candles might be seen through the hole in the dome of the church. An hour after McBride and the others had left he had had to hustle the Pope down into the vault when he had heard the police cars going up the lane to the villa. He had pulled the slab into place above the steps and waited, the torch lit and the gun aimed at the Pope; it was twenty minutes before the carabinieri had come down to look at the church, but their search had been perfunctory and they had soon left. He had then taken the Pope back up into the church until darkness had come. When they had returned to the vault they had had a meal of salami, cheese and bread, and drunk half a bottle of wine. They had talked easily to each other and Toohey had been reminded of an almost forgotten memory, of the days after he had first got out of jail back home in Sydney. He had gone on the track, tramping the bush, and there had been other nights when he had shared a meal with a stranger, both of them hunched about a small fire under some bridge. He had been broke and sometimes felt sorry for himself, but Christ, how simple life had been then!

'No, I'll call you Father, if that's okay. I can't come at the Holiness bit.'

'Father will do.'

'I once knew a priest when I was doing time back in Australia. He used to come to the jail once a week, talk to me, give me smokes. He never tried to bother me about religion, but somehow I never felt I oughta call him anything but Father.'

'Was he a good man?'

Toohey shrugged. 'He could've been. I've never passed an opinion on a good man. It's the bastards of the world that worry me.'

'They are the ones who worry me too.' Martin smiled gently as he leaned back against the second-tier tomb behind him; the marble front of it had been smashed by vandals and the skull of Pietro Pericoli (1812–1868) grinned over his shoulder with the eternally mirthless smile of the dead. 'But I also have to worry about the good. They are the more demanding.'

'What do you mean? They ask for something in return for keeping the commandments?'

'Something like that. Though precious few of them keep *all* the commandments. I sometimes feel that not all those tablets given to Moses were of stone – some were made of glass, they have been broken so easily.'

'That one about adultery – they don't seem to have taken much notice of that.'

'*Thou shalt not kill* – that commandment is broken too often.'

Toohey said nothing, all at once reminded of Belfast again.

'I dedicated myself to peace when they made me Pope. I hoped my voice – my papal voice, not just mine – would have some effect. I spoke for Christ – ' He shook his head, aware that his voice had been crying in the wilderness of war. There was no major conflict going on anywhere in the world, but man was still at war with his own kind: the mark of Cain was just another scabby scar, unnoticed among other blemishes on the face of Man.

'Why did you take on the job?'

'You don't refuse such a – a job when they nominate you for it. Depending upon your conceit or your humility, you can never be sure that it isn't a direct word from God.'

'Did you think it was?'

'Yes,' Martin said firmly. 'But I still don't understand why He chose me. And now I'm not sure that He doesn't feel He made a mistake.'

'I thought you blokes taught He never made a mistake?'

'He gave us free will – all of us. Perhaps that's where He made His mistake. When I was in Dachau I used to ask myself how a merciful God could allow men to treat other men as they were doing. It was a Jewish rabbi who told me that when God gave Man free will, men could not complain if other men abused that freedom. I think that was my first real lesson in humility – and courage.'

Toohey nodded, only half-convinced. The metaphysics of good and evil had never engaged him; he had the amorality of the honest thief, you took what the mugs of the world made available. It was you against them, and if it was a case of you *or* them, as it had been with the demon in Belfast, it had to be the other bloke who copped it. That, he supposed, was another of the results of free will.

He looked at the third man in the vault, the only one of them who really knew if there was a God at all. Pericoli lay stretched out on another tomb, his soft black hat over his face, his hands in their yellow string gloves crossed on his chest. The Roman aristocrat looked like all the dead-beats Toohey had seen asleep on the benches back home in Belmore Park in Sydney or along the Embankment in London; more elegantly dressed, but just as careless as any of them of tomorrow. Jesus, he thought, I wonder if that's the answer, just to be stone cold dead?

Then he heard the sound of the footstep on the marble floor above. He was on his feet, swiftly and silently, the gun aimed at the opening at the top of the steps. He shook his head warningly at the Pope.

'Turk?'

Then Ryan appeared in the opening, came heavy-footed down the steps, looked around him curiously.

'What's the matter?' Toohey put the gun back in his belt.

'Seamus not here?' Ryan sat down beside the Pope, nodding his head at him in a little bow. 'Do you mind, Holiness?'

Martin gestured a welcome, watching the big Irishman carefully. Ryan was worried and nervous, his left hand opening and shutting constantly as if he were trying to relieve it of cramp.

'I waited for him at the road junction in Frascati, but he didn't come. Everything went well on the train – I think. Only it was Fergus who brought the money, not that monsignor we'd asked for.'

'Was it some sort of trick?' Toohey's voice rasped in the quiet chamber; his mood had abruptly changed, was as tense as that of Ryan. 'You think him and Smithy have double-crossed us, shot through with the cash?'

'Fergus wouldn't do that,' said Ryan.

He has faith in McBride, Martin thought. But then so had I and look where I am now. He began to think of escape again. He glanced quickly towards the back of the vault, wondering where the dark gallery led. One torch lay on the steps beside Toohey, who had resumed his seat there; the other, like a silver thighbone that had fallen from one of the tombs, was at Pericoli's feet. He would need one of them but, with his swollen instep, he doubted his ability to move fast enough to grab it before Toohey or Ryan could intercept him. He no longer believed that Toohey would shoot him: he had that much faith in the little man. But if he did run, where to run to?

'The police must have picked up Seamus,' said Ryan. 'Yes.'

'If they'd done that, they'd be here by now. That bastard wouldn't go to jail on his own – he'd want us for company.'

'You're wrong, Turk. He had his faults, but he was a good IRA man – '

'He was a bastard,' said Toohey flatly. 'If the Father wasn't here, I'd say worse. If the crunch has come, he won't care a bugger about the IRA or anything else but himself.'

Ryan was silent for a long moment, then he said mournfully, 'What do we do, then?'

'Sit and wait.' Toohey looked at his watch. 'Till midnight. If Smithy and Fergus ain't back by then – '

'What do we do then?' said Martin.

Toohey looked at him, brow wrinkled. 'What's it got to do with – '

'We're all dependent on each other. If we all go back together, you will have spared my life and perhaps I can do something for you. No,' he added strongly, 'I *shall* do something for you.'

'They won't take any notice of you, Father. The mob's afraid of forgiveness, they think it's a sign of weakness. They'll bust a'gut yelling for justice and me and Des will spend the rest of our days in jail.' Toohey looked off into the darkness, in the same direction the Pope had gazed a moment ago. His hand went to the gun in his belt, but he didn't look down at it. 'I think I'd rather finish up down here. At least I could make it quick.'

'Not me,' said Ryan, and blessed himself. 'When I die I want the Church to bury me.'

'Think about it, Turk,' said Martin.

'I've been thinking about it ever since we bloody kidnapped you!' Toohey's control snapped for a moment. He got up from the step, stood with his feet apart like a man ready to run. Then he looked about him and his shoulders slumped as he admitted the race was almost over. 'Christ, can't you see I wish we'd left you where we found you!'

'Take me back, then.'

Toohey shook his head, like a man in pain as much as in doubt. 'Not yet. Not yet. We'll wait – ' He looked at his watch again, but it was only a gesture: the face of it was a blur to him, time no longer meant anything. 'It won't be long.'

2

'How did you know I'd be coming here?' said McBride.

'I just assumed you would be. Or rather *hoped*. I went back to watch your apartment, but the police were there. Then I remembered you said you garaged your car on the Via Lombardia. I found your car. It took a little time, especially trying to avoid the old man in the office.'

'How did you know it was my car? There are a dozen Alfas in that garage.'

'Letters in your glove box, Herr McBride.' Kessler sat crosswise in the cramped back seat, the suitcase wedged in beside him. 'Drive carefully, please. We do not want the police pursuing us.'

'Where do we go?'

'That is what you show me. But if you take me somewhere and Kurt Stecher is not there – ' In the driving mirror McBride saw the gun come up to the back of his neck and he felt the skin tighten there. Kessler glanced out the window. 'I seem to recognise this road. Are we going to the Villa Pericoli again?'

'Yes.' There had to be a destination: he couldn't expect to drive around Rome, like a taxi driver on the gyp, waiting for Kessler's patience to run out. But when they reached the villa he was determined he was not going to hand over the Pope. The killing had to stop, even if he himself died in the stopping of it.

Traffic was coming into Rome, people heading for dinner and a night out. McBride drove against a train of lights; help went by with derisive toots of horns. Two girls stood by the roadside, their wares hidden under their topcoats; on chill nights like this their trade depended on good will and past experience. The moon was full and bright, throwing the countryside into sharp relief; a ruined tower, two arches of an aqueduct, slid past in silhouette like a moving diorama of the past. Then they were turning off the main road into the lane that led up to the villa.

McBride tensed himself, knowing the moment had to come soon. Then the headlamps showed the car parked in the lane, too far out from the bordering wall for him to squeeze by it. He pulled up, kept the engine running.

'Put out your lights and stop your engine. Whose car is that?'

'I don't know.' He had never seen the car before, but he guessed it was the one Ryan had rented in Frascati. Des had done a bad job of parking it, as if his mind had been on something else when he had driven up the lane. Did he know that Smith was dead?

Kessler was leaning forward, looking out to either side of the Alfa. 'What is that through the trees there?'

McBride tried to keep his voice careless. 'Where? Oh, that. I'm not sure. It looks like some sort of ruin.'

'What sort – ' Then the gun was pressed against McBride's neck and Kessler whispered, 'Not a sound or I shall kill you!'

273

McBride saw the dark shape coming cautiously through the olive trees from the tiny church. He recognised the walk of the man rather than his shape: it was Ryan. He wanted to cry out, but his throat and mouth were suddenly lined with cracked leather; all at once he didn't want to die, no matter what the price might be for staying alive. His thoughts of heroics had turned out to be spurious; he was really only concerned for himself. And in the dry bowl of his mouth felt the worst of all tastes, self-contempt.

Ryan came to the wall, keeping within the shadow of a tree. 'Fergus? Is that you, Fergus?'

'Wind the window right down,' Kessler whispered.

McBride, with an arm that felt as if it were broken, wound down the window. 'It's me, Des.' His voice was a croak; he hoped Ryan would catch the note of warning in it. 'Move your car. I'm going up to the villa.'

Ryan clambered over the wall. 'No need for that, Fergus. We're still over there in the little church. We – ' He stopped as he saw the second figure in the Alfa. 'Is that Seamus with you? Christ Almighty, Seamus, you had us worried. Yes – '

He died with an affirmation on his lips that meant nothing. Kessler took the gun away from McBride's neck and shot Ryan in the chest; the Irishman fell back against the rented car, slid down and lay beneath the front wheel like a pedestrian who had been too slow in crossing the lane. McBride turned his head quickly, reaching for the door handle, but the gun came back, striking his ear and ripping skin off it. He could smell cordite: it was another of the stinks of death.

'Get out, slowly and with your hands up.'

McBride opened the door and got out with the stiffness of a man who might have been driving for hours without stopping. He thought for a moment of slamming the door back against Kessler, but the latter anticipated him. 'Move away a little more, please.'

Kessler got awkwardly out of the car, but the gun in his hand never wavered in its aim at McBride's back. 'We'll leave the money in the car. When this is all over you can just drive away with it.'

Bitter humour stabbed McBride. 'Why don't you take the

money and go? There's fifteen million Deutschmarks in that case – you can have the lot.'

'No, Herr McBride. I did think of taking a little of it, then I decided that would be dishonest, so I didn't open the case. I am not a thief, but I did not want to be tempted. It is all yours, payment for giving me Kurt Stecher.' The gun was pressed into McBride's back. The silencer must have been loosened a little when Kessler had smacked McBride across the ear; he felt the German tightening it. He tensed, preparing himself to duck aside and swing back at Kessler. But he waited too long: the gun was jabbed into his back again. 'Over the wall, please.'

McBride stepped over Ryan's outstretched legs. Moonlight came over the olive trees, splashed on the thickened, scarred face; the eyeballs shone like white pebbles, separated by the thick black shadow of puzzlement between the brows. McBride climbed over the wall, moved on when Kessler followed him. They came to the church, paused in the shadow of the mound of rubble that sloped up against one wall. The gun once more dug into his back and he stepped into the church, hearing the grit on the marble floor scrape beneath his shoes.

'About bloody time.' Toohey's voice came up from the vault. 'Down here, mate.'

McBride blocked, but again he didn't have the nerve; the gun jabbed hard into his back. He moved across the small chamber, guided by the glow of light coming up from the vault. He went down the steps, wondering if he could fling himself to one side and trust to luck that Toohey would shoot first; but Kessler was right behind him and Toohey stood at the foot of the steps, his gun stuck in his belt. McBride gave up hope.

Toohey, backed away, put a hand to his gun. 'What the – '

'I shall kill Herr McBride if you try to use your gun. Take it out and drop it on the floor.'

Toohey, with an unintelligible curse, threw his gun on the floor, stepped back as McBride was forced down to the bottom of the steps. Kessler came down, backed away against a wall and looked across at Martin sitting on the tomb against the opposite wall.

The Pope stared at the tall thin man, the spectre from the past. 'He even looks like him! It could be him!'

275

'Is that all you have to say?' Kessler felt weak and unsteady, like a man who had finally scaled his own Everest and was not sure what to do in his triumph.

'Is there anything more I can say? Except that I am truly sorry for having had no charity when it was asked of me?' The two of them spoke German to each other. But something more than language set them apart from the other two men in the vault: a ghost whom one had loved and the other, for one regretted day, had hated.

'You murdered a good man.' Kessler abruptly began to weep; he raised the gun. 'I loved my father – '

McBride never knew where the strength in his legs came from; one moment they were blocks of wood, the next he felt the muscles bunch in them. He flung himself at Kessler, knocking the gun upwards. It went off, even the silenced explosion of it booming in the narrow confines of the vault. Kessler swung away, still clinging to the gun. Martin and Toohey jumped towards the darkness of the catacomb leading out of the vault, Toohey grabbing the flashlight from the feet of Pericoli as he went past. Kessler fired again, the bullet zipping past McBride's face so close that he felt the burn of it against his skin. He twisted away, fled down the gallery of the catacomb after the beam of the flashlight bobbing like a swarm of fireflies ahead of him. Kessler had fallen down against the steps; McBride heard him scrambling to his feet, but he didn't look back. He ran on into the darkness, crashing against the walls, plunging headlong once but bounding up again, chasing the light and the two running silhouettes ahead of him. There was a thundering crash behind him and something flew off the black invisible roof above his head: Kessler was shooting at him with Toohey's gun.

'Put out the light!' he yelled, realising he was outlined against the bouncing glow ahead.

The light suddenly went out and he skidded to a halt, abruptly blind in the blackness. He put out a hand, felt for the damp, evil-smelling wall, touched something cold and hard: ran his hand along it, felt the bump on the end of it and knew, without seeing it, that he was handling a thigh bone. He drew his hand away as if burnt, looked back and saw the light bumping its way down towards him. Kessler had found the second flashlight.

'This way!' Toohey's voice came rolling down the gallery.

McBride, still looking back towards Kessler, saw the light stop. He dropped flat to the floor; the bullet whined off the wall above him and the sound of the shot reverberated like the crack of a cannon. He lay for a moment, the dank earth close against his face: this was the smell of the grave, this was the entry to death. He shivered, afraid again, got up and began to stumble down the gallery, one hand running along the wall. He felt the smoothness of marble, skulls, ribs, all equally cold; once he heard the clatter of bones behind him as his hand slipped, dragged a skeleton to the floor. Then his hand stopped, felt something familiar: a metal candlestick encrusted with wax. He felt up, grabbed it as he touched the four or five inches of candle stuck in it.

The light flashed for a moment up ahead, like the baleful grin of lightning. He flattened himself against the wall, crouching down: the bullet went by above his head and the shot crashed down the long corridor again. Kessler was coming slowly after them, not hurrying, as if now he had them here among the dead he had all the time in the world to put them to death.

McBride raised himself, stumbled on, carrying the candle but afraid to light it. The gallery turned suddenly to the right and he bumped hard against the wall; he felt his way round the bend and suddenly yelled, 'Flash the light, Turk!' The light flashed on and he ran desperately towards it, screened for a few seconds from Kessler by the bend in the tunnel. He caught up with Toohey and the Pope, grabbed the latter's soutane, and at once Toohey snapped out the light.

'Hang on, Father,' the Australian said, and the three of them moved down through the long blackness like pilgrims who knew neither their way nor their destination. Behind them Kessler suddenly yelled something at them in German, a cry of rage unintelligible to any of them; then the light came round the bend of the gallery, blazed down at them. McBride dropped to the floor, dragging Martin down with him; but Toohey was too slow, the Pope losing his grip on the little man's jacket as he fell down. Toohey stood for a moment looking back at the light; then he flinched as the bullet hit him and he fell back under the thundering wave of the shot. McBride jumped to his feet, keeping close to the wall, pushed the Pope ahead of him.

'What about – ?'

'Run, for Christ's sake! Kessler wants you, not Turk – ' He kept talking as they stumbled on into the darkness; the flashlight was somewhere on the floor with Toohey. 'If Turk's still alive, Kessler's not going to waste another bullet on him – '

They blundered into the wall again, turned along it to their left. At once McBride looked back: the glow of Kessler's torch was lost for the moment. He took Smith's lighter from his pocket, lit the candle. They were in a largish room, really no more than a widening of the gallery; the catacomb here had an altar in it, a marble edifice that looked untouched. Tombs lined the walls; above them faded frescoed saints gazed dolefully at the ceiling, as if the promise of Heaven was not enough. Three galleries opened off on either side of them, their dark interiors not illuminated by the weak glow of the candle. McBride pushed Martin towards one of them.

'In there!' he whispered urgently; and snuffed out the candle as he saw the beam of Kessler's flashlight hit the bend in the wall behind them. 'I'll distract him – try and find your way back – '

The Pope didn't move for a moment; McBride felt the protest in the stiffened stolid body. Then Martin slipped away in the blackness and McBride turned the other way, moved like a blind man with his arms outstretched in front of him till he found the opening to a gallery. He stepped into it, flattening himself against the wall. He could feel his heart beating heavily, found all at once that he was having difficulty breathing the dank dead air. God knew what gases lurked here in this darkness; centuries of poisoned air thickened the atmosphere. Conceivably Kessler had only to retreat to the entrance vault, sit there and wait for them to die – it would not be wrong to say they died from natural causes. But he knew that Kessler did not want that sort of revenge: it would be too impersonal, the Pope had to die at the end of a gun.

278

The beam of the flashlight probed its way into the outer room; then McBride heard the slow plod of Kessler's boots. He pressed himself still flatter against the wall, watching the glow of the torch grow brighter. He held his breath, felt all his muscles begin to ache with the effort to control them; his stiff clumsy fingers reversed their hold on the candlestick, grasped it tightly like a club. The torch beam swept around the room, settled on the altar; then it dropped to the floor, turned away from McBride. It followed the footprints in the dust on the stone floor, straight into the opening opposite. The beam swept up, aimed like a gun at the gallery; but it was not a gallery, just a short narrow cubicle. The Pope was trapped in it, outlined against its back wall, a faded blotched Christ behind him with arms raised in benediction.

Kessler raised the gun: the gun Toohey had dropped, Smith's gun. McBride shook his head in anguish: that would be the final bitter irony, it was too much to bear. He leaned away from the wall, raised his arm and flung the candlestick. It hit Kessler high on the left shoulder, bouncing off, not knocking him down.

He spun round with a yell of surprise and pain, firing at McBride as the latter flung himself forward. The bullet tore through the outer flesh of McBride's shoulder; but he didn't feel it. He hit Kessler hard in the stomach and the German fell back against the altar. The torch fell to the ground, bouncing away; the beam slashed the walls, came to rest pointing back the way the three men had come. Kessler fired again, but McBride was too close to him this time; the shot went wild and McBride grabbed the hand that held the gun. Kessler let go, too readily; McBride relaxed for a split second, surprised. The German wrenched himself away, grabbing at the pocket of his raincoat. McBride saw the gun come halfway out of the pocket, caught for a moment by the bulky silencer. Then his own hand, almost of its own accord, found the gun that had been dropped: it lay on the altar step, an offering. He grabbed it, brought it up in a reflex action, pulled the trigger in the same robot-like way. The sound of it in the room was tremendous: Kessler staggered back as if hit by the explosion itself rather than the bullet. He fell against the wall, slid down it; paused for a moment in a sitting position, then slowly fell over. Silence rushed back into the room. McBride slumped down on the altar step, too empty to be sick, the gun still clutched in his hand like a leper's clapper-bell. In his dead hollow mind a voice, his father's, was echoing: *the gun is the only way.*

He began to shake his head from side to side. He did not look up as he heard Martin approach him, did not respond to the comforting hand that lightly touched the top of his head.

10

Pope Martin the Sixth was once again celebrating his name day. He bowed his head beneath Bernini's great canopy that humbled any man who served Mass on its altar. *Domine, non sum dignus*: Lord, I am not worthy . . . Watching him, McBride thought: Every man his own judge. But Martin would always sell himself short: he was far worthier than a lot of popes who had celebrated Mass on that altar.

The crowd stirred, caught up in the underlying emotion of the moment. There was no overflow of brilliant colour surrounding the altar as there had been a year ago when the bishops had been here in St Peter's in force. For this day Martin had declared there was no rank in the Church he led; the crowd lapped at the altar steps, rich man, poor man, cardinal, clerk. Several of the Curia cardinals had stayed away, all offering excuses as obvious as their pride; but most had taken Martin's edict to heart, had seen the need for the public expression of humility. The Church was the universal church, every man's, and on this day Martin was opening it to all who claimed their place in it. Moroni was dead and Fellari was retired, but De Luca and Victor were lost somewhere among the crowd. In the stalls a bus driver knelt beside the new Cardinal Secretary of State, an Englishman; cardinals, archbishops and bishops bent their heads among those they served in Christ. The Church had once been like this and this was a magnificent gesture. But that's all it can be, McBride thought: a gesture. Tomorrow the bureaucrats would take over again; no institution could beat them. Heaven and Hell had them, he was sure: he prayed for immortality to avoid them.

'What are you praying for?' Luciana whispered beside him.

'Nothing,' he said; and changed the prayer. 'I'm just saying thanks.'

'We should,' she said.

Indeed we should: twelve months had not altered that fact. He closed his eyes and the murmuring, shuffling, coughing around him faded in his ears. Certain events of the past would always belong to the present; he would never be able to separate them as long as he stayed here in the tiny world of the Vatican from which there was no escape. At least not in the foreseeable future, not till Pope Martin died.

'Why didn't you go back to your apartment as you said you would?' della Porta had said, full of suspicion. He had been waiting in Cardinal Moroni's office when the Pope and McBride had reached there.

'It was just as well I didn't. You would have taken me to headquarters to question me – '

'You have nothing at all to do with the IRA?'

'Nothing.' A doctor had been summoned to look at the flesh wound in McBride's shoulder; it wasn't serious, but the doctor was suggesting a day or two in hospital. McBride hid his face behind the doctor's bulk as the latter applied a dressing. 'I admit my father belonged to it, but I never have.' That was a half-truth, anyway. He attacked with a confidence he hadn't felt in weeks: 'Your father, General, was a top Fascist. Does that make you one?'

Della Porta ignored that. 'We can check on those other men – '

'I shouldn't do that if I were you, General.' Martin sat in his chair, sipping the tea Sister Caterina had brought down for him. He looked tired and wan, his soutane dirty and mud-streaked, his instep swollen and scratched above his slipper. But he had refused to go up to his apartment, to retire to the rest that he sorely needed, until the police were finished with their questioning and McBride, too, could go home to his bed. 'We have no real evidence that those men had anything to do with any organisation. I do *not* want this to have any political overtones – ' There was no mistaking the demand, almost command, in the Pope's voice. He had no authority over della Porta, but one look at the Carabinieri chief showed that he was not going to argue. 'Kessler was the central figure in this dreadful business and he had nothing at all to do with the IRA.'

Della Porta made a slight bow of acknowledgment. He looked back at the American. 'I still don't understand why you concealed from us that Kessler paid you a visit today.'

'I would have told you eventually, General,' said McBride. 'But he had threatened to kill Signorina Pericoli if I told the police – I was afraid he would go to her apartment, try to kill her even though you had a guard there. He was mad, General. Insane.'

'Did he say anything about trying to kill His Holiness?'

'No.' The doctor stood directly in front of him, shielding him from della Porta. But looking sideways he watched the Pope's face for any reaction. There was none, Martin just went on sipping his tea. 'All he was after was the ransom money. He knew what that gang was up to and he was going to hijack it off them. You know who his father was – His Holiness has told you that. Maybe it was some sort of revenge, to get away with all that money.'

'I wish it could all be forgotten,' said Martin.

'It can't be, Holiness,' said della Porta. 'Unfortunately world headlines can't be swept under the carpet. Now that you have been returned safely, you will continue to be headlines. At least till another catastrophe.'

'Mr McBride deserves *his* headline,' said Martin. 'It was he who got me back safely. We must never forget that, General.'

When Kessler had been shot Martin had been the first to recover. He had moved past McBride, touching the latter's head lightly, picked up the flashlight and laid its beam on the German. The dead man's chin rested on his breast; the Pope knelt down and gently lifted the gaunt face. The eyes were closed and tears glistened on the cheeks; the expression was remarkably soft, that of sad disappointment. Forgive me, Martin had said silently.

He picked up Kessler, holding him like a child in his arms. 'He's skin and bones. He might almost be one of his father's victims.'

McBride stood up, stiff and clumsy. 'Leave him here. Why – ?'

Martin shook his head. 'I brought him to this, Fergus – he is not your responsibility.'

McBride took the flashlight and led the way back down the gallery. They came to Toohey lying face down on the floor. McBride bent down and picked up the Australian; the little man was dead, he had died underground after all. McBride and the Pope, with their burdens, went down the long gallery, past the tombs and frescoes, past the skeletons that grinned at them in the glow of the torch: the last laugh of death, the one that Toohey and Kessler would soon be sharing. They reached the vault and laid both men down.

McBride looked at Count Pericoli, then said, 'There's Des Ryan up in the lane.'

'So many dead.' Martin shook his head, looked ready to weep. 'All because of me.'

'No,' said McBride. 'Don't blame yourself for all this. Don't even blame yourself for Kessler.'

'I am my own judge of myself,' said Martin. 'At least until I am as dead as they.'

McBride saw there was no argument: Martin was already donning his sackcloth. 'What do we do now?'

Martin wiped the sweat from his brow with his sleeve. 'We go back to the Vatican.'

'I know that. I had no intention of trying to run away.' It was the truth: the thought had never been an intention. 'But I'm not going to tell them the full story, Holiness. I want my girl kept out of this. She's already been through enough – '

'You've both had your punishment, I think. The police need not know about Signorina Pericoli's connection with my kidnapping – she has lost her father, that is enough. They will ask questions, but I'll leave you to cover up for her – I shan't contradict whatever you say. As for you – ' He looked at this young man who had disappointed him so much. There could never have been a close relationship between them, his own position demanded loneliness as its price; but it diminished any man, even a pope, to see another man ruin his life. Faith was more than just belief in God; it was belief in men too, because that was where love, the expression of faith, lay. 'It will be up

284

to yourself to convince the police that you had nothing to do with Mr Toohey and those other two men.'

'You are allowing me to do a lot of lying.'

'I think in this case the truth could be too dangerous. If we can avoid it, we don't want anyone making political capital out of what has happened to us.' McBride remarked the papal *we*; Martin was more concerned for his office than for himself. 'I haven't yet thanked you for saving my life.'

McBride squeezed the strong hand that took his. 'You're forgiving me too easily. There's something else, isn't there?'

Martin nodded, his face suddenly grey and old in the glow from the flashlight. 'I am making up for the charity I lacked all those years ago.'

'You can't let me go scot-free.' It was not just the desire for sackcloth and ashes; he knew, somehow, that there had to be punishment as a protection. 'General della Porta, of the Carabinieri, is no fool – '

Martin was silent for a moment, then he said, 'You will work for me from now on, as my personal press secretary. If I am your *jailer*, can the General interfere?'

McBride smiled, an effort but sincere. 'You really know how to dole out the penance, don't you, Holiness?'

'If not a Pope,' Martin returned the smile, 'then who else?'

They left the three dead men in the vault and went up and out of the Chiesetta Sant' Augusto. McBride lifted the body of Ryan into the back seat of the rented car and closed the Irish man's eyes. Then he and the Pope got into the Alfa, McBride backed it down the lane, and they drove back to Rome through the moon-bright night.

There was consternation when they drove in the Porta di Santa Anna. As the Pope stepped out of the Alfa he was recognised at once; a cry went up and several men fell to their knees. To McBride the scene that followed was almost medieval. Swiss Guards, their pikes at the ready, forced their way through the hysterically jubilant crowd; somewhere a bell began to ring and within five minutes, as the news spread, the bells all over Rome began to respond – Martin raised his hands, the rapidly gathering crowd fell on its knees and he blessed it.

The blessing over, the Swiss Guards moved in around Martin.

But he stopped them, came back to McBride. 'Come, my son. You are our charge now.'

He was the Pope again, full of authority and dignity; even his mud-streaked soutane, his pyjama legs showing beneath it, did not detract from his aura. He strode across the courtyard through the kneeling crowd and McBride followed him, the Guards in a solid barrier on either side of them. As they stepped into the elevator Martin gestured that he and McBride were to ride alone.

'We shall go and face General della Porta at once – I heard one of the Guards say he is with Cardinal Moroni.' The doors closed and the elevator began to ascend. 'Tomorrow you will be a hero – that may be another part of your penance, if that's what you are looking for.'

'All I am looking for is peace,' said McBride. 'That was what I was looking for when I got involved in this whole damned mess.'

All that had been a year ago. McBride had embraced his religion again, but he knew he was still a poor Catholic; he just hoped he might be a better man. As the Mass now came to an end he and Luciana began to move out of the Basilica. They came out on to the front steps and General della Porta, resplendent in a new, perfectly fitting uniform, stopped beside them.

'A beautiful Mass. I hope The Lord answers His Holiness's prayers for peace. The headlines this morning aren't encouraging. More bombs in Northern Ireland, for instance. The IRA seems as if it will never give up.'

'So my father used to tell me,' said McBride. 'But I never listened to him.'

'When is the baby due?'

'Another two months,' said Luciana. 'We hope you may come to the christening, General. His Holiness himself is going to perform the baptism.'

'Delighted,' said della Porta, and looked at McBride. 'If I may be so bold – if you are looking for a godfather – ?'

That's all we need, a cop in the family. 'We'll be honoured.'

'Will the baby have an Irish or an Italian name?'

'American,' said McBride. 'George or Martha Washington McBride.'

The General smiled and they began to walk down the steps. 'We should have seen more of each other this past year, signore. The events of last November will always be a bond between us.'

'You sound as if you regret it's over.'

'No, I'm glad it is. We got His Holiness back and that was the main consideration. But a policeman always likes a case tidied up and this one never was, not to my satisfaction. I still think there was someone in the Vatican who helped that gang break into the grotto in the first place.' They came to his car; the aide got out and opened the door. 'Good day, Signora McBride. Try and make the baby a girl – one as beautiful as its mother. You are a very fortunate man, Signor McBride. But then I suppose you know that?'

McBride watched the knuckle at the moustache, but he kept his smile innocent. 'I know it very well, General.'

Della Porta saluted and got into his car. McBride stood and watched it drive away across the Square and down the Via della Conciliazione, the road that a year ago was to have been their escape route.